SHADOW OF THE DAGGER

CIA Operatives—Book 1

ENDORSEMENTS

Anne Greene's archaeological adventure is a fast-paced romantic mystery that kept me hooked until the very last page. Her multi-layered characters with noteworthy quirks and attributes added depth and interest at every turn. I found myself rooting for the romance sparked between Nicole and Josh and loved the interplay of faith between them. Looking forward to the sequel!

—**Catherine Finger**, author of the *Jo Oliver Thriller* series

Anne Greene's *Shadow of the Dagger* grips the reader with tension heightened in each scene until it explodes in a thrilling climax. But readers will also be gratified by the author's in-depth knowledge of Turkey's geography, history, and culture carefully woven into the fabric of the novel.

—**Donn Taylor**, author of *Lightning on a Quiet Night, Murder in Disguise,* and more.

This is the first Anne Greene novel I've read. Won't be the last. *Shadow of the Dagger* jumps right into tension and never lets up. Vivid details, fascinating characters, and tight writing style push the story forward. Greene immerses the reader in the exotic Turkish culture, history, and ancient traditions, including the confining rules for women. She also portrays the breadth of beautiful countrysides and cityscapes with the intriguing architecture and confusion of mazes and corridors.

Good pacing of changing POV scenes. Suspense couples with smoldering, yet controlled romance scenes. A complex plot brims with inner and outer conflicts, mistrust and betrayal. Nicole Phillips is a gutsy heroine, full of faith, and I so relate to her directional dyslexia.

—**Janet Chester Bly**, author of *The Trails of Reba Cahill* Series

From modern Istanbul, with its cosmopolitan attractions and creature-comforts, Anne Greene draws the reader into the deception of Old World intrigue. Nicole, an unknowing and distraught young Texan trying solo to locate her missing brother, must seek out the hard men who know about the disappearance. Josh, a worldly-wise, Turkish-speaking American, steps in to help. But can she trust this too-handsome man and his too-convenient appearance? *Shadow Of The Dagger* is a stranger-in-a-strange-land thriller, a winding mystery of personal angst with larger, international import. A former resident of the region, Ms. Greene masterfully weaves her knowledge of Turkish culture into the fabric of this compelling and entertaining story which the reader will be hard-pressed to put down before finishing.

—**James Yarbrough**, author of *Mystery At Grantham Lake*

Anne Greene expertly spins a tale of intrigue and romance and drops her characters into a spiral of danger and emotion within an exotic setting. A must-read book.

—**Linda Wood Rondeau**, author of *Hosea's Heart*

Shadow of the Dagger is a suspenseful tale of intrigue, deception, and danger, skillfully intertwined with current events and ancient history. The good guys are real and believable, while the bad guys are mean and nasty—just the right combination to keep readers engaged. I highly recommend this book.

 — **Donna Schlachter**, historical suspense author/**Leeann Betts**, mystery author

SHADOW OF THE DAGGER

CIA Operatives—Book 1

Anne W. Greene

ELK LAKE PUBLISHING INC
Plymouth, Massachusetts

Cover and Interior Design: Derinda Babcock

Editor(s): Cristel Phelps

Author Represented By: Hartline Literary Agency

PUBLISHED BY: Elk Lake Publishing, Inc., 35 Dogwood Drive, Plymouth, MA 02360, 2019

Library Cataloging Data

Names: Greene, Anne W. (Anne W. Greene)

Shadow of the Dagger—CIA Operatives: Book 1 / Anne W. Greene

400 p. 23cm × 15cm (9in × 6 in.)

Description: Her husband is dead, her brother kidnapped. She's alone in Istanbul and must try to rescue him. Is the American who wants to help her friend or foe.

Identifiers: ISBN-13: 978-1-951080-18-1 (trade) | 978-1-951080-20-4 (POD) | 978-1-951080-19-8 (e-book)

Key Words: CIA, Suspense, Mystery, Action/Adventure, Antiquities, Kidnapping, Turkey

LCCN: 2019945613 Fiction

DEDICATION

I dedicate this book to my wonderful husband, Larry.
Thank you for our love story.
Thank you for supporting me in this great adventure
of being an author.
You are a gift from heaven.

ACKNOWLEDGMENTS

Thank you ...
Deb Haggerty, my publisher;
Cristel Phelps, my editor;
Derinda Babcock, my cover designer;
and my critique friends.

For I can do everything through Christ who gives me strength.
(Philippians 4:13 NLT)

CHAPTER ONE

"My marriage can't end this way!" Nicole Phillips gripped her brother's arm as the helicopter door opened. Her tears blurred the desolate, wind-swept slice of Texas land abutting the Mexican border.

The hope she'd nurtured since the police helicopter left the Dallas Police Station wilted like the yellowed sagebrush dotting the arid earth. More tears veiled the officer holding up his arms to assist her off the chopper. She stumbled. The unsteady step down to the rough ground jolted her. She ducked her head beneath the *whump, whump, whump* of the helicopter's blades.

Her brother thudded to the ground beside her.

She followed Ian and the policeman away from the blasts of wind created by the spinning blades. Her cowboy boots kicked up dust as she walked across several hundred yards of empty flat land. She and Ian reached a dip in the vast, open landscape. Scattered wreckage glinted in the sunlight.

Behind her, the helicopter shut down.

A cold chill settled over her. She hugged her arms to her chest. "It's a mistake. This can't be Paul's plane."

With strong, gentle fingers, Ian squeezed her shoulder. "Nikki, there's no mistake."

She raised her face toward her newly-deaf brother, so he could read her lips. "Of course, there is. Don't look so worried. Paul's fine. Fine."

Her husband had been missing ten days, six hours, and thirty-five minutes. No, Paul wasn't fine. She brushed numb fingers across her eyes and blinked hard at the piles of metal. "Surely, that can't be all that remains of a plane?"

"I'm afraid so, Sis." Ian shrugged.

"I can't believe it." Nicole clenched her fists and shook her head. "This scorched earth is no place to say goodbye." She gazed at Ian. "No place for a man like Paul to die."

"Not much left." Ian's scratchy voice sounded strained—unlike the usual well-spoken words he practiced each month at rehab. An early diagnosis two years ago had given both of them opportunity to learn lip reading and signing before silence shut Ian from the world of hearing.

"Why here?" Nicole choked, swallowed, then forced words through her constricted throat drier than the desert beneath her boots. "Even if mechanical trouble forced Paul down, he could have skid-landed here. He wouldn't have crashed. This doesn't make sense."

Ian rubbed his square chin. "You're right. The crash here is more than strange."

Her boots crunched on the burned grass as she circled the scattered pile of twisted metal and shattered plexiglass. Stark shadows and deadly quiet added to her sense of unreality. "Nothing here adds up," she signed.

Ian's long strides shortened to match her steps. She loosened her hand on his sleeve but didn't let go.

"Bizarre." Ian stooped by a metal fragment.

"Ma'am." The police officer loomed beside her.

She'd forgotten him.

"This way, Mrs. Phillips." He led her to a jagged, misshapen piece of metal hidden by a sheared off bush. "The FAA ruled this crash an accident. Said the plane was out of gas."

She knelt, touched the metal, then jerked back.

"Careful, sun's baked it hot." Ian's warning came too late.

Nicole rubbed her stinging fingers. With the tip of her nail, she traced the still legible scarlet-painted *S.* Her heartbeat slowed, turned bleak, deadened.

"I'm sorry, Nikki." Ian's baritone voice shook.

"Summer's Girl," Nicole whispered.

Ian held out his hand and tugged her to her feet.

"Sorry, ma'am." The police officer's hat shielded his eyes. His mouth was set in a hard line. "We searched the area but …" He shook his head. "… couldn't find any remains. We think coyotes …" he paused and cleared his throat. "Wreck's been here a few days. There's blood …"

The policeman's voice drifted into background sound. Paul's plane found but not Paul. Perhaps he was still alive. Nicole gazed around the vast emptiness and said vaguely, "Paul and I talked of having a baby."

Ian laid gentle hands on her shoulders. "Nikki." He drew her against his chest.

Her knees threatened to buckle. She leaned into her brother's shoulder and spoke into his crisp dress shirt. "Sometimes …" She remembered Ian's deafness and lifted her face to him so he could read her lips. "Sometimes, Paul loaned his plane to one of his buddies."

Ian shook his head, squinting against the harsh sunlight. His blue eyes brimmed sympathy. "Not this time." He lowered his voice. "But this was no accident."

CHAPTER TWO

The year had passed quickly. When had the leaves budded?

Nicole glanced at the stack of unopened mail on her glass-topped table. A tight band wrapped around her chest. She groaned. Not another one! So, the first letter hadn't been a prank.

She pulled in a deep breath and picked up the top envelope. Though sunlight bathed her cozy kitchen nook, bouncing off the soft yellow walls like liquid gold, the warmth failed to chase her goosebumps. She stared at the flowing script addressed to her.

"Oh, Father God, help me," she murmured. "I don't think I can stand any more stress and pain." She gripped the envelope in her icy fingers. "Lord, you carried me through the worst period of my life. Now this happens. Please, please, let my life return to normal."

She ripped open the flap and shook out the single sheet of paper.

Dear Ms. Phillips,

You realize by now your burglar alarm does not deter me from entering your house. You have a map that belongs to me. I demand it back. If you do not send my map to P.O. Box 33, Dallas, TX 75206, you will die. The map is mine.

A barb slashed her heart. She slammed the note onto the table. What map? She sank onto a kitchen chair and stared at the letter. What map?

Should she call the police again?

No, they'd already said they could do nothing unless a third break-in occurred and the intruder stole something. Nikki dropped her head into her hands and rubbed the tight muscles at the back of her neck. The grandfather clock in the living room chimed ten times.

She straightened. Her employment contract had also arrived. She'd ignore the letter and get on with her life. She rose, crumpled the paper, and headed for the trash can. She shook her head and smoothed the paper. Stalking into the living room, she deposited the letter in the drawer where she kept important papers. On her return to the kitchen, she glanced at the framed diploma announcing her new PhD over the fireplace. Too ostentatious. She'd take the document down soon. But not immediately. She'd worked hard to earn that Doctorate in Archeology.

She scooted onto a kitchen chair and picked up the thick envelope from the university which lay atop the stack of junk mail and travel brochures. She slit open the envelope and checked the last page for her signature and that of the university president. Then she flipped back to the first page and stared at the fruit of the last seven years' worth of hard work.

The unique, three-distinct-chime melody from her cell signaled her deaf brother's text. She reached across the contract and grabbed her phone.

IAN: NIKKI, YOU'RE IN DANGER. COME TO TURKEY WITH ME.

A familiar dart of fear made her shudder.

NICOLE: OH, IAN, WHAT'S WRONG NOW?

She texted and waited the few seconds for her words to be typed on Ian's special vibrating, light-up cell phone for the deaf. Her cell beeped.

IAN: I'M STILL AT DFW AIRPORT. PLANE TAKES OFF IN TEN MINUTES. I GOT A MESSAGE FROM PARKLAND HOSPITAL.

A shadow spread across the sunny kitchen. Fear fingers prickled her spine. She gripped the phone so hard her nails bit into the case. She hated hospitals. Hated the cold antiseptic atmosphere. Hated the devastating news doctors brought into waiting rooms. Crushing her memories into a vault inside her brain, she forced her thoughts from the past.

NICOLE: WHAT'S UP?

Outside her kitchen window, two squirrels raced each other up the rough bark of her Magnolia tree as if horrible events didn't occur during daylight on a beautiful Texas spring day. She tapped her fingers on the glass table, waiting for Ian's next text.

IAN: SOMEONE MURDERED MY NEW INTERPRETER. THE MULTILINGUAL ONE FOR THE DEAF.

Her sudden jerk almost made her drop the cell. *Oh God, please not another death.* She stiffened her shoulders and grasped the edge of the table to keep from turning into a quivering lump.

NICOLE: WHAT? WHEN?

IAN: I HADN'T MET HIM. THIS MURDER IS NOT EVEN DISGUISED AS AN ACCIDENT.

Nicole's shoulders slumped. Her fingers shook.

NICOLE: WHAT'S HAPPENING TO US?

Her insides renewed the tremulous dance that started with Paul's mysterious plane crash.

IAN: DON'T KNOW. YOU'LL BE SAFER WITH ME INSIDE THE COMPOUND. I NEED YOU WHERE YOU'LL BE PROTECTED. DIG'S SECURITY PATROLLED. NEED A PASS TO ENTER. WHOEVER'S DOING THIS KNOWS WHERE YOU LIVE. I NEED YOU. YOU CAN HELP WITH THE DIG.

She rubbed her forehead. Safe? Were they safe anywhere? She rose. Standing in her peaceful kitchen, gazing across the sunny back yard, another death seemed unreal. Their parents died in that late-night car wreck shortly after Paul crashed his plane. Last month, someone broke into the house. Twice. Though the police weren't concerned, she'd grown more and more cautious, making certain she set the alarm and locked the door. She made a wry mouth. Useless precautions after the second letter came today. And now this murder.

Why kill Ian's interpreter? Had whoever sent me the threatening letters attempted to kill Ian but murdered his interpreter by mistake? Was all this death about a map?

NICOLE: YOU WANT ME TO SPEND THE SUMMER AT THE ARCHAEOLOGICAL DIG?

She hadn't set foot on a plane since Paul's crash. She wasn't afraid—more like apprehensive. She flipped through the contract on the table, wanting so badly to deny this murder. She just wanted to enjoy a work-free summer and teach at the university this fall. Live a normal life.

IAN: NIKKI. PLEASE. WE'LL BOTH BE SAFE IN ISTANBUL.

Was he right? Her brilliant brother usually was. She sighed and glanced at the travel brochures. She'd planned to surprise Ian by spending several weeks with him in Turkey. Why not go early and stay? Escape the creeping sensation which crawled up her neck each time she returned home from running errands. Was someone watching her? This murder and today's letter proved she had more than a case of nerves. For some reason she and Ian were in danger, and the local police could offer no help. Maybe she *would* be safe in Turkey. She had a free summer. Ian needed an interpreter, and she could do that for him.

Nicole: Okay. I'll take the first plane I can book.

She dialed the airline and secured a last-minute flight to Turkey leaving Tuesday evening. She had her passport, a day to pack, and a discounted seat. She would view this trip as a vacation.

She sighed. If only life could return to normal. At twenty-eight years old, she simply wanted to teach archeology and live a quiet academic life. These past months had knocked her to her knees.

But Ian needed her.

As her last surviving family member, Ian could ask her to die for him, and she would.

Tourists milled about the huge display room in Istanbul, Turkey. Ian McKenzie touched an intricate tile-decorated wall. He was actually here in the famous Topkapi Museum, inside one of the hundreds of rooms of the ancient palace of Ottoman sultans.

He stood within the quiet circle of his recent deafness, inhaling history as he might have the perfume of a beautiful woman.

He gazed with narrow-eyed concentration at the world famous Topkapi Dagger. In the artificial light of its display case behind the throne of Sultan Ahmet I, the dagger's huge eye sparkled as if the weapon peered through the hidden folds of life.

He braced his legs, locked his thumbs into the belt of his khaki shorts, and stared at the dagger's golden hasp. Leaning closer, he studied the antique watch embedded in a massive emerald atop the dagger's hilt. The card below read: *Designed 1741.*

Ian moved to a matching display case across the room. His temples pulsed. The plaque beneath the jade sailing vessel studded with precious stones read: *Nineteenth century gift from Tsar Nicolai II.*

His breathing quickened. The cryptogram on the treasure map pictured both ship and dagger! He rubbed his jaw, puzzling over the mystery. What was the connection?

Paul had secretly passed him the map when his brother-in-law feared for his life. Now thanks to possessing the map, he and Nicole were both in danger. Chills tripped up and down his spine, goosebumps sprouting on his arms. He glanced around the crowded room. *Thank you, God, no one in Turkey knows I have the map.* The ancient document must lead to priceless treasures.

The display room, the famous dagger, and the jade sailing vessel, all marked on the map, spelled out the riddle's secret. He rubbed his chin, churning the muddle in his mind. He would solve this puzzle. He owed it to Paul.

From his peripheral vision, he glimpsed a red-uniformed palace guard herding tourists from the room like a fierce Sheltie nipping sheep. He glanced at his watch. Too early for closing. What was going on?

As the room emptied, he hurried toward the door.

Four men, wearing three-piece suits and white turbans, cut him off. Anxiety pricked his gut. The armed guard slammed the single exit door on the last tourist's heels then turned the key in the lock.

Ian's mouth went dry. He yelled, "Hey, wait! Let me out!"

But the black-bearded men blocked his way. He sidestepped one bouncer-type. "Sorry." When the man pivoted back in his direction, Ian amended his English to "*Uzgun.*" The Turkish word felt awkward on his tongue.

Another man, the size of a small truck, lunged forward and slammed a massive shoulder into Ian's side.

With a groan, Ian stumbled to his knees. *Oh Lord, Help!*

The man glared down.

Ian watched the man's thin lips snarl through his thick, black beard. The words Ian lipread knotted his stomach.

Lights flickered out. Darkness swept the room except for the glimmer pulsating from the display cases. Springing up from his knees, Ian scanned the dusky room for a way out.

Arms folded across his chest, the palace guard blocked the locked exit.

Ian started to call out, but an expert punch cracked against his chin.

Dazed, he staggered against the display case. The burglar alarm vibrated along his spine. Three men crowded him against the trembling glass. Dropping into a defensive crouch, he faced them, fisting his hands. He tried to look formidable and growled, "I won't go easy!"

But he did—no match for the butt of a .357 magnum slamming his temple. Terrific pain. A billion stars exploded inside his head. He folded forward and entered a long, dark tunnel with no landmarks.

CIA Headquarters, Langley, Virginia

Josh Baruch shook hands with his old friend. How long had it been since their last Air Force Reserve training? "Catch you for lunch again soon, Buddy."

"Yeah, see ya." Rex grinned, nodded, and strode off down the sidewalk.

Josh turned toward the high glass arches of the Langley Station doorway. Inside, he passed through the metal detectors into the atrium, empty except for the armed guard. He nodded. "Danny."

"Doc." Danny punched the up button on the elevator.

The doors hissed open, and Josh stepped inside. He exited at the third floor. Glancing up, he saluted the hidden camera guarding the suite. He slipped his keycard into the slot and slid through the door. A year of practice entering his office complex made maneuvers automatic.

"Hi, Glenda." He offered a half smile to the receptionist.

Glenda smiled and patted her lengthy auburn hair with her long-manicured nails. "Back from lunch so soon, Dr. Baruch?"

"Can't stay away." Josh ignored her flirting. Attractive as she was, he'd worked too hard on his woman-dodging image to tarnish it.

"Can't be your CIA Intel work that's irresistible. Must be my charm." Glenda motioned to the monitor connected to the guard cameras at the front and rear doors. "You look good on TV. Maybe you should moonlight."

He ignored her comment. Long after the other single women at Langley had given up trying to date him, Glenda still worked all the angles. He tugged off his suit jacket and slung the grey linen over one shoulder. "Did I receive an answering cable from the DI?"

Glenda nodded her head "Our esteemed Director of Intelligence answered that there's nothing new since your last report on nuclear weapon sales to the Mideast."

"Thanks." Josh brushed past her desk, strode through the small reception area, turned into the hall, and walked the few feet to his office. He tapped in his private code, stepped inside, and leaned against the door.

Before he reached his desk, Glenda buzzed his intercom. "From our operative in Turkey. Something about a missing archeologist. The commo doesn't appear important. Just another alert that won't require CIA action. Should I pass the message on to Hal?"

"I'll take a look." Josh hit the hidden button to unlock his door.

Glenda thrust a typed sheet at him.

Istanbul, Turkey: American Archeologist, Ian McKenzie, reported missing after visiting Topkapi Museum, Monday, 19 June, eleven hundred hours. No terrorist group claims credit. Our sources in Istanbul suspect German art dealer responsible. Phone records indicate sister arriving Wednesday, twelve hundred hours, Istanbul International Airport. Local police involved. Expect kidnapper to contact sister. NCIA.

Josh reread the commo and lingered on the *NCIA*. He scrubbed his hand through his hair. Okay, so it's *not* a CIA case. His stomach tightened. This was *his* own personal vendetta.

As he surfed his options, he ducked his head and massaged his temples. The German art dealer had to be Helmut Meier.

Strong, conflicting emotions rushed through him until, frowning, he leaned forward, clicked on his computer, and glared at the screen. Okay, so this kidnaping, or murder, wasn't connected with his Intel specialty. He maneuvered the mouse on his desk. If he used a few weeks' vacation, what could the CIA say?

Plenty. If he screwed up. By the time they found out he worked the case, with any luck he would have enough evidence to send the murderer to the pen for life. And avenge his brother. He clenched his fingers into a tight fist.

Josh typed in his airline reservation, scooped papers into his attaché, and glanced around his office. What else might he need? His job in Intel didn't equip him for covert work. He wasn't privy to anti-terrorism weapons or gadgets. He had no network of trained cohorts. As an Intel Analyst, he would be on his own.

But he was smart. He smiled wryly. Hadn't had smarts enough to keep Helmut Meier from murdering Scott. Okay, maybe he wasn't so smart. But he was persistent. With this lead dropped into his lap, he'd put Meier away. Permanently. Josh jerked his jacket from the back of his chair. Plus, he'd escape the desk and see some action.

He glanced at the office laptop. Nah. Packing it would tip off his DI. And if the computer fell into the wrong hands, the information within would have international repercussions. Big time. No go.

He lifted Scott and Suzanne's wedding picture from his desktop. The memory of Suzanne's betrayal still shot darts through his heart. He flicked the widow's face with a hard finger, cracking the glass.

"I'll get that creep for you, Scott." Josh slapped the picture face-down on his desk and punched the secret button. With his shoes cracking like gunshots on the marble floor, he rushed out the door.

"If Meier doesn't catch me first."

CHAPTER THREE

Inside the Istanbul Atatürk Airport, Josh rested his long body against the window frame of Gate 21's baggage claim room. He stared at arriving passengers and dealt with second thoughts. He was way out of his league. What made him think he could pull off this caper?

He glowered at the flat grey wall. *Man up! What's the big deal?* All he had to do was locate the sister, use her as bait to lead him to Meier, collect evidence, and snag Scott's murderer. Easy. Josh closed his eyes and pinched the bridge of his nose. Meier would walk free of this crime as he had Scott's murder, unless *he* locked the brute behind bars.

Knowing Meier, the monster would contact the sister, either for money or for whatever the art dealer needed. John pulled in a deep breath. If no one made contact, he was dead on the runway.

He straightened and scanned the passengers streaming in. To bag the kidnapper, he would have to charm the archeologist's sister. *Charm?* He frowned and raked a hand through his hair. He'd avoided women for over a year. Since his brother's widow … he shook his head. He wouldn't go there again. But he *would* do what he had to do.

The arriving passengers slowed to a trickle. Businessmen in rumpled suits, Middle Eastern locals, and a few families with children. No woman alone. Maybe she wasn't on board. His heart thudded like a plane engine about to stall. Perhaps he'd missed the sister.

Flexing his jaw, he attempted to relax his clamped teeth—tried to ignore the hostility burning inside his chest. To bring Meier to justice, he'd dropped everything at work and risked losing his job. He rubbed his chest, then stiffened.

A woman alone. A swarm of bees stung his gut. If he'd been an operative, he'd have a picture. But he wasn't. And he didn't. This had to be her.

She wore a skirt that skimmed her knees above movie star legs. He lifted his gaze to the rest of her. She looked good. Too good. Sunny blonde hair swung loose and hung down her back. Tall and slender, she had the kind of curves that drove men wild. He swallowed.

Ignore the sister's looks. Hadn't he learned yet that women couldn't be trusted? He pushed away from the wall and stepped behind a pillar. She probably wouldn't notice him in the press of the crowd, but he couldn't take chances. Ha! Who was he kidding? He did take chances, or he wouldn't be here.

As she stood on her side of Customs, her expression looked eager, and her big sky-blue eyes sparkled.

Lurking behind the pillar felt deceitful. He didn't like the sensation, but this was business. He slid onto one of the fixed airport chairs, lifted a newspaper from the adjoining seat, and watched her over the top edge of the Turkish tabloid.

The passengers selected their luggage and cleared the room, which left the woman he hoped was McKenzie's sister alone in the baggage area. Her sparkling eyes and smiling lips sobered. Glancing around, she hugged a hardback book to her chest, collected her bags, and worked her way through the short line at Customs.

When she entered his side of Customs, he tossed the newspaper aside and tailed her. He stopped across the room from where she stood alone, again searching the diminishing crowd. He angled toward the wall, leaned casually, and waited.

The few Turks and Middle Eastern nationals still in the Customs area kept glancing at her. No question why. She was a woman no man could miss. A knockout in western clothes. Too provocative in this part of the world.

He rotated his tight shoulders. So, she didn't know how to dress in Turkey. He made a wry smile. He'd remain focused on snaring Scott's murderer—the devil the underworld called the Viper. Though watching McKenzie's sister scrambled his brain, he had to keep his eyes on her. He couldn't afford to lose his only lead.

By now, a frown worried the young woman's forehead. She twisted the strap to her shoulder bag with jittery fingers. The tiny digital camera dangling from her wrist trembled.

Josh rubbed his hand over his jaw. Why hadn't the Turkish police met her and informed her about her brother? Who dropped the ball?

Most of the crowd had filed out. Her frown grew. Her fidgeting increased. Finally, she called a porter to carry her bags, then hurried outside.

Where were those policemen? Josh sprinted to catch his bait and stopped short on the sidewalk. A driver shoved the last of her bags inside a small bus. Cursing himself for being a novice in the field, he waved to a waiting cab.

Speaking Turkish, he ordered the driver, "Follow that bus!"

He dropped onto the taxi's torn upholstery. The driver turned and winked, then zoomed into heavy traffic. Lumbering buses and cabs kept the other vehicle a good fifty yards ahead. Leaning forward, Josh shoved Turkish lira near the driver's face. "Don't lose that shuttle!"

The taxi driver hit the gas.

"*Teshekur ederim.*" Josh thanked the cabbie. He eyed the small bus's tail lights and gripped the back of the ragged front seat. "Keep them in sight."

When her bus stopped and her driver unloaded her bags, he spoke in Turkish again, "Drop me at this end of the block."

Heart beating at full throttle, he climbed from the cab and rocked onto his toes to see over the crowd. In the flurry of people congesting the sidewalk, she stood in the middle looking lost.

Behind her a simple brass plaque etched with the words, *Asya Hotel*, identified a black marble building with double glass doors. He memorized the site and name of her hotel, one of hundreds in Istanbul.

A muscular Turk stepped out of a shadowy doorway and zeroed in on her.

Josh's stomach tightened. The Viper wasn't losing any time. Was that Turk with the gun butt protruding from his holster, half-hidden by his hand, planning to kidnap her in broad daylight?

Josh broke into a run.

CHAPTER FOUR

Standing on the busy sidewalk, luggage jumbled around her feet, Nicole gazed at the hotel. Was this the right place? Had the shuttle driver understood her English?

Heat from the midday sun scorched through her sandals. She clutched the book tighter to her chest. The sights, sounds, and scents of this foreign city made her acutely aware she was alone. And a long way from Dallas. To top that off. Ian hadn't met her at the airport.

Above the traffic din, the high-pitched voice of a muezzin on a loudspeaker called faithful Muslims to prayer. Women, heads covered and wearing long black gowns, tagged the heels of their black-suited husbands. Tourists haggled with vendors tending pushcarts. Two men greeted one another with a kiss on each cheek. From sidewalk vendor stalls, the sights and aroma of fresh baked bread and meat sizzling in spices made her mouth water.

The scene would have been exhilarating—except worry for Ian scattered her thoughts. Why hadn't he met her at the airport?

Her breathing accelerated. She must stop hyperventilating. Tomorrow, she and Ian were to take a rental car to the dig. He should be here. She lifted her chin. She would trust the Lord. He'd promised he wouldn't take her through any trial he hadn't prepared her for. Already, he'd been with her through massive deep waters. He'd proved faithful, but could she survive more?

"Stop!"

She started. A tall, dark-haired man raced toward her through the snarl of pedestrians. He shouted, "*Tehlike! Tehlike!*"

He didn't look like a Turk.

Before she could guess what the charging man wanted, someone from behind slammed against her. A whiplash jolted her, and the strap to her shoulder bag snapped.

The thief evaporated into the crowd, her purse cradled like a football in his robe-covered arm.

"Hey! Stop! Help!" Loss and a sense of vulnerability flashed through her. She would not panic. She would remain calm.

The man who had shouted rushed toward her.

Her heart pounded. On the plane, the flight attendants had warned Turkish purse snatchers worked in pairs. The running man must be after her camera.

As the man thundered toward her, she took her stance. When the runner reached her side, she grabbed his arm. Utilizing the force of his rush, she flipped him.

He sprawled flat on his back.

Her move worked!

Her gratification was cut short.

As he fell, the man caught her hand between his arm and his body. Her feet tangled with his. She fought for balance, wavered, and collapsed on top of him.

He groaned, whooshed out air through puffed out his lips, looked dazed, and shook his head.

She shoved against his chest. "Thief! Leave me alone."

"Thief? I came to help."

She kicked and squirmed, trying to untangle her limbs from his big body. "Let me go!" After the long plane ride, Ian not meeting her, and losing her purse, this was too much. Her throat constricted, and tears prickled her eyelids.

"Mind getting your elbow out of my gut?" A baritone voice gasped.

She struggled to her feet. "Who are you?"

"A friend."

Amusement danced in his eyes.

His dark good looks made her shiver.

He flashed a smile, then sprang to his feet.

His cavalier demeanor unnerved her. "What? Do you think you're some kind of hero?"

He bowed. "Hero, no. But you could make rational men forget their manners."

Nicole hated come-on lines. She had withstood way too many. "You have a lot of nerve!"

"In my profession, nerve and fast reactions save lives."

She glared. "If you're not an accomplice, then help me get my purse back!"

"Too late. Thief's disappeared into any one of a hundred hiding places."

Turning from his dark intensity, a sinking sensation hit her like a punch to her stomach. Her so-called rescuer was right. She glanced up and down the street, then appealed to the swarthy-skinned men sprinkled among black clad women who had formed a ring around them. "Help me. I need a policeman!"

Several onlookers raised open hands and shrugged.

"Apparently, unlike me, they don't speak English." Her would-be rescuer crossed his arms over his chest. "I'm also fluent in Turkish. I'll be glad to help you."

His cocksure attitude boosted her exasperation. "Mr. ...?"

"Joshua Baruch." He touched his forehead in a salute. "I had hoped to stop that purse snatcher, but your karate moves sent me into a tailspin."

"Compliments of Mr. Toshika's night class." The familiar, vulnerable shaky feeling she hated returned. Had she manhandled the wrong person?

Baruch gently squeezed her arm. "Let me guess. You've lost your passport and your money. Everything a tourist needs was inside your purse?"

She slid her arm free. Wrong. She'd hidden her passport and ID in the wallet around her waist. But she had to get her money back. Had to tell the police where her hotel was located. That would be difficult due to her directional dyslexia. She glanced around the foreign scene for a street sign and found one with an unpronounceable Turkish name.

Baruch tapped her shoulder.

"What?" She pivoted to face him, to memorize his features in case she needed to identify him to the police. He was irritatingly handsome with large, dark eyes, straight brows, a slender nose, and full, firm lips. His slight grin and his manner indicated events transpired to his liking. Though clean shaven, stubble showed beneath the taut skin of his square jaw. With his olive complexion, he looked Mediterranean. Yet his English sounded pure American.

"I'm here to help." He smoothed his rumpled shirt and flicked dirt from his khaki pants.

She couldn't read his expression.

"I'm a fellow American." His lips tightened. "Jewish."

As if his heritage mattered in her predicament. Still, he was from the States. Her exasperation faded. She gathered her composure around her, but it lay limp as silk in a rainstorm and felt as transparent.

In the States, she avoided this type of man. Even before Paul, she hadn't trusted fine-looking men. Especially men who held a high opinion of themselves—like this one.

But she had no one else until Ian showed up. "You said Josh Baruch. From?"

"Here in Istanbul on a short vacation. I thought you needed rescuing." He rubbed his back. "Although, I could be mistaken." His expression remained deadpan. Only his eyes twinkled.

"You're right. I just arrived in Turkey after a twenty-hour trip, and my brother didn't meet me at the airport." She hated the way her voice broke. "Now my purse is gone." Out of politeness, she refrained from adding, *and a strange man accosted me.* "I'm worried about my brother. It's not like Ian to be late."

She turned from Baruch's intrusive eyes. "And this city is huge and foreign. I don't know my way around." *And you, Josh Baruch, make me extremely wary.*

His hand cupped her elbow and guided her away from the gawking pedestrians. "Let's not provide any more entertainment for the locals." He gestured to a bellboy to carry her three bags inside.

"Okay. I'm for that." Contrary to her better judgment, but pinched by circumstances, she let the American escort her through the double glass doors into the modest hotel.

"I think you're handling this situation well. You've lost everything you need to survive here, and you worry about your brother? *Chutzpah!*" He winked.

"Thanks." Spunk? No, she had only her trust in God and needed to rely on every bit of her mustard seed faith until Ian arrived. "Where can my brother be?"

He didn't answer.

After the noise and heat of the streets, the cool, inviting atmosphere of the hotel embraced her. In the narrow lobby, black leather couches clustered around a large glass cocktail table. Not so different from a Texas hotel. The bellboy stood by her bags as if guarding them from an invading army.

Josh Baruch steered her toward a dapper Turkish clerk behind the hotel's registration desk. While her heart beat like a bird trying to escape a cage, Baruch leaned against the marble counter as relaxed as a model in *Gentlemen's Quarterly*.

Or more like a wildcatter drilling for oil. He looked to be a man who operated outside the bounds of standard practice, a fearless man who lived on the edge. Though he dressed in khaki slacks and white polo shirt, Baruch appeared out of place in the cozy hotel atmosphere. Oh, she recognized his type. He was every bit as daring and adventurous as her late husband.

She wanted nothing to do with the reckless, danger-loving type. His authoritative, take-charge manner irritated. But he spoke English and Turkish. Until Ian showed up, she needed him.

She didn't need the tingling awareness she experienced when he stood close. The man obviously knew his way around women and the effect he had on them, the curse of attractive men. Another reason she avoided them.

"What's your name?" Baruch smiled. "After we get you quartered inside your room, we'll ring the police."

"I'm fixin' to do just that."

Baruch must have meant his expression to be reassuring. "Can't call in the cavalry unless I know your name."

"Nicole Phillips."

A startled look swept Baruch's face.

Why? She turned to the desk clerk and spoke slowly, hoping the man understood English. "I have a reserved room."

Baruch leaned toward her. "You're from the south."

She nodded. "Texas. Can't hide my Hill Country accent."

The deskman pushed a register toward her.

She signed the ledger. "My brother and I will pay our bill when we leave."

She caught the guarded expression that stole across Baruch's face. What was that all about?

"You're in luck! Few people check passports once you're inside Turkey." He frowned. "But you'll need yours to leave the country."

She had her documents, but that wasn't his business. "After I get my key, I'll call the police from my room." Nicole rubbed her eyes. The long trip and the shock of not seeing Ian had drained her. "You seem familiar with Turkey."

"I visit here one month every year to fulfill my Air Force Reserve pilot's training. Plus, I was stationed in Turkey at Incirlik Air Base while on active duty."

"Really. That explains how you speak the language so fluently." Summoning energy, she turned to the desk clerk. "What's my brother's room number, please? His name's Ian McKenzie."

"Right." Baruch muttered. He skimmed a big hand through his hair.

Was the fleeting look on Baruch's face relief? Strange.

The desk clerk handed her an old-fashioned brass key with the number stamped on its wide bottom edge. "Your room four twelve."

She could barely understand his heavily-accented English. "Thanks."

"According to the register, your brother's room is next to yours, number four thirteen." Baruch pointed to the key safe behind the desk and spoke Turkish to the clerk.

The man handed Josh the key to Ian's room.

"Did Ian leave me a message?"

Josh spoke in Turkish to the clerk, then turned to her. "No messages."

She clutched the old-fashioned key until the metal bit into her hand. The threatened headache took hold with a vengeance. *Heavenly Father, where is Ian?*

The desk clerk jabbered a long string of Turkish.

Josh leaned against the counter and interpreted, his face open and friendly. "Your brother dropped his key at the desk before he left Monday morning. Mr. McKenzie was the first person down that day. He mentioned seeing the sights." Baruch's dark brows jutted together.

She gnawed at the long nail on her index finger, then tried to sound calm, but her voice trembled. "Monday morning? Ian didn't spend the last two nights here?"

"Apparently not." Josh gave a reassuring smile.

She jammed a hand across her mouth.

Baruch drummed his fingers on the desk. "Don't panic. Your brother might have checked in after this guy got off duty." He lifted an eyebrow. "Then there's traffic. Traffic in Istanbul is risky. Turks are notoriously fast, fate-driven—"

"No! No. Something's happened to Ian!"

"Okay." Baruch's voice turned soothing. He dangled Ian's key. "Let's check your brother's room for messages. Then we'll call the police and report your purse stolen."

She tried to hide her gnawing suspicion Baruch wasn't quite what he seemed. "Why are you helping me?"

"You're as unpredictable as a crosswind landing." He shrugged and reached into his back pocket, pulled out his wallet, and flashed his American driver's license and his pilot's license. "Here, check this out."

She caught his hand as he started to stuff his wallet back in his pocket and peered closer. As far as she could tell, the identification appeared authentic. He lived in Virginia.

"You don't trust me, do you?"

"It's a long story, but … I don't trust anyone." The dangers of the past year crashed through her like a fatal accident, making her longing for Ian almost physical. She needed his brilliant mind to answer her questions, needed his comforting presence to prove he was safe. She needed him safe.

Rumblings of laughter rose from deep within Baruch's chest. "This must be your first time out of the States, or you'd know Americans hang together in foreign countries."

His laughter helped. "You're right. I guess my naiveté shows."

He thrust out his hand. "Let's go, Texas."

She ignored his hand.

He led the way to the elevator, and she studied him from behind. As his loafers struck the marble floor, she categorized him as a man comfortable with commanding and getting his way. After a year of terror, she didn't mind having such a man help her. She frowned. Her new semi-acceptance of this American put her on edge, as if she were betraying Paul.

But Baruch seemed okay. Beneath his faux-charm, Josh struck her as kind. She liked his dark, twinkling eyes and the way his hair showed signs of waves. When he punched the elevator bell, his wide shoulders strained the fabric of his shirt.

Groaning noises drifted from above as the elevator moved down. When Josh pulled the doors open and stood aside for her to enter, she hesitated. "That tiny elevator looks as substantial as an ornate hat box. We could take the stairs."

"It's okay. These elevators are sturdier than they look. German made. They complain, but they get the job done." He bowed. A dare. "After you."

She walked inside with Josh on her heels. The bellboy pushed in after them, jamming all three suitcases into the tiny space. Crammed against Baruch, who was sandwiched between the bags, bellboy, and her, she was conscious of his masculine scent.

They didn't speak during the slow ride to the fourth floor.

She stepped out, glad to be on solid ground and away from the press of his body. "I must seem like a Texas country girl to you." She certainly felt like one.

He raised an eyebrow. "Country girl? No way."

They filed through the dimly lit hallway—footsteps soft on the worn carpet. The bare tan walls looked depressing. The unfamiliar foreign atmosphere of the upstairs, with all the rooms lined on one side facing a blank wall, intrigued her. Under different circumstance, she could enjoy travel in foreign countries.

When they stopped in front of room four-twelve, Josh lounged against the door frame while she inserted the old-fashioned key.

He folded a bill into the bellboy's hand. The boy smiled. In accented English he pronounced, "If you have need of a item, ask Rashid."

"Thanks, Rashid. We can locate the lights."

The bellboy nodded and left.

Josh dragged her luggage into the tiny room, lifted her suitcases onto the bed, and swung around to face her, a flush on his cheeks. He took her arm, fingers warm against her skin. "Let's go check out your brother's room."

She didn't budge. Only extended her palm. "Ian's key, please."

Josh slipped a hand into his trouser pocket, retrieved the key, and folded her fingers over the metal. His lips parted in a display of straight, white teeth. "Let's see if we can track down that errant brother of yours."

Her heart lifted. He made this nightmare seem a game. If only this proved to be that simple. They left her room and walked into the hallway. She fit the key into Ian's lock, and Baruch shoved the door open.

He entered first. His tall body blocked her view, wide shoulders brushing the insides of the doorway.

Staring at his back, heart thudding, she spoke through a tightened throat. "Please let me by."

He didn't move.

She pushed past him.

Then stopped dead. Fear for Ian gathered like a grey mist to settle with a chill in her heart.

"Someone's ransacked Ian's room."

CHAPTER FIVE

"Dear Father God, no!" Chills shivered Nicole's spine, then spread to her hands. Her fingertips grew icy.

Ian's tiny hotel room looked as though whirling dervishes had whipped through. Every dresser drawer hung open. His clothes lay scattered on the floor like discarded rubbish. Bed clothes draped mostly off the bed. Broken tiles swung from the ceiling. The cupboard door sagged by one hinge, and the grey carpet resembled wrinkled skin. Raveled edges gaped where the thick material had been ripped from the floor. The light above the dresser dangled by its cord like a dislocated eye.

Josh tugged her around to face him, expression a mask. Eyes grim, his voice was silk slit by a sharp knife. "Just *who* is your brother?"

She stumbled against him. Swayed.

Josh's hands gripped her shoulders.

She would not faint. She dropped her head to his shoulder. She couldn't lose Ian too.

"Take it easy." Josh's voice came from far away. He eased her down to lie on the disheveled bed, walked the few steps into the bathroom and brought back a damp towel to put on her forehead. He massaged her cold hands.

He opened the sealed bottle of water sitting on the bureau and handed her a glass. The single upright bottle had contrasted sharply with the devastated room. This detail seemed important as she struggled to adjust to the sense of unreality sweeping through her. She tried sitting.

"Why is your brother in Istanbul?" Baruch's brown eyes bored into her.

"Ian just completed his Masters. Archeology. University of Texas." The familiar words brought order to this frightening event. "Ian snagged a job at a dig in Antalya. Working with the Turkish Government." Her fingers had a life of their own as they clenched and unclenched rumpled sheets. She stilled them.

"How long has he been in Turkey?"

"A few days. We planned to meet at the airport earlier this afternoon, then see the sights in Istanbul. Saturday, we were to travel to the dig." She shook her head. Something awful *had* happened to Ian!

She swung her legs over the side of the bed. "We need to call the police. Send out search parties."

"Easy."

"Ian needs me. He ..." She struggled against a rush of devastating emotions. "He's hearing impaired."

A startled look crossed Baruch's face.

"He can't read Turkish on foreign lips. Foreigners pronounce English differently. That's why I'm here. A few days ago, someone murdered his interpreter. I'm taking his place." Why sit here jabbering? She frowned against her headache, fighting the lost feeling drifting through her.

"Go on," his warm tone encouraging.

"I barely had time to make arrangements and pack." She rambled, grasping for solid ground. Life had grown surreal again. She couldn't lose her baby brother. *Oh God, please keep Ian safe.*

"Was your brother born deaf?"

She shook her head, trying to focus on Josh's questions. "No. We have a family history of genetic deafness. The problem's progressive, beginning about age eleven. Ian was completely deaf by twenty-one." Despite the warning clanging in her brain, she babbled on. "Ian speaks clearly as long as he continues speech therapy. If he doesn't, he forgets the sound of words."

"And you?"

She hardly knew what she answered. "Spared the defective gene." Her voice rose. "We must call the police. Do something. Help me find my brother."

"Take it easy. I said I'm here to help. Why would anyone be after your brother?"

"I haven't the faintest idea!" She jumped to her feet and searched for a phone. "Who did this? I have to find a phone."

"Whoa. Slow down. I need some background information." Baruch sat on the bed, pulled her next to him, and took her hands.

His strength and calmness restored a measure of her composure.

"Describe your brother."

"Tall. Almost your height, only more slender. Extremely intelligent." She glanced down. Baruch held her hands firmly.

"An Einstein, eh? I've got the picture. Tell me more."

"Sandy-haired. Attractive. Women flock after him. But he's shy with them."

"Afraid?"

"Yes. He's never dated much. His lack of hearing makes him skittish." She pulled her hands free. "We're close. More so since ..."

"Since?"

"I lost my husband last year." Josh's interest seemed so genuine. A rock in the shifting sand. Why was she spilling so much information to this stranger? She'd never excelled at keeping her mouth shut. Think. She must have time to think. And pray.

Noting the stern contours of his face, she shifted him in another direction. "Please, find me a telephone." She jumped up and headed for the door. "There must be a telephone in the lobby."

"There is. Do you speak Turkish?"

Her steps faltered. She squared her shoulders and stopped, hand on the doorknob. "No, but you do. How well?"

"Fluently. I'll help you make the call, but first I need more facts. How old is your brother?"

"Twenty-four."

His penetrating eyes assessed the room. "Not many clothes or personal effects. Think this is all he brought, or were some things stolen? And your husband, did he die of natural causes?"

Anger flashed through her. "This has nothing to do with Paul's death!" Jerking open the door, she ran from the room and was halfway down the hall toward the stairs when Josh caught her arm.

"I'm trying to prepare you. Turkish police prefer not to get involved with foreigners' troubles. Too much paperwork. But they'll grill you. They'll want to know why your husband died … why your brother is missing. Suspicion may fall on you." His tone sounded gentle, but he smoldered like a lighted stick of dynamite.

CHAPTER SIX

Frankfurt, Germany
Near Ramstein Air Base, home of the 86th Airlift Wing.

"Suzanne?" With a creak of expensive leather, Helmut Meier leaned back in his massive chair, ruffled thick fingers through silver hair and silently thanked whatever gods that be for his wife's greed. His gaze lingered on the graceful arch of her neck and the pale cameo of her face framed with masses of black hair.

"Yes. Exquisite." Suzanne, head bowed, eyed the treasure.

Helmut smiled. His present wife resembled a mother peering into the face of her loved infant as she gazed at the ancient mosaic tiles he'd placed on his enormous mahogany desk.

"Smuggled from Turkey?" Suzanne lifted a disdainful lip.

"Yes." He shifted his gaze to the mosaics. "The new dig is rich. A buried city as important as Ephesus. Mosaic inlaid rooms filled with statuary and jewels." He stroked the tiles with a tender finger.

"Greek or Roman?"

"Greek. But we have one small problem."

"We?" Her delicate brows arched. "Helmut, I remind you. You signed a prenuptial contract not to involve me in your export-import business."

Helmut snorted. She was quick. But dear, intelligent Suzanne was no match for him. He possessed intuitive insights that had transformed him from a beer garden waiter to the third richest man in Europe. He read people's imperfections as easily as other men read the daily news. He tightened his lips. Then he exploited those flaws.

"My dear. Of course." Heaving his massive bulk from the chair, he breached the space between them and grasped her fingers. "You enjoy the good life my money buys, but you don't taint your lovely hands with my business."

The challenge Suzanne must accept from him—her part in his private war against Major Joshua Baruch—made his heart race and his blood heat. He licked his lips.

Her lips turned down at the corners. "Helmut, you promised."

Today, everything about this woman excited him—surprising after a year of marriage. He pulled her close. "My love. My faithful wife."

Suzanne pushed away.

Settling back into his chair, he tugged her head down and rubbed his whiskers against her soft cheek. "At this moment, you are of more value to me than all the mosaics hidden by antiquity."

"How sweet."

Ignoring her sarcastic tone, he closed his eyes. Heady sensations of power from his anticipated victory over Major Baruch spread a flush through his body.

Less than two years ago in the historic part of Frankfurt on Königstrasse, the major had brought his brother and his brother's wife, Suzanne, into Helmut's Antiquities of the World shop.

Helmut steepled his fingers over his muscular girth. Fortunately, the major, his brother, and Suzanne loved antiquities. They had been intrigued by the few treasures he'd smuggled out of Turkey. Back then, he'd been smitten with Suzanne. With her willowy grace and liquid eyes, she personified everything beautiful in Jewish women. Suzanne's haunting loveliness presented an instant challenge. Her marriage to the major's brother added to his fun. "I do appreciate you so, dear Suzanne."

"You are a man who values fine things." She tossed her head, flipping shining dark curls over her shoulder.

"And you hold the same values as I, my sweet." The first day he'd met her, he'd probed her personality for weaknesses and found Suzanne had a driving passion to possess fine things.

"You belong in my world." He encircled the curve of her waist and breathed in the scented skin. Suzanne's beauty had nudged him into disposing of his second wife. Little Natalie. So sad to die so young.

Suzanne twisted away to stand behind him.

He so enjoyed recalling how he'd lured all three Baruchs to his estate for weekend rides, giving them their choice from his stable of Arabians. When the major and his brother—what was his name—had been called to the States for business, he invited Suzanne to his mansion.

He'd dazzled her with precious jewels, flown her to the German-Austrian border to see King Ludwig's fairytale castle, and squired her to quaint towns like Idar Oberstein. The major's brother hadn't a suspicious thought in his head. Perhaps he'd thought Helmut too old for sweet Suzanne.

When Suzanne would settle for nothing less than marriage, he'd ordered the major's brother killed. He could dispose of Suzanne when she outgrew her value.

He caught her hand. "I had no delusions. Money bought you, my prize."

For a short time—far too short—Suzanne aroused his dormant passion. The test he was about to give her fired him anew.

"My sweet bride." He swiveled his chair to face her. "I am the wealthiest man you will ever meet." He turned her palm over and displayed the nine-carat diamond sparkling on her ring finger. "And so, you will remain my devoted wife."

"Indeed."

She tried to pull her hand free, but he wrestled her onto his lap. "I need your help."

"You sound serious."

"Deadly."

Already her eyes sparkled wariness. Like an alert fox, she scented danger. Hiding his elation under a lazy gaze, he searched her face. He'd not mentioned her ex-brother-in-law since their wedding. "How long since you've seen the major?"

She jerked. He allowed her to leap up. Slipping into position behind him, her soft hands tightened on his neck. "I haven't spoken to Joshua since you and I married. At least a year. Not after he left Germany." She frowned. "He's no longer full-time Air Force, but I don't know how he makes his living."

She gazed out the bank of windows that overlooked his formal gardens. Her delicate mouth thinned.

His trusted intuition jangled alarm. "No? Not even a phone call?" Rising to his entire six-foot-five inches, he jammed her into his arms.

Standing on the sharp edge of danger, desire filled him as it had when he was young. Women had once been his weakness. These days only the use of force or the uncertainty of risk excited him.

"No, Helmut. Why should I contact Joshua?"

Helmut crushed her to him and whispered into her lovely ear. "Do you still nurture feelings for the major?"

"Of course. I *was* wed to his brother three years." She pushed against his embrace. "I still care about Joshua's welfare."

He released her. They stood toe to toe. "Do you care enough to save the major's life and earn a scandalous sum of money?"

Suzanne pulled delicately back to gaze into his eyes.

Most men would have cowered.

She did not. "What do you want me to do?"

"My intelligent, practical beauty. How like you to come straight to the point. No games. I'll lay my cards on the table as well. You may play them or not."

Suzanne's expression hardened. She crossed her arms, her back stiff. "And if I don't?"

"That would be sad, my sweet. The major would suffer an unfortunate accident. I can afford no wild card destroying my organization."

"You wouldn't!" Her dark eyes belied her denial.

"Not if he cooperates. If he doesn't, you need think of him no more. The major will no longer exist."

Suzanne stepped back from him until her spine touched the bank of windows.

"I prefer not to be pushed to that extreme." He savored the lie, knowing just how much he would enjoy disposing of the major when the time came. "Unfortunately, he knows too much. The fact is, yours will not be his first offer. The major has already refused me."

She faced him like a tiger held at bay by his training whip. "Why Joshua? Why can't you leave him alone? Find someone else to do your dirty work."

"Your concern might cause me to reconsider." He chuckled. "But I believe you won't jeopardize your present life for any sentimental concern you might have for the major."

He explained her mission.

"Helmut, you are a devil!"

"Had I been a vampire and bonded you to myself with a fatal bite, we could not be more attached." He held his thumb and index finger a fraction of a milliliter apart. "And yet, there is the slight possibility I am wrong." He smiled. "Therein lies the risk. And the thrill." He squeezed her arm until he knew it hurt. "You are the major's one chance to live."

Her face turned pale as the ramifications of the situation became clear. Then, her expression melted into anxiety. "Joshua will hate me if I trap him into accepting your plan ... and he'll die if I don't."

How astute he was, how transparent other people. Feelings of god-like power permeated each cell as neurons fired in a heady rush until his face flushed. What pleasure Suzanne provided! "My dear. Don't expect the major to welcome you. But be assured, you hold his life in your capable hands." Suzanne would not leave him. He bound her by stronger ties than love.

"I know Joshua. He will never agree to your plan ... even to save his life."

"The major has a fatal flaw, my dear. He wears a white hat. And he still loves you. That's the leverage you will use." He drew his wife close and bit her soft neck. Suzanne would either ensnare the major into working for him or entice him to a rendezvous with death.

CHAPTER SEVEN

Nicole gritted her teeth, tilted her chin high, and tossed back her long hair. "My husband died in a plane crash. The circumstances are not related."

"You're sure?" Josh folded his arms across his chest.

"Certain." Was she?

"And Ian's clothes? Nothing's missing?"

"Ian has little interest in what he wore. I don't suppose he packed more than shorts, a few shirts, running shoes, a dress shirt in case he found a church …" She stopped mid-sentence. Josh probably attended synagogue. Saturdays.

"Just these few clothes?" Josh cocked an eyebrow and motioned to the clothes strewn around the room.

Her suspicion bounced. She might give information he needed to … what? What if he knew where Ian was? No stranger could be this concerned. He had to have ulterior motives. She crossed her arms over her chest. She'd pretend to trust him. He might lead her to Ian.

"What do you think is missing?" Josh leaned against the wall.

She surveyed the room. "I don't see Ian's tools."

"Tools?"

"Picks, brushes, notebooks, maps. Most of his luggage would have consisted of his archaeological equipment." She glanced around again. "I don't see any."

Josh mused, "No note, no equipment. Before we call the police …" His jaw squared, and his mouth thinned. "… let's see if we can discover any clues."

"Us?"

"We'll touch nothing. Preserve everything exactly as we find it."

"Why us?" Her suspicion skyrocketed. She turned toward the door.

"This isn't the States. Trust me on this."

"Yeah. Right." She unslung her camera and snapped pictures of the destroyed room.

"Good move." He took out his cell and snapped different shots of the room.

"Thanks." She pulled in a deep breath. The shambled room yanked at her heart. Mouth trembling, she spied one of Ian's rumpled shirts on the floor. Resisting the temptation to hide her face in its clean, American folds, she tried to loosen the icy fingers gripping her heart. "What could have happened to my brother?"

He glanced up from examining the lock on the door. "Looks bad. I think someone's kidnapped him."

Nicole tried to maintain a level voice. "You think?" *Why did you let this happen, Father? Kidnapped! What ransom can I pay?*

She steadied her inner quaking with deep breaths. "When I first became a Christian, I thought nothing bad could happen to me. Then I lost my husband. And a few months later, I lost my parents."

Josh nodded. A deep line formed between his dark brows. "Yeah. You were no longer protected by faith in your own invincibility." His voice softened. "The same naïveté sends pilots into combat with the belief they won't die."

"Yeah. Something like that." She snapped a few more pictures. "Now, I know differently. Bad things do happen to Christians." She pulled in another deep breath. "But God will see us through this. And he will protect Ian." She felt better. At least she'd opened the door to sharing her faith with Josh.

Josh's eyebrows rose, and a smile twitched his lips. "I understand your loss of innocence. I'm a survivor too."

"You've been through rough times?" A flash of sympathy warmed her.

"Nothing I want to discuss." He sorted through the cluttered mess. "Whoever dismantled this room did a professional job. I doubt the police will find fingerprints." He peered at the door jamb. "Don't expect Turkish authorities to wear latex gloves and bag evidence."

"Do they even fingerprint?"

"I don't know how sophisticated their investigation will be. I do know they don't read Miranda rights when they arrest." He handed her his ballpoint pen and a handkerchief. "Use these to lift things as you search. Try not to disturb anything."

He flicked open the longest blade of a Swiss Army Knife and turned over one of Ian's shirts. "I once had to rescue one of my men for writing *Turks suck* on a restaurant window." His mouth twisted. "Then I pulled the fastest transfer on record to whisk him out of the country. Authorities could have thrown him into a Turkish prison for eight years for that stupid slur."

"For graffiti?" Using the tip of Josh's pen and his handkerchief, she rummaged through the mess in the cupboard. Conversation distracted her thoughts from mental images of Ian kidnapped, hurt ... or worse.

"Yeah. Most Turks are Muslims. They're ticklish when someone smears their name, especially those they label Christians.

By Christian they mean infidel, non-Muslim." He glanced at her from his crouched position by the bed. "That includes Jews."

"Why would a soldier write that graffiti?"

"Drunk. Incirlik Air Base is Turkish-owned and run, although we build the buildings and maintain the airstrip. Turks suffer our presence because they need our military support." Josh stood on tiptoe to inspect the light fixture. "When they no longer need us, they'll kick us out. Meanwhile, they wreak havoc with our training. Makes life ... difficult."

"So, you're Air Force. Reserve did you say?"

"Right. I enjoy several months training at Incirlik Air Base every year."

Respect for the man sifting through the debris hit her. A bud of trust wound through her heart. She nodded. Any other time, she would have found Josh riveting. Now, interest was inconvenient. If Josh were going to help her find Ian, she preferred he behave as a friend, nothing more. She frowned. Not that he had been anything other than a gentleman, even from the start.

She opened the bathroom door. The thoroughness of the intruder's search jarred her. Tile by tile, someone had pried up the floor. The medicine cabinet lay across the sink, glass door broken. The smashed toilet bowl cover spread in huge chunks around the stool. Plaster littered the floor like burial mounds, crunching under her feet.

"Strange no one heard any destruction noise going on here." Josh shook his head. "Maybe the kidnappers had inside help."

"Can we check that out?"

"Might be a lead. I'll follow it. More likely a dead end though. If they had inside help, no one is likely to talk."

"What are we looking for?" She wrinkled her nose at the old room's moldy odor.

"Any clue." He followed her into the bathroom. "A scrap that isn't from your brother's stuff. A footprint." He raked his fingers through short hair and grunted. "Anything unusual."

Dropping to hands and knees, he eyed the wall behind the ripped-out tiles under the sink. "The Turkish police may choose to say, 'Allah doesn't will for them to inspect these rooms.'" He stood.

She met the dark intensity in his eyes. "Allah's will is involved?"

"Sure. You're dealing with fatalistic Muslims. This investigation might be up to us. I think *we* can find your brother."

Her stomach sickened. "Us?" The lost feeling ratcheted back. "Without police help?"

"Turks are masters of delay. They'll dillydally. The trail will cool. Trust me. Whoever snatched Ian will contact us." The muscles in his jaw jutted. "Then we'll find them."

"And Ian."

"Of course."

She lowered her eyes and brushed past him to search the other room. Was Josh more interested in finding the kidnappers than rescuing Ian?

"Still no note?" Josh called from the bathroom.

"No note. I thought kidnappers always left them."

"We'll hear from them."

She turned over piles of clothes, lifted torn panels from the floor, and replaced everything as found. Nothing.

She plunked down on the tangled bedclothes atop the ripped-open mattress.

Josh folded to sit beside her. "They searched for something small. A piece of paper? A jewel?" He leaned forward, elbows on his knees, and massaged the back of his neck.

She piled two ravaged pillows between them. Even with his mind on Ian, the man radiated serious magnetism. "Ian hasn't

49

even visited the dig at Antalya. We planned to fly there together. He has our tickets."

Josh narrowed dark eyes and pinched the bridge of his nose. "That city's well excavated. I'm not aware of any dig going on there now."

She gripped her hands together.

Josh squeezed her shoulder. "But I'm not privy to every excavation in Turkey. It's conceivable there's a new one." He closed his eyes. Fatigue lines showed on his face. "How does an unknown grad garner a plum job in Turkey?"

"Ian met Professor Alexandros in Austin."

Josh's brown eyes flew open and held questions marks.

"At the University of Texas. Ian took archeology classes from the professor. Ian's brilliant and eager. The prof must have liked him."

Josh sprang from the bed as if he'd forgotten something and strode inside the bathroom.

She jumped up and found him on his knees eyeing ripped up tiles.

"Find anything?"

He turned, face flushed from bending, and held a hair aloft. He grinned.

"Hadn't we best leave it for the police?"

"Nope. Hand me a tissue. I hope the Turks have a lab, so we can get this analyzed. Your brother has sandy hair?"

"Yes. We have identical hair color. What color is that?"

"Black."

His searching look unsettled her shaky stomach.

"I'd say your hair is more like honey, thick and silky."

She made a wry face. "Why don't you stick to the search?" Seemed he expected every woman he charmed to fall for him.

"Prickly." He sent a crooked grin. "Sorry. I'll work on not complimenting you." He cleared his throat.

She stiffened. "Prickly when scared." He didn't look sorry. She lifted heavy hair off her hot neck. "Most Turks have black hair. Maybe this room wasn't cleaned well." She fumbled through litter until she found a roll of toilet paper, then handed it over.

He held the strand up to the bare light bulb. "Coarse texture. Might be fake." He rubbed his jaw. "Maybe a wig."

"You're right!" She almost hugged him. "We really have uncovered a clue!"

"Yeah." Pulling off some tissue, he wrapped the hair strand and then tucked the small packet into his pants pocket. "Men disguised as Turks might have kidnapped Ian."

"Of course. Men with lighter hair. We're on to something. I know it."

"Yeah." He wiped his hands on his khaki pants. "That's it then. Let's go."

They filed through the tiny bedroom and into the empty hallway. She locked the door behind them.

In front of her room, Josh paused. "Rest in your room until the police arrive. You look shaken. I'll fill them in on what we have. They'll question you." With a warm finger, he tilted her chin up. "They may give you a rough time."

If he continued this tenderness, how long could she hold back tears? "I'm okay. I'll go to the lobby with you."

"You rest. I'm off to phone the police."

Why not? She was tired. Besides, she badly needed to pray.

He strode down the hallway toward the elevator, punched the button, waited a few seconds, pulled the door open, and without a backward glance entered the old-fashioned elevator.

She gave a deep sigh, turned the key in her lock, and opened the door, half-expecting to see her own room a disheveled mess.

No, just as she left it. Now instead of looking dismal, the tiny space welcomed her with quiet arms, a sanctuary in this bustling country of ten million strangers.

Thank you, God, for Josh. I think you must have sent him.

CHAPTER EIGHT

Ian woke, gradually. Wished he hadn't. Pain stabbed his right temple and radiated down his neck and shoulder. His arms were bound behind him, his ankles tied, and his knees jammed halfway to his chin.

Absolute darkness. Uncomfortable pressure around his eyes told him he was blindfolded.

Attempting to stretch, he discovered he couldn't. Confused, memory a blur of pain, he fumbled for order through the chaos in his mind.

Throbbing in his head subsided to a prize-winning headache. The constant bumping and rough upholstery beneath his cheek alerted him he must be wedged inside the trunk of a jouncing vehicle.

Why?

A flash of memory jerked him back to the Topkapi Palace Museum. Nightmare events. He panted in the heavy heat and nausea gripped his stomach. No one knew he had the map, and he didn't look like a rich tourist. So, why kidnap him?

The vehicle jolted, smacking his head into the trunk lid. With shooting pain, a new thought punctured his consciousness. Nikki must have arrived at the *Havaalani*, the airport.

Sweat broke out on his forehead and drenched his heated body. *Father, please guide her.*

He willed his pounding heart to slow. In the suffocating, stagnant air, bile rose in his throat. T-shirt and shorts clutched like sticky hands to his skin. His mind functioned as if he stood brainstem-deep in mud. Must be drugged.

He flexed swollen hands, wincing as they received a minute supply of blood. Enough to throb. He tried rolling off his side but was wedged too tight to move. He must have spent hours hogtied inside this trunk. Where were they taking him? What were these guys after?

Had to be the map.

He rubbed his forehead against the fuzzy floor like a dog worrying a bone, trying to dislodge the blindfolding tape. No luck. His efforts increased the pounding inside his skull. His thoughts short circuited.

What if the kidnappers grabbed Nikki?

The tape binding his mouth muffled his shriek. Fearful images built in his mind. He worked the ropes shackling him, but his struggles only coated his body with sweat. His tongue clung to the roof of his mouth. His wrists and ankles grew bloody.

Father, please protect Nikki.

Feeling more alone than she'd ever felt, Nicole pressed against the closed hotel door and let choked-back tears slide. She sank to her knees beside the bed, buried her face in the bright woven cover, and cried. Face and hands wet, chest heaving, she opened her heart.

Oh Lord, please protect Ian. Please guide me to him. Give me wisdom. Please, spread Your comfort and strength through my soul … and give me peace.

Little by little her nerves released, leaving her drained of energy. She wiped her face with her fingers and tossed back her hair. She poured a glass of water, swallowed two aspirins, and stretched out on the bed.

A commanding knock on her door made her jerk. Her hand flew to her throat.

"Open up, Nicole! It's Josh." He pounded again.

She ran to the door. The man outside represented danger. Not bodily but emotional—the kind she was far from ready to experience. With her emotions so vulnerable, she didn't want to be alone with him. She needed to talk with a police officer who would track Ian and end this ordeal.

"Nicole. Are you inside? Are you okay?"

"Yes. Are the police with you?" She put a careful hand on the doorknob.

"Let me in."

She turned the key, pulled the door ajar, and peeked into intense black eyes. Where was a safety chain when she needed one?

Josh pushed past her into the tiny room. She braced her back against the wall, against the vitality he brought with him. Against the distrust.

An almost imperceptible line between his brows deepened. "When you didn't answer, I thought someone kidnapped you too. Why didn't you let me in?"

"Where are the police?"

His face tightened.

She couldn't read his expression.

"They're not coming."

"What?" The shrillness in her voice warned she perched on the brink of hysteria.

"Ease up. We're going to them. They're understaffed and refuse to leave the police station." He frowned. "Whatever you're doing to calm your nerves isn't working."

"I won't lose control." She hugged her arms. "I can't."

He stepped closer.

She forced herself to stare into his eyes that were less than a hand's breadth away. The color wasn't black but deep, warm brown with golden specks. She held her ground, though her senses screamed retreat. "I'm—"

"You're the most wholesome looking girl-next-door, WASP, American girl I've met in Istanbul." His voice roughened. "And I haven't seen gorgeous legs like yours in a long, long time."

A blush heated her cheeks. He said WASP as if the word were praise. She tightened her lips. She'd been away from single men far too long. "Please stick to business."

Josh grinned a movie-star grin and braced a hand against the window frame. "Didn't your travel agent warn you not to wear short skirts here? In the outlying villages the men could stone you." The crease between his eyebrows deepened, and his gaze slid away. "Or rape you. After watching MTV, Turks think all American women are prostitutes." He scrubbed his hand over his face. "You're fair game, and they're sharpshooters. In Turkey, Americans live by Turkish rules."

"No travel agent. Spur of the moment plans. And I'm one of those born and bred Texans who's never been outside our state."

"Just my luck."

"You could charm a kitten out of its milk."

He flashed an apologetic smile.

Evidently her sarcasm wasn't lost on him.

"Sorry, I didn't intend to blurt that out. I'm not the most diplomatic pilot around."

A tiny shock pinged her chest. He was apologizing. "Fine." She tossed her hair, turned away, and massaged her temples. She needed to sweep the Josh static from her mind. She walked to the curtainless window and gazed into the rear of several tall apartments on the other side of a narrow alley. People cluttered small balconies fringed with lines of handmade Turkish rugs which swung below hanging pots of bright flowers.

"Please, please forget the come ons." Hands anchored to the window frame, back toward him, she spoke to the window. "I'm ready to leave."

"Josh Baruch at your service until we locate your brother." His breath stirred her hair. "We'll find Ian before my vacation ends."

She smothered a gasp. "It will take that long?"

"Might."

"Let's go." She pushed by him.

He blocked the door. "After you change clothes. Do you have another skirt?" His cheeks reddened like a boy caught fishing a *no trespassing* lake. "Not a short skirt—more like one that falls to your ankles?"

"Yes. Your grandmother would love wearing it."

His grin looked sheepish. "Sleeveless shirts won't fly either. Long sleeves keep prowling Turks at bay."

"What? In this heat! Archaic." She stiffened. "What else do chauvinistic Turkish men decree?"

"Some like their women to cover their hair. But none expect that of foreign women."

She groaned.

"What does it take to gain a smile?" He lifted an eyebrow. "Look, I just gave up my vacation for you. You've got no one else, and I'm a sucker for a beautiful woman in distress." A dimple creased his cheek. "Not that I run into one that often."

She smacked her hands on her hips. "Nobody asked you to give up your vacation. I'm perfectly capable—"

"Sorry. Poor choice of words. Change clothes and let's go. I'd prefer to finish at the station before dark. Maybe we'll learn something about your brother by then."

He apparently had scant faith they'd hear from Ian. But God was on their side, so she did. And okay, so he wanted a smile. She smiled her sweetest. "Wait in the hall."

"Right. Hurry!" He stomped off and slammed the door.

She slid around the edge of the bed, unzipped one of her bags, grabbed a long, brown broomstick skirt and a soft cream blouse with three-quarter length sleeves, and changed. Then splashed her face with cool water.

Where was her shoulder bag? She scanned the bedroom. Bother. She'd never see that purse again. Lifting some cosmetics from her suitcase, she dabbed her cheeks and lips with coral, and ran a comb through her hair. She mugged her reflection. "Wholesome looking WASP? Huh!"

She stuffed compact and lipstick into her brown leather hip pack. And, of course, her cell was gone, along with the international phone package.

Fingering the tassel hanging in front for quick opening, she sighed. Her fanny pack felt way too light without her gun. Since Paul's death, Ian insisted she carry a nine-millimeter. After the break in and threatening letters, she preferred carrying. She liked visiting the range and perfecting her skill and hadn't hesitated when Ian suggested she take Tai Kwon Do classes. Did Ian know things he hadn't told her? *Was* Paul's death linked to his disappearance?

She had no idea, but she didn't believe in coincidences.

She surveyed the room. A mess. Her bags sprawled open— contents scattered across the bed. Hairbrush and perfume littered the wooden dresser. She preferred leaving things neat. Since Paul died, she'd found tidy less lonely than messy.

An impatient knock.

She hurried to the dresser and picked up the room key. Soon the police would find Ian. Josh was a distraction. After they talked with the Turkish police, she would ditch Josh.

CHAPTER NINE

Nicole opened the door.

"Hi." Josh's deep voice greeted.

He appraised her with what appeared to be an experienced eye. His gaze felt as intrusive as the female guard's hands at the airport after she walked through the security gate. The woman had patted her down as if she were a convict entering prison rather than a tourist entering Istanbul.

Josh's heavy glance strayed to her fanny pack. "You're packing a weapon?"

"Only my lipstick."

A smile cracked his intent expression. "Feeling better?"

"Regaining equilibrium, thank you. At last, I'll have police help."

"Ouch. Search and Rescue's not enough for you. I'm doing my best."

His smile disarmed her, and hard-won emotional barriers tumbled. She hid defeat with a sassy expression.

"Before we leave, we set a few ground rules." He waved an index finger. "First, don't go anywhere alone. Another woman provides some protection, but a male companion is safe." He bowed. "You'll be treated with courtesy and respect as long as you're with me." He expression hardened. "No joke. A woman alone is an invitation."

So much for her plan to ditch him.

"That's limiting."

"Turkish rules." He grinned, teeth even and white against tan skin. He held the door open.

She locked up behind them, braved the adventure of the elevator, ignored his extended arm and hurried toward the downstairs lounge.

"In Turkey, we leave the room keys here," Josh murmured as they strode toward the main desk. "But Turks don't ask you to leave your passport."

"Fortunate for me." She surrendered her key to the deskman and hustled to where Josh waited, glass front door open.

Outside the hot air greeted her like an unwanted acquaintance—clinging, and impossible to escape.

CHAPTER TEN

The car jerked to a stop, throwing Ian against the interior of the trunk. In less than thirty seconds a burst of cold air rushed across his body indicating the lid had snapped open. Goose bumps prickled his skin.

Rough hands grabbed his ankles. Other hands clutched his shoulders and dragged him out of the trunk, scraping his arms against something.

He inhaled a deep breath. They carried him up an incline through sharp air that bit his bare arms and legs. The blindfold tape held so securely he couldn't tell daylight from dark. He fought rising panic. Without eyesight, he was cut off from the world.

Forcing himself to get a grip, he prayed. *Lord, please give me clarity of mind and the ability to face whatever comes.*

He calculated the distance they carried him. The jerky upward way had him at almost a sixty-degree angle, almost perpendicular. Frigid air this time of the year meant high altitude. Mentally, he consulted a Turkish map. Couldn't be any of the Aegean, Mediterranean, or Black Seas coastal areas. Might be one of the three mountain ranges crossing the Turkish plains. They had traveled too far to be in the Ararat Range. But he could be in the Pontus Mountains that divided central Anatolia from the shores of the Black Sea or perhaps the Taurus Mountains in southeastern Turkey.

As they carried him, the men slipped, cursed, and slid, so the terrain had to be rugged and probably snowy.

A chill shivered him. Wherever they were, his sixth sense assured him the area was remote. Best guess, Taurus Mountains.

The thugs's steps evened out. Warmer air replaced the biting cold. The smell of kerosene and candles swirled around him.

The men threw him down onto a straight-backed wooden chair, then shoved his bound arms over and behind the back of a chair. Splinters scraped his arms.

He groaned.

Someone passed another rope around his chest several times securing him to the chair.

After lying so long with restricted blood circulation from the shackles, his head spun and his muscles ached. Absolute silence and complete blindness walled him inside a dark prison. Fear clutched his chest.

His captors ripped the tape off his mouth.

Pain slashed through the lower part of his face. "What's going on? Who are yo—

A blow to his stomach knocked the wind from him and sent his chair sprawling on its back, pinning his arms beneath him. Fighting for breath, gasping, and battling panic, he forced himself to concentrate on details. The rough, uneven floor gave him a mental picture of a wooden hut like those in western ghost towns.

Before he recovered his breath, they dragged his chair upright.

Expecting another blow, he faced the silent void and gasped, "If you're interrogating me, you can stop. I can't hear you. I'm deaf."

Shock waves whirled around him in the dense silence.

"You've made a bad mistake. I have nothing you want."
Like an artifact brushed from eons of dirt and brought into

the spotlight of modern day, his head cleared. He'd just made a mistake. Since they couldn't know about the map, they must have kidnapped the wrong person. When they discovered their error, they would kill him, hide his body, and return to find the man they had mistaken him for. Swallowing against the terrible dryness in his throat, he racked his brain. What could he tell them to make them think he was worth keeping alive?

"I could be wrong about having nothing you want. Take off the blindfold, and we can talk. I read lips."

The floorboards vibrated under his sneakers. His captors were moving about. A burst of cold air wafted to his face. The outside door must have opened and shut.

Soft fingers touched his parched lips. Delicate perfume floated among the heavier odors of men. A swirl brushed his bare knee.

A woman!

Something hard pressed against his mouth. Water trickled down his chin. He gulped it. "Thanks. I'm hungry too."

Thirst somewhat slackened, another pressing need surfaced. Because of the woman, his cheeks burned. His urgency told him he must have been in the trunk an extremely long time, perhaps twelve hours. "I have to relieve myself."

He detected no movement.

"Do you speak English? Ingiliz?" He tried every language he knew. "Bathroom ... banyo ... tuvalet ... toilette."

Nothing happened.

Finally, rough hands ripped the ropes from around his chest and freed his ankles. Someone yanked him upright and pushed him across the room, out the door, and into the cold. His wrists still lashed behind his back, a burly form flanked each side. His feet and legs responded like blocks of wood. He stumbled on rocks, sneakers sliding in snow that filtered into his shoes. The wind bit his bare legs and arms.

They stopped—in the open as far as he could ascertain by the whip of the wind and the snow wetting his skin. The men wrestled with the ropes around his wrists and untied them. He flexed his swollen, numb hands. Someone reached around him, unzipped his shorts. Face flaming, he struggled not to wet himself. *Dear God, don't let the woman be watching.*

Inconsequential at such a time but embarrassing.

Shivering, he stumbled back to the hut between two men whose broad shoulders brushed his own. If his captors saw him as a person, a human being, he might stand a better chance of remaining alive. He spoke, "Y'all are tall for Turks."

A shove sent him to his bare knees on cold, wet rock.

Inside the hut, the two men jerked him to a halt. Both men gripped him by an arm and shoved him across the room. They kicked his feet out from under him. He landed flat on his back on a hard-spongy surface. They jerked his hands above his head and tied him spread-eagle to posts. A bed. Even without blanket or pillow, the bed offered more comfort than the car trunk or the chair. He flexed his cramped legs.

He tried to make his voice casual. "This is your luxury suite, right? First Class. Triple A."

The bed sagged. A flowery scent, sweet and clean. A woman.

Gentle fingers brushed back his hair and touched his face.

"Strip off the blindfold, will you? It shuts out the world." His words hurt his dry throat.

Instead she traced soft fingers along his jaw.

The mattress sprang up where she'd been sitting.

Had someone pulled her away? He tensed, expecting another blow. Minutes passed. Nothing happened.

"Hope the food's first class. I'm ready for it." He felt their presence in the swirl of heat from their bodies. They had to be big men.

"If you're asking me questions, I can't hear. Take off the blindfold, and we can straighten out this problem. Do you speak Turkish, French, Aleman, Español?" Already his arms ached from their stretch above his head. "Who are you? What do you want?" He stuffed fear down from his chest to his quivering stomach.

A heavy body sagged the mattress. His legs slid down the depression and landed against a broad, muscular thigh. Harsh hands thrust deep into his pocket and lifted his wallet.

The man moved, no doubt sorting through his wallet, reading his passport, driver's license, and credit cards. Cold sweat broke out on Ian's forehead. They would find Nikki's name, address, flight number, and hotel, which he'd jotted down and slipped into his billfold. Nikki!

A sharp pain. Ian grunted.

The kidnapper had stuck a knee into his side. Big hands patted him until the man discovered his money belt. The man pulled the band tight and snapped it.

A painful sting. Ian ground out between clenched teeth, "Enjoying yourself?"

With the thug's knee still jammed in his side, he pictured the kidnapper thumbing through his and Nikki's tickets to the dig in Antalya.

"Not as much money as you're used to collecting? I admire the way you guys cleared the room at the Topkapi. Professional job." He tried to squirm free of the thug's knee. No luck. The jerk increased the pressure. "Mind moving your knee?"

Someone stripped off his wet sneakers and socks. The water-proof packet containing the map he'd hidden there would now be in his captors's hands.

The knee in his side lifted. The mattress sprang up.

Relief. He sucked in a deep breath. The men must be celebrating their discovery.

Harsh hands grabbed his ankles, pulled his legs taut and tied his ankles to the foot of the bed.

"And I thought the other way was your luxury treatment." He was stretched tight between the bedposts.

A kick in the ribs made him gasp.

Fear clawed at him like a vulture's talons digging into roadkill.

CHAPTER ELEVEN

Nicole's senses numbed. Where was Ian? With him missing, Istanbul's charm and hubbub looked filtered, like sunlight through a dusty windowpane.

Despite the heat, the city purred with life. Outside the Asya Hotel, the narrow street shadowed by tall buildings provided Josh and her respite from the sun.

"City's a great mix of old world and new."

She tried to match Josh's enthusiasm. "Captivating."

Countless kiosks, selling goods from tablewares to bolts of cloth, offered an open-air market. They walked between portable carts loaded with fresh fruit, nuts, and kabobs of barbecuing meat. The delicious scent of juice seeping through layered slabs of browned lamb started her mouth to watering. How long since she'd eaten? She stopped in front of the cart.

"Hungry?" Josh smiled.

"Starved." An answering smile slid to her lips. Anxiety bubbled on the back burner of her mind, but her tummy rumbled.

Josh ordered. "*Gün aydin. Elma iki kebobs, efendim.*"

The vendor's eyes assessed her.

Josh frowned and slid his arm around her shoulders.

The Turk turned away. "*Serefinize,*" he muttered. Taking a large, sharp knife, he sliced thin sections of meat from the savory lamb. His stubby fingers laid the lamb slices on bread shaped like a long, fat pita, wafting an oven fresh aroma.

"*Ekmek.* Pronounced eck meck. Bread." Josh's deep voice sounded relaxed. "Taste's great. Good dipped in humus or dripping with honey or in a sandwich. But when ekmek cools, the bread grows stale. Have to eat it warm." He dropped his arm and propped a foot on the cart, apparently relaxed and in his home turf.

The proprietor wrapped their kabobs in paper and offered each of them a fat sandwich and some napkins.

"*Tesekkür ederim,*" Josh thanked him and handed the man a handful of lira.

The vendor beamed.

"*Allah ismarladik,*" Josh said.

"*Güle güle,*" the proprietor answered, appearing to accept whatever Josh had said. The man followed them several steps along the crowded street, bowing, and smiling.

Nicole took a bite, and savoring the succulent kabob, threaded through the crowd beside Josh. They trudged up the sidewalk's steep incline. At intervals, they picked their path through concrete that had crumbled into stones.

"Careful. Watch your step."

As she worked her way over collapsed stones, Josh cupped his hand under her elbow. His touch raised her confidence.

The walkway disappeared into a stairway passage leading down to a tiny shop tucked into the side of the tall building. "These basement shops look intriguing." She wended her way with downcast eyes to avoid falling into one of the hidden stairwells. Wares strewn in casual heaps on the walk forced her to edge into the honking traffic that sped through the narrow street.

She finished eating her kabob before they reached the corner. She'd stared at the buildings and signs to locate landmarks to help retrace the way back to the hotel.

Directional dyslexia had many disadvantages, especially with Turkish names so difficult to pronounce.

Across the intersection, a large mosque raised four slender spires like delicate fingers to a cloudless blue sky. She read the street signs aloud. "*Fevciye C.* And the cross sign says *Veznneciler C.* Both are impossible names to remember."

"C stands for *caddesi* or main street." Josh pointed down a short, landscaped walkway. "That's the Schzade Mosque or *Cami* as the Turks call mosques."

She stared like a tourist. "Beautiful."

"Don't worry, we'll grab another taxi to your hotel." Josh took her arm to help her over concrete blocks piled on the sidewalk. On the other side, he snugged his hand into the small of her back, guiding her.

His hand felt intimate. Did he take every opportunity to touch her? Any other time she'd discourage him, but traffic encroached on the sidewalk, and he provided a human barrier between her and rushing cars.

Obstructions forced them to edge out into traffic again. He grasped her hand.

Holding his hand resembled seizing a live wire. Her heart fluttered. Josh was so alive. In in the mists of memory this time with Josh would glitter.

A man of the world like Josh wouldn't remain intrigued with her. She was too conservative ... too cautious. Even if he were interested, she couldn't be. The timing couldn't be more wrong, and he wasn't a Christian. She didn't need him complicating her thoughts when Ian's life hung in danger. Dear Ian, with his serious approach to living, so careful to hide any tender feelings except toward her. Her sweet, sentimental brother. The last of her precious family.

Josh released her hand, pulled a small map of Istanbul from his pocket and spread the creased paper against the side of a building.

"Where did you get the map?"

"Picked it up at the hotel desk when I went to the lobby to call the police. I've seen most of the touristy spots," he grinned, "but I've never been to the police station."

His grin did funny things to her heart. "Find it?"

"Yeah. It's a way." As they passed a peddler standing by his cart, he stuffed the map into his hip pocket.

The man asked in broken English, "You buy shoes?"

"A taxi. We need a taxi. Where can we find one?" Nicole spoke with slow, distinct words.

The merchant gazed at her with blank eyes. Apparently, he'd spoken all the English he knew.

"*Lütfen, nerede badem taksi, hanim?*" Josh waved his hand.

The shoe salesman pointed up the street. "*Çok teşekkür ederim. Çok naziksiniz.*"

Josh nodded. "At the next corner." He took her elbow and lengthened his steps.

When they reached the corner, Josh stepped out from the curb and held up a hand. A cab screeched to a halt.

With its crude hand-lettered *Taksi* painted in red across its battered door, the vehicle didn't strike Nicole as a promising ride.

Josh opened a rear door.

She stooped and slid inside. At last, they would get to the police.

Josh eased in from the other side.

The cabbie craned his neck to glance at her, but directed his words at Josh. "*Ne tarafa gidecegiz?*"

Josh leaned forward. "*Polis lütfen. Acelem var.*"

"*Polis karakol?*" The driver wiggled his grey-flecked black mustache.

' "*Evet. Yerebaten Caddesi,*" Josh directed, then leaned back on the thin seat cushion. His shoulder brushed her, setting off a shock wave.

The cab lurched off, thundering open tailpipes and rattling battered metal. Blasting the horn, the driver skidded into heavy traffic.

Nicole grabbed the wobbly above-the-door strap. "He drives as if he races the Indy 500."

"Yeah. I think the Indy's easier to drive than Istanbul traffic." Josh steadied her with an arm around her shoulders.

"You've raced?"

"Some. When I was young. Before I joined the Air Force. Amateur stuff."

"Oh." A pilot and a race car driver. Definitely not her type.

The cabbie's horn cut into conversation. The driver forced his way through the traffic, making a fourth lane where only three existed. They flew west across town. Another driver behind them forged ahead, creating a fifth lane.

Nicole gripped the door strap with both hands. "This is madness!"

"Typical Turkish driving." Josh kept his eyes on the traffic.

She scrunched her eyes shut rather than watch the maniacal driving, held on and bounced against the battered cushions. *Lord, please keep us safe.*

"Not like Texas traffic?" Josh joked.

"Far worse." She gritted her teeth. "I'll never take another cab."

With no air conditioning, hot wind rushed through all four open windows accompanied by the noise, clatter, and smell of the city. Nicole clamped one hand over her long hair. Still strands whipped her face as she breathed the humid foreign breath of the city.

She watched Josh rather than traffic. He looked cool, relaxed, and confident, watching the fast-moving traffic. How could he look so comfortable? Her legs felt clammy under her long skirt, and her arms itched with heat rash beneath her three-quarter length sleeves.

"Traffic's murder." Josh grinned his devilish grin. Then he muttered, "Sorry, poor choice of words." He supported himself against the sudden lurches and breakneck stops, with his free hand grasping the back of the lumpy driver's seat. A sudden lurch threw them together.

He laughed. "Turkish traffic's the closest thing to battle I've experienced."

"You've no combat experience?"

"None. Missed everything but peacekeeping duties."

She downplayed her anxiety about the demolition derby they were experiencing with another question. "Are you married, Major?"

A flush stained his smooth olive complexion. His expression tightened. "No."

The finality of his voice forbade further discussion of his marital status.

She attempted to ease the tension grown between them. "Where's your hometown?"

"No hometown. I'm an army brat. My father moved every couple of years. I earned a double degree in Math and Criminal Justice at Cal Tech, Fullerton." He smiled, but his open brashness had disappeared.

Her throat squeezed. Had a woman hurt him? If only she'd curbed her curiosity. Another good reason to guard her heart from him. A wounded man often turned cynical.

She had to regain a more impersonal footing. "Do you have any hobbies?"

The car careened around a corner. His arm tightened around her shoulder. He hadn't moved any closer, but his presence monopolized their space.

He propped a steadying foot on the center floor hump and gave a sardonic smile. "Antiquities and art. Turkish artifacts. Hittite, Greek, Roman, Byzantine." He chuckled. "I could give lectures. Been to many archaeological sites in Turkey."

"Really? Who would have believed *you* have an interest in art?"

"Don't I fit the stereotype?"

What was wrong with her? She didn't want to think about him. Not with his arm around her. Not with Ian missing. Not with her uncertainties about Paul's death. "Far from it."

Traffic howl increased, making conversation difficult, so she rode in silence until curiosity overcame her. "What's that?" She nodded toward an eye-shaped blue glass, painted with an egg-yolk-pupil, dangling from the driver's rear-view mirror. Each time the cab lurched, the emblem cracked on the window.

"The evil eye. Superstitious Turks believe the talisman wards off evil. I don't know its history, but the eye's sold as a souvenir wherever tourists shop." His brown eyes twinkled. "If someone raises their hand with thumb holding down the middle fingers here, they're not making the University of Texas' hook 'em horns sign. They're weaving a charm against the evil eye."

"You know Texas?" She clutched his shirt as they careened around a corner.

He raised a brow.

She blushed.

"Stationed at Lackland a few years ago."

"Oh, San Antonio!"

"You got it."

The *taksi* drove between the gates of a high wire fence onto a dirt road winding through a junkyard of cars smashed into twisted shapes. Dust rose to blanket the *taksi* then sifted inside through the windows. Josh reached across to roll up her window.

"Thanks! I didn't expect dust." She blinked her lashes clear.

At the end of the road near the back of the high wire fence, a forlorn building squatted in the dirt, almost hidden by broken cars and tiers of battered bicycles. The *taksi* jolted to a neck-snapping halt.

She didn't even try to hide her shock. "*This* is the police station?"

"Doesn't inspire confidence." Josh glanced out the window. "I suspect those smashed vehicles are impounded." His voice rumbled dry as a desert wadi, "*Inshallah*–if God be willing— didn't work for these drivers. I'd hate to think God wasn't willing for all these drivers to go home in one piece."

She nodded. So, Josh believed in God.

Their cabbie turned, teeth white beneath black and grey-bristled mustache, giving him the appearance of an aged but cunning walrus. "Four hundred thousand lira." He held out a grimy hand.

Nicole gasped. She would owe Josh a lot of money. She would wire Dallas for money after she left the interview with the police. She didn't want to owe Josh anything.

Josh peeled a pile of bills from his wallet and waved them beneath the driver's nose. "Wait here for us, and I'll double these." He repeated his bargain in Turkish.

The driver's grin grew larger. "*Tesekkur ederim.*" He bobbed his head. "Wait, yes."

"*Rica ederim,*" Josh jumped out and ambled behind the cab to open the door for her.

Grateful to be alive, she took the hand he held out. The drab adobe building, whose open door and screenless windows gaped to the sun-glaring heat, looked depressing. She distracted her growing agitation by focusing on Josh. "Your Turkish seems fluent."

"Not as fluent as it should be, merely adequate." Josh grimaced. "It's not a difficult language. But Turkish isn't related to any other language I speak, so I haven't picked up as much as I would have liked. However, I get by."

"What other languages do you speak?" She slowed her steps, suddenly in no hurry to enter the unpainted building, even to take advantage of the shade. The police station looked too different from what she'd expected. Different even from what she read in mystery novels. How could anyone in this junkyard help her?

They walked past scores of impounded motorcycles.

"A little Hebrew, some German, high school Spanish. I minored in French and Russian in college. I get around wherever I am."

"I bet you do."

Josh cocked a dark eyebrow but let her sarcastic comment pass. "Ready?"

She grabbed a deep breath. "Let's go."

CHAPTER TWELVE

Nicole pressed a hand to her heart as she led the way to the open door beneath the hand-lettered sign that read *Polis.*

Josh followed her into a small room floored with concrete. A fan beat the hot air, offering little more than its whirring noise.

Nicole lifted her eyebrows. "A Turkish police *woman?*" she whispered.

The uniformed woman stood by the open window administering a breathalyzer test to a young Turk.

The Turk palmed some bills into the woman's hand then backed out the door.

Josh grinned. "But no women pilots yet."

His joking answer barely reached her ears.

Square in the middle of the room, a youngish man in a rumpled business suit lounged behind a scarred desk. His brownish-red head bent, and his chiseled features gazed at a single paper. Except for a black rotary phone, the desk was as bare as the rest of the room.

"Inspector?"

In answer to Josh's question, the policewoman waved her hand toward the seated man.

Disappointment savaged Nicole. This was the man on whom she'd pinned her hopes? He looked not much older than she.

He glanced up.

She gazed into piercing grey eyes. As their eyes locked, ambition stared back at her. And something else. Something unreadable, yet unsettling, hid behind that powerful drive to succeed. An expression she should recognize but couldn't.

The policeman jumped to his feet, knocking his swivel chair against the wall. His eyes masked into a blank, slate grey, and his face grew impassive. "Detective Nikolai Pavlik. Kolya to my friends." He waved toward the policewoman. "This is my assistant."

With a quick movement, he reached inside his suit jacket, flashed his identification, then slammed the wallet on the desk. He grasped her extended hand with a gallant movement and bent to kiss it.

Coming from him, the gesture seemed appropriate.

"I command this precinct in the historic area of Istanbul. I am at your service."

She eyed the bulge under his jacket next to his left biceps. "I'm Nicole Phillips." She turned toward Josh. "And this is Major Josh Baruch."

Josh stepped forward and thrust out his hand.

The two men shook, sizing up each other like male dogs on leashes.

Josh dropped his hand, picked up the black ID folder inside the wallet and scrutinized the policeman's credentials.

The detective brushed Josh aside with a perfunctory nod and turned his full attention to her.

His intense gaze felt as intrusive as if he flashed a spotlight on her.

"You are the tourist with the missing brother and the missing pocketbook?" His manner seemed gracious.

"Yes."

"Tell me what happened."

As she related her story, Detective Pavlik focused his eyes on her.

A few times Josh interjected information she omitted.

As she spoke, she glanced around the humble room to avoid the detective's unrelenting scrutiny.

Detective Pavlik asked all the questions she expected, noting answers on a pad he fished out of an otherwise empty desk drawer. Beside the window, the policewoman caressed a rifle. She remained silent. Probably couldn't speak English.

Josh's face darkened. Breaking into the questioning, he shot out, "Pavlik, you're not the policeman I spoke with earlier on the phone."

"Oh, no, Major Baruch. The policeman you spoke with called me in. I am a specialist, you see. In missing persons. And I have taken over your case. You expected a Turk, of course." The detective favored Nicole with a you-and-I-share-a-secret charismatic smile.

He seemed charming, businesslike, and shrewd. But obviously, he didn't like Josh any more than Josh liked him.

Josh continued scowling but nodded curtly.

"I was born in Georgia, in Hanak, just across the border from Turkey. While yet a young man, my parents moved to Turkey to obtain a better life." Pavlik's chiseled, almost handsome, face clouded. "The economy in Turkey, you see, was thriving, and my parents sold Russian carpets. So, I speak Turkish and Russian well, and my English is not so bad, do you think?"

"Although you have a slight accent, you do speak well," Nicole admitted.

Josh didn't comment.

From Josh's defensive attitude with his arms crossed and a frown pulling his brows together, apparently Detective Pavlik annoyed him. True, Detective Pavlik centered his concentrated savoir-faire on her, but she *was* the one with the missing brother. Josh's mind-set was unreasonable.

Josh stepped across to the desk and sat on the edge, his arms rigid, a hand on each widespread knee, inserting himself between her and Detective Pavlik. One muscular leg brushed her skirt. He projected a strong barrier between Pavlik and her, forcing the detective to speak to Josh.

At any other time, she would have laughed at the rivalry for male dominance.

"You took over after my phone call, Pavlik? The other man, Onon Halil Zeheb, mentioned he would remain here all evening."

"Yes, this is true." Pavlik tipped his swivel chair and faced the laser blast shot from Josh's eyes. "Under-detective Zeheb desired me to take over the case, you understand, as I am the more experienced in searching for missing people." He barked a string of Turkish to the policewoman.

She nodded and held up a hand as if under oath.

Josh clicked his mouth shut, but his expression remained belligerent.

Detective Pavlik continued questioning her.

Finally, the detective stood, again knocking his chair against the wall. "Please, Mrs. Phillips, won't you sit down. You look tired." He shoved the swivel chair around the desk close to her. His gravelly voice changed timbre, sounding as if he offered her the choice seat at a posh restaurant. "Allow me to offer you use of my chair, as I have no other. I insist, you see."

Grateful for his thoughtfulness, Nicole sank into the wooden seat, still warm from his brawny body.

The two men exchanged dagger looks.

Detective Pavlik plumped down on the center edge of the desk, between her and Josh, his broad back to Josh. He continued questioning as if the two men had not rattled swords.

A stir of amusement rippled through her.

"And what distinguishes your brother from the other tourists visiting Istanbul? Does he have any identifying marks or outstanding habits?"

She frowned. She'd given an explicit description. What else might a man find different about Ian? She slapped a hand on the desk, of course! She signed with her hands as she would have when speaking with Ian. "My brother's hearing impaired. I forget most of the time because he reads lips so well. We both sign but seldom need to. Because, like I said, Ian reads lips."

"Ah!" Detective Pavlik narrowed his eyes.

Josh's scowled.

"And do you speak Turkish, Major?" Detective Pavlik didn't turn toward Josh.

"A few words. I know how to ask for the bathroom."

"Oh, he's much better than that. He speaks—"

"A few other words tourists need to know," Josh cut in. "Nothing to brag about. Just enough to impress the ladies."

Irritation surged through her. Why was Josh acting like a ... a puzzle? First, he behaved as if he had to defend her honor from Detective Pavlik, then he acted like a casual pick up. Time she took control of the interview. "Are you going to give Detective Pavlik the hair we found in Ian's bathroom?"

Josh drew his lips down at the corners. "Sure." He reached into the pocket of his white polo, retrieved the tissue-wrapped hair, and handed it over.

Men. Acting like wolves marking their territory. But she needed them both. Would they refrain from killing one another?

After he unwrapped the hair, Detective Pavlik picked up the black old-fashioned phone from its cradle and dialed. He grunted a long series of Turkish words into the mouthpiece, then hung up. After bawling more Turkish to the policewoman, he smiled at Nicole. "She speaks no English, you see."

The policewoman took the tissue-wrapped hair from the detective, slung her rifle over her shoulder, and strode out the door.

Josh growled, "Are you sending that to a lab for chemical and DNA analysis?"

"Exactly. We have sophisticated technical equipment at our central office."

"Glad to hear that." Josh nodded in the direction the silent policewoman had gone. "She seems well-armed. That's also a 9-millimeter Beretta with a fifteen-shot magazine she wears in her specially-engineered holster."

Pavlik's face reddened. "We are not a third world country." His ears reddened, and he clenched his hands. "You know your arms, Major. As does Officer Zeynep. I assure you, she's an excellent shot with that Beretta." The detective hitched his own hidden holster and moved his thigh higher on the desk.

Nicole remembered Berettas from her course in firing her own gun. Berettas were accurate, reliable weapons with a long range—sleek, heavy, and deadly. But she kept quiet. She was no expert. Besides the two men already tore at each other's throats. No small wonder Josh never made the diplomatic corps. He was an expert at ruffling feelings.

Folding his notepad, Detective Pavlik heaved his muscular body to his feet, smoothed his suit over the bulge under his armpit, and cleared his throat. His voice sounded rocky as a cement mixer. "I will write up my preliminary report this evening. In the meantime, Mrs. Phillips, don't expect to see your pocketbook again. You must visit the officials at the American Embassy in Ankara and make a new passport, you understand." He smiled warmly. "I hope nothing else valuable was lost." He took her hand and held it between his large, hot ones. His piercing grey eyes softened from storm force to gentle drizzling rain.

"What about my brother? Are you going to look for him? We shouldn't waste any time. Ian—"

"I've already started, you see. My men search his room as we speak."

Nicole shook her head. "What? I thought you didn't have enough personnel to check Ian's room today."

"Happened before I was called in, you see. I have my own men at my disposal. Your case has graduated to a higher level."

Logical. She rose to leave. "Thank you."

"When you hear from the kidnappers, call this number. No matter what the hour, you understand." Detective Pavlik scribbled on the bottom of the paper still lying on the bare desktop, tore the sheet off, and handed it to her.

"I will. Of course, I will." She folded the paper and slid it into her hip pack. She gave Pavlik a smile and shook his hand. "Your help takes a weight off my mind."

Josh grabbed her other hand and herded her outside to the dusty yard. "I'd say Pavlik is a defective on the police farce," he whispered.

She squinted in the sunshine. "Detective Pavlik seems competent."

The detective walked out into the heat. "Oh, Mrs. Phillips."

"Yes?" She turned.

So did Josh.

"Since your brother is missing, you must know something. Are you keeping important information from me?" As he approached, the smiling detective straightened his tie, then smoothed his long reddish-brown hair. "Perhaps something else you did not think important." Detective Pavlik's hypnotic eyes drew her out.

"No ..."

Josh tugged on her hand.

Ice slid down her spine. New doubts jumped out. Obviously, Josh didn't trust Detective Pavlik. *Was* the detective in league with the kidnappers? Or was she paranoid, sensing danger wherever she turned? *What information did Ian have?* "No. No, nothing."

"I will be in touch, you understand." Pavlik lifted a hand in farewell.

Josh hustled her into the waiting taxi. With a screech of tires, the driver took off spitting a gravel and dust fog at Pavlik.

Once back on the paved street, Josh scooted across the lumpy seat and gripped her shoulder. "We'll have to find your brother ourselves."

"We do?"

Josh scowled. "We can't trust Detective Pavlik."

"Are you sure?"

"Not entirely certain. Enough that I know we have to find your brother ourselves."

After all the horrible events in her life ... she didn't trust anyone. The detective seemed okay, though a little odd. Josh seemed charming, though too pushy. The country's customs were different and strange to her.

She was confused and hurting. Who could she trust?

And yet, she must find Ian. She stiffened her shoulders. She would.

CHAPTER THIRTEEN

Sighing deeply, Vashti pulled open the wooden door at the remote cabin where the men guarded the prisoner. A tear slid down her cheek. No more freedom for her.

"Vashti! Past time you return from market."

She sometimes found it difficult to understand Brun's heavy German accent. This time she understood perfectly. "I return in excellent time." She kept her voice soft, liking the way her Turkish-slurred-English sounded different from her irate man's harsh German accent. "You could not have done as well." Brun sprawled in the large overstuffed chair with his feet propped on the ottoman as if she had left only a few minutes before, rather than almost a day.

Not surprising. The men had little to do inside the cabin. She stripped off her gloves, blew on cold fingers, slipped out of her heavy coat, and threw the fur across the backend of the ancient couch sagging beneath the weight of two muscular men.

She glared at Gunter and Franz who lounged at either end of the sofa, a game of cards laid out between them on the center cushion, just as they had been when she left.

Both looked up and ogled her.

Her husky Brun coughed, shoved his hands on the arms of the overstuffed chair, and heaved himself up. He strode across the room, grabbed her in his too-powerful embrace, lifted her until her eyes leveled with his, and buried his great head in her neck.

She tried to return his greeting with enthusiasm, walking the thin line between acceptance and encouragement.

"Ach. Brun, you are one lucky mobster," Gunter grumbled from the couch.

He and Franz resumed their card game, eyeing her with guarded glances. They feared her robust giant, Brun. Her protector ... and owner.

Brun set her down with care.

She let her dimples play games in her cheeks and made her dark eyes look sultry with promise to make him feel the richest of men. Leaning close, she let the perfume of her hair drench his nostrils.

"I missed you," Brun whispered. "I want to carry you into the bedroom. Escape this boring guard-duty."

"Brun, you know I return as soon as necessary." Vashti pouted, making her full lips inviting. She snuggled into Brun's arms, pulled his head down, stood on tiptoe, and nibbled his earlobe. "Not in front of the others," she breathed. "Please behave yourself."

Brun's face reflected the electric shock of her teeth on his sensitive earlobe. Frustrated desire burned his face.

She pushed against his arms. She must be more careful with her German volcano ready to erupt.

His expression as petulant as a spoiled child, he let her slip away.

Vashti glided to the open fire, bent, and rubbed her chilled hands. She glanced around the room at the empty beer bottles scattered in heaps. She spoke to no one in particular. "Men leave such mess."

"Ach, Vashti, when do we eat? We wait for that Turkish cooking you dish up." Gunter didn't look up from his cards but tossed his words out as if her cooking were the only part of her he desired.

Both she and Brun knew better. Eying Gunter's dyed-black beard which looked so strange contrasting with his light brown hair, she challenged the cold grey-blue of his eyes. "When I'm ready."

"Keep your dirty eyeballs off my Vashti," Brun roared, his face crimson.

Gunter constantly pushed Brun for top-dog status. Only a thin margin separated the three men, but Vashti knew Brun would control that coveted top position if he had to kill Gunter.

"Men." Contempt spread through her as she glanced from where she crouched in front of the fire into the tiny, poorly equipped kitchen she had left spotless. Dirty pans overflowed the sink. Spoiled food cluttered the makeshift table. Hand prints blackened the ice box door. And the crude wooden cupboards swung open with rice, spices, and coffee beans scattered as if someone had made a frenzied search.

She glanced at Brun. He was as responsible as the others for the mess. He hung his head.

But she kept her gaze away from the couch. The two men always watched her from behind their cards. She hated them ... and their hot-eyed inspection.

"I do no cooking until kitchen cleaned." She made her voice firm and loud, pretending she had authority. "Someone must bring food sacks from truck."

The men on the couch groaned but threw down their cards. Brun looked annoyed.

Again, she walked a thin line. Frustrated to the point of exploding, her Brun needed little to ignite his fury. As the tallest and strongest of the four Germans inside their tiny cabin, he ruled by brute force. Sooner or later one of the other men would go for her. And Brun would stop him. Shivers quivered her spine.

Brun's neck blotched red. He clenched his massive hands at his sides. "Little Liebchen. You can be so demanding."

Her desire for cleanliness wasn't what bothered him. This cabin gave him no privacy. For that she praised Allah.

"Stepp!" Brun roared far louder than necessary for his voice to carry into the bedroom.

A chair clattered in the next room—Stepp caught napping. His slender, muscular form appeared in the doorway. Even though his self-confident face looked much younger, he sported the same dyed beard as the other three. His blond hair shone white in the flickering kerosene light. "Yeah, boss?"

"Dummkopf. Get out into the kitchen and clean the dishes. Vashti won't cook in that mess." Brun straightened to his full height.

Insolence slid from Stepp's face like mud down a rain-washed hill. He whined, "Guarding the prisoner's my job. Am I the only one who can work?"

Brun stomped across the tiny room, gripped Stepp's arm, and bellowed, "Dishes, *now*!" He slung the smaller man across the room to slam headlong into the kitchen doorframe. "We're starving!"

Rubbing his conked head, Stepp entered the kitchen and rattled pans. He muttered, "Hungry for more than food."

"Too cocksure, you are, Stepp. Next time do as I command. You will learn." Brun scratched his dyed black beard.

"Gunter, go outside and bring in the groceries. Franz, get more firewood. This place is cold." Brun glared at the two men,

They slapped cards on the pillow and stood.

"Wood's stacked by the door," Gunter answered. "Franz, haul it in … and bring in the groceries."

Gunter's dead-eyed stare locked gazes with Franz.

Franz jutted his jaw and stomped toward Gunter but stopped.

Vashti pulled in deep breaths. Once again, she'd watched the pecking order reestablished among the four burly men.

Dragging his feet, Franz shrugged into his coat.

Gunter picked up Franz's thrown-in deal and shuffled the cards, his thick hands working swiftly.

Brun stepped toward the captive's bedroom.

With Brun's back to the main room, Gunter leered at her and whispered, "That slender figure of yours has curves stacked in all the right places."

Her skin crawled as if lice raced over her body. She flicked Gunter a warning look, slid into the bedroom, pulled on an oversize sweater from the heap on the table.

"You can't hide from me. I could draw your curves blindfolded," Gunter murmured.

She shivered. Not from the cold. Although the bedroom *was* cold. Its only warmth drifted in through the open door from the fireplace at the far end of the main room.

As she gazed at the prisoner, she forgot Gunter. The young man lay just as she had left him at daybreak, hours ago. His wrists and ankles tied to the four posts of the bed looked chaffed raw. Red welts rose under the tight ropes. He wore only a T-shirt emblazoned in gold with the words *Dig for Knowledge* half tucked into khaki pants that stopped at his bare knees. Shorts, Americans called them.

He shivered in the freezing room.

She jumped as a hand touched her waist. Jerking away from Gunter, she hissed, "Don't touch me."

Edging into the small bedroom, Gunter followed step for step, backing her into the rough wall.

She struggled to push him away, but Gunter bent to suck the hollow of her neck.

"Halt!" A massive hand grasped the back of Gunter's shirt and dragged him from the room as easily as a rag doll.

She watched, her heart beating wildly.

Brun hauled Gunter across the room, his heels digging on the uneven wooden floor. Brun jerked open the door letting in a blast of cold air, flung Gunter outside into the snow, and stomped out after him.

Her heart slowed, then warmed. "Thank Allah." She moved to the doorway.

Brun beat and kicked Gunter.

Gunter whined through bloody lips, "You win. You win. I keep hands off Vashti. She belong to you. I won't fool with her."

She felt no pity for the bloodied man.

"I not fooling with you!" Brun kicked Gunter in the stomach as he lay groaning in the snow. Then, Brun kicked him in the head with steel-tipped shoes.

Neck distended with bulging veins, his chest heaving, Brun stomped back into the cabin.

Her protector resembled an angry bull. She relaxed the death grip she had on the bed post.

"Button your sweater," Brun roared at her.

Cringing from his tone, she buttoned the last button of the overlarge sweater, glanced over her shoulder at the prisoner, and crept out the bedroom door. Head held high, she scurried through the tense main room and into the kitchen.

Gunter stumbled back inside the hut.

Much later, after she fed the four men, Brun dragged the overstuffed chair closer to the fire. She and Brun snuggled into the cushions.

Stepp cleaned the kitchen.

Facing their endless card game, their latest hand of cards flattened against their chests, Gunter and Franz slept, snoring like buzz saws.

Vashti looked forward to the peace night brought to the cabin. Light filtered in from the kerosene lamp in the kitchen and flickered from the fire in the fireplace.

Brun snored.

She disentangled herself from him and tiptoed into the kitchen. "Did you feed the prisoner while I gone?" She whispered to Stepp, giving him a teasing, lighthearted smile as if they were brother and sister. Stepp posed no threat since he feared Brun.

Stepp winked. "I don't coddle him like you do. Not one of my strong points." He glanced toward the tiny bedroom where the prisoner lay tied.

She threw him a cutting stare, unfocused as if he were not there. Contempt for his methods choked her. But she couldn't let him know the depth of her disgust. "You're certain he is deaf?"

"Sure. He can't hear for nothing. Fun to startle him. He never knows what I'll do to him next. Keeps him tensed up."

She deepened her scornful glare.

Stepp giggled. "Must feel scary, not seeing and hearing nothing. But he rattles on all the time." Stepp's mouth drew down at the corners. "Mostly he says what he tells me are Bible verses."

She moved around the tiny kitchen retrieving the plate of food she had hidden for the prisoner and filling a glass with bottled water. "You tired of guarding him? You cold in there? I think you like to rest by fire while I feed him?"

"I like to torment him."

Wrinkling her nose, she let her long hair veil her expression and headed for the tiny bedroom, her hands filled with the heaped plate and the glass of water. "As you wish. I think you tired of that room."

Stepp nodded and gave her a long, slow wink. "There's always tomorrow. Looks like we'll cozy-up here longer than anyone thought. I'll catch some *z's* next to the fire while you feed the kid."

Her lip curled even as she smiled for his benefit. "He look young to be an archeologist?"

"Yeah. But who listens to Stepp? The new man on the block as the Americans say. Brun says the kid's the one Viper fingered." Stepp waved a hand from where he sat cross-legged by the fire. "My American slang is good, don't you think? I dig American cinema."

Vashti grunted and pushed through the doorway. She felt Stepp's eyes follow her. He tormented the prisoner ... she could do nothing to stop him.

Inside the bedroom, icy fingers bit into her. Poor man. When had they taken him out to relieve himself? Not in the past five hours. Perhaps not all day.

She liked his build, his muscles drawn tight as his arms and legs were stretched to the four corners of the frame. His shoulders looked wide and strong, and his body tapered to a narrow waist and straight, muscular legs. Even his bare feet were handsome as they poked up toward the ceiling. Fine, blond hair grew far more thinly on his arms and legs than hair on the men in her Turkish family or even the Iranian men she had glimpsed at market.

The prisoner's fine blond hair fascinated her. Plate and glass in hand, she contemplated the man, slowly becoming aware of the smile on her lips. The young man charmed her because he could not see her. She hated the way men ogled her. In the beginning, Brun had been different. He had gazed at her like he wanted to protect and care for her, not like the Turkish men she knew ... with their burning eyes. She wished the prisoner were not tied, but she was glad his eyes were taped. His hair fell in unruly spears over the binding. His sand-colored hair falling over the blindfold flew straight to her heart. Not dull-hued like the Germans but full of life. Like sunshine.

She placed the food and water on the cluttered table, smoothed back his hair and uncovered the ugly bruise on his temple. The blindfold across his eyes half-hid his fine, narrow nose, but his full, pale lips and strong cleft chin showed his beauty. She had never thought a man handsome before. Only repulsive.

His teeth had been white and his breath sweet a few days past. Now golden stubble covered his cheeks and chin like tundra in the high Taurus mountains. And his lips were cracked and dry. A musky, masculine odor floated to her nostrils. Inhaling, she decided she liked his scent.

"Hello," he said in a hoarse baritone. "I knew it was you. I smelled your perfume when you came in. You've been gone a long time."

She almost answered before she realized anew he could not hear her. How alone he must feel, cut off from sound and sight. The thought sliced her soul. She sat on the mattress and squeezed his hand.

"How can you speak with clear words when you cannot hear? Your voice sounds as normal as Brun ... only far more pleasant." She knew he couldn't hear but she needed to talk.

He returned her squeeze.

A warm feeling cheered her. She squeezed back.

A smile curved his lips.

She'd never seen a smile like his on a man's lips—only leers, grins, sneers of invitation, but never a smile like the prisoner's.

"Your smile is an angel's smile." She traced his lips with a light finger. "The Koran say angels sometime take the form of men. If I ever saw an angel, you are an angel. Your smile is ..." She searched for the right description. "... sweet. Not sweet as a woman's but like a smile Mohammed might have smiled." She touched his hair. "You have no trace of lust, or greed, or ... or any of those. Only resignation ... and pain." A strange ache punctured her heart. An ache that would not stop.

"I call you Lara," he said. "After the Lara in Dr. Zhivago. That's an old American movie. I'm glad you're here, Lara. I missed you." He coughed. "I count the hours. Days are warmer than nights, although neither are much to brag about. We must be in the mountains." He squirmed on the bed. Occasional spasms shivered his body.

Vashti wondered about Lara. What kind of woman was she?

"I figure from the length of time I was in the trunk, we're in the Taurus Mountains."

She slapped his hand. She must warn him not to talk about his surroundings. About how much he knew.

He frowned, puckering the duct tape with his forehead. Then his frown died, and he nodded. "You don't want me to reveal what I suspect."

A thrill shot through her. He understood. She slid off the mattress, tiptoed to the cluttered table outside the bedroom and pulled a blanket from the pile of sweaters, coats and blankets. She glanced into the main room. Brun snored in their big chair. Stepp lay curled by the fire under a blanket, and Gunter and Franz sprawled on either end of the sagging sofa. Hefty levels of snoring vibrated through the room.

Tiptoeing back to the prisoner, she spread the covering over his shivering body.

He smiled. "Thanks, Lara. I can't repay you for your kindness."

She sat on the hard mattress, took the glass, and pressed it against his lips.

He lifted his head and gulped the entire contents.

So, Stepp hadn't given him water. On purpose. In her heart, she called a curse from Allah down on Stepp.

Pressing the spoon to his mouth, she fed him. First the rice, then the sandwich.

Like a wild wolf he ate.

She called down another curse upon Stepp and the other men who didn't care, including Brun.

"Thanks," he said. "Do you have more? I'm still hungry."

How could she tell him the four Germans had eaten everything? They would have taken his portion had she not hidden his plate. German men ate far more than Turks.

She tiptoed into the kitchen and refilled the glass.

He drank, then thanked her. "Y'all are one of God's ministering spirits, Lara. You can't know what your being here means to me." He shifted on the bed. "I wish I could see you."

She cradled his face in her hands and kissed his forehead. The first kiss she had ever willingly given a man. Then with a flash of inspiration, she lifted his bound hand. With her index finger, she traced in his palm. "I am Vashti."

At the end of each word she let his hand drop, then lifted it again to show another had begun.

"Vashti." He spoke her name with reverence.

She slapped his palm. Then tracing, she told him, "Do not let them know you understand. They will kill you."

She saw his jaw harden.

CHAPTER FOURTEEN

Inside the jouncing taxi, Josh watched Nicole's delicate face transform from hopeful to shaken to distrustful. Now he'd done it. The suspicion in her blue eyes hit him like a rabbit punch to the gut.

He should never have told her they had to find Ian themselves. Along with destroying her faith in the Turkish police, he'd undermined the fragile trust he'd instilled regarding his role in finding her brother.

Not smart. But then he'd not had time to prepare for this job. He played his part blind.

No excuses. Even had he prepared, he couldn't have foreseen his immediate reaction to Nicole. First mistake. Now he was stuck. But he must treat her with the dispassionate charm his mission demanded. No muddling emotions with this job. He must sever his feelings to catch the Viper. Like surgery ... cool, professional, total. No halfway measures. No tender feelings.

"You're scaring me."

Her soft voice pulled him to his senses. "Sorry. You've got to trust me. We can't count on the defective detective." He touched her hand. When she pulled away, he knew he'd blown his chances. An unexpected knot gripped his heart. He had to regain her trust while keeping a tight leash on his multiplying sense of responsibility for her.

Though the cab bucked heavy traffic, and the cabbie glanced through the rearview mirror, Josh couldn't help himself. He cupped her chin and tilted her head until she gazed at him. Her light brown brows arched over eyes like lakes of deep blue water. Troubled water. Her slender nose dusted with freckles, rounded forehead, and delicate high cheekbones looked too vulnerable. The knot tightened around his heart.

Could he see this mission to the end? Could he let her walk into danger?

The whir of helicopter blades woke everyone inside the cabin.

Brun landed on his feet, almost dumping Vashti from the overstuffed chair they had shared for the night. He stumbled over Stepp, bundled on the floor by the dying fire.

The man stretched like a cat, a smile on his thin face.

Franz and Gunter groaned, faces tight and closed.

Brun sprinted to the window, jerked back the dangling beads, and stared into the lightening dawn.

His eyes hurt with the glare of the landing pad's lights that flooded the sheltered side of the mountain. He cursed as the helicopter landed in a blur of swirling snow, its blades slowing to whining death.

He turned toward where Vashti curled inside the chair, looking confused. She combed slender fingers through thick, dark hair and watched him, her face childlike in the tangle of time between wakefulness and sleep. Tucking her bare feet into the double chair, she clasped her knees with her arms, her young face anxious, but her big eyes full of trust.

Trust in him. She trusted him. Brun cursed louder. In German.

Jerking on his shoulder holster, heavy with its .357 magnum, he strode across the room to the wooden door, threw the iron bolt, and banged the door wide. Frigid air gusted in. He stuffed his shirt into his pants, licked dry lips, and waited.

He fisted his hands and cursed beneath his breath. Why had the Viper come? "*Guten Tag*," he greeted the big boss.

Three identically well-dressed men pushed past Brun into the tiny cabin. Clones. If a man didn't know better, he'd mistake them for lawyers. Slick. Sophisticated. Their leader owned a shock of silver-white hair.

Brun grunted. He'd often realized he wasn't smart, but he knew one thing. He didn't want these men around Vashti.

She shrank back against the chair cushions.

He wanted her invisible.

Gunter and Franz stood to face Viper and his two bodyguards.

The guards stared them down, alert, hands resting on 9-millimeters inside unbuttoned shoulder holsters.

The Viper never took his eyes off Vashti.

Giant that he was, Brun had to look up to few men. But he had to tilt his head to lock eyes with the Viper.

Stepp leaped up, white-blonde hair standing on end, and slipped through the doorway into the bedroom where the prisoner was tied. In the dead silence, Brun heard Stepp rustle around, probably shoving his .38 into his belt.

"Morning, sir. Good to see you, sir." Gunter kissed feet as the tall, silver-haired leader lumbered past him into the bedroom.

No matter Gunter played up to the Viper. Brun shifted to the bedroom door. Until he muscled his way to top position, Gunter had been in charge under Viper. Gunter accepted Brun was in charge. For now.

Their cosmopolitan boss didn't bother answering. He turned his concentrated attention to the prisoner.

The archaeologist tensed—hands knotted into fists.

Brun jutted his jaw. How had the kid known someone entered the room?

Firelight from the main room masked the bedroom with shadows. From his place in the doorway, it seemed to Brun the Viper overwhelmed the area, dwarfing Stepp.

Gazing around the Viper's shoulder, curiosity stirred in Brun's mind as the Viper pulled his 9-millimeter from inside his cashmere topcoat.

The Viper pointed the gun at the kid's temple.

Good. If the Viper shot the kid, he and Vashti could leave the cabin. Shoot, he silently urged.

Just as Viper's finger squeezed the trigger, the boss swiveled the gun barrel up. The gun roared.

Dummkopf Stepp covered his ears.

The shot tore a hole through the roof. Broken tile and plaster fell on the kid, whacking his face and body. He struggled against his ropes, blood seeping from cuts where tiles shredded his skin.

From the other room, his Vashti screamed. Brun wanted to comfort her. Not with the boss present.

The kid coughed and yelled. "What's going on? Earthquake?"

"Deaf as a sphinx." The Viper jerked the kid's arm where his wrist was bound to the bedpost. "Too loose."

Stepp lunged forward and hitched the ropes tighter.

The kid grimaced and set his lips. His face looked pale.

Jerking off the blanket, Viper flicked the kid with one end.

The kid yelped. A purple welt rose on his bare leg.

Brun cursed under his breath. Had to be his Vashti. When had she dumped that blanket on the kid? He'd lay down the law.

"Release the prisoner," Viper commanded. The massive silver-haired man lifted his expensive snakeskin shoe. One of the clone bodyguards polished the toe with his silk-suited forearm.

"Gunter! Franz! Untie the kid," Brun ordered. For once, the two obeyed without squawking.

When the ropes fell to the floor, they jerked the kid into a standing position. He slumped between them.

"Grab him!" Brun ordered.

Gunter's muscular arm cinched the kid's neck.

Franz forced the kid's arms up behind his back. They dragged him upright to face Viper.

Brun rattled the lucky dice he always carried inside his pocket. With Lady Luck's help, the kid's presence would blind Viper to his Vashti. Whatever happened, he and Vashti could leave soon.

Viper circled the kid, staring at him with his tight gaze.

Viper got what he wanted. Brun had never seen him fail. He smiled. Today would be no different.

The kid was tough. Not tough enough to stand up to the Viper. No man could.

Over his bent knee, Franz worked pressure on the kid's arms.

The kid locked his jaw and latched his lips.

Brun had seen men's bones break under that pressure. Whatever Viper wanted from the kid—he would get it.

"Force him to his knees." Viper smiled.

Brun grunted. The boss planned to play before he got serious. Brun edged toward the door. Could he leave the room without Viper noticing? Get Vashti out of the cabin?

Franz applied pressure to the kid's arms to almost the breaking point.

Gunter jerked his hold tighter around the kid's neck, shutting off his air until the kid sank to his knees. Gunter released his neck lock.

The kid gasped and coughed, gulping air. Sweat coated his forehead.

"It'll take more than that," Brun said. A slight stir of admiration for the kid held him where he was. He'd been through these interrogations many times. They all ended the same. Viper got what he wanted. Then Brun cleaned up after, getting rid of the body.

"Sir, we thought we might have nipped the wrong man. This one's so young. Doesn't look to be more than twenty-four." Brun rattled his dice. "He's the one showed up for the appointment though." Brun tried not to fidget. "Kid got to the Topkapi fifteen minutes early. He looked around. Tensed up when no one showed. Then he got interested in the gizmos in the museum."

Always, he had a hard time swallowing around the boss. Free hand toying with his shoulder holster, he didn't take his eyes off the big man. "Didn't have no trouble snatching the kid. No trouble getting away. Went down smooth as beer."

Viper glared as if he were a fly to be swatted. "He's the right man. I set McKenzie up with the archaeological job. I realized he would retrieve the map from wherever he'd hidden it and bring it with him to the Topkapi. The man's a genius. I know he solved the cryptograph. The question is ... will he talk?"

Brun nodded, rubbing his cheek to hide the twitching. He moved to block Viper's view of the overstuffed chair.

"Place McKenzie's head on the floor," Viper ordered. "As an archeologist, even a new one, he'll understand."

Gunter jammed a swift knee into the prisoner's back.

Franz jerked his arms higher behind him.

McKenzie's forehead smacked the floor with a hollow thump.

Viper drove a heavy foot down on the back of the kid's neck.

McKenzie let out a low moan.

"This stance is sculpted on every excavated Assyrian wall. The victor and the defeated foe. I need only slice off McKenzie's head with my scimitar." Viper chopped his empty hand down above the kid's throat.

Still pinning the kid's neck to the floor and watching pain contort his face, Viper ordered, "Tie him to the chair."

Stepp raced to bring more rope.

Gunter wrenched the kid upright and slammed him into the straight wooden chair.

Viper stood motionless, licking his lips.

Franz and Gunter yanked each twist tight until it bit into the kid's body.

Brun hoped they would force a grunt of pain from the kid and get a smile from Viper. He needed the boss in a good mood.

But the kid spoke up in a gutsy voice, "You've got the map, but you'll never figure the crypt—"

Viper smashed him so hard in the mouth, the chair crashed to the floor, and the kid blacked out.

Brun shrugged. Viper enjoyed interrogations. Brun edged back toward the door. He had to get his Vashti out of the boss's sight.

Viper ordered, "Bring me his things."

Brun scooped up the kid's wallet and documents from the cluttered table and handed them over. Then he returned to block the door and Viper's view of the other room. And Vashti.

The boss shuffled the papers in massive hands, looking over the kid's driver's license, passport, tickets to Antalya, and the note with his sister's name, date of arrival, flight number, and hotel. Brun had them memorized.

Viper held the document high in his big paws. "Ach—at last. As I suspected. Paul Phillips passed the map to McKenzie." Viper tossed the other documents into the fire. "I don't need these—thanks to the tail I have on Mrs. Phillips."

Brun watched the papers curl, burn bright, then sift into hot ash. Jaacov must be tailing the woman.

"Nicole Phillips." Viper raised his massive well-groomed head and smiled. "Ach, so, both marks accounted for." His eyes gleamed. "You see how a small murder forces Mrs. Phillips into my hands? Mrs. Phillips could not resist signing for her deaf brother after his interpreter died." Viper winked. "Good job, Gunter"

Stepp interrupted. "Yeah, Boss. And we got her purse. But some guy foiled our plan to snatch her."

Brun shook his head. Dummkopf. Trying to credit himself for a botch-up.

Gunter and Franz hung their heads.

Viper faced Brun. "McKenzie won't talk without a great deal of persuasion. Where do these Scotsmen find their strength? Ah, well. There's a more interesting way. Why be prosaic when one can be creative?"

Brun shook his head. What did Viper mean?

"We'll pick up the girl. This time no foul ups." Viper smiled. "McKenzie will reveal the secret to save his sister's life."

Brun thought of his father, the only man alive he'd ever feared other than the Viper.

"After that, I have plans for her. Someone wants Ms. Phillips enough to kill for her." Dumping the kid's small pile of Turkish lira on the wooden floor, Viper crunched the paper money underfoot and shouldered his way through the bedroom door.

Brun froze.

The Viper meandered to the overstuffed chair. His gaze slid to Vashti.

Brun's stomach turned over. He swallowed.

The boss rubbed the back of his knuckles.

Brun knew from experience how knuckles stung after smashing a fist into a face.

The Viper stripped off his cashmere topcoat, tossed it to Gunter, and motioned his clones to do the same. He handed his 9-millimeter to Franz. "Clean it."

Franz scurried.

With the map dangling from one large hand, Helmut Meier towered above Vashti.

She huddled in the chair, face white, eyes wide.

Brun trembled.

"Woman, get me a drink." The Viper's voice sounded hard and cold like his gun.

Brun stiffened, hand sneaking toward his own gun.

Vashti jumped. As she crawled out of the chair, her heavy sweater, which she'd used as a blanket, slid to the floor exposing her graceful, slender body. She dashed to the kitchen.

Brun kept himself from chasing her and covering her with the sweater. He stood still.

Helmut Meier, the Viper, hoisted himself down into the double chair, filling the cushions with his muscular body. His eyes never left Vashti.

It seemed to Brun the boss skewered her like a shish kabob.

Vashti brought the drink and handed the glass to the boss. The Viper. Helmut Meier.

"Is this top-drawer Raki?"

She nodded.

"Well, bring the water."

Vashti stumbled as she hurried to the kitchen. She brought a bottle of water and poured a small amount into the glass of Raki. The clear liquor turned milky.

Brun stalked to the chair, ready to intervene.

"Ach, lion's milk." The Viper saluted Vashti and downed the potent drink in one gulp. "Another."

Vashti scurried into the kitchen and brought the bottle of Raki. Her hands trembled as she poured another drink.

Few men, including Brun himself, could drink more than one small glass without losing some mental acuity. Viper's first glass had not been small.

Brun smiled. Good, maybe he'll get drunk and forget his Vashti.

Vashti's gaze skittered from Viper to him. Her big eyes pled silently for help.

Brun nodded.

She backed into the bedroom.

He moved to stand between the room and Viper.

The Viper sipped his second Raki, then turned to the map in his hand.

Brun let out his breath.

"Lights." Viper tossed back the rest of his drink.

Franz laid down the gun he was cleaning. He jumped to trim the kerosene lights, leaving an acrid odor in the room.

Viper spread the treasure map on his massive knee, pulled a pair of diamond-studded half glasses from his silk vest, and peered down.

Gunter held a lantern close.

Minutes later, Viper muttered, "Aah." He leaned back in the deep, overstuffed chair, refolded the map, and placed the waterproof paper in his vest pocket. His heavy face turned thoughtful. He sipped his drink. "Cigar."

One of the clones hurried to his side.

Ambition to rule it over them pulled at Brun. One more brilliant job for Viper and he would.

Viper selected a Cuban cigar from a slender box the clone held out to Meier.

He puffed the stogie into life. "Who was the man?"

Gunter shifted his gaze and frowned. He cleared his throat. "We're still running a check on him. Can't find out much. Almost like he don't have a history."

"You have his name?"

Brun almost felt sorry for Gunter. Almost.

"Hotel clerk said he gave the name Josh Baruch," Gunter's dead eyes remained flat.

The cigar fell from Viper's mouth.

Brun shrugged. Name meant nothing to him.

Viper tilted his head. "Here's a lesson for my knightly men." He leaned forward. "Listen up. A man such as I must choose between attractive options when presented with a new twist in plans." He smirked. "Ach, what might I have become if I had used my talents legitimately—ambassador, president of the UN, king of the one-world government. Who knows?"

He waved his huge hand. "Sit, my jolly knights. We will discuss new plans." He turned glittering eyes to Vashti. "My dear, come out and stand in front so I may admire your loveliness. Stepp, join our round table."

Sweat dripped from between Brun's shoulder blades. He didn't budge from his position between Viper and Vashti. She huddled behind him, her quick breathing warming a spot just above his spleen.

Viper cleared his throat and raised an eyebrow at him and Vashti. "We must delay our sport with the prisoner since you bungled getting his sister." His heavy, motionless body conveyed disappointment. "I must keep the young man alive a few more days. He holds the key to the cryptograph in his mind." Viper puffed his cigar. "He'll talk when we show him his sister."

Stepp, cocky as if he wore a Gestapo uniform, swaggered in.

The clones Meier brought with him pulled the couch closer to their leader and sat. Gunter, Franz, and Stepp dropped to the floor in a circle facing Meier, like boy scouts at a campfire.

"Sit, Brun."

Brun's blood pounded, making his temples ache. He sank to the floor. Viper could push him so far. No further. He grabbed Vashti's hand and tugged her behind him.

The fire died, and the room cooled. Daylight slanted through the beaded window curtain, showering iridescent colors across Viper's hard face. Chill swept through the room. Brun pulled open his heavy sweater and tucked Vashti inside with him. He dared not leave the circle to tend the dying fire.

Tied to a chair at the far end of the room, the kid regained consciousness and sneezed.

"And there you have it, my shining knights. You each understand your job and your timetable. If any of you fail, my plan fails." Viper stared at each man. "I do not tolerate failure."

Brun shrugged. They were dead men if they failed. They all knew it. He nodded.

Meier reached into the inner pocket of his expensive suit jacket and pulled out documents and Turkish lira. He handed passports, plane tickets, and wads of cash to Franz and Gunter. "I expect a report twice daily. You have my radio frequency. Gunter, destroy the Turkish garb used when we kidnapped the prisoner. Repaint the Medical Emergency Vehicle at our body shop and change the plates. Use the surveillance equipment and radios on your new mission. Franz, erase everything from the computer. Leave no records."

Meier stared at each man in their campfire circle. "Get rid of the black dye. Shave your beards." He turned to Gunter. "Gunter, you are my dark knight, tried and found loyal. Though you botched your assignment, I offer you this final chance to redeem yourself. Use your cunning, resourceful mind. I depend on you. Leave now!"

Dead-eyed Gunter, Brun's enemy, stood, bowed at the waist, took the documents, pulled on a parka, and strode outside, letting in a blast of cold air.

After the cabin door slammed shut, Meier turned his withering gaze to Franz. "You play my white knight. Do not betray me, Franz, even with a thought. I am trusting you with my jewel. You are my eyes and ears. Do not let Suzanne out of your sight. Report to me three times daily. No cell phones. Call on the red phone if there is trouble. On your way."

Franz slipped into his coat and strutted from the cabin.

"Ach, and Sir Lancelot stays with Ms. Phillips."

Brun grimaced. Who might Lancelot be? Jaacov? He dared not ask.

After Gunter and Franz left, Stepp looked at Meier like a dog begging for a bone.

Viper appeared not to notice. He slouched in the chair and leaned his head back on the overstuffed cushion.

Stepp drummed his fingers, picked lint off his clothes and tapped his foot, light eyes darting from Meier to the kid tied in the chair.

Brun hunkered on the wooden floor, his anxiety building with each breath.

Meier's two clones gazed into the ashes of the dead fire as if they had nothing on their minds.

Viper stirred. "Warm the 'copter," he ordered his lawyer-type clones. "We're leaving."

Without a word, the two pulled on cashmere topcoats, leather gloves, and slammed the door behind them.

Brun clenched his hands. The tic beneath his eyes double-timed. His heavy body wanted to relax. Wanted to go to bed. With Vashti.

"Stepp, do you enjoy guarding the very handsome young man?"

Stepp froze, tapping foot in midair. "Yes, sir!"

Viper's smile curdled Brun's stomach.

"Stepp, I know I can trust you with guarding the prisoner." Meier's voice softened to a whisper. "Do not be easy on him. You understand?"

Stepp nodded.

Viper motioned for Stepp to bring the briefcase lying beside the door.

Stepp set it at Meier's feet.

Viper pulled a long, padded box from his briefcase and opened it. Rows of syringes glistened in the firelight. "Though the prisoner is blindfolded and deaf, he's far from dumb. As I said, he's a genius. I want his mind cloudy until Gunter and Franz bring Ms. Phillips." Meier raised an eyebrow. "The drugs will soften his defiance. Every man has a breaking point. He will talk."

Stepp nodded. Padded box cradled under one arm, he slunk to his post in the bedroom.

The Viper glanced at Brun. "You can easily dispose of his body. With drugs in his bloodstream, no big investigation."

Brun felt Vashti shiver.

Viper gazed at Vashti.

Brun's gut tightened. Trying to distract Viper, he stomped to the couch and dropped with a thud that shuddered the ancient structure.

Vashti eased down beside him, curling to make herself small, her pale face betraying fear.

"Brun."

Every muscle in Brun's body twitched. He hunched his shoulders, feeling like a whipped dog given poison meat.

"Tell her I want her to dance," Viper whispered.

Vashti's face turned ashen. Her big eyes begged Brun.

He refused to meet her gaze. "He wants you to dance." A pulse beat violently in his temple.

Viper's voice was water sliding over ice. "Tell her to change into her costume and dance. Now!"

Brun's throat constricted. He growled, deep inside his chest, a low, animal growl that curled his lip and narrowed his eyes. "Costume, now." Hate for the Viper flooded his veins. But ambition ripped through his hate. The man held his future in his hands.

Vashti trembled. But she stood.

Stepp burst through the bedroom door, Vashti's filmy costume clamped in his fist.

"Give the costume to her, Brun." The Viper smiled.

Reeling like an aging man, Brun pushed up from the couch and stumbled over to tear the costume from Stepp's hand. He thrust it toward her and watched Vashti stumble into the dim bedroom, costume dangling from her fingers like a fisherman dragging an empty net.

"Music, Brun," Meier smiled. "Vashti must have music. Start her CD."

Moving with a jerk and a lunge, he found the CD player and pressed the button for Vashti's music. Turkish music, played on the *saz*, boomed in the small room.

"Where did you get her, Brun?" Viper ran a hand through his silver hair.

"I bought her."

"Tell me about it." The Viper leaned back in the overstuffed chair, hands steepled over his ample midriff.

Dogged determination edged Brun's voice. "Her father sold her to me."

"Why did they sell her? Is she a bad girl?"

"No. She refused to marry a rich old man. Her parents didn't want such a disobedient girl in their home." He turned toward the closed door to the bedroom. "I heard she was for sale, so I went to look at her. I bought her the same night." He growled, low in his throat.

Vashti thrust her slender leg, clad in transparent gauzy material, through the opening. Viper sat forward, his eyes glittering as he watched the ancient dance. From time to time he blew puffs of air through pursed lips. His cigar dropped from fingers that clutched the arms of his chair.

Brun rubbed his furrowed brow. His shoulders slumped.

When the dance ended, Vashti's slender chest heaved.

Brun longed to snatch her, carry her out of the cabin, and out of Viper's sight. But he sat glued to the couch.

Viper clapped. "Very good," the velvet voice purred. He pushed his enormous body to his feet. "I have but one more command, Brun, and your lovely harem girl will live. Tell Vashti to put on her shoes and coat and wait for me in the 'copter."

CHAPTER FIFTEEN

"I'll spend the night in your room—"

"No way!" Nicole raised a stop-right-there hand.

Josh shook his head. "It's common sense. Your life's in danger."

Tension snapped between them like charged air before a lightning strike. Since their return from the police station, Josh had stuck closer than Anthony to Cleopatra. "I need to rest. With you around I don't figure I'll get any. No."

"For security."

"No."

"Look, as long as I'm with you, the kidnappers don't dare lay a hand on you."

"It's not their hands I'm worried about."

Josh swore. "Okay. I'll sleep in Ian's room." He shook his head. "There's only a thin wall between us. If anyone breaks in, bang on the wall. I'll come flying." He braced a palm against her door. "You're making a mistake." He scrubbed a hand over his face. "Only a *shiksa* insists on separate rooms."

"Shiksa?"

"Gentile girl." Still grumbling, Josh backed out and slammed the door.

She walked to her window and gazed up into the night sky. Could Ian be staring at the same moon? Was he close by or miles away? Missing four days now. If he'd been kidnapped, why hadn't she heard from the kidnappers? Where are you Ian? *Father, God, please protect him and keep him alive.*

She refused to think of any other possibility.

Moonlight played on the rooftops and napped on the terraces of the buildings angled toward her. She let her eyes wander to the apartments where lights glowed behind sheer curtains. "Are you observing me through your back windows as I watch you?" she whispered. A chill made her shiver. Or were kidnappers monitoring her movements? She stiffened her shoulders. They wouldn't scare her from her search.

Reaching down, she unlatched the tall, narrow window and swung the glass open to the night. A cool breeze blew in bringing soft blurs of sound. A couple in the fifth-floor apartment across the way glided around their terrace in a graceful dance.

She glimpsed their faces, cheek to cheek, tuned to one another, happy in togetherness. Her heart caught. Her chest clamped into a painful knot. Without Ian, she had no one.

Shutting her window, she pulled the drapes.

She sat on the edge of the bed. She'd never sleep. When her head touched the pillow, she tossed and turned through the long night, drifting off to dream in the wee hours of morning.

Pounding on her door startled her awake. Slipping into her short silk robe, she stumbled across the entry to answer, her mind groggy with slumber. She cracked open the door. "Josh?"

He stood outside in the hall—one hand braced against the doorframe.

"You look," she cleared her throat from morning huskiness, "awake." And incredibly alive. And painfully handsome. His brown eyes smoked intensity. His chambray shirt was pressed, and his navy slacks had sharp creases. He smelled of soap and masculine aftershave.

"Sorry to disturb you, but it's eight. The hotel serves a complimentary breakfast until nine."

His words sounded casual, but his face flushed with attractive color.

He spoke as if he couldn't catch his breath. "Knowing your shortage of cash, I thought you might want to take advantage."

Yesterday's events jolted her awake. "Any news?"

Oh, Ian, are you eating breakfast? Are the kidnappers feeding you? Are you warm, sheltered ... alive?

"Not yet."

"What's the plan?"

"Will discuss that at breakfast."

"Sorry, I guess I overslept. Didn't get much sleep last night. Worrying." Brushing hair out of her eyes, she realized she wore her pink robe over shorty pajamas. She stepped behind the door, as much to block his ultra-masculine presence as from modesty. Stifling a yawn, she closed the door until it barely cracked between them. "I can't believe I slept so late. I'll meet you in the lobby in fifteen minutes."

Moving fast, she showered and dusted her face with powder. She ran a comb through her hair and twisted the sides back, letting the rest hang free down her back. Choosing a tawny, long-sleeved silk shirt almost the shade of her hair, she matched it with tan slacks that fit loosely on her slender frame. She hooked on a wide leather belt with a leopard buckle that accentuated her small waist. A brush of coral lipstick, a touch of blush, and she was ready. The skinny mirror showed she looked neither dowdy nor demure. But no one could claim she hadn't dressed modestly. She lifted her chin at her reflection.

If Josh could take her breath away, the least she could do was pay him back.

When she entered the lobby, the flicker of approval in his expression sent a twinge of gratification to her chest.

He stood, firm lips unsmiling, dark eyes flashing, a frown spoiling his brow.

She tilted her chin higher, daring him.

But he said nothing about her appearance.

"Dining room's this way." He slipped his arm around her waist and guided her past the ornate elevator cage to a spiral stairway at the far end of the lobby. They descended the steps and entered a charming mauve and tan room with arched ceilings. Small, white-clothed tables lined each side, separated by black wrought iron to the ceiling, giving each table an ambiance of cozy solitude. A banquet table filled the room's end, breakfast buffet spread onto its snowy cloth.

She felt guilty. Perhaps Ian had nothing to eat. The thought stole her appetite.

"Two?" An ultra-polite, uniformed waiter seated them at an end table.

Filled tables signaled their lateness. Josh stared at the other diners. He kept his voice low. "American tourists occupy all but two of the tables."

She glanced around. Easy to spot the Americans. Most wore slacks and long-sleeved T-shirts. One man sat alone—his head buried behind a newspaper. She could see only his bright yellow shirt. "Which two?"

Josh nodded to a table across the room. "Turkish businessman. Notice the trademark moustache, and he's reading a Turkish newspaper."

"And the other?"

Josh tilted his head toward a table to their right. A blond couple talked and laughed as if they were the only ones in the restaurant. She caught a few German words.

"Okay. I'm impressed. You did that very quickly. Are you sure there's no one here watching us?"

"Reasonably." He opened his mouth as if he planned to say more but a waiter approached.

With impeccable accuracy, the waiter poured strong-smelling Turkish coffee into their cups and left the silver pot on their table.

"This place beats the *lokantas* I'm used to." Josh sipped hot coffee.

"Lokantas?"

"Local eateries." He stood, pulled out her chair, and followed her to the buffet. "Try the *beyaz peynir*, the white goat cheese. Salty but tasty."

Walking in front of the buffet table, she chose several of the small, white squares of cheese along with sliced cucumbers so fresh she could smell the crispness, huge black and green olives marinated in oil, and warm ekmek.

"Turks serve fruit for breakfast," Josh explained as he piled melon, lush strawberries, and watermelon on his plate. "At the local lokantas, lunch and dinner are meat, rice, and bread. Turks eat a lot of meat."

She picked a few strawberries from the artful presentation. "I'm not hungry."

"You need to eat. Keep up your strength. We don't know what the day will bring." He filled her plate.

With a stacked plate in each hand, they filed back to their table.

The white-jacketed waiter poured fresh-squeezed orange juice into their goblets.

Lifting his glass, Josh touched hers in a toast. "*L'Chaim*, to life."

Relaxed for the first time since she met Josh, she forced herself to eat. "Breakfast is different. But delightful." This morning she felt thankful for his company. He brought order where her life had become so disordered.

"I read this morning's paper. Nothing about your brother. As Detective Pavlik suggested, the police and the Turkish media want to keep his disappearance out of the news. Bad for tourism." Josh dribbled honey over his ekmek.

She was glad Ian's kidnapping hadn't made the news. She knew what notoriety headlines created—what rumors they spawned. She had no wish to repeat that experience. She forked food around her plate. Josh's appetite seemed unaffected. His table manners were excellent. She liked that in a man and clung to anything that might make her world seem more normal. "So, what's the plan?"

"After we eat, we'll head for the Citizens Consular Services, since the American Embassy's located in Ankara. We need to get you a new passport, although no one here checks for passports except to enter or leave the country."

She sighed. "I suppose I should have told you. I carry my passport in a hidden pocket along with my return ticket and a little cash. I still have it, but I do need to wire home for more money."

Josh's full lips curved into a smile. "Well done. We'll head for a bank then."

They spoke of inconsequential things as if Josh tried to keep her thoughts from dwelling on Ian. Because of his teasing and entertaining travelog, remnants of her appetite returned. With half a heart, she chuckled at Josh's latest joke. They smiled and chatted as if they had no cares. If only that were true. Would she ever laugh and chat again with Ian?

Most of the other diners filtered out, but the lone man in the yellow shirt continued to read his newspaper. He must have been nearsighted because he wore thick glasses and held the paper close to his face.

The day stretched before her, empty with no word from Ian's kidnappers. No way to search for him. "I want to check with the police to see if they've learned anything."

Josh drained his coffee cup and nodded. "Before we leave for the bank, I'll phone the police. Maybe something's turned up." He slipped lira under his cup. "*Bakhshish.*" He winked, "A tip. You may as well learn some Turkish."

He bent in his seat to return his billfold to his hip pocket, and a chain around his neck dangled over his chambray shirt.

She reached across the table, caught the cool circle in her fingers, and tried to read the symbols engraved into the gold. "What's this?"

"Two Hebrew letters. Spells *L'Chaim.*"

"Like your toast. What does life mean?"

"Different things to different people. To me, the word means there are no second chances. A person can't sleepwalk through life. We Jews have a saying *Tikkun olam*, translated 'repair the world.' I do what I can to help."

"You wear a white Stetson and ride a white horse to help damsels in distress?"

He grinned. "Yeah. That's me. Last of the good guys." His face grew thoughtful. He reached across the table to take her hand.

She decided this was a gesture of comfort, no more. In ordinary times, she backed away from such a man, particularly one who could make her forget her own name, if he chose. A man who was Jewish, not a Christian. But these weren't ordinary times. She needed Josh's help. Even though she didn't totally trust him.

But she could test the water. "What would you have done today if you hadn't run into me?"

He stiffened. His fingers tightened around hers, then loosened. He placed her hand gently on the table. "Oh, tourist-type things. Turkish bath, shop for brass, take tours to archaeological sites."

His manner seemed evasive, and his chocolate brown eyes refused to meet hers. He brushed bread crumbs into his hand and studied them.

"Don't you have plans that need rearranging or canceling? People you needed to meet for your vacation?"

"Nope. This little vacation was strictly a loner."

"Oh. But I thought—"

"The kidnappers are obviously professionals."

"Why do you think that?" A nag of suspicion reared its ugly head at his quick change of subject. He hid something. She couldn't let him sucker her into completely trusting him. Though her heart sang a different song.

"They left the scene clean. We've no clues except that single strand of hair we found." He rubbed his square chin. "They'll make a mistake. When they do, we'll find Ian."

"We again? Detective Pavlik seems competent. Why don't you trust him?"

"Competent? I don't know. There's something about that jerk I don't like. Can't put my finger on what. After the bank, we'll return to the hotel and wait for the kidnapper's next move. Unless I miss my guess, the police won't have any new information."

He shoved back his chair. Before she could rise, he came around, and helped with hers. "Let's check the desk first."

Eager to start the search, she hurried from the charming candlelit room. And thrust the nagging doubt about Josh into a file in her mind marked *investigate and proceed with caution*.

He circled her shoulder with his arm as they climbed the spiral staircase and entered the lobby.

"You have no faith in Detective Pavlik's ability to—"

"Mrs. Phillips. You have a message, Mrs. Phillips." The deskman's loud voice echoed through the still hotel lobby. "You have a message, Mrs. Phillips."

Heart fluttering, she hurried to the desk and extended a hand to the smiling man.

With a flourish, he handed her the message.

About to open the folded sheet, Josh's hand closed over hers. "We best read this in private."

"You're right." They power walked to the antique elevator, crowded inside, and pushed open the door at the empty mezzanine. Comfy chairs, soft lighting, and well-placed pictures welcomed them.

She sank into a cushioned chair. Her hands shook. Grabbing a deep breath, she unfolded the note. First her eyes refused to focus, then she read.

MEET ME AT THE HAREM INSIDE THE TOPKAPI. TODAY 10:30 SHARP NO POLIS! ALONE

The typewritten words in capital letters on plain bond paper tied her stomach in knots.

Cold sweat beaded her forehead.

CHAPTER SIXTEEN

The note shook in Nicole's hand.

Josh wrapped his warm fingers around her chilled ones. He took the paper and read it. His jaw worked.

To stop her knees from trembling, she clasped them and hugged tight. Hope and fear played hide and seek in her heart, pumping adrenaline. "Ian is alive!"

Josh stood legs braced, shoulders squared, hands clenched. Excitement gleamed in his dark eyes, a half-grin exposing white teeth. He looked like a rock in a storm, a thoroughbred at the starting gate, a trained pilot ready to fly a combat mission. Like Amanda Greene's assistant in *Intrigue,* Josh was in his element—a masculine, alert male.

"I'll go alone. I suspect a trap. Whoever's got Ian may want you."

"Why me? I don't have a clue about what Ian's involved in."

Josh plunged down into the chair beside her. "What better way to make him talk than threaten his sister?" A frown furrowed his dark brows.

"What do you mean, 'make him talk?'" She didn't like the sound of this.

Josh wouldn't meet her eyes. He clenched his hands and looked uncomfortable.

What did he know? "What information do the kidnappers want from him?"

Josh rubbed his nose. "*If* they wanted to make him talk." He pulled at his ear.

"You! What do you know? What aren't you telling me?"

"Woman, what does it take! I'm on your side!" His olive skin flushed. "I'm a sucker for helpless, beautiful women."

"I'm not helpless." She tried to track his slip of the tongue. What was his angle? "Why are you sticking as close to me as wraps on a mummy?"

He threw back his dark head and laughed, a deep-throated laugh that roared through the mezzanine. "Only an American girl would see herself in this situation as ..." his deep voice mimicked a higher timbre "... not helpless." Shaking his head, all trace of laughter gone, his eyes pierced her. "You have no money, you don't speak the language, you don't understand the customs, so you put yourself in danger by walking down the street ... and you don't feel helpless?"

He leaned forward, held his head in both hands and mumbled, "You *are* very beautiful." He faced her. "I hesitate to mention the most sinister aspect of your situation. Your life is in danger."

His expression unnerved her.

"You will lock yourself in your hotel room, and I'll meet the person or persons who sent this note." He rested an arm across the back of her chair, his fingers touching her shoulder.

"What do you mean, make Ian talk? Talk about what?"

Josh's shoulders tensed. He swallowed and rubbed a palm against an outstretched leg.

"You know something regarding Ian's disappearance. Things you haven't told me!"

He met her gaze. "By the looks of Ian's room, the kidnappers are searching for something. If Ian isn't talking, they can force him to ... by hurting you." His eyes drifted from hers. "We can't take that chance. We can't let them kidnap you."

His explanation sounded logical. Yet, a sixth sense she hadn't known she had sent goosebumps tiptoeing her spine—as if she walked over someone's grave. Eerie. Josh hadn't come clean. What wouldn't he tell her?

"They're expecting *me*." Despite her best efforts, her voice trembled with suspicion. What was Josh hiding?

"They'll work with me," he growled.

"If that Russian is a Turkish police officer, they'll think you're one also. They specified *No Polis*."

Josh's eyes narrowed. A cloud settled on his face. "You may be right." Burying his head in his hands, he appeared lost in thought.

Her mind jumped from possibility to possibility, like a cat leaping from branch to branch up a tall tree. Why wasn't he straight with her?

Josh sprang up. "Here's the plan. I'm certain we're watched."

A shiver chilled her spine. She hugged her arms to her sides.

"I'll make a show of leaving by the front door, then sneak in the back entrance." He flashed a smile.

Didn't reassure her.

"Then I'll change clothes. We don't want the kidnappers to know I'm keeping you under surveillance. I'll stick less than fifty feet from you at all times." He held out his hand to help her up.

"The police?"

"Right, we'll contact them and shoot them the details. Then you meet the kidnappers at the Harem. I'll tail you. I won't let you out of my sight." He grinned as he punched the elevator button.

"I thought a woman couldn't travel alone here."

"I'll show you a few ways to get by for short periods. It's risky. But I'll remain close. Any trouble, and I'm on it."

"It's a plan. I can't think of a better one."

"I'd give a million bucks to have my sidearm," Josh grunted. "You'll walk alone, so wear a head scarf. That'll deter most Turks for a while. American women seldom cover their hair. And keep your head lowered. When you are alone, never, never look a Turkish man in the eyes."

They entered the elevator. He put a comforting arm around her shoulder and grinned.

Woman-charmer grin. He was still trying to make her forget his slip of the tongue.

"You know why a Turkish man keeps his woman veiled, don't you?" His eyes sparkled.

"I can guess." She tried to match his lightness, but her heart hammered against her rib cage.

"To hide the woman's emotions." Josh winked.

"Woman's emotions?" She was hooked.

He looked pleased as he was about to deliver his punch line. "Yeah. The Middle Eastern man thinks he reads body language so well that with the slightest encouragement he will force himself on a woman. He thinks he knows what the woman wants. Their men keep them veiled to protect the women." He pushed the door open at their floor. "Maybe we should buy you a veil."

Color rose to her cheeks. "Seems the woman is better protected if the man controls his urges."

"That's the Western way. Or it was until the last decade or so."

"And you?" She tried to pass her question off in the joking vein he had drawn her into, but a serious undertone crept into her voice.

They walked the long hall to her room.

"Me? I'm a confused Jew." A curious, uncertain expression flickered over his face. "I seek modern truth but strive to live by ancient standards. I'm out of step with the world." His mouth hardened. "I'd like to find the type of foundation my namesake had. Where everyone else saw giants in the land, Joshua relied on the strength of God."

Wow, Father. I guess that means you want me to share with him. Just tell me how. Please!

"You haven't found that kind of faith?" God must have sent Josh to hear the gospel. And to help her. God was in control.

"Nope. Probably doesn't exist." His hard-edged tone stopped any more conversation as effectively as a burst from a stun gun. "I need the key to Ian's room." He held out his hand.

She dropped the key into his upturned palm, her mind mulling his flash of vulnerability. His search. And his skepticism.

He walked her to her door and waited while she unlocked it.

"Okay. You stay put. I'll leave the hotel, grab a taxi, then circle back. After I change clothes, I'll knock on your door, and we can head over to the Topkapi. Any questions?"

"No. Just something I need to tell you. I get lost in a revolving glass door. I've no sense of direction."

Worry puckered his brow, but he wisecracked, "No revolving doors in Istanbul. If you need directions, stop, and I'll find a way to speak with you. Anything else?"

"No. But hurry. The kidnappers expect me to leave."

"Right. See you soon." The grin he flashed looked eager.

She watched him go, then went inside. After rummaging in her luggage for a scarf, she sat on the bed to wait. So, sure-of-himself Josh had questions about life. Deep ones. She smiled. Josh now seemed much more accessible.

She slid her Bible out of the top compartment of her luggage and flipped through to the book of Isaiah. Hadn't she heard Isaiah was the place to start explaining the Scriptures to Jews? Isaiah fifty-three?

Forgive me, Father, for not walking closer to you. I've let my sorrow come between us.

Peace stole over her. Peace she hadn't known since Ian failed to meet her at the airport. Peace she hadn't known since Paul turned up missing and was presumed dead. God had remained silent in the face of her anger—and her questions. But now his peace filled her heart.

Ian was alive. God wanted her to share her faith with Josh. For now, that was enough.

Eyes closed, she ran her fingers over the fifty-third chapter of Isaiah and clung to the peace that warmed her to her toes.

Lord, help me to walk with you. Not only for the wonderful peace you give, but so you can guide me to Ian and help me share my faith with Josh.

He knocked.

Breathing a prayer and steeling her emotions against the reaction she invariably had with her first glimpse of Josh, she slid the chain free and opened the door.

He stood in the doorway, panting, his chest heaving as he stuffed a T-shirt, with UT AUSTIN emblazoned on the front, into a pair of rumpled khaki shorts.

"Ready for this?" He pulled on a blue Dallas Cowboys baseball hat and twisted the bill to the back.

"Ready!"

He bent to hook the sandals that flopped on his feet. When he straightened, they strode to the elevator. After pushing the button, he slipped on aviator sunglasses. "How do I look?"

A giggle bubbled up inside her. "As collegiate as Ian. Where's your military bearing and razor-sharp creases?"

An impish grin lit his face. "Could you rub a dab of Bengay on my sprained dignity? I'm not used to damsels laughing at me."

She shook her head and laughed outright, knowing her laughter could easily slide into tears. The last time she'd seen that T-shirt, Ian had worn it. "All you need is my camera hanging on your wrist, and you're the stereotypical tourist."

"Great idea. I'll run back and get it."

She passed him her key just before the elevator arrived. "Did you see anyone suspicious?"

"No one except that goofy dude in the yellow shirt who ate breakfast same time we did. He waddles when he walks, so I nicknamed him *Ducky*." The elevator door started to close but Josh held it back. "Wait for me outside. Best we aren't together when we leave the hotel." He grinned, then jogged toward her room.

She waited in the lobby next to the double glass doors until he clambered down the stairs with her camera hanging from his wrist. The embroidered American flag on the strap winked at her.

He nodded.

She tied on her scarf, pushed open one of the heavy double doors, and strolled into the sunlight. Halfway along the block, she stopped to gaze into a store window.

"I'm right behind you. Don't look back. If you run into trouble, I'm here for you. Think of me as your guardian angel," he whispered. He stood with his back to her examining a vendor's cart filled with melons.

"I hope not a fallen angel."

He growled, "You're a hardheaded woman."

She turned away.

Josh breathed, "*Allah esmarladik*. Put yourself into the hands of God."

CHAPTER SEVENTEEN

Outside the hotel, a grey-bearded kiosk proprietor stopped Nicole. He smiled, flashed a watch, and asked in broken English, "You buy?"

She took the watch and pretended to look it over. She had to reach the Topkapi by ten, then find the Harem by ten-thirty. But which way to go and how far? The watch read nine-thirty.

Catching up to stand beside her, Josh tipped his head back and clucked *no* when the same proprietor swung a bra in front of his eyes.

Josh spoke Turkish to the man.

He must have asked directions to a taxi. Nicole sighed. Taxis here frightened her.

The salesman pointed to a cobblestone street crammed between tall buildings.

She glanced at Josh.

He nodded and turned away, pretending they were unacquainted.

Forcing herself not to look back to check on Josh, Nicole hurried toward the alley-wide street.

The cobbles wound upward, a narrow knife between ancient stone walls. She climbed. Though she'd jogged every other evening after school in Austin, by the time she reached a series of crumbling steps cut into stone, her breath came in gasps. Worn with age and slippery with small pebbles, high and wide apart, giants or mountain goats needed these huge steps. She clambered up, her heart racing, negotiated a narrow turn, and puffed up another steep series of stairs. She was alone. Seemed few tourists ventured here.

When she reached the top, she made an abrupt right turn, then stopped dead. The cobbled road, cluttered with trash, ended against a stark brick wall.

Two swarthy men with dark eyes under heavy black brows glowered at her. Drooping walrus mustaches covered the upper portion of their grim mouths.

Fear stabbed her. She glanced back. No Josh in sight.

The two men closed in. Their breath fanned her face. One man fired rapid Turkish, then pointed to the stone wall. Hoping they didn't plan to pin her against it, and rob her, she fled the direction they pointed.

"*Chekiš,*" one man yelled

She stumbled closer to the stone wall. A long, low tunnel opened before her. An acrid stench of urine bit her nostrils. She peeked inside. She didn't want to stumble onto any Turks with their pants around their ankles.

The tunnel looked empty. Her quick steps echoed, then she was through, treading back into a street buzzing with people going about their lives. She uncurled her fingers and relaxed.

Men threw her dark glances.

She pulled her scarf around her face and lowered her eyes. Although her hair and part of her face were covered, still she attracted attention. Few women walked these streets, and no other woman walked alone. Hurrying over the uneven sidewalk, she melted into the moving jam of humanity.

A Muslim family trudging in front hampered her progress. Two black kerchief-headed women wearing long black coats, their swollen ankles and flat-slippered feet peeking from under their somber clothes, herded three children through the crowd.

A handsome Turk with groomed ebony hair, wearing the blue serge suit cut too long and too loose that appeared to be the male's uniform, stalked in front of the women.

She'd been told modern Turks were allowed only one wife. Conservative Turks kept their women either working in the fields or confined to their home. *Thank you, Lord, for America.*

The family group slowed her progress to a snail's pace. Taking advantage of the situation, an enterprising young Turk saluted her, grasped her arm, smiled showing his white teeth, and asked, "Where you from, Amerikan?"

Josh had warned these street introductions led to an extended conversation in which the Turk asked your name, your business in Istanbul, and ended by offering to guide you through the city. All spoken politely, leading up to the inevitable invitation, "Come into my shop and we will sit down to *çay* and make a lasting friendship, honorific *alba*—honored sister. Then you buy." Having completed his pitch, the street salesman then propels you into his shop.

Josh had said, "Hawkers are harder to get rid of than enemy planes in a dog fight. Don't talk to them."

She followed his instructions, kept her eyes downcast, and the salesmen stopped hounding her.

Everywhere she looked, male shop proprietors waited on male customers. This area of the city appeared to be for residents not tourists. At outdoor cafes, men sat at small wooden tables drinking *çay*, playing games or talking.

She frowned. Her internal directional compass spun like a roulette wheel. The streets were mazes. How could she find her way? She'd have to memorize more landmarks.

She passed a low trough with water splashing from a brass lion's mouth. A man sat in a marble alcove near the fountain, his sandals beside him, and washed his feet. He looked as if he prepared to enter the nearby mosque to pray.

She was lost. Rising on her tiptoes, she searched above the crowd for Josh. Darn, where was he?

The street, lined with open-doored kiosks, displayed wares in the Turkish way of having the same type of shops huddled together. So confusing. No landmarks. The cluster she strode past all displayed animal pelts. She stopped to touch the long silky hair on one of many goatskin fleeces hanging across the front of a shop. Wrinkling her nose at the pungent odor, she peeked from behind a dangling skin.

No sign of Josh.

If he hadn't warned her not to walk alone in public, she would've had no qualms, except about getting lost. Head down, she ran into the shop's proprietor. He stood so close she could see the individual hairs in his walrus mustache.

He said something.

She couldn't understand, so she shook her head. Then remembered *no* was signified by clicking the tongue and a single backward tip of the head that looked to her like an emphatic nod.

The weathered man pulled the fleece from the rack and laid the smelly thing in her hands.

She held the pelt up, sidestepped the proprietor, and peeped out again.

Still no Josh. Her heart hammered. She had warned him about her directional dyslexia. He knew she got lost. Where was he? She searched the faces of the men doing their shopping. No one seemed interested in her except a few dark men whose bold eyes stared so hard, her ears burned.

She almost missed Josh, standing in the shadow of a different kiosk stocked with identical goat skins. She let out a long breath. She was such a boob.

He signaled with a thumb's up sign and grinned.

She tossed the fleece into the startled proprietor's arms and turned in the direction she'd been heading.

A street jammed with darting traffic faced her. On the opposite side, taxis lined up like planes at Dallas' DFW airport. She thinned her lips. No more cabs for her.

Her thoughts jumped ahead to her fearful meeting. She must face it. Would the meeting mean the end of hope?

For now, thanks to God's peace in her heart, she had the courage to overcome whatever hurtles lay ahead.

She pressed on toward the street's center island. A raised platform provided a narrow oasis above the snarl of traffic for people to wait for the tram. She stepped in line at the tram kiosk.

"A ticket to the Topkapi Museum," she told the ticket agent, fishing the lira Josh had given her from her fanny pack.

"Topkapi," the agent repeated as if he heard it many times a day and often dealt with foreigners who entered his country without learning his language. "Two thousand lira."

She thumbed through her slim pile of bills until she found one with the number needed. Did that translate into two cents or two dollars? She didn't know. Whatever the cost, she must get to the Topkapi Palace Museum and the Harem in time.

Gripping her ticket, she watched traffic zoom past the stop sign at the corner near the tram booth. A Turk stepped out in front of a speeding vehicle. The car screeched to a halt. The Turk crossed the street. Traffic sped up until other Turks merged into traffic and ground the autos to a halt while they crossed the street. Turkish drivers sped through stop signs and red lights with no apparent remorse.

The trick must be to step out and pray. Edging into the company of a group of Turks, she darted with them in front of a moving car. The car screeched to a halt inches from her legs.

"Hang on, Ian. I'm on my way," she breathed, her heart pounding.

She joined people thronging the tram platform. Men jammed around her with a sprinkling of school children in neat blue and white uniforms. The girls giggled at the boys, and the boys made faces back. No one pushed. Cars whizzed by in both directions so close she felt heat from their exhaust.

Silently the tram pulled to an abrupt stop. Doors whooshed open amid a general rush to enter packed cars. She squeezed on board and grabbed an overhead bar. Just before the doors swished closed, Josh slid inside. Her stomach stopped trembling. She found herself pressed against three men who tried to avoid jostling her.

Behind her, Josh relaxed against her in a protective way. He was in top shape—fit beyond reason, honed to the point of hard-muscled incredibility. Of course, a military man would be. Still, his closeness gave her reassurance.

People rode in complete silence. Pressed against Josh inside the swaying tram, she found herself feeling thankful he'd noticed her at the airport, glad he'd followed her, and happy he cared enough to make her his project during his holiday. *Thank you so much, God, for sending Josh to help me find Ian.*

But she *was* attracted to him—too much so. She depended on him, thanks to her directional dyslexia. Finding Ian might rest in Josh's hands. Detective Pavlik had a full load of police business which demanded his attention. Whereas Josh could concentrate on finding Ian. He knew the country, the language, and the customs. She peeked at his reflection in the tram window.

If only she could shake off the nagging doubt that Josh had an ulterior motive in helping her.

The tram slid to a smooth stop, and the door opened at the street called Yerebatan Caddesi.

"This is our stop," Josh whispered, his breath tingling her ear.

His gentle shove started her moving. She slithered through the densely packed riders and worked her way out the door.

Outside, she lingered until she glimpsed Josh squirm through the closing door just as the tram started to speed. Her breathing eased.

"Toward the sea," Josh whispered, then hung back.

She trekked along the sidewalk toward a slice of blue sparkling in the sun. Sniffing the salty ocean breeze of the Bosphorus fondling her face, she smiled, and raised her chin to the sun.

"Move! Don't draw attention to yourself." Josh whispered. "In a world populated by women, you'd be a standout. Here you can't avoid the spotlight."

She rushed down the steep walk until she caught up with a group of German-speaking tourists. Josh must not get out of the barracks very often if he thought her that attractive. But his words stirred her heart.

Ignoring a few irritated glances, she mixed with the Germans, matching their pace down a modern walkway flanked by a wide street buzzing with manic traffic. In makeshift booths along the sidewalk, proprietors sold trinkets and souvenirs. Where the hill reached bottom then rose, the Germans growled and muttered among themselves and frowned at her. She slowed and hung back, but not so far as to appear apart from their group. At the summit of the hill, a beautiful ancient turreted wall guarded by twin towers distracted their attention.

She drew a deep breath, letting the exotic building burn its image into her mind. Beneath a brick rampart, a five-story-tall arched Baroque portal opened into the palace fortress. A sign naming it *Imperial Gate* hung in the archway's center.

Guards carrying assault rifles eyed each person entering the giant wooden doors.

Her curiosity spiked as she passed between the vigilant guards and entered the citadel. "Exquisite," she breathed. A sense of awe filled her as she meandered between lush formal gardens.

She was here. If only Ian were with her. He'd share her appreciation of the bursting history and unique antiquity. She glanced at her watch. Twenty minutes until deadline. She had no time to sightsee. She must make mental notes, so she could find her way back. She hurried along a broad stone walkway through beautifully landscaped gardens.

She joined tourists who looked to be from around the world and stared at new buildings which housed a *tuvalet* or restroom, a gift shop, and the ticket booth.

"One ticket, please."

In return for her lira, the agent handed her a brochure and a map.

She stared around. Was anyone spying on her. Seeing no one suspicious, she read the brochure as she walked.

DURING THE OTTOMAN EMPIRE FOUR THOUSAND PEOPLE LIVED INSIDE THE TOPKAPI PALACE. THE GROUNDS AND PALACE CONTAIN A NETWORK OF IMPERIAL BUILDINGS INCLUDING COURTS, PAVILIONS, MOSQUES, AND GARDENS. THE FORTRESS STILL BOASTS ITS BYZANTINE WALL WITH SHOOTING BREACHES AND GATES THICK ENOUGH TO WITHSTAND THE EROSION OF TIME.

Would the brochure offer any information concerning where Ian was kept? She hurried faster and read.

THE COMPLEX IS LOCATED ON A PENINSULA HIGH ABOVE THE SEA OF MARMARA WHICH CONNECTS THE AEGEAN TO THE BLACK SEA; TO THE NORTH SPARKLES THE GOLDEN HORN, AND TO THE EAST THE BOSPHORUS SEA SEPARATES EUROPE FROM ASIA. SULTAN MEHMET II BUILT THIS PALACE AS HIS RESIDENCE IN 1467, AND IT WAS USED BY SUCCESSIVE SULTANS UNTIL 1839.

She checked the map. Where was the Harem? Oh, there.

Fifteen minutes left. She slowed. Would she find Ian inside? He had to be alive or his kidnappers wouldn't approach—

"No use putting off the contact." Josh hissed from near her elbow. He stooped to adjust his sandal. "It's got to be made."

Her cheeks burned. Where had he come from? She turned her steps toward the scary meeting. The map said she'd take the gate to the second court.

As she passed beneath the imposing arched gate, she craned her neck to catch its name, *The Gate of Salutation*. Flanked by twin octagonal towers, the entrance reminded her of a Medieval castle. She tugged off her hot scarf and tried to pinpoint the Gate in her mind for her return trip. It had been to her right from the gated entrance so would be to her left when she returned. Right?

Inside the second courtyard, a tree-shaded area opened out with six paved paths leading different directions. She hesitated beneath stately trees. Why must the way be so confusing? Music from water fountains played, and birds sang in the trees.

Nicole ran a finger over her open map. Path one led to the stables of the sultans and ended at the *Gate of the Dead*. The second path led to the *Carriage Gate* and to the *Harem*. Which was the second path? Path number three led to the *Privy Council*. Blast her poor sense of direction! The structures formed a long wing with walls inlaid with cobalt tiles. Might Ian be hidden there? She shook her head. He could be anywhere inside this huge expanse.

Path four led to the gateway to the *Third Court* and paths five and six to the *Grand Palace Kitchens* where priceless porcelains were displayed. Surely the Harem wouldn't be near the kitchen.

She spun around checking each red-tile-roofed building domed with silver. She studied the map and walked, trusting she'd found the second path.

Hope trickled through her veins. She must be getting close. She hurried through the *Gate of White Eunuchs*. She knew from her minor degree in history there, ensconced on costly Turkish carpets, the sultans held open-air court. They strolled beneath these same covered colonnades, saw the brilliant hues of these vast tulip gardens, and heard the tinkling melodies played by these ornate fountains.

Josh hid his whisper behind a fit of coughing. "Get moving or you'll have a squadron of men on your tail. Then I'd have to gun them down."

She startled. Where had he come from? His appearance nudged her thoughts into a different direction. Josh, with his backwards baseball cap, shorts and camera looked as harmless as a college student—a lean, muscular, handsome student but ...

She shook her thoughts back into focus. These musings were diversions to calm her racing heart. She knew it. She was in ...

Denial. She couldn't face life if she found Ian dead. There, she'd put her fears into thought. Now go forward and find him. Yet, her feet seemed rooted.

Brushing past her elbow, Josh knelt in front of her. He focused her camera on the *Gate to the Sublime Port* and grunted loud enough for her to hear, "You have to buy a ticket to enter the Harem, and the ten-thirty group goes inside in less than five minutes. You best get yourself to the Harem." He nodded toward her right, snapped his picture, and stood in a swift movement of rippling muscles. His stride away shouted impatience.

Five minutes. Her heart drummed. She would like nothing better than to wait an hour ... two hours.

Deja vu.

She couldn't deal with finding Ian like she'd found Paul. This whole experience was too reminiscent of the trip to the site of Paul's plane crash. She'd had the same sense of unreality and expectancy. The same rising hope. When she'd seen the charred remnants of the Cessna 210, she'd lost all hope.

No one could have survived the crash that left Paul's plane shattered. But without a body, she had no sense of closure. No sense of being a widow. She'd never quite believed he was dead.

At any time, Paul Phillips might walk back into her life.

CHAPTER EIGHTEEN

Nicole sighed. Not knowing was exquisite torture. She was neither married nor free. If only Paul would walk back into her life. Or his body would be found. She had no closure.

Her hands shook. She was terrified to meet with Ian's kidnappers. If only Ian were not scarred, mutilated, or dead. Dear Ian, with his gentle blue eyes and his infectious grin. His shyness with her friends ... around *any* girl. And the almost miraculous way they communicated, seldom needing words, their minds in sync.

She clenched her hands, desperately wanted to prolong her hope. She stiffened her back. She would face whatever lay in store.

Josh hissed, "Go!"

Taking a deep breath, Nicole jogged toward the Harem.

She ran up the paved walk through the *Carriage Gate* to a recessed building where a crowd waited. Breathless, she stopped in front of the ticket office just as the Turk closed the window and reached to lock it.

"Please, two tickets." She held up two fingers and waved the wad of lira Josh had given her.

The Turk frowned, stared at his watch, glanced at the waiting crowd, then looked her over with that male superiority she so often encountered here.

Remembering Turks loved blondes, she half turned, letting him see the hair hanging down her back.

His smile grew until the man grinned broadly beneath his bristling mustache. Opening the ticket window, he held out two squares of thin paper printed with pictures of the Harem.

"How much?"

The man answered with a long jumble of Turkish words punctuated with smiles and nods.

She shrugged. The door to the Harem opened and people poured into the building. So, she handed her thin roll of bills to the ticket seller.

The Turk counted out the lira he needed, then handed her change, closed his window, clicked the lock, and pulled the shade.

A muttered oath sounded behind her.

Without turning she held both tickets up, her hand spread so Josh could see she had a ticket for him. From the corner of her eye she saw him follow her into the surging crowd.

He shouldered her as they pressed in to enter the narrow door.

She slipped him a ticket.

They were the last two to enter.

Inside, three Turks stood on a raised dais offering tours in German, Turkish, and English.

She, Josh, a tall, fat woman with garish red hair, and several middle-aged couples followed the English-speaking Turkish tour guide.

Their group milled together in the atrium.

The guide, his English heavily accented, instructed them on the Harem's history.

Nicole stared at the massed people for the contact she'd come to meet. Her heart hammered.

"The word *Harem* is Arabic," their young guide began. "Harem means forbidden. We Turks called this *House of Felicity*.

Before Islam, Turkish people were monogamous. But after Ottoman Empire in tenth century conquered us, we accept Islam and adopt Arabic Harem. Our esteemed leader, Ataturk, banned harems in 1926."

"This complex holds four hundred rooms for sultan entire House of Felicity. His sons, the princes, lived next to Harem in structures named *kafes*."

"Three hundred young, attractive girls lived in Harem. Our people brought young girls, aged five and six, from conquered lands or from slave traders. Sultans called new girls *acemi* or beginner. *Cariye,* or concubine, was girls' next step. Experienced girls called *kalfa.*"

"Princes enjoyed intimate relations with girls." The guide grinned. "Each girl receive expert training."

Nicole squirmed under the guide's gaze. He stared at her as if he were a prince and she was one of the Harem girls.

Josh sauntered across the room and slouched in front of her, blocking the guide's stare.

In her secret, inner heart, she thrilled. She hadn't known such protectiveness since Dad died.

The guide frowned but continued. "Concubine sultan preferred became *ikbal,* or favorite, and owned special apartment inside Harem. Sultans prize Caucasian girls because of pale beauty."

Nicole shivered. How many countless little girls over the centuries had been forced to live and die inside harems for the sole purpose of serving men? She glanced around and mugged a wry face at Josh. Where was her contact?

Josh shrugged and spread his hands.

The guide led them through labyrinth-like stone passageways deeper into the Harem. The other two tour groups had moved out of sight.

The Turk's accented words droned on. "Today, visitors can see small part of Harem."

Was Ian inside these chambers, hidden in one of the rooms not shown to tourists? Nicole sharpened her awareness. Somewhere she would find a clue to lead her to him. So far, nothing but the confining isolation of the Harem.

The guide turned his head to answer a tourist's question.

She turned the knob of one of the closed doors. Locked.

And she was lost. If she discovered Ian, no way could she lead him to freedom.

"We enter guardroom of *Black Eunuchs*. Sultan castrated all Harem guards. Chief Black Eunuch was most powerful man in Harem and responsible for discipline. He was fourth highest in empire. The Chief Eunuch, not real man or real woman, filled with hate against both, instigate intrigues."

"Ah! The Ottoman reputation for intrigue and murder," Josh murmured.

She took a chance and whispered, "Do you think the kidnapper is in our group?" None of the Americans looked like kidnappers. Judging from their conversation, the grey-haired, portly couples seemed a congenial party who had known each other most of their lives.

"I'd guess not. Our contact must plan to meet us somewhere."

The pounding inside her rib cage accelerated.

The guide's droning voice receded to background noise. She tried another closed and locked door. She met Josh's gaze and shook her head.

The look in his eyes multiplied her drumming thoughts, the knot in her stomach, and the goose bumps pricking her arms.

Her last trace of suspicion regarding Josh dissolved. Deep inside, in a place she'd thought protected, fondness sprouted. She couldn't let Josh get emotionally close. He knew nothing of

Christianity. What bad timing. She mustn't act like a love-sick girl. She must concentrate her attention on finding Ian.

How could she find Ian in these rooms recessed with hidden passages?

"Sultan bathroom," announced the guide as they entered a beautiful white marble bathing area that opened into a massage room and then a dressing nook.

The red-haired woman broke into the guide's lecture. "Now, *this* is what I call a Turkish bath!"

The guide offered a thin smile. "Sultan used gold baroque bedroom when he visit Harem. Fountain with tiles from Vienna. Behold!" He waved a dramatic hand, "Baldachino bed."

"Impressive. I'll wager the good old sultan seldom slept in his palace bedroom," the red-haired woman sang out.

The tortured life of so many young girls, however long dead, was no joking matter. Nicole frowned at the woman. How could that tourist be so insensitive?

"Because of nomad life Ottoman Sultan live, rooms sparsely furnished. They must, at a moment's notice, empty closets, roll up beds, and toss all on saddled camels. In emergency, sultan leave bedroom through secret door." The guide touched a hidden lever behind an ornate gold mirror. The mirror sprang open, revealing the entrance to a dark passageway.

The red-haired woman's jaw dropped with a full-throated "Pshaw!"

Nicole's heart sank.

Josh reflected her despairing look.

How would they find Ian with secret passageways and sealed-off rooms? When would they meet their contact? What ransom would he ask? She ached to see Ian. To know he was alive and whole.

Reluctant to leave the hidden passageway, she trailed the guide.

He pointed out inlaid cobalt tiles, egg-sized encrusted jewels, and glorious handmade Turkish carpets.

The Harem struck her as drafty, callous, and sinister. The gold-plated armchairs, Venetian crystal, and lavish English clocks didn't lighten the atmosphere of gloom. Ghosts of anguished women paced the stone passageways and reclined on the Turkish sofas. The high-ceilinged, ornate rooms remained a foreboding prison.

Which hid Ian.

"Fountains inside Harem prevent eavesdropping near rushing noise of falling water. We enter *kafes*, wing of crown princes. Rooms for twelve princes. Royal princes not permit to bring children into world. A pregnant girl must abort her baby."

Nicole smashed a fist against her lips to hide her gasp.

"Twelve Harem women service each of twelve princes. Many babies murder."

Nicole's breakfast rose in her throat. Her nerves strung tighter than violin strings. The slightest touch of a bow would make her scream. Exploited girls and aborted babies. So much evil. And how many kidnappings?

As if he sensed her tension, Josh held both thumbs up in encouragement.

Laughter gurgled up. Was she getting hysterical?

The others in the group looked up from investigating the mother-of-pearl inlaid shutters with interested stares.

Nicole turned away.

Their guide led them through a confusing array of narrow stone passageways, one opening into another, often with as many as three doors leading out.

The familiar lost feeling choked her. Was Ian inside one of these sealed rooms? Imprisoned where she could never find him?

She locked gazes with Josh. All trace of teasing had vanished from his expression. Instead, his dark eyes smoldered compassion.

Knowing her face often mirrored her thoughts, she glanced down pretending to read the brochure she clutched. She couldn't let Josh see the tears pricking her eyes.

With a smothered shriek, the redheaded woman slipped on the inlaid tile floor and almost fell.

Nicole and the group stared at her.

Loud and ill-favored, the redhead had sought attention from all of them.

Nicole would be glad to see the last of her.

The guide took a sharp turn.

She found herself back in the sultan's lavish blue-tiled bedroom.

The young man stopped in front of the gold Baldachino, roped-off bed.

She stole a glance at Josh.

He stared, stone-faced, at the mirror which hid the secret passageway.

"Our tour is over, but I have a special surprise today for this English-speaking group."

Josh cut an expectant look toward her.

Her heart pounded.

"Chief eunuch train concubines with music talent to dance for sultan. When sultan bored, he order dancers brought. After girls danced, they touch forehead to floor before sultan."

The guide paused for effect, cleared his throat, pulled a tape recorder from his pocket, clicked on music, and stared at the mirror on the hidden door.

The door popped open.

Nicole felt almost as if the past moved up to engulf the present.

A slender leg encased in transparent nylon slipped through the opening and posed. The taut leg, slender-muscled, ended in a foot clad inside a pointed Turkish slipper. The toe touched the inlaid tiles. A shapely bare arm encircled with silver bracelets tinkled through the door. As the music echoed inside the immense room, a lovely girl slid through the portal. Her skin was alabaster pale. Masses of black hair flowed in waves to her waist, undulating with every movement. In a world of veiled women, she seemed to be clad in less than she was. She wore a pink bikini-type costume. Transparent nylon ballooned from the top of her long thighs to where it hugged her ankles. Gold bangles swayed from the bottom of her bra with each movement. A diamond glittered inside her bare navel.

She floated across the room to stop in front of Josh. She smiled behind the veil falling from her hair, one corner of which she held in front of her lips. Then twitched a tiny titillating quiver of her stomach.

Josh's face reddened.

With a graceful movement, the girl held out her hand, and with a flick of her index finger coaxed Josh to dance.

He planted his feet and refused.

The dancer gave a saucy flip of her nearly naked hip.

A flood of emotions boiled inside Nicole. Naturally, the dancer chose Josh. He was the only young male in the room. She wouldn't choose the married older men.

As she danced sensuously, the girl coaxed Josh again and again.

But he stood rooted like a tree staring at her.

She was breathtakingly beautiful with large, dark eyes, delicate bone structure, and full lips. But she was so young, little more than a teenager, her face innocent as a child's.

Nicole's heart went out to her.

An innocent face with an enticing body. She danced through the room in absolute control, holding every man there in the exotic palm of her little hand. When she performed the tiny movements with her stomach, no man in the room withstood her enchantment. Their tongues all but hung out.

The dancer cornered Josh, her face chaste, her body performing centuries-old movements guaranteed to captivate. In that enormous sultan's bedchamber, she smiled for Josh alone. Designed to bewitch, her pristine face transformed with a provocative wink. Again, she crooked her finger.

Again, Josh mutinied.

The guide did not.

Young, handsome, full of pride and Turkish rhythm, their guide joined the belly dancer. She cajoled him into removing his shirt and taught him vigorous movements she hadn't used before, turning him into a ridiculous parody of herself.

The tour group laughed and clapped, freed from the power of her dancing.

At last, looking sheepish and sweating, the young guide backed out of the dance to the tour group's clapping, jeers, and catcalls.

Like a switch being thrown, the girl transformed back into an alluring woman. She seduced each staring man with the ancient power of her movements.

Sultans and pashas, harems of attractive girls with almond eyes. She entranced.

Nicole frowned. Of course, she did. The girl had been professionally trained.

Then with a sweet smile, the girl confronted Nicole. Bowing, she eased off one of her bracelets and placed the band in Nicole's hand.

Nicole closed her fingers around the cool, silver bracelet, and the scrap of paper the dancer passed to her.

Tears glistened in the girl's eyes.

Nicole trembled. *She knows where Ian is. She cares about him!* Nicole reached for the girl's hand.

But the dancer scampered away.

Josh didn't appear to have seen. He looked dazed, his eyes fixed on the dancer.

The girl whirled to face Josh. She floated the long veil across her face, pulled it from her hair then twined the opaque cloth around Josh's neck. She enticed him until his ears turned red.

Scarcely more than a child, the belly dancer gave one last flick of her stomach, backed across the room, and out through the mirror.

Nicole expelled a breath.

The obnoxious red-haired woman trilled, "The sultan would have chosen that one for sure." Her wide, red-lipsticked grin leered.

Nicole wished the girl were safely in school, not dancing in front of a bunch of strangers.

The guide tucked in his shirt and wore his pride again. "That dancer older than Harem girls. Sultans to train virgins long before girl could become pregnant."

With that horrifying remark, uttered as if he spoke of a girl learning her ABCs, the guide led them out of the Harem and out of the building.

Nicole lifted her face to the sunshine. She'd stared evil in the face.

The note burned inside her clenched fist. The kidnappers. At last. She had to read it. But she wanted to be alone.

And she was afraid.

The kidnappers hadn't provided a shred of proof that Ian was alive. She nodded to Josh—certain he would follow. She tracked several unobtrusive signs to the *Konyali* Restaurant at the edge of a cliff. Her emotions clashed between hope and terror. She needed to regain her composure before she read the message.

The *Konyali* turned out to be an outdoor restaurant with a panoramic view of the Bosphorus, Istanbul, and the Sea of Marmara. She shadowed a waiter through the long terrace, then slid into a chair at a table for two facing the sea.

Far below, the blue, blue water sparkled in the sunshine. Across it, the Asian side of Istanbul gazed at her with inscrutable Eastern eyes. But the sea breeze spoke of life, promise, and a different world for women. She felt as if she had stumbled through a past as pulsating with life as the present.

Were girls still enslaved in harems? Was the teenager she'd just seen one of them? Why had the girl looked at her with such pity? She pushed that question to the back of her mind. After coffee. Not yet.

When the waiter took her order, she asked for coffee and *Kadinbudu Köfte,* hoping the dish would be something she could eat. What appetite she'd had, she'd lost when the dancer slipped her the note. But she needed time. And to use the table, she must order.

The smiling waiter left.

She glanced at the most magnificent panorama she'd ever seen. One of God's glorious creations.

Beneath her, spread as far as she could see, sparkled the Sea of Marmara. Palaces and quaint seaport villages, tucked into tiny bays, lined both sides. Two enormous bridges spanned the sea and connected Europe with Asia.

She searched the other tables for Josh, but he wasn't anywhere in sight. No worries. He excelled at mingling and disappearing into a crowd, then popping up to startle her.

Her coffee arrived. When she sipped the hot Turkish brew, her fingers trembled. Sucking in a bracing breath, she unfolded the note.

CHAPTER NINETEEN

No Polis. Rent a car. Drive to Antalya with Major Baruch. Await further instructions from contact.

Ian wasn't here. The kidnappers knew about Josh.

Nicole refolded the note. Her mind whirled, not able to sort things out. Where could she find order in this bedlam?

She gazed down the sheer drop to the sparkling sea girded by the ancient fortress walls of the palace. A ferry steamed under the enormous expanse of the Mahmet Bridge. Further in the distance, almost lost among hazy clouds, the Golden Horn, the Bosphorus, and the Sea of Marmara blurred behind her held-back tears.

She hadn't found Ian!

To numb the pain, she funneled her thoughts away from the note. The solidarity of history always brought comfort. Byzantium—Constantinople—Istanbul, this ancient city had been called three different names. Each name recalled the three great periods of their history.

This time history didn't help. She'd pinned her faith on finding Ian here. The more hours that sped past, the less certain she was that she'd rescue him. If only she could have arrived in time to save Ian from being kidnapped.

Her practical nature reasserted itself. She faced a turning point—she could surrender to her overwhelming feeling of helplessness or stand on the promise of God.

She chose. She *could* do all things through Christ who strengthened her. He wouldn't ask her to do more than she could handle. He would help her contend with her fear for Ian. He would give her strength, though she felt so very unqualified for this task. One step at a time.

She was not alone.

Her vision cleared. Everything her blind eyes had missed became etched on the hard disk of her mind.

The strange man Josh dubbed *Ducky* waddled through the tulip garden, his face admiring, his eyes on the brilliant hues. As if she'd acquired a sixth sense, she noted the obnoxious red-haired woman sitting quietly two tables away. Odd. Out of character with the woman's earlier conduct.

She stiffened. On a terrace far below, almost at sea level, sat Josh. Five tables clustered under a shady nook beneath an ancient olive tree that grew from the living rock just above the soft slurring of the ocean. When she leaned forward with her elbows on the glass table, she could watch him.

He lounged alone at a table for two. Riding on the brisk wind, the murmur of voices, mingled with the whisper and scent of the sea, floated up from the terrace. What was Josh doing down there?

With his back to the rock, he faced the bottom steps that ascended two steep levels to where she dined. He looked relaxed and as inconspicuous as a single man could in the company of tables occupied with couples. He'd taken off the Dallas Cowboy baseball cap, and his dark hair blended into the shadows of the sheltering tree. Lounging, knees spread, both elbows on the chair arms, he gazed out to sea as if he were a tourist who wandered into a nest of lovers by mistake.

But for all his studied relaxation, something about his attitude suggested tension. He was out of sync with the hand-entwined couples conversing at the other tables. With stiffened shoulders and tightened hands, he looked rigid, even as he strove to appear relaxed.

Her lunch arrived. She toyed with it, forking a few morsels into her mouth as she concentrated on Josh.

He should be here. She must learn not to depend on him. She would put her trust in God and the fortitude and brains he'd given her.

With God's help, she'd lived through Paul's death. As she searched for Ian, she'd find her strength in God once again.

The note shook her confidence to the core. No more denial. Her intuition had been right. The message suggested Josh collaborated with the kidnappers. They knew he was with her and wanted her and Josh to stay together.

Before the belly dancer slipped her the note, a trusting, vulnerable part of her had refused to believe Josh was involved in kidnapping Ian. She'd been a fool to trust him. She had to make a clean break with Josh.

But the note's terms puzzled her. Meet the kidnappers without the police. Certainly. Yet, they'd not asked for money. And they'd given no assurance Ian was alive. Major Baruch was to accompany her to Antalya.

She could add two and two. The kidnappers ordered Josh to ride with her so he could guard her and make certain she obeyed instructions. Deep in her heart she'd known their meeting had been too coincidental. Her stomach churned. She laid her fork on the tablecloth.

A movement on the top tier of steps leading down to the terrace by the sea caught her attention. Other people had descended the double tier of steps, but this woman caught her eye. Tall and slender, she had dark hair disheveled by the breeze. Dark glasses couldn't hide her beauty. She wore designer slacks and a white gauzy blouse. Her white-strapped high heels clicked on the stone stairs. Touched by sunlight, her nails glistened blood-red.

She walked with self-assurance that would have set her apart, even had she not been so attractive. The mysterious woman looked a Nefertiti or a Queen Esther—a woman a man would kill for.

Brilliant sunspots bounced off an enormous diamond on her left hand. Whoever she was, there was little doubt Nefertiti wallowed in wealth.

The woman swept over the uneven paved ground between the two tiers of stairs then continued down.

Nicole's heart sped into erratic beats. She was headed toward Josh.

As the woman neared Josh, she passed a waiter and spoke. The waiter grinned, dropped the tray he carried toward another table, and dashed to the bar.

Queen Nefertiti reached Josh's table.

He stood. Both hands gripped the edge of his table, then he shoved them into the pockets of his shorts.

The woman tilted her head at Josh and smiled—the smile of a woman accustomed to dazzling any heart she chose. Her smile brimmed invitation with no strings attached.

Nicole's heart fluttered like a wounded bird. Feelings for Josh surfaced. Yet, he was somehow involved with Ian's kidnapping. And with this woman.

Throat tight, she watched Josh seat the woman with her profile facing Nicole. Then he moved around the table to face the woman.

Nicole leaned across her own glass table and stared down at them.

Josh dropped into a chair. His movements, the first awkward ones Nicole had seen him make. His obvious discomfort in the woman's presence fired off a barrage of questions inside her mind. What was this woman to Josh? Why were they meeting? Did Nefertiti know Ian's whereabouts?

The waiter arrived with two drinks, served them, and made some remarks to the woman.

Her tinkling laugh rose on the wind.

All pretense of relaxation gone, Josh neither smiled nor spoke.

The woman talked to Josh, toying with the straw in her drink.

Josh's face hardened into a grim expression. His hands gripped the chair arms. He didn't touch his drink.

So, the woman wasn't a date.

The lovely woman laughed and chatted.

Josh's color deepened. He crossed his arms. Twin lines creased his dark brows. His gaze never left the woman's face.

Nefertiti leaned across the small table close to Josh and whispered into his ear. She touched his arm.

Josh thrust his hands to the table as if they had grown too big, and he didn't know what to do with them. He pushed his drink around the glass tabletop until she layered both her hands over his.

Then Josh bent toward her and spoke.

Nicole's heart forgot to beat. Loneliness captured her, gripping her before she could run from it. The couple had been together less than five minutes, and the woman owned Josh.

The queen touched his cheek, speaking with intensity.

Josh's eyes narrowed. Color flooded his face. He jumped to his feet, upsetting his chair. "No!" His bellow reached the upper terrace.

Nicole's heart fluttered in hope.

Couples at other tables glanced up and watched the pair argue.

The waiter scurried over and righted Josh's chair.

The woman lowered her face into her hands, and her shoulders shook.

Josh slanted into his chair, his face a mask. Whatever his thoughts, he hid them. He watched the woman sob. At length, he leaned forward and spoke.

"Interesting scene, would you not agree?"

Nicole bit back a yelp and knocked her luncheon plate to the edge of the table.

The red-haired woman from the Harem tour flopped into the empty chair across the table, her back to the sea. "Don't be alarmed. I'm Nikolai Pavlik." The Russian-Turkish police detective spoke just above a whisper. "In disguise, don't you see."

Gathering her equilibrium, Nicole managed, "Detective." Relief pumped through her bloodstream. "Why are you disguised?"

"Please call me Kolya, as my friends do. A bit embarrassing to appear like this, but I had to speak with you. Without the major's knowledge, you understand. He is suspect, of course."

"Josh? You suspect Josh is one of the kidnappers?" The detective was good, already onto Josh.

"But of course. You must not tell him of our meeting. For that reason, I wear this masquerade. Because of my work, I must be a master of disguise. You never surmised, of course."

Nicole shook her head. The police detective suspected Josh just as she did. She sighed. The fluttering hope in her heart died.

"You look lovely. I would kiss your hand, but under the circumstances such contact might look startling."

"Yes, it would." With his nose to the scent, Kolya personified a cold-blooded greyhound. If any man could find Ian, this man would.

"Mrs. Phillips, that woman who met Major Baruch is his former-sister-in-law. His murdered brother's widow." Kolya nodded to where the mysterious woman sat with Josh. "German police suspected Major Baruch murdered his brother but had no proof."

"Oh." Nicole's mind blanked at whatever else the detective said. *Had* Josh murdered his brother? Her heart whispered, "no."

Kolya's voice turned from gravelly to smooth, "Quite so. Quite so. You knew Major Baruch's brother was murdered?"

Nicole forced an answer through her tight throat. "No."

Kolya glanced to where the former sister-in-law sipped her drink. "Major Baruch is preparing to leave, I think."

She stared down at the couple.

Kolya held out his hand. "But more to the point. May I have the note?"

Already off-balance from what she'd just learned, the deep voice, coming from a heavyset middle-aged woman, disconcerted her. And Kolya somehow knew she'd received a note. Her hand shook as she handed him the note. Steady, she ordered herself.

Kolya's fingers felt hot.

He read and reread the message, folded the paper, then bent and slipped the paper inside his red high-heeled shoe.

"I'm instructed not to involve the police."

"Of course. An additional reason for my costume. However, not involving me would be quite dangerous for you. You realize you could disappear here in Turkey without a trace? Or you could turn up dead." Kolya's eyes flicked over her. "But then, for the killers, there would be the inconvenience of a body."

His piercing grey eyes drilled into her. "More likely the kidnappers would hide you inside any number of ... what? They are called brothels in the States, I think."

Nicole sucked in a breath.

He reached over to touch her hand.

A chill ran through her. The sense of things unspoken under his words unnerved her. Kolya thought she was in grave danger.

"In Turkey, a girl who is an encumbrance to her family or unwanted by her husband ... or dangerous, say in her knowledge of a crime, can be imprisoned inside a harem." He opened his purse and took out a mirror and reapplied his lipstick while checking behind his back. "With few questions asked. I fear the disappearance happens more than we like to believe, you understand." He smiled.

"You think that could happen to me? An American?"

"You understand there would not be a search made for you for a rather long time. Do you think your parents will start such a search? They have been dead these past two years. There are only you and your brother, and he is, of course, missing."

"How did you know about my parents?"

"I have made inquiries, you understand. My job. Checking your background. Your husband died—his estate is closed. You're planning to return to the University of Texas to teach. You have no long-term male friends. In short, you see, you have no one in America who expects you or would miss you if you failed to return."

Chills slid down Nicole's spine. Kolya was right!

"And in Turkey there is, alas, no one who would miss you. Except myself, you understand." He squeezed her hand. "And the major has other interests to sidetrack him." He stared at the twosome still whispering together on the terrace for lovers. "Can you trust him? I think not. What do you know about the major?"

She tilted her head. "Very little really."

His eyes warmed. "So, that leaves me. It is my job to keep you safe ... and to find your brother."

"How did you find out so much so fast?"

Kolya gave her hand another reassuring squeeze. "I'm a detective, you understand."

The waiter arrived and bowed to him. "Did you wish to change tables, Madam?"

Kolya pitched his voice higher, "Why, yes, thank you. And please bring me a Raki with water. I've always wanted to try one of those Turkish drinks you hear so much about. What is in it?" He giggled.

The man was a superb actor. And he had no accent. Surely, the versatile man could help her find Ian.

"Very good, Madam. Raki is a potent anise-flavored liquor distilled from grapes. The taste is like the Greek liquor Ouzo." The waiter turned to Nicole.

"Nothing for me but my check, please."

After the waiter left, Kolya spoke in a low voice, "Whoever abducted your brother wants something else. And they haven't found it yet, you understand?"

CHAPTER TWENTY

Nicole's heart sank. "They might kidnap me to make my brother talk?"

"You are an intelligent woman, Mrs. Phillips. I'm impressed." Kolya glanced at her barely touched lunch. "The mutton should not be wasted."

"I have no appetite." She pushed her plate away.

"So sorry." His eyes beamed sympathy. Then switched to businesslike. "You don't mind hiding your plans from Major Baruch, Mrs. Phillips?"

"A little. But no, if you think it best. Please call me Nicole."

The masculine hand with painted red nails tapped his painted lips.

She blocked her thoughts from peeking into the frightening black hole of present-day harems. She must concentrate on less terrorizing events.

Here sat a man she could trust. A solid man. Experienced. Like an older brother. Backed by his own company of men to search for Ian. How she wanted him back! Ian with his naive trust in people and his whole-hearted trust in God. God wouldn't disappoint Ian's trust.

The detective dabbed his lipsticked mouth then leaned closer and whispered. "I checked into your husband's death and uncovered some interesting facts. For instance, no body was recovered."

Pictures of the crash site flashed through her mind. The anguish, uncertainty and heartbreak of those days bombarded her, then doubled because of her concern for Ian ... and now for herself. Pricks. She gazed down. Her nails bit into her palms.

"The insurance company settled. Unusual—and for such a large sum of money. However, they paid quickly. Why do you suppose they did that?" Kolya leaned back in his chair, patting his red wig as if he were a middle-aged woman, concerned for her hair in the tugging wind.

Even face to face, she couldn't distinguish his normal features. He was skillful in the use of theatrical make-up. Surely, he was as accomplished in the other aspects of his detective work. He would find Ian. Soon.

"I don't want to discuss insurance and my missing husband. Have you checked out Major Baruch?"

"Ah. We are in the process. This man is a mystery. Not a person to trust. Seems as if he has no past or present. But we pursue information about him."

Had Josh hidden it? Her heart raced.

"Now, please help me do my job." Kolya's voice carried an air of authority.

"Of course. I'm more anxious than you to find my brother."

"I think Major Baruch is an accomplice to the kidnappers, if not the Viper."

She spilled the coffee she reached for. "The note appears to corroborate that."

"I want to keep him under surveillance."

She nodded. "Josh might lead us to Ian."

"Quite so. Don't let the major to know you suspect him," Kolya whispered.

She nodded.

"Act normal. Make your assistant think he helps you. You understand? Tell him nothing."

"I understand." Nicole's neck muscles grew rigid. Her head throbbed.

Below on the terrace, Josh jerked to his feet like a puppet pulled by invisible strings, turned his back on the woman, and stalked to the stairs.

Nicole tried to focus on what Kolya said, but found it hard to concentrate, with disillusionment crowding her thoughts. She must get his instructions straight.

"I must leave now. I do not want Baruch to see us together. Even disguised. Don't leave until I signal. And fear not, I will be near at hand." Kolya rose from his chair in a tangle of lumpy dress and oversize purse.

She managed a thin smile. She had police help.

Kolya waddled away.

She sipped cold Turkish coffee and watched the detective clump on his high heels to the end of the terrace, then stop by the waist-high brick enclosure to gaze at the sea.

Keep Josh in the dark. Could she do it? Yes, she could do all things through Christ. But she'd prefer to dump Josh and drive to Antalya alone.

Unanswered questions swirled inside her mind. Why had Josh met with his former-sister-in-law? Nicole massaged her temples. Why had he risked her seeing him? Had he killed his own brother? Hard to believe.

Rubbing the frown from her brow, she leaned forward to stare at the woman sitting two-stories below in the secluded alcove. Was Nefertiti waiting for Josh to return?

Nicole tapped her fingers on the tabletop and in time with her beige leather pump on the in-laid tile floor.

"Need anything more, Miss?" The waiter stood at her elbow.

She covered her coffee cup with her hand.

"The woman who left paid your bill." The waiter smiled and left.

Moving her water glass in circles on the table, Nicole leaned forward to watch the lower terrace. Where was Josh? She shook her head. Josh—an accomplice. Maybe even the ringleader. The concept made sense. Yet disappointment stung like a knife in her heart. Okay, she *would* string Josh along so Kolya could keep an eye on the charming deceiver. Josh wasn't the only one who could act.

She wouldn't dwell on her keen sense of loss. Instead, she mulled over the other instructions Kolya had given before she left the table. She was to go to the archaeological museum next door to pick up the keys to a rental car fitted with a signaling device the police would monitor. Then wait an hour before returning to her hotel. Drive with Josh to Antalya without rousing his suspicions. Tell him nothing. Act as if she trusted him. Difficult. He so easily broke through her defenses. But she would try.

She lifted her coffee cup to her lips. Oh, it was empty and probably had been for a while. She set it on the saucer. At Antalya, the kidnappers would contact her. She'd find out what they wanted, give whatever it was to them, and free Ian. Kolya would step in and arrest the kidnappers ... and Josh. Her heart constricted.

Now she knew which side Josh was on and what she had to do. Her back rigid, she tapped her nails on the glass.

She refused to think of Josh.

She'd concentrate on Ian. Visions of Ian bound, hungry, thirsty, or beaten by his captors tormented her.

Oh God, please protect Ian. She scrunched her eyes against hot tears.

What did Ian know about a mysterious map? His kidnapping had to be connected to the threatening letter she received in Dallas. He must have the map. How did he get involved in something this dangerous? Where was he? Ian couldn't be dead. She'd find him.

She rubbed her fingers over her eyes. Was it possible Paul wasn't dead? Had his plane crash been staged as Kolya intimated? She massaged her arms to stop the shivers.

If Paul were alive, why hadn't he contacted her? Why had he let her collect the insurance money? Was he a criminal? Did Paul kidnap Ian and now wanted her too? Perhaps to disappear together. He must know she wouldn't, nor would Ian. Would Paul? She hadn't known Paul well. There hadn't been time before his death. And he'd been gone so often. And they'd dated such a short time.

A movement below caught her eye.

Queen Nefertiti summoned the waiter. After the woman paid her check, the waiter bowed, kissed her hand, and with a wide smile escorted her to the bottom step of the terrace.

Conversation among the other tables stopped as she passed.

Nefertiti didn't move through space, she dominated and used it as a stage. Each movement could grace the cover of Vogue. She left an aura of sexuality lingering behind like some women leave the scent of perfume. She carried beauty as if it were her name.

Nicole's heart sped.

The queen was Josh's former sister-in-law. He might have murdered his brother because of her. Nicole fingered her tight throat. She shouldn't care.

She let out her breath and grew aware of the shushing sound of water against the shore, the sun sparkling the brilliant sea, the fresh air, the aroma of exotic food, the quiet hubbub of conversation ... and the passing of time. When would Kolya signal her to leave?

He hovered at the edge of the terrace, hanging over the brick enclosure with his slip showing under his tawdry dress, as if engrossed in the sea and the view of land where Asia met Europe.

She glanced around, trying to appear as if she sought nothing, restless and anxious to get on with the search. Why did Kolya wait? Couples and families ate, talked, and snapped pictures on cameras and cell phones at the many tables. None looked suspicious or threatening. However, in the bright sunlight, even Kolya appeared innocuous.

At that moment, a man she hadn't noticed before detached himself from the shadow of the serving building on the lower terrace. He wore dark slacks and a white, open-necked shirt. He blended with the waiters. He only needed to pick up some menus. Or he resembled every male tourist in the restaurant. He only needed—

Nicole pulled in a deep breath. He did. He slid a small camera from his pants pocket and flipped the strap over his wrist.

He could be photographing Josh's former sister-in-law, or he could be her bodyguard. Either way, he followed her up the stairs.

A surge of excitement gripped her. She glanced at Kolya, but his back was turned. Shading her eyes, she stared at the man as he took the terrace stairs two at a time. He stood well over six feet tall, was clean shaven with light brown hair. Although he had a muscular build, he moved with the agility of a cat. His craggy profile looked nondescript, but his blue eyes were unflinching in the hard sunlight.

Hair rose on the back of her neck. Except for the single-minded determination oozing from every pore of his strong body, he could have blended into any crowd.

Bodyguard. That's Nefertiti's bodyguard. Strange he didn't stay closer to her. Appeared as if he didn't want her to know he followed her. Or was Josh having her tailed? What did Nefertiti have to do with Ian?

Kolya patted *her* hair, pulled lipstick from *her* purse, painted *her* mouth, then gripped *her* watch as if *she* were late for an appointment.

Nicole's signal to leave. Pulses fluttering, she tugged her sunglasses from her fanny pack and stood.

As she left her table, a couple with three children crowded up to take her place. Nicole smiled at their happy faces and walked from the terrace.

Striding through the colorful gardens outside the restaurant, sweat dampened the back of her neck. Away from the sea breeze, the day had grown hot. She calmed her racing mind with details of the flowers, the tourists, and the bus loads of school children. But her thoughts insisted on returning to Josh.

Where was he? She was supposed to bait him into going to Antalya with her. Him with his charm and appeal. All a charade. She'd been so deceived.

Reaching the fortress gates, she passed the two guards.

Each cradled an assault rifle in the crook of his arm and ogled her.

Lowering her eyes, she dug into her fanny pack, pulled out her yellow scarf, and tied the silk around her head, babushka style. Chauvinistic men.

She blended with the crowd, then edged in to join a group of Germans, staying in step with their five men, six women group.

Anger churned inside. Some friend Josh turned out to be. One of the kidnappers. What if he didn't come? She tried to shake off her disappointment, not let his deception bother her. But regret seeped through her irritation.

As instructed by Kolya, she found the sign that pointed to a quaint cobbled road that led to the Archeology Museum. The steep descent proved shady and pleasant. She passed a boy vending homemade pretzels from a tray balanced on his head. The ancient stone arch behind him and the narrow-cobbled street beneath his Turkish shoes, created a memorable picture. One Ian would love. But Josh had her camera.

Blast him! He was probably off giving instructions to his hoods. She must be careful. She grimaced. She couldn't show her anger or let him know she was on to him.

She pushed thoughts of his handsome face aside. Fortunately, she'd discovered his true identity before she had become too intrigued with him. Not thinking of him wasn't easy.

She concentrated on the archaeological museum. She raised a brow. The building was magnificent, one of the most important in the world. Ian would visit here after she freed him.

Alone, she too easily became lost. To memorize her way back, she stared at the three enormous U-shaped buildings, surrounded by formal gardens, and scattered with authentic Greek statues. Greek architecture with long, graceful, porches studded with pillars faced her. Huge sarcophagi were spaced in front of the wide walkway.

She found the ticket booth almost hidden inside a rose garden. "A ticket to the museum, please."

The swarthy man stared back with the hot glowing eyes of so many Turkish men. His walrus mustache gave his face a ferocious, pirate-like expression.

She dropped her few remaining lira into his callused palm. The man's gaze darted over the area.

"That's all the money I have left. Isn't it enough?" She despised the snap in her voice. Too many frayed emotions.

The man muttered a string of unintelligible Turkish, sounding as if he scolded her. Then his tone turned beguiling and flowed into melodious speech.

What? She glanced behind her to see if Kolya waited nearby to help. The walkway and the garden were empty. An uneasy feeling tickled her spine. A bird chirped. She shifted her weight.

The man inside the booth shoved a ticket in her direction and fumbled with her money and his change. The scent of roses sweetened the air, sweat dribbled down her neck under the scarf and impatience crawled up her skin like aphids on a flower. Still the man shuffled his fingers through the money and stared at her.

She wanted to reach through his cage and shake him. He was her height and almost as slender with bony shoulders spiking through his white shirt. Turkish men weren't husky, and this one was slow and scary looking. Probably because of his moustache and staring eyes. He had a paranoid look. Fanatical.

The man shoved money toward her.

She reached for the small pile. Her fingers touched two keys on a ring hidden among the lira.

A chill hit her as she put the money and keys into her fanny pack. How had Kolya managed this? She hadn't seen him talk with anyone.

How many people knew who she was?

CHAPTER TWENTY-ONE

Nicole glanced at her watch. One o'clock. She had an hour to kill while Kolya set his plan into motion. She'd visit the Archaeological Museum. Better than sitting on a bench fretting.

She skimmed through a few of the many large rooms in the central building. Normally she would have spent two, perhaps three days investigating the artifacts, ranging from a cornerstone of the Jerusalem Temple inscribed by Herod destroyed in A.D. 70, to relics from a partially excavated Troy.

Her mind, tuned to less than one-quarter attention, she viewed the sarcophagi uncovered in the Royal Tombs at Sidon, considered the greatest archaeological discovery of the nineteenth century.

She turned her back on Alexander's tomb. Formed like a Greek temple, the edifice dated from the fourth century B.C. She checked her watch. One forty-five—the time Kolya said she should leave.

As she started for the door, her thoughts tumbled over one another. She glanced at the bas relief of Alexander with a lion's pelt hanging over his shoulder. She must return with Ian. Nothing would stop them from exploring this fabulous museum.

Retracing her steps, she inspected the few people touring the magnificent halls. None looked suspicious. And where were Kolya and Josh? The narrow statue-filled halls offered no place to hide.

As she exited the main door, sunlight blinded her. At the head of the stairs, she stopped between graceful Greek pillars and fumbled in her fanny pack until she touched the rim of her tortoise shell sunglasses. She slipped them on. Even tinted lenses failed to filter the intense light. She squinted.

Where was the hotel? Should she find a cab? Take the tram? But what direction?

For the millionth time in her life, she felt helpless. Why was she born with this directional handicap? With her internal navigational map skewed, she got lost in a department store. If she thought a destination were to the right, it turned out to be left. On a straight street, she had only to turn two corners to become confused.

At the bottom of the stairs she hesitated. Where was the Rose Garden? What? Rose gardens bordered each building.

Great. Where to now?

She walked a few steps along the walk between sarcophagi on one side and statuary on the other. Where was the exit? Why hadn't she paid more attention? The stone masonry dwarfed her. Gardens grew everywhere. To the left, a curving walk meandered into trees. That way?

Totally lost, she followed the cobblestone walk. As she rounded a corner, a movement scraped behind her.

A man's hand shot out from between the thick cover of trees and clamped over her mouth. His other hand encircled her waist.

She sank her teeth into his palm and her elbow into his midriff.

He groaned, grunted, shook her teeth out of his palm, and dragged her deeper into the trees.

She struggled, but he was far too strong. She stomped on his foot—targeting his instep.

He groaned louder and loosened his hold on her waist.

She twisted to glimpse her captor. Josh! She went limp. "Sorry. I didn't expect you to show."

Josh held his stomach, his face squeezed in pain.

"I hope I didn't hurt you." She straightened her clothes. "You frightened me."

Bent over, his complexion red, Josh tried to catch his breath.

Watching him, her fear dissipated like fog beneath sunshine. She smiled. Josh always underestimated her.

He panted, "Lady, you pack a wallop!"

She smiled her sweetest smile. "You're lucky I didn't spray you with mace."

"Yeah, lucky."

She would act gullible. Perhaps she could find out something. "Where have you been? I thought you said you were my bodyguard."

"Maybe you don't need a bodyguard," Josh muttered. "Where are *you* going? Did the kidnappers contact you at the Harem?"

Anger, impatience, and something she couldn't identify drenched his voice. He seemed distracted. "I'm the one who should be angry."

His bad mood leaped between them and became contagious.

"Josh, you scared me to the next timeline by grabbing me." Was his anger directed at her? It seemed more nebulous. Still, like fire ant bites, his ill humor burned and irritated. She smothered her feelings, jammed her hands on her hips in mock exasperation, and joked, "You were too busy eying the belly dancer to notice the contact. Yes, I did receive a note inside the Harem. I'm to drive to Antalya. They'll contact me there."

She held her breath. Would he volunteer to accompany her, or would she have to snare him into going?

Josh's face puckered as if her words didn't taste good. His eyes smoldered banked fires. She expected them to shoot flames like air-to-air missiles or whatever fighter pilots shot these days.

But he leaned back against a tree and massaged his stomach. "Let me see the note." His quick words sounded brusque.

"I don't have it."

"Where is it?"

"I told you what the note said."

"Where is it?"

The unmistakable command forced her to offer a misleading answer, not exactly a lie. "It was windy on the terrace."

"You let the note blow away!" Pure skepticism flickered behind the anger in Josh's eyes. He jerked to attention. "Are you being straight with me?"

"I'm trying."

Josh lowered his head, slid down the tree trunk to sit at its base and tugged off his sandal. He rubbed his instep.

If only he would tell her everything. His betrayal shot burning arrows into her heart. If only he were a friend. Now, she would have to raise her defenses higher.

He gazed up, his eyes impossible to read. "Who gave you the note?" He watched her with the intensity of a sniper targeting her in his crosshairs.

"Someone slipped it into my hand."

"Someone?" Steel honed to a fine heat blazed behind the cold in his eyes. "The belly dancer. When she passed you the bracelet."

It was a statement not a question, so she didn't answer.

"Okay. What did the note say?" He rubbed his foot.

"I told you."

"You're making this difficult." He sounded resigned.

"I'm sorry. That's not my intention."

He was silent, his head bowed. Sliding his sandal on, he took his time as if thinking of the best way to answer. "I'll rent a car and we'll drive to Antalya. That's about a day and a half hard driving. If we work fast, we can find your brother."

Her words spilled out. "I've already arranged for a car. It'll be parked in front of the hotel by the time I return and pack."

Josh's attitude grew quizzical. "How—"

"Where did you disappear to?" She had to sidetrack him from his questions.

He grunted. "Private business. The guide at the Harem told me a Mrs. Meier wanted to meet me on the lower restaurant terrace. I figured you'd be fine in the restaurant for a few minutes. I wasn't gone long. I started tailing you when you left the restaurant."

Josh's betrayal clutched at her heart. "Private business? I thought we agreed to be straight with each other."

Was he the kidnapper's accomplice? The note proved they knew Josh was with her. If Kolya hadn't warned her, she would have told Josh everything. She was too attracted to him to judge his real character.

"You're a great one to talk about being straight with each other!" Josh glared. His brown eyes unwavering, dependable.

Of course, he'd appear trustworthy ... even knightly ... certainly attractive. All her instincts prompted her to trust Josh. Since her directional instincts were always wrong, perhaps her intuition was as well. She couldn't chance Ian's life on intuition. Kolya's suspicion and the note implicated Josh.

She tilted her chin and dared him. "I think it best you stay in Istanbul and continue your vacation. I appreciate the help you've given me, but I don't want to inconvenience you further. I can drive to Antalya alone. I'll wire home when the kidnappers demand ransom money." Flames burned her cheeks. "I don't need you any longer." Smiling, she extended her hand to shake his. "Goodbye." She wasn't such a bad actress. Would he take the bait? She had to obey the kidnappers and take Josh with her. If she appeared too eager, he'd be suspicious.

"You've got to be kidding!" Josh shot up from his sitting position and grabbed her arms.

She pulled away. "I can handle this myself." She peeked at him from under her lashes.

Josh's jaw hardened. His voice cracked as if he summoned a desperate effort at nonchalance. "American women. You think you can do anything." He pressed his thumb and forefinger against the bridge of his nose and closed his eyes. When he opened them, he worked up a smile. "Remember, you can't travel alone. You don't know the language. I can't figure how you managed to rent a car. And these kidnappers aren't playing games." He grinned crookedly. "There, that's settled. I'm going with you." He touched her cheek with his warm fingertips. "Have you contacted the police?"

She stepped away from his tender touch that flew straight to her heart. "The note ordered me not to contact the police. And you flatter yourself. I know it's hard for a hot dogger like you to understand, but I *don't* need you. I'm perfectly capable—"

He huffed a noise between a grunt and a snarl then stormed, "Woman! You're unreasonable. I'm going with you."

Soft as a fading whisper, Nicole decided. She would discover some information before she capitulated. "I'll let you come on two conditions." She waved a finger under Josh's nose. "Number one, tell me about your secret business meeting so we can be honest with one another."

Josh's face tensed. He shoved his hands into the pockets of his shorts. "Okay. Play hard ball. What do you want to know?"

She barely breathed. "Who was your private business with?"

He sighed and swallowed. "An old ... acquaintance. We reminisced." Josh's chest heaved. The rage in his eyes contradicted his soft tone. "Not a pleasant meeting."

"And?"

"Nicole ..."

Her knees wobbled. This was the first time he'd spoken her name with tenderness. The man wielded enormous power over her. She stiffened her resolve.

His voice changed. "It *was* a business meeting. A ... a mission they want me to accept. I couldn't decide. I have to contact them with my answer."

Her heart hammered. Josh had said *them.* More people than his former sister-in-law were involved. Who? "Does your mission have anything to do with me?"

"Why do you think that?" Josh gazed toward the Topkapi Palace and didn't meet her eyes.

She blurted, "Are you in league with the kidnappers?"

Josh's eyes turned suicidal. "No! Look. You need my help. I'll not let you drive to Antalya alone!"

He appeared ready to die for what drove him. "For some reason you don't trust me," he glowered. "My name is my integrity, and it's at stake here as well as your brother's life. I'm going with you, like it or not."

He backed against the tree. "But first, I have to make that contact." Glancing at his watch, he frowned and rubbed the back of his neck. "We'll take the tram as far as the University of Istanbul Plaza. Split at the plaza while I make the contact, then meet on the far side." He cupped her elbow. "Let's go."

CHAPTER TWENTY-TWO

Nicole smiled.

Josh's hand felt warm and strong as he propelled her back to the cobbled road and in the opposite direction from which she had come.

Darn. She *had* chosen the wrong path.

"What's the second condition?"

"Separate rooms," she answered firmly.

Josh threw back his head and laughed. Then his brown eyes pinned her. "Look, Angel, I don't know what kind of man you're accustomed to dealing with, but I'm senior officer in charge of this mission. These goons are kidnappers, perhaps murderers. You're in danger." He rubbed a large hand across his cheek. "Think of me as your shadow, your fortress, your own private Search and Rescue team." He paused as if weighing his words. "But don't think of me as attracted to you."

The glow his protective words had generated in her foolish, defenseless heart blinked out.

"Too much is at stake. We sleep in one room and take turns staying awake." Josh's face tightened, his eyes narrowed, and his jaw jutted.

She almost agreed. But strength she hadn't known she possessed, surfaced. She couldn't let him take charge. "No deal. This is where I strike out on my own. Goodbye, Major Baruch. It's been *different* knowing you." She turned her back on him and strode down the cobblestone road toward the gate. *Thank you, God, Josh headed me in the right direction, so I could find the way out.*

Josh caught up and grabbed her arm.

Not a person was in sight. "Let me go. I'll scream."

He pulled her against him, pressed a hand over her mouth, and whispered into her ear. "Scream and I'll gag you with your scarf, sling you over my shoulder, and lug you out of here. Now, will you come? You want the kidnappers to see us together?"

Nicole tried to wrench free. His brown eyes looked intense and dangerous. Her nerve weakened, but she hung tight.

Hard muscles in his arms hugged her against him. His heart hammered against her back. "Give me your word you won't scream, and I'll let you speak."

Beneath his hand, she nodded.

Josh dropped his grip over her mouth.

She hissed, "I'm supposed to trust a man who threatens me?"

"You've got to. I'm all you have. That police detective's probably working with the kidnappers. It's too coincidental how he took over your case after I spoke with the other investigator. I smell *bakhshish*."

"What?"

"Money under the table. A bribe. You can't rely on him."

"And you're the man I should trust? Ha!"

Quick as a Los Angeles landslide after rain, his stone-faced impassivity slid into contrition. "How can I prove I'm on the level?"

"Not by issuing orders and gagging me."

He released his bear hug but gripped her arm.

"Okay." She shook her hair out of her eyes. "You've proven you're bigger and stronger. I'm not going to disappear. Let go."

He released his fingers, his eyes watchful.

"Tell me, Major Joshua Baruch, did your private business have anything to do with me?"

"And you tell me, Angel, how did you manage to rent a car while you were inside the museum, and why aren't you being straight with me about what happened to the ransom note?"

"Seems we have a stand-off, doesn't it?" She tucked her blouse beneath her leopard belt, tossed her hair back, and gazed at Josh with her sweetest smile.

"Not exactly." Josh took her arm and propelled her down the cobbled road toward the gate. "Your refusal to answer fills in the blanks. Somehow Detective Pavlik contacted you at the Topkapi. You gave him the note, and he supplied you with keys to a rental car, probably one equipped with a surveillance device." He walked fast, his brow puckered.

His intensity dialed down. His expression brightened. He grinned. "The Russian detective planted thoughts into your mind that I wasn't to be trusted. What a jerk!"

"Who would have suspected such an active imagination?" But her cheeks heated.

"I'm right! Your face broadcasts your thoughts." He slid his fingers down her arm and grasped her hand.

"Does my expression also announce I still don't have a logical reason to trust *you*?"

"Why don't you chalk up my helping you to my Jewish heritage? We Jews feel we have a mission on this earth to help people. We try to bandage a damaged world." He grinned his incredible magnetic grin. "I'm suckered by those unable to help themselves."

"Suckered?"

"Okay, okay. I'm the sucker. I'm the one sticking my neck out ... because, as someone I once knew pigeonholed me, I've got a fatal flaw. I fall for beautiful women in distress."

"Fall for?"

"Driven to help."

Though disappointed at his definition, he seemed so open, and he had the right shade of chagrin, she almost believed him. Blasted wolf in sheep's clothing. But she let him hold her hand.

They reached the closed gate, and Josh flung the wooden doors open for her to walk through. They picked their way down the steep cobbled street and started the upward climb. She stumbled on a loose cobblestone.

Josh put his arm around her to steady her, but she shook him off. "Tell me about your private business meeting."

Josh stopped and gently pushed her against the ancient fortress wall that paralleled the road. He placed a hand on either side of her, and towering over her, gazed down into her eyes.

But she couldn't read his expression.

He sighed. "You win. While you ate lunch, I talked with a messenger. She gave me a business proposition."

His impassive face told her nothing. "You already related that much."

His warm breath fanned her cheek. She inhaled his masculine scent.

He sighed again. The stubble on his jaw darkened his complexion.

Oh, he was way too attractive.

Indecision fought in his eyes, with it compassion, then capitulation. "The woman is my brother's widow, remarried too soon after Scott's murder. She said the kidnappers are threatening your life and your brother's if ..." He looked away. His Adam's apple rose and fell inside his tanned neck.

"If what?"

"If I refuse to smuggle antiquities from Turkey for them."

"What?" This was so far out in left field, she couldn't grasp the concept.

Again, his eyes turned death-defying. "I'm to meet a contact inside the University of Istanbul Plaza in a few minutes with my answer."

Nicole's mouth went dry. His explanation seemed too farfetched to have been made-up.

"As an Air Force Search and Rescue pilot, I fly into the Kurdish part of northern Iraq. Their plan is for me to drop off certain Turkish antiquities in Iraq during a routine flight. The Kurds then transport the treasures into Syria. From Syria, the loot will be sent to Cyprus, and then to the States or Europe. The Viper approached me once before. I refused." Josh shifted his hands on the wall, moving even closer. "Now he's using you and your brother to force me into working for him." Red flushed his stony face.

"After I complete one job for him, Meier promises to release Ian." His voice roughened. "But if I finish that one, he has only to turn me into the Air Force to ruin my career or to the Turks, and I'll rot for ninety years inside a Turkish prison."

He backed away and half-turned from her. "With those threats hanging over my head, he thinks to force me to smuggle for him."

Nicole's face burned. "What? How? I'm confused. Why would that man expect you to put yourself in danger for Ian and me? You don't even know Ian." She breathed the question, "Do you?" She blinked up at him. "Why would you risk so much for us?"

He leaned against the ancient wall. "Because ..."

She stiffened. Anger flamed through her. She pushed him. "So, you *are* a plant! This is all part of an elaborate plan. You knew my identity at the airport, followed me, had my purse stolen, and lured me into trusting you."

His eyes softened. "You trust me?"

"Did. For a brief moment." She grimaced and backed away from him.

But he grasped both her hands. "No. You've got it all wrong. I swear, I knew nothing about the smuggling until I met Suzanne at the restaurant. I ... I was attracted to you at the airport, and I could see you needed help."

He pressed his lips together as if he'd said too much. As if that attraction no longer mattered. "I've found the world's a very small place." He dropped her hands. "My meeting you was a fortuitous coincidence for the kidnappers. Meier works on a man's weakness. He's clever and powerful and dangerous."

"You don't expect me to believe in a coincidence?" Nicole raised her brows and shook her head.

"Woman believe what you like! We must find your brother in the next few days. We can trust no one. Certainly not Detective Pavlik!" He muttered under his breath, "The jerk's more interested in you than in finding your brother." He stalked on, motioning for her to follow.

Nicole's thoughts spun. Smuggling? Could Ian be involved? Not her Ian. He was a Christian and way too straight for any kind of criminal activity. Whatever the truth, Josh was key to finding answers, and answers meant finding Ian. And Kolya wanted Josh with her.

She'd play along. "Wait," she begged.

Josh stopped.

"Okay. Ludicrous as it sounds, I believe you. I'll come peaceably, Sheriff." Her silly heart did believe everything he said. *Lord, please show me the truth. I don't know who to trust.*

Hand in hand, they threaded through the crowded streets.

"You said the Viper. You know the kidnappers?" She was already breathing hard from their fast pace.

Josh scarcely moved his tight lips. "Yeah."

"Shouldn't we notify the police?"

He stopped so suddenly she stumbled against him. "What did the note say?" It was a command.

"Not to involve the police."

He nodded. "We'd best do as they say. I don't have a good gut feeling about Pavlik." His smile looked forced. "What else? Tell me verbatim what the note said."

"Not much. Drive to Antalya. Contact will follow. No Polis."

Josh nodded. They worked their way up the sidewalk trying to avoid bumping into people. "The note said Ian's in Antalya?"

"No. They didn't mention Ian."

They entered a beautiful park filled with families sitting, strolling, and visiting together as they meandered through the spacious walks and gardens.

Nicole couldn't help but notice the Turkish families. The lilt and passion of their speech livened the park. Turkish men seemed proud of their children. A pang shot through her breast. Children. How she longed to have her own. With the recessive gene that caused deafness, would she ever dare? Paul hadn't wanted to chance having babies, and her clock ticked faster each passing day.

A uniformed man with a shining silver samovar of **çay** strapped on his back, thrust glasses in their faces. *"Size yiyecek bir sey ikram icecek?"* He wiped the two glasses on his shirttail and held them out again.

"Hayir." Josh clucked "No." They hurried on. "Not a word about Ian? Will he be in Antalya?"

"I ... I assume so. They said I would be contacted."

Josh nodded. "They didn't say." His lips tightened

"He's alive. He must be alive!" Josh's grim expression made her heart pump too fast.

"They'll keep Ian alive, at least until I finish one job for them. After that ..."

"They'll kill him?" She tried to keep the tremor out of her voice.

"Depends on whether he tells them what they want to know. As long as he doesn't, they'll keep him alive."

As they left the park and crossed the street, they jogged. Shoppers on the crowded sidewalks and the inevitable hawkers blocked their way. They dodged past tiny shops with leather coats, socks, sunglasses, cooking pots, and men's underwear piled on the sidewalk in haphazard heaps. A wheeled cart filled with silver and brass bangles crossed the sidewalk. They sidestepped into the minefield of heavy traffic.

Back on the sidewalk, a bread vending cart barricaded their path.

"Smells too good to pass up. I didn't have time for lunch." Josh bought a pita and offered her half.

"No, thanks. I'm not hungry."

He munched as they continued their trek.

She thought he looked the part of a soldier, eating as he marched toward battle. Once again, a flame of faith in him sputtered into life. He held her hand with a protective tenderness that made her throat tighten. But whose side was he on?

Swallowing the last of his *ekmek*, Josh gestured with his free hand. "The University Plaza is at the top of that hill."

She lagged, breathless, still mulling the different possibilities of his story.

As they approached the bottom of the steep stone steps leading up into the Istanbul University Plaza, a woman, her head wrapped in a devout Islamic turban and wearing full legged pantaloons, sat cross-legged on the limestone block of the bottom step looking pitiful. She lowered her head over a small boy lying in deathlike stillness in her arms. The woman thrust out an open palm to Nicole.

With a sidelong glance at Josh, she reached into her fanny pack with her free hand to fish out some lira.

A large white van, red lights flashing, with *POLIS* printed on the side, screeched to a halt at the curb beside them. Armed policemen flung open the four doors and jumped to the street.

CHAPTER TWENTY-THREE

Nicole stared.

Mouth wide in a silent scream, the beggar woman sprang to her feet.

The *dying* child opened his eyes, picked himself nimbly from where he had slid to the stone step, and both sped off.

Two of the policemen caught up with her, grabbed the woman's arms, spoke roughly to her in Turkish, then freed her.

After smiling her gratitude, the woman and her son disappeared through a different crowded street.

Wait! Now the boy looked identical to scores of other healthy, active boys who wandered the streets plying more productive, if not more lucrative, trades.

What a sap she was. Was nothing in Istanbul what it seemed?

"Turks live in extended families." Josh grinned. "They take care of their own—the old, the sick, and the disabled. Turks respect each member of their family. They don't have to beg, but a few like to swindle tourists." He stopped at the edge of the walkway overlooking the plaza.

Nicole swiped at her red face.

Josh apparently dismissed the incident. He searched the crowd.

A shoeshine boy selling perfume approached. "For your lovely woman, sir. Genuine Chanel Number Five. Smell. You see." The boy sprayed Nicole's hand before she could pull away.

"What your name, mister? I Rayard. You come from Germany? You are soldier. You not fool Rayard. Rayard recognize walk. And haircut."

Josh squeezed her hand, his signal for her to rush on and ignore the young man.

The boy attached himself to them. "What you need? Rayard is guide. Come into store. Cost nothing to look. Father sell Turkish carpet. Rayard serve you **çay**, *Raki.*"

Josh ignored the boy as he towed her down a flight of stone stairs and onto an enormous plaza. They threaded through vendors spread in rows, selling everything imaginable. Beautiful tall buildings surrounded the square. A sign above the center building read *The University of Istanbul.*

They plowed between packed vendors. In front of them, two policemen rousted vendors from their pallets forcing them to move out. Didn't work. After the police left, the vendors migrated to another spot and laid out their wares on blankets and the bare stone blocks.

Josh scanned the plaza, his face tense, a muscle in his lean jaw flexed. As though he were a tourist, he pulled Nicole's camera out and appeared to take shots of the congested square.

Vivid splashes of color from carpets, embroidered cloths, and flashes from knives and cookware caught her eye. A few quaintly dressed women in black robes were sprinkled among the men. Clouds of smoke hung above each vendor's area as the men smoked one pungent cigarette after another.

"Turks smoke, everywhere all the time," Josh mumbled, shading his eyes as he searched the crowd.

She and Josh passed university students picking their way through the vendor jungle as they cut across the plaza to class. Nicole felt more at home with the students, who looked quite cosmopolitan, than she had since she'd arrived in Istanbul.

Almost like American university students, although they seemed more serious and dressed less casually.

"This place crawls with undercover police," Josh whispered. "Every university student is under surveillance by a secret policeman. The Turkish government fears an independent mind."

"Really?" She gazed with new eyes at the crowd. Josh was right. She knew little of life in Turkey. Nothing was the way it appeared.

They stopped. Josh shifted from one foot to another, holding the camera. "I'll wait here to meet my contact." He stepped into an open area in the center of the plaza. "Cross to the north side and meet me on the steps of the main building." He nodded toward it. "The one with the clock tower. Try to look like a tourist. I don't think my contact will show with you here."

She pushed through the crowd. If she didn't resemble a tourist, what did Josh think she looked like? Two hawkers attached themselves to her. She ignored them, except to give periodic backward shakes of her head.

Without Josh's hand holding hers, staving off the staring men, she felt alone and unprotected. Glancing around, she searched for Kolya. He was nowhere in sight. She pulled out her scarf and tied the silk around her hair. Faking an interest in some handmade jewelry, she turned to see if Josh had made his contact.

What answer would he give? Would he gamble rotting for the rest of his life inside a Turkish prison or risk the end of his military career for her and Ian? Or was that story concocted to make her trust him?

Where was he? Not where she'd left him. His dark hair blended with the crowd, and his shorts, T-shirt and ball cap resembled so many other tourists. Would he disappear and leave her and Ian to the mercy of the kidnappers? What would keep him from that? She had no idea how to find her hotel or in what direction the tram was. She fumbled among the silver jewelry.

"I give you good price."

Startled by the merchant's voice, she dropped the silver necklaces. "No. No thanks. I'm just browsing." She ambled toward the clock tower then stopped beside a collection of copper pitchers with long curved handles. The clock tower turned out to be a graceful building. Several steps above the plaza, the building stood serene and majestic, unfazed by the seething, noisy crowd below, like a confident teacher ignoring unruly students.

She climbed the steps to the clock tower building and stood beside an ornately carved door. She sat on the top step and searched the milling multitude for Josh. If what Josh said was true, she couldn't jeopardize his career with her problems.

Josh materialized from the crowd. "Let's go." He grabbed her hand and pulled her to her feet, then power walked so rapidly she had to jog.

"Is this the way to the hotel?" she panted.

They ran down the steps, leaving the plaza and trotted up a winding street.

"We're taking the ferry."

She'd seen a large boat steam up the Bosphorus through the Sea of Marmara when she sat at the Topkapi lunch terrace. "Why?" Breathless and with a stitch in her side, she worked to keep up.

"They're playing hard to contact. They sent a boy to tell us where to go next."

"They know we're together?"

"Yeah. We don't need to pretend anymore." He smiled tenderly.

He glanced around—his eyes narrowed. "Where's your tail? I don't see the trusted Detective Pavlik cat-footing behind you."

"I don't see him either." She clamped her lips to keep from telling him that Kolya was a master of disguise and might be close without their realizing. She hated keeping secrets from him. But Ian's life hung in the balance. She couldn't risk telling Josh after Kolya had warned her not to.

"You can bet he's following us. My contact probably spotted him and is trying to lose him. Hurry. The last ferry leaves in less than half an hour."

They squeezed into a tram. During the short ride to the sea they crammed so close, his sense of virility crashed into her like shock waves.

Josh glanced down, an accusing expression on his intense face. "The great detective didn't plant a surveillance bug on you, did he?"

Her startled look answered his question.

"I may have to search you." The devilish twinkle in his eye warned her he was capable.

She shook her head. "Kolya never came near enough. So, don't even think about it." With his body curved around hers in the packed tram, she felt the athletic length and breadth of him.

His devil-may-care glance warned. He lifted a hand and let it slide down her back leaving a warm trail.

"No," she hissed.

He chuckled wickedly. "Just business." His breath brushed her ear.

"Satisfied?"

"No surveillance bugs."

Her nerves jumped. If he teased her with such liberty in a crowded public area, what could she expect alone with him in a hotel room?

At their stop, they slid off the tram an instant before the doors closed. Then jogged, hand in hand, toward the quay lining the sea. A salt breeze freshened her perspiring skin.

Josh glanced back over his shoulder. "I see a few German tourists and some Chinese carrying cameras. Unless he guessed our destination, we lost Pavlik."

Nicole wasn't so certain. Should she tell him of Kolya's ability to disguise?

On the top deck of the ferry, an awning shaded them from the sun. The sea breeze grew to a stout blow. Gorgeous scenery slid past on both sides of the sparkling water. They glided by lush gardens, priceless palaces, and under two bridges that rivaled the Golden Gate. She perched on the wooden bench, her hands gripping the rail.

Why were they on the ferry? They need to be on their way to the hotel, the car, and Ian. Why had she let Josh take her on this wild goose chase?

"Ancient caravan routes followed this waterway. Agamemnon, Genghis Khan, Darius, and Alexander the Great battled and forged history here."

She smiled wanly—for once not interested in history.

"Paris fought for Helen in Troy. And in Antalya, Anthony met Cleopatra." With gentle fingers, Josh nudged her hair back from where wind streamed strands around her face.

She had to say something. "Right. And in the south, Saint Nicholas converted the heathen and gave gifts to children."

"You know your history." He put his baseball cap on her head to shade her eyes from the sun's glare off the water.

She adjusted the cap. "And in the Far East rises Mount Ararat where Noah's Ark rested. Somewhere near is the source of the Tigris and Euphrates where Eden lay. Have you seen any of those places?"

"Yeah. I climbed Mount Ararat and waded the Euphrates." He laid his arm across the wooden bench behind her back. "We've a lot in common. I like history. These sites are great to visit." His hand massaged her shoulder. "Hope you and Ian will see them together." He gazed at the twin wakes left by the ship's prow cutting through the sparkling sea. "Have you heard the Muezzin broadcast five times a day from minarets to call Muslims to prayer?"

"When I arrived, I did." She peeked behind them over the waters of the Golden Horn to the Old City of Istanbul silhouetted against the receding sun.

He reached for her hand, squeezed it, and smiled.

Inside his warm hand, she realized how cold her own was.

"What happened to the Christians?" She gazed back at Istanbul.

"What Christians?"

Ottoman palaces, mosques with slim minarets, Koran schools with cupolas, and domed Turkish baths outlined between the sky and the sea slid past. Seeing these places was as if she peeked into the world of Arabian Nights. "The descendants of the Christians who attended the Seven Churches of Revelation. The children of the ones Paul converted on his missionary journeys."

"I don't know anything about Paul or those churches. When the Turks conquered the land, they persecuted the Christians. In the 1920s, Attaturk deported the rest to Greece."

The ferry blew its horn, and she shivered. Exotic Turkey held a world of intrigue, kidnapping and danger, veiled faces, and harems. "The Turks sent all the Christians to Greece?"

"A type of ethnic cleansing."

"Are there no Christians in Turkey now?"

Josh quirked his eyebrow. "Anyone not Muslim, they consider Christian. Protestants you mean?"

"Anyone who has put his faith in Messiah. Jews, Catholics, Orthodox Greek, Protestants, whatever denomination."

"Messiah?" He frowned, opened his lips as though he planned to say more, then didn't.

"What about Protestants?"

"There might be a few Orthodox churches around. But even the Hagia Sophia's been converted into a mosque. I think there may be a few churches recognized by the Turkish government, but the only Protestants I know of meet on base. Besides the chaplains, Incirlik Base has several churches." He smiled wryly. "I hear many of the pilots' wives talk to their housekeepers and gardeners about *the Lord*." He held up his fingers to mimic quotation marks. "I haven't run into any of them myself. And they don't talk about Messiah." His expression tightened, and his eyes warned her off.

She ignored his signal. "You mentioned you were looking for the faith of your namesake." She moved on the hard bench, and his arm tightened around her.

"Yeah."

"Yeshua. You know, the spy who entered Canaan with faith was not the only Yeshua in the Bible." *Lord, please give me the right words to say.*

"Are you speaking of what you call the Old Testament?"

She took a deep breath. "I'm speaking of the old and the new. Prophesies from Genesis through Malachi center on Yeshua, Messiah. And the New Testament shows Jesus as the fulfillment of every prophesy."

"I think you know the Writings better than I do." He scratched his head and scrunched his shoulders.

She would do this. Make him listen. "Did you realize the prophet Micah announced Yeshua's birthplace at least five hundred years before he was born?" She closed her eyes, recalling the passage. "But you, Bethlehem Ephrathah, though you are small among the clans of Judah, out of you will come for me One who will be ruler over Israel, whose origins are from old, from ancient times."

"Many have come, calling themselves Messiah." Josh frowned. "They caused a lot of Jews to be murdered by the Romans."

"From Bethlehem? In fulfillment of prophesy?"

"I don't know. For a Jew, the greatest heresy is to accept the Gentiles' Jesus."

"Jesus isn't only for Gentiles. He's the Anointed One, David's ever-so-great-grandson. Our New Testament opens with the record of the genealogy of Jesus Christ, the son of David, the son of Abraham."

Josh's expression looked intense, though he gazed over the water.

She forged on. "An angel appeared to Joseph, stepfather of Jesus, and told him his wife-to-be to be, a virgin, was pregnant with a son conceived by the Holy Spirit."

Josh stirred and looked around.

She spoke faster. "Joseph was to name the child Jesus, Yeshua, because he would save his people from their sins. His people ... the Jews."

"Yeah? Something to think about." Josh dropped his arm.

Her shoulder felt lonely.

"But Gentiles worship a Trinity." Josh crossed his arms in front of his chest. "My God tells me, 'Hear, O Israel: the Lord our God is one Lord.'" His eyes flashed. "I was born with that, raised with that. I believe that." He stood. "I'll get some coffee."

She breathed easier after he retreated and prayed for him.

She was not accustomed to sharing something as personal and precious as her faith. But Josh walked a dangerous tightrope ... for her.

CHAPTER TWENTY-FOUR

As the ferry sidled up to a short dock fronting an enchanting village, Nicole's heart beat in her throat. Who would Josh contact? The sooner they met, the sooner they could leave Istanbul, drive to Antalya, and free Ian.

She leaned over the rail and stared at white-washed, red tile-roofed buildings lining the dockside. Beside her, Josh's shoulders tensed.

A few passengers disembarked. Tourists dressed in leisure wear headed down the dock toward a small restaurant. Bright orange and red blossoms, banked high against a charming stone fence, surrounded the restaurant. A white paved path led from the dock toward the island village.

"Winsome," she breathed.

"Yeah, but no contact. We have to ferry on to the next port."

The boat slid away from the dock and continued up the Bosphorus. It zigzagged to similar docks, first on the European side, then on the Asian, stopping at a dozen such resorts, each unique. And each time Josh grew more silent when his contact didn't show. He repeatedly glanced at his watch.

"Almost three. Either this trip is a delaying tactic, or someone's still tailing us. We'll have to drive all night to reach Antalya." He paced the deck. "I'm going to check out the other decks. Stay put."

Before she could object, he was gone. Fifteen minutes later, he returned.

"Nothing. There's an hour wait at the last stop. Then, the ferry makes the return trip. Either they meet us soon or we're stuck here for a while." He strode the deck in front of her, a frown creasing his forehead.

"Oh, look, Josh." Nicole touched his arm. "There, high on that mountaintop." She pointed to a brooding castle that commanded the entrance to the harbor.

"Yeah. That's the medieval stronghold to the Black Sea. Two castles stand guard." He pointed. "See atop those steep rocks on the other side of the Bosphorus. That's the other one. This channel runs to the Black Sea." He propped a foot on the bench and leaned over the rail. "Here's our last stop, the town of *Anddolu Kavagi*. My contact better be here."

"Yes. We've got to head out. This trip is a waste of time."

"Don't worry." He took her hand and walked her to the prow.

After the ferry tied up, the crew threw out the docking lines, secured them, and dropped the boarding ramp. She and Josh joined the few people left aboard and trooped off.

A few men from the village trotted up to greet the crew with a kiss to the forehead and both cheeks. Turks seemed quite emotional. After the hugging and formal kissing, the crew scattered with them into the nondescript village.

She scanned the dirt road leading up the steep mountain to the castle. "Looks like we're the only ones on this trip to visit the village shops."

"Yeah. Want some coffee?"

"I'd love something cold to drink."

They walked to a short pier where a set of chairs waited at a wooden table. From her seat, the sound of the ocean lapping on the rocky shore soothed her restlessness.

In front of her, a knot of men remodeled a storefront sign. Two leaned out the open window on the second story and lowered ropes. Men on the ground tied the ropes to a large sign. The men upstairs yanked up the sign. One rope slipped, and the sign tumbled back to the sidewalk. Undaunted, the Turks started again. They laughed, joked, and apparently discussed strategy in their lilting language and appeared to have time to kill.

She drummed her fingers on the table. Time slowed to an elderly pace. Several men, full of pride and years, sat in the shade of a large tree playing a Turkish board game.

"With their grey beards and bald heads fringed with grey, they resemble grizzled sailors from the coasts of Maine." Josh ran his hand through his own short hair.

"Do they? You've traveled there too?"

"Yeah. Military family. Military life. I've traveled the world."

A vendor stood at his counter waiting to dip ice cream into uneven homemade cones. A man clad in the inevitable long baggy pants and loose Turkish shirt detached himself from the group working with the sign and came to take their order.

Their cokes arrived in doubtfully clean glasses. Unchilled. No ice. Josh tapped his foot and kept glancing at his watch like a New Yorker waiting for a taxi.

The sun reached past the castle guarding the hill above them, tiptoed across the newly hung sign, and sat heavy on their shoulders. For the umpteenth time, she thought of the woman Josh had met. Now was as good a time as any. She needed answers.

There was no delicate way to ask. "What happened to your brother?"

Josh startled. His frown deepened.

Perhaps she shouldn't have ventured where angels feared to tread.

Like a man facing medieval inquisition, a dogged look hardened Josh's face. "Scott was murdered. He'd recently opened an antique shop in Frankfurt. A mom and pop business."

His hard words through stiffened lips barely reached her.

"Police found Scott's body washed up on the banks of the Rhine River. He had a bullet in his head."

"How long ago?"

"A year."

"What happened to his wife?" She had to discover how Josh felt toward his former-sister-in-law.

"Two weeks after police found his body, she married a rich man. No more questions."

His flat words stopped her. She dropped her head, finished her coke, and felt as antsy as Josh acted. "Let's get some ice cream."

They sauntered to the ice cream counter. The owner boasted one melting container of ice cream. With no coolant inside his display booth, the ice cream looked unappetizing. Nicole turned away.

The ice cream vendor leaned across the counter spoke in a low voice, "Major."

Josh stiffened.

The man motioned Josh close and whispered.

Josh jerked his head and clenched his fists. Was he going to punch the vendor? Instead, he smashed one hand into the palm of his other and stormed over to the men tinkering with the store sign.

She followed. "What did the ice cream salesman tell you?"

Josh slammed his fist into the palm of his hand. "The Viper will meet us in Istanbul, inside the cisterns. This trip was bogus." He strode to the knot of men still working on the sign. He spoke Turkish.

The men shook their heads.

Josh pointed to a few small motorboats lining the dock.

The men shrugged and shook their heads.

Josh's eyes blackened into deep holes.

The men stepped back, turned, and scrambled up the steps.

Josh returned and stood in front of her.

"What happened?"

"I asked if there was a boat to rent. They said there was only the ferry. I asked if one of those other boats were available. Said I'd pay. Just for a quick trip back to Istanbul. They said all their boats needed repair."

"Now what?"

"We check the stores." Josh stomped along the paved road to a dilapidated door and barged into a small shop selling ladies' clothes. He soon came out. His face red, his fists clenched at his sides.

Nicole trotted beside him, visiting the remaining shop. But no one had a boat to rent.

He strode back to the white chair near the dock and slumped on it. "We wait. The Viper bought off the few people with boats. He stranded us while he completes some devious plan."

"All the boats?"

"He has the resources."

She slipped into a chair beside him. "Then why did he kidnap Ian? We don't have much money for ransom. Only the amount my husband left in insurance money."

"That's the question. We know he's using Ian as hostage, so I'll do his dirty work. But that was an afterthought. Why did he nab Ian in the first place?" Josh pinched the bridge of his nose. "I'd forfeit a month's pay to have my gun." He rubbed his face. "For now, we're forced to play by his rules. Until we find your brother."

"Doesn't knowing this Viper give us an edge in figuring his next move?"

"He's ruthless in getting what he wants. Soon, I'll stash you in a safe place. So long as I comply with his wishes, I think you're safe. But I need to do recon on who's tailing us and how many there are."

She mulled his words. He tried hard to convince her she was safe, but how certain was he? "What if whatever the Viper needs from Ian is more important than your smuggling antiquities from Turkey? What would prevent him from kidnaping me and using me to force Ian to do whatever he wants?" If only she could talk to Kolya.

"Too many questions we have no answers for." Josh massaged the back of his neck and glanced at his watch.

Forgetting to hide her inner feelings, she looked at him, her heart in her eyes. "Josh, don't you think—"

A lightning change transformed his face. "You trust me." His grin erased a few shadows from his expression.

"How can I not, when you risk so much for us?" Her stomach fluttered, and her cheeks burned. "But I think we should contact Kolya and tell him what the Viper is forcing you to do. I think—"

Josh slammed his feet on the walk and straightened. "You two must have had a cozy meeting." Josh shook his head. "No. First, I don't trust Pavlik. Then, if he is on the level, what can he do? We don't know where Ian is yet. If Ian doesn't tell Meier ... forget you heard that name!" A vein throbbed in Josh's forehead. He slumped in his chair frowning. "The less you know, the safer you are." He dropped his head in his hands and fell into a deep brood.

Meier? Josh mentioned his former-sister-in-law was Suzanne Meier. Was his brother's widow married to the Viper? How bizarre! Was that why Josh wanted to catch him? Was he as interested in Suzanne as in helping her? While she, blast her foolish heart, cared about him. He might love Suzanne Meier. *Oh God, why did you let me fall into this mess?*

When the ferry reappeared, they boarded and steamed back to Istanbul. Then headed, as directed by the ice cream vendor, to the underground cistern.

"This isn't the tour of Istanbul I planned to take," Nicole quipped as they skipped down the steep steps and entered the cisterns.

Dank, chill air stirred up goosebumps on her arms. Naked bulbs hanging across the water lit the huge expanse. The cavern looked as though it extended for miles beneath the city. Thin concrete piers crisscrossed the water. Doric columns, standing deep in water, held up the ceiling. Nicole gasped. Some of the columns dated to Roman or Greek days. One lay sideways in the water submerging the carved head of Medusa with her snake-crawling hair.

Their steps echoed eerily on the narrow concrete pier. Nicole shivered.

She pointed. "They're here." Her excited whisper drew Josh's look, not downward at the bottom of the stairs where the man sat, but at her face.

"How do you know?" His intense eyes looked distrustful.

Her face heated. "I ... I saw that man at the Topkapi."

Josh stared at the muscular man wearing black slacks and an open-necked white shirt, looking like a businessman now, with an attaché case beside him on the seat. He sat near a closed drink kiosk in an alcove below them. He was alone. He pulled a newspaper from an attaché and soon seemed engrossed in reading.

"Are you sure?" Josh whispered as they descended the steps toward the man.

She nodded. "He pretended to act as a waiter at the restaurant."

"So, he's your tail. Strange he let us see him." Josh took her hand as she walked behind him on the narrow concrete pathway, past the man, and deeper into the underground cistern.

"No. He's not my tail."

Pointing at a carving on a nearby column, Josh pretended to be a tourist. "Not your tail?"

She stooped to see if she could touch the water with her extended fingers, not wanting Josh to see her face.

His voice hardened into a command. "Whose tail?"

"The woman who met you at the Topkapi. I saw her, Susanne, your former-sister-in-law."

"You saw Suzanne?" He frowned and said nothing for a few heartbeats. "Information you withhold from me might cost your brother his life."

His tone spiked shivers along her spine.

"Tell me everything you know."

Before she could answer, the lights went out.

Josh squeezed her hand. "Don't move. You could end up in the water."

They stood still. The sound of water dripping from the ceiling broke the dead silence. Total darkness engulfed them.

CHAPTER TWENTY-FIVE

"What now?" Josh muttered.

Dankness closed Nicole in, cool and penetrating. Her eyes should adjust soon to the darkness.

Beside her, Josh's breathing quickened.

She lifted her hand toward her face but could see nothing.

Josh reached for her, searching, then grabbed both her wrists. "Don't move. You could fall off the pier and into the water."

Right. They stood more than fifty feet below ground. Without the artificial bulbs, there wasn't the faintest glimmer of light. She fought rising panic. So that's why Josh's breathing had harshened.

"I should have left you outside," he whispered.

"Too late now." She'd do yoga breathing. Deep, slow breaths. Full inhalations.

"Hold on. Maybe the problem's an electrical short. But more likely ..."

Twin specks of light flicked toward them.

Shoes slapping on concrete echoed in the stillness.

Nicole moved closer to Josh, the toes of her shoes touching the thin tongue of concrete that ended in nothing.

His strong hands held both her wrists. Lights wavered toward them. Hope and fear fought in her breast as she shivered in the black dampness. Water dripped nearby.

"Father, protect us," she prayed aloud.

The full force of twin flashlights glared into Josh's face. She saw nothing except Josh, with his eyes blinking and narrowed against the dazzling light.

Out of the darkness a rough hand jerked her arm, almost toppling her off her feet. But Josh held tight to her wrists.

"Release the girl." The resonant voice had a distinctive German accent.

"Your business is with me. If you want my answer to your proposal, leave Nicole out of this." Josh's voice sounded strong, reassuring.

"Your funeral, Herr Major." The accented voice came from the darkness.

Behind the light flashing in Josh's face, the indistinct form of a light-shirted chest. A giant.

The hand gripping her upper arm increased pressure.

"Ouch," she yelped. She bit her lip to stifle a whimper.

The unknown man held tight.

Josh tightened his grip on her wrist. "The Viper himself."

Undercurrents of hate swirled around her, passing from one man to the other as the two men clutched her in a tug of war.

"How do I know Ian McKenzie's still alive?" Josh stood outlined in the light, feet planted, hands gripping her wrists.

"Use your brains, Major. He's no use to me dead. Neither is this pretty lady. I salute your excellent taste. But we both know your fatal flaw, don't we?" The massive man paused. Silence thickened around them until the German spoke again. "You can choose to walk away, again. Uncomplicating your life. Although, alas, poorer and, did I mention ... you, the lady, and her brother, dead?"

Nicole sucked in her breath. These Germans planned to kill Josh too.

The giant's voice donned a sarcastic overcoat. "You will learn wealth grows on you. Becomes a means, a master, if you will. But you, Major Baruch, pretend higher standards."

Jerks on her arm emphasized his words. She winced. Was the man going to yank her arm out of its socket?

The German's voice hissed sarcasm. "Your driving need is to be Sir Galahad, to save the damsel in distress and her brother." The scorn slid into a contemplative tone. "Perhaps I underestimate the white knight. You know more than I think."

Silence sank between them.

Nicole wrenched her arm, trying to drag free from the Viper's painful grip.

"Perhaps, Major, you do know who this woman is? Aha! You're after the same thing I am."

The Viper's gloating voice sent ice chills through her veins.

Josh's stone-stern face, spotlighted by the flash, didn't wince. His full lips pressed into a tight line, his jaw squared, and his unflinching dark eyes narrowed.

Darting feelings permeated the blackness surrounding her. Suspicion, anger, challenge, and stark hatred spoke so loud she almost heard their voices.

"Want I should make him talk, sir?"

The other man's staccato voice caused Nicole to glance at him. She caught a flash of his face before he lowered his light. The *bodyguard* she'd seen following Josh's former-sister-in-law beamed the other light into Josh's eyes.

Both men towered over Josh. What could she or Josh do to stop them if they decided to kidnap her? Her legs trembled. She stiffened her knees, willing herself to be strong, drawing strength from Josh's face.

Josh's voice sounded firm, as if he were not blinded by the light—outnumbered and out armed. "I've followed red herrings all afternoon. I've an answer to your blackmail. But it's no go if you touch Nicole."

A thrill strengthened her quivering core.

"Ah, yes. But you see Major Baruch, I don't want witnesses to your answer," the Viper's voice raised an octave. "Permit my friend here to escort the young lady to the upper level while we discuss my offer."

Josh didn't loosen his grip on her. "And have her disappear. Think again."

"So, black knight against white knight. How dangerous for you, Major."

"Give Nicole a flashlight. Leave her here. Three of us will walk to the end of this pier and talk. When we're finished, you and your henchman take off. Then Nicole and I will leave."

"You overestimate yourself, Major Baruch. I can collect the girl any moment I want. I could have taken you both a dozen times today."

Nicole's throat tightened. She felt Josh stiffen.

"But, contrary to the rumors you have heard, I prefer the use of persuasion to force. And with the integrity you've built into your career, you are above suspicion with the military. You can become a valuable asset to me." The Viper shifted position and dropped her arm.

The sigh of relief was her own.

"This time, we'll abide by your rules, Major." The Viper flashed his light on her. "But be clear about this, when you work for me—I write the rules." The giant seized her arm again. "The little lady gets no flashlight."

Nicole's mouth was so dry she squeaked, "I understand."

The Viper dropped his crushing grip on her. Josh released her wrists. She clamped her teeth to keep them from chattering. What would happen to Josh?

The three men walked away—their circle of light trained on Josh. At one point, the light played on the standing water under the pier, some five feet below the men. They moved further away, footsteps loud in the dark.

The last two days had strengthened her as surely as the darkness blinded her. Her trust lay in God, who controlled all events. But if they injured Josh and she lost control now, she'd endanger his life.

Father give me power over my emotions, discipline my mind. Cast out my fear.

The flashlights bounced in the distance, turned a corner, and entered a different concrete pier. The group stopped. The lights flicked off. She stared toward the murmur of male voices echoing in the vast cistern.

What would Josh answer? What *could* he answer?

How awful he jeopardized his life for her. The kidnappers would murder Ian if Josh refused. Was this all a hoax? The note had made her so certain Josh instigated Ian's kidnapping. Yet the Viper threatened Josh's life. What if Josh did smuggle and were caught? She'd heard reports of the dismal conditions inside Turkish prisons. No food unless the prisoner had money to pay for it. Torture. Sodomy. Isolation. Would Josh take such risks for her?

A thought flashed through her mind. Perhaps Josh *was* after something else. Did he seek whatever the Viper wanted that everyone thought Ian had?

Father show me the truth. Please give me discernment.

Time stretched out and dragged. Fear for Josh gathered in her chest like water in a blocked dam, threatening to flood her self-control. Cold sweat filmed her forehead. She was no use to Ian captured. If the kidnappers came back for her, she would fight. Use her Tae Kwon Do. They wouldn't expect that.

Together she and Josh might break free. If they left her as Josh ordered them, she would never put herself in such a vulnerable position as this again.

Where was Kolya? Maybe Josh was right. Maybe the detective wouldn't be much help. He hadn't been yet. She and Josh would find Ian. Together.

Loud voices shattered the blackness, but she couldn't understand the German words. Even Josh spoke German. Sounds of a scuffle, pushing and grunts of pain punctured the darkness. Then the distant flashlight snapped on, spotlighting Josh flat on his back on the concrete pier with the Viper's massive knees on his chest.

She wanted to run to Josh, but her feet rooted to the cement. She dropped to her knees, felt her way with her hands, and inched along the pier in the pitch darkness, her eyes on Josh.

Both shadows bent over him, lights trained on his body lying beneath them on the concrete. A sharp, droning noise, screaming loud as a jackhammer in the silence, set her teeth on edge. The sound echoed inside the cavern. Seconds churned into minutes. Still, the whirring battered her ears.

What were they doing to Josh? She crept toward him.

The noise stopped. The *bodyguard* rose and extended a hand to the massive shadow of the Viper.

Josh rolled over, then staggered to his feet.

The flashlight flickered toward her as all three men approached. Her heart hammered. She sucked in quick breaths and stood at the crossroad between her walkway and the pier where the men approached. Then the two men, taking their light with them, headed in the opposite direction.

"Josh," she called.

"Keep talking, I'll come toward your voice."

She babbled on.

Scraping sounds came toward her as Josh worked his way closer. Before he reached her, his raspy breathing underscored her ramblings.

"Don't move." His voice sounded hoarse.

"What—?

"No questions. Trust me." He touched her arm, then gripped her hand in his sweaty palm, and towed her toward him. He held her in his arms as the light disappeared farther and farther down the cavern away from them, leaving them in complete blackness.

She put her arms around his neck.

He touched his lips to her forehead, leaving a burning brand. "Hold still. We don't have a choice. Trust me." He whispered against her cheek.

Their light disappeared.

She closed her eyes, shutting out the frightening darkness and snuggled against his chest. Strange how safe she felt in his arms. Protected. Cherished.

The cavern lights flashed on. She blinked, adjusting to the light, then leaned back in his arms and gazed into Josh's face.

His eyes beamed lasers in the direction the two men had gone. He breathed in irregular pants. His arms loosened, his hands slid down her back, and he grasped her hand. "This way."

Her dry throat barely let her speak. "You're hurting my hand."

"Sorry." Josh's grip relaxed.

She and Josh wound their way through the massive cisterns labyrinth until they found a steep flight of concrete stairs that promised to lead to street level.

"Up here?"

He shook his head. "We'll walk underground to the next exit."

"Okay by me." She was only too glad to put distance between themselves and the two kidnappers. Even though light illuminated the high archways and the strips of cement crisscrossing the water, they strode hand in hand. She should have followed them, but her legs had no strength. "What happened?"

"We follow their instructions."

Josh's curt answer didn't reassure her. "What was that awful noise? Are you hurt?"

CHAPTER TWENTY-SIX

Josh sighed, and thrust his left arm, fist tight, inner wrist up toward her.

Nicole gazed at his taut forearm, bronze and masculine under the naked bulbs. Just above his watch strap a raw tattoo glared. A black slash of lightning marred the lighter skin of his wrist. Blood reddened his skin, smearing the shining image.

"I'm initiated into the Viper's elite group of storm troopers. It's half a swastika. I'm to get the other half after I complete my first job. What better way to prove in court I'm one of the bad guys?" Anger seeped from Josh's attitude.

"Oh, Josh! I'm so sorry. As long as I'm alive, I'll make the truth known." Horror for him gripped her heart. "It's inhumane, what they did."

Josh's jaw bulged. He shook his head as if a tremor shivered him. "The irony's not lost on me. A Jew wearing half a swastika." He sounded angry, but he flashed her a crooked grin. His brow creased. "You're in more danger now. Your witnessing that little scene gives the Viper another reason to make you disappear."

The fragile thread that bound her to life loosened. "You're right." Respect for Josh bubbled into pride. Though the German's marked him with a swastika, he'd thought first of her. And proved himself a faithful ally.

Her heart fluttered. This time not from fear. "Let's get out of here." Her pulse jumped at the touch of his hand.

"Right." He pointed to a set of stone steps not far away. They ran.

Outside, the afternoon sunlight dazzled her.

"The hot air feels good." His fingers touched her arm where bruises darkened her skin. "You're skin's cold."

"Excitement will do that. Now that the danger to you is over, I feel more alive than I've felt since Paul's plane crash."

"You thrive on danger?"

Nicole shrugged. "Maybe. And you?"

"We'll shortcut through the covered bazaar," he spoke over his shoulder. "Save your questions until we're inside the rental car. We've got to run."

As Josh darted through the busy streets pulling her along, she began to imagine he'd led her by the hand for most of her life.

His intense eyes scanned the area. Bolting into heavy traffic, he tugged her across the street as if they were intrepid Turks. A car screeched to a halt within a hairbreadth of ramming Josh's knees.

Breathless, her heart thumped so hard she counted the beats. She raced beside him to a series of concrete steps leading between ancient buildings. After they scampered down, she gasped, her mouth wide in a smile.

"The underground bazaar," Josh motioned to the stone passage with high arched walls that met at the ceiling.

"It's a fantasy from the Arabian Nights!" Brass hookahs, brass tea sets, and brass ewers hung in tiers from the walls. As they hurried by, merchants behind their wares waved them over. Glass cases filled with brass lined the stone walls.

"Seljuks and Aladdin. Right out of history and fiction," she panted as they rushed deeper inside the bazaar.

Josh huffed, "Honest merchants, but they expect a hard bargain."

She realized he loved these people and their culture. Her fear for him lessened in this exotic world peopled with men from storybooks. And for her, Josh took on a new persona. Fearless hero.

She guessed the covered bazaar was not what poured the excitement into his eyes. He'd just sold his soul. How could he be excited? Apparently, he loved adventure. The more dangerous, the better. Even stranger. So did she. And she had thought Paul crazy.

She followed Josh through the wide, arched passageway which soon opened into two others, all crowded with shoppers. They zagged into another ancient, stone passageway jammed with small booths, tourists and Turks.

"The spice bazaar," Josh waved a hand as they dashed through.

An exotic scent emanated from scores of brilliant red, yellow, and orange colored spices spilling from the open mouths of huge burlap bags. She trailed her hand through a bag of vivid red beans. The tantalizing odor followed them as they bolted past. Was this really her? She enjoyed her new-found serendipity. Where was her fear? She reveled in the courage God gave.

Turks in embroidered vests hawked their wares as far as she could see along the stone-floored passage. Bright silk canopies of various shades billowed above the different shops.

"This bazaar covers a maze of sixty-five streets." Josh paused to let her catch her breath. "If we're followed, we can lose the kidnappers in here." His eyes flicked past her to search the mob behind them. "We've got four thousand shops to hide in."

"Are they following us?"

"Viper's a control freak. He'll want to know our every move. Yeah, I'm certain they are." Josh scanned the passageway they'd just scurried through.

Her senses felt so alert she imagined she could see around corners. They approached a fountain with a lion's head spouting sparkling water. A young Turk dried his feet, flung out his prayer rug, knelt, and bowed until his forehead touched the mat. He ignored the noisy crowd.

Suddenly, she knew why she felt so liberated, so heady with excitement. She trusted Josh.

He hurried her through that passage and another lined with silver merchants. Other passageways branched off in a complex network of people and wares. The two of them sped through leather goods and turned into an avenue past shops sporting Turkish carpets laid on the stone pavement, with more carpets in thick rolls climbing to the arched ceiling.

As they dodged merchandise piled in their way, Josh continually glanced over his shoulder.

"Are you certain you know where we are?"

"Don't worry. You're with the world's best land navigator." Josh flashed a smile.

They raced through other confusing corridors. They passed three men lying on couches in a tangle of hookahs, puffing opium. A sign above them read *Sark Café*. All three looked at them with vacant, brown eyes. The essence of blood-red poppies permeated the air with its seductive odor.

"The breath of Istanbul," Josh puffed. He darted into a small doorway, pulled her inside a clothing store, appropriated a pair of women's pantalooned trousers, and thrust them toward her. "Put on these *salvars*."

She wrinkled her nose but tugged the loose brown pants over her slacks.

He tucked a brown shawl around her shoulders. "Tie this *carsaf* over your hair."

She slipped the scarf over her hair and tied the ends under her chin. "I got you. Disguises." She flattened herself against the shop wall.

Josh jammed his long legs into a loose-fitting pair of trousers. A jacket large enough to cover his broad shoulders proved harder to find. He donned a shapeless blue serge, stuffed Ian's baseball cap into a pocket, and counted out bills to the beaming proprietor. He flattened himself against the wall next to her and grinned.

Sharing dizzying adrenaline, she smiled back.

The owner approached Josh with a tray and a drink. "*Hoš geldiniz.*"

Josh greeted, "*Tešekur ederim.*"

The man poured clear liquid into a small glass, then poured water into the liquid.

"Raki," Josh muttered in her ear.

Nicole watched the raki turn from clear to cloudy white—as opaque as an opal.

"Lion's milk, the Turks call this," Josh murmured. "I can't offend this man by not drinking."

He sipped the tiny drink. "It has quite a kick." He returned the half-full shot glass to the tray.

"You drink more!" The proprietor, a big Turk, with the inevitable mustache and gallant manner, beamed.

"Very good, but no more." Josh handed back the glass.

The Turk threw a thimble of water over his shoulder. "He believes the gesture will make us return." Josh glanced out the door and up and down the passageway.

Nicole smiled. "Interesting." She stood a breath away from Josh. "How long until we leave?"

"Now. Let's hope we lost our tail." Josh stepped out the open door. His back stiffened and his hand tightened around hers.

She entered the stone passageway before she realized he'd meant to stop her.

A powerfully built man with the flat eyes of a person who kills without qualms stared at her. His calm assurance tied knots in her stomach. She faced a murderer without pity or remorse.

His heavy arms crossed over his hulking chest, he leaned against a shop displaying basket-woven trays brimming with red peppers and tomatoes.

Josh turned right and sped up the passageway. His hand gripped hers.

The man fell in behind them, not bothering to hide his intentions.

"That's three. Another of the Viper's black shirts. Have you ever seen this one?" Josh paused and handled a bright yellow pepper.

"Never." Where was her helpful adrenaline when she needed the energy? The man's eyes had left a paralyzing effect, as if her senses lay frozen beneath a primordial glacier.

Josh's hands gripped her shoulders. He shook her gently. "They need us. They won't kill us yet. Don't spazz out on me." He held her hand in the familiar, protective way and guided her through the dense crowds. "We might lose him now your golden head's covered. Try to keep up."

They wound through so many stone passages they must have lost their tail. Nicole couldn't see the killer. After a long trek, she clamored after Josh up the stairs that led to the street and squinted in the sun. They mingled with the crowd. Stopped by loud honking, Josh jumped back, treading on her toes. A car zipped past.

Despite the heat, her hands grew cold. The killer's eyes must have unnerved Josh.

Once across the street, they jogged a weaving path through the throng on the sidewalk.

Slowed by the crowds, Josh pointed to an enclosed balcony with a window overlooking the busy street. "That's for wives cloistered from male eyes. Women became captives, once they married."

Josh wanted to distract her. "So, married women watched the world of men behind latticed shutters," she gasped, breathing hard.

He pulled her on. "Reminds me of an old Russian proverb, *'marriage is the tomb of love'*."

"Must have been a real tomb for Turkish women." Had she jogged across all of Istanbul? Then, she felt better oriented. "Look the Mosque, the one near my hotel!"

"Wondered when you'd recognize where you were." He opened the double glass doors for her.

"At last!" Sweating under her extra clothes, the air-conditioning cooled her face.

"We've no time to eat." Josh checked behind them. "No sign of our tail. I think we lost him."

She picked up her key at the desk. Then raced Josh up the stairs, along the hall, and into her room. He stuffed her possessions into her suitcases while she slipped off the *salvar, carsaf* and shawl.

In the bathroom, Josh changed into his slacks, loafers, and polo shirt.

In minutes, they rushed back to the lobby desk where Josh paid her bill. "I know, I know. You can pay me back later." He flashed a grin, then held out his hand. "Key to the rental car, please."

She hung on to the key. "I'll drive. I'm an excellent driver."

"No doubt. But can you lose our tail? Don't look now, but Dead Eyes just walked up to the bar."

Nicole dropped the keys into his palm. "Blast. See if you can lose him."

"Smart girl."

Inside the car, Josh tried to lighten her grim tension. "Let's see if I can use the Turk's search and destroy method of driving to lose that bozo." He gunned the car into the stream of traffic.

A Turk driving in the lane beside Josh punched a new lane in front of him. Josh screeched to a halt, throwing her forward in her seat. "Turks hold a fatalistic view of life I can't accept." He kept his eyes glued to the congested snarl of cars and both hands gripping the wheel.

Curiosity nibbled around the edges of her anxiety. "What is your life view?" She hung on while Josh ricocheted through traffic as if angels guarded them.

"I'll answer that when I have an answer. What I seek may not exist," he gritted.

A driver barreled into their lane from a side street, scraping the rental car's front bumper.

Nicole held her breath.

Josh pumped the brakes in time to avoid hitting another car that made a left turn into his lane. He hurtled through one narrow street after another.

She rolled down her window, letting hot air beat against her face, and stared behind them. "I don't think we're being followed." Horn blasts and exhaust fumes filled the air, but the rental car had no air conditioning, so she left the window open.

A Turk leaned on his horn and plowed by as if he proved his manhood by jockeying for position.

"Take a look at the map and tell me where we hit E-80. Once on E-80, at Sapartica we turn south toward Antalya." Josh shoved the map in her direction.

Nicole searched the map. "I can't find it."

"Keep searching."

"There's the sign." She pointed to a small street sign with an arrow pointing to E-80. Josh hit the brakes and swerved onto the road. She fell against his shoulder. Behind them horns blared.

They left the crazy city and settled to a fast speed on a wide, well-paved, four-lane highway. Josh stiffened. His knuckles whitened as his hands tightened on the steering wheel.

With no attempt to hide their presence, a late model black sedan screeched onto the highway, sped up, and tailgated them. Nicole leaned forward. Through her rear-view mirror she saw three large men packed into the car. Dead Eyes drove.

Josh hitched his head in their direction, his jaw taut. A muscle jerked under his day's growth of dark beard, but his eyes flashed excitement. "They must have a professional driver. I couldn't lose them."

He reached over and squeezed her hand. "My plan was to hide you here in Istanbul." He rubbed the back of his neck. "Couldn't evade them long enough."

Although the road was wide and empty of cars, he concentrated on driving.

Hot wind whipped her hair. From the way he avoided looking at her, he must have something important to say. She was certain she didn't want to hear it.

"The Viper wanted to take you. I bargained with them and bought us some time. There's no question now. They want *you*, Nicole."

CHAPTER TWENTY-SEVEN

Was it day or night? Ian had no idea. No light penetrated the blinding duct tape. He urged his drug-slowed mind to reboot. How long had he been bound to the chair?

A very long time.

The sadistic one had played havoc with him when the guy gave him that gouging shot in his carotid artery. The left side of his neck throbbed. Nausea spiraled through his body.

His hands and feet felt numb. Not the rest of him. Ropes bit into his flesh like fire ants. He licked his cracked lips with a thick, fuzzy tongue too large for his mouth. His throat burned.

When the vicious guard fed him, he offered tiny morsels. Teasing. The grinding of his stomach accelerated when his captor waved delicious smelling bites beneath his nose. He opened his mouth but found empty air. The scent of food twisted his grumbling stomach twenty times a day.

The duct tape shut him off from light, the ability to read lips, and etched a ridge into his skin. His not being able to see, to make sense of his dilemma, stretched every nerve.

Where was Vashti?

He fought the void much as he had fought the silence when he'd lost his hearing and the last whisper of sound had been forever stilled. He'd overcome that disability. He'd handle this predicament too.

He must formulate an escape plan. The guard no longer bothered taking him outside in the frozen snow to relieve himself. Not that he needed to with the little water and food they gave him. That way out was blocked.

The drug they'd injected confused his thinking. Time had become a meaningless wave that rose higher and higher as the narcotic in his blood thinned. Now as the drug wore off, pain hit so hard his breath hissed through his teeth.

He forced himself to focus his mind like a laser, narrowing his thoughts from the pain of cutting ropes, a pounding head, the gut-eating, and the thirst—the increasing agony of thirst. He must have a plan.

Answers. He needed answers. They had the map. Now they wanted him to reveal the secret of the cryptograph hidden between the map and the Topkapi. At some point they would take off his blindfold and attempt to force him to talk. He wouldn't.

He was certain now Paul had died because of the map. Ian had the responsibility to return the document and the code to the Turkish government. With today's delicate balance of power, all a Third World government needed to gain nuclear and military weapons was the untold wealth contained inside the Topkapi. And he'd puzzled out the secret unguarded entrance encoded in the map.

With Russia's arms up for grabs to the highest bidder, some country wanted this map and his knowledge. Perhaps not a Third World country. Might be Germany. Germans were known middle men who sold arms between Russia and the Middle Eastern countries.

He didn't know. His hazy mind couldn't muddle it out. Time was on the kidnappers' side. As his body grew weaker, so would his will. The only reason he still lived was because he'd solved the puzzle of the cryptograph. They hadn't.

These were no ordinary kidnappers. The leader knew archeology. The brute had forced him to submit to the Assyrian method of the victor planting his foot on the neck of the vanquished.

Which pointed to his professor at UT. He'd been a fool to think Professor Alexandros dropped a plum job like Antalya into his lap. He'd suspected there'd be a string attached, but he'd been too greedy for his first field job to question his good fortune.

He'd been set up. Whoever killed Paul Phillips had planned the whole thing—from his getting tapped for the dig in Antalya, to meeting the kidnappers at the Topkapi. They'd banked on his ability to decipher the code. They'd probably watched as he did it. Waited for his face to reveal he'd solved the cryptograph in his mind. The four men had closed in afterward. So much for why.

The question now was how to escape. Vashti had gone as had the leader and at least four of the men who'd tied him to the chair. That left the big man and the sadistic guard. He hadn't sensed the big man lately. Perhaps only the guard remained.

How deep was Vashti involved? A strange emotion akin to disappointment hit him. She'd seemed to be on his side, and he'd depended on her communication and help. There'd been a bond between them he'd wanted to pursue. The first bond he'd ever established with a woman, and he hadn't even seen her face.

His thoughts returned to escape. He must be positive about who still guarded him.

The sadistic one and the big man with the footsteps that rocked his chair. He felt certain that was all. So cold. He couldn't stop shivering. He set his teeth against the constant chill.

The floorboards vibrated under his feet. Light steps. The mean one. Ian stiffened, expecting lightning blows. What abuse would Sado inflict now?

"Lord, please give me strength," Ian prayed aloud.

Had Sado brought water? Ian wrenched his thoughts from water. He'd be disappointed. He had to find a way out.

"I need to go outside," Ian croaked through dry lips.

Stepp frowned. The kid's praying got on his nerves. He set the tumbler of water on the floor. When the kid quit praying, he'd get water. Stepp grinned. The kid couldn't hear him, but he'd taken to talking to him anyway. Gave him a feeling of power. How often did a guy like him get to lord it over a genius? "Forget it, pal. I ain't gonna untie all those ropes for nobody. Deaf as a doorknob. How'd you know I came in? You got radar or some kind of ESP?" He liked to parody cinema characters to amuse himself.

Pent-up boredom fueled his quick movements as he added still another rope around the kid's chest and hitched it tight. "Time for another shot. Viper said a man should enjoy his job. So, the shot can wait. No fun tormenting a half-conscious victim."

Stepp glanced into the adjoining room where Brun sat hunched in the overstuffed chair glaring into the crackling fire. The big man clenched and unclenched his ham-like hands as they hung between his legs.

"Brun's in another world. Brooding over his Frau. He don't care what goes on in here. Long as you don't get away."

Stepp stood spread-legged in front of the kid. "Boring as a museum inside this cabin. A man's entitled to have a little diversion."

His first blow caught the kid in the stomach just below where his ribs divided. The chair skittered back and hit the wall.

Nicole heaved a deep sigh.

"It'll be dark in less than an hour." Josh glanced over from behind the wheel and smiled. "We have to drive all night. You want to sleep now and take over when I get tired?"

Nicole admired his chiseled profile and the ease with which he accepted the car filled with armed men tailing them plus his new position in the Viper's employ.

"I'm tired but too nervous to sleep." She checked her rear-view mirror hoping for a glimpse of Kolya, but no other car followed the black sedan tailing them. She grimaced, disappointment stabbing her.

They rode in silence. Perhaps now she could discover information she desperately wanted to understand about Josh. "Tell me about yourself."

"Like what?" His jaw clenched, and his eyes narrowed.

She'd take a safe approach. Start him talking, and then hit him with the real questions she wanted answered. "Tell me what it's like to be Jewish. You're the first Jew I've had the opportunity to know."

"I'm a guy, just like any other guy." A thoughtful expression settled on his handsome face softening the angular lines. "But born Jewish means living in two different worlds, the Jewish world and your world." He shot her an appraising look.

She nodded to encourage him.

He seemed to relax. "We follow a separate calendar. Ours marks us as living in the 5700s rather than the 2000s, because our history is ancient." Humor lifted his lips. He loosened his grip on the steering wheel. "Judaism isn't so much a religion as being connected to an extensive extended family and to an ancient history." He glanced at her, twinkles flashing in his eyes. He raised a jaunty brow. "We fast on Yom Kippur, close our shops for the High Holy Days, and eat herring, chopped liver, and lox. That part is good."

"And the other part?"

His humor faded. He frowned, and his voice deepened to a muted growl. "It's knowing I'm different. An outsider." He stopped talking as if he'd revealed too much. The car shot forward as his foot tensed on the gas pedal.

Nicole hoped he would continue. When he didn't, she prompted, "How an outsider?"

"Sure you're interested? It's cursed boring."

"Cursed?"

"Sorry. An expression I picked up from my RAF buddies."

How little she knew of him. Not only did she want to fathom how his Jewish heritage set him apart, she wanted to comprehend everything. All that made him Josh. She nodded. "Don't try to sidetrack me. You can tell me later about your RAF friends."

A thin edge sharpened his voice. His hands tightened on the steering wheel. "You asked for it." He cleared his throat. "I took Hebrew lessons once a week throughout my elementary and high school years. Hebrew's as familiar to me as English." He shrugged. "For what purpose?"

"You can read the Old Testament in the original language."

"Right. Friday nights, we gathered as a family with Grandfather Baruch. Mom lit candles, cut the *challah* and said *berashahs*. Father, Scott, or I read the Torah."

She let the unfamiliar words pass, thinking he spoke of food. She didn't want to offer him an out. "And?"

"Saturday morning, I attended services."

"Services on Saturday made you an outsider?"

"No. They taught me values like being a good person, caring for others, honoring the family, and getting together for holidays." He grinned.

His glance communicated he enjoyed discussing the easy things. Her heart fluttered. This glimpse into Josh's soul gave her more than she expected. These days, a man with values was a treasure. His confession made him so human, less controlling. Reassurance flowed through her. She trusted Josh. She had the Lord, Josh, and Kolya all helping her. "Tell me about life as an outsider?"

His voice sounded too even. "Problems started in public school. My parents couldn't afford the private school Jews attended." A muscle jumped in his jaw.

A rapt feeling stole over her. Now Josh had started, he would spill the whole story.

"In the off-base school, kids taunted me with *sheenie, kike, dirty Jew,* and *Christ killer.*" He shook his head. "I didn't even know what those words meant."

Nicole snorted. "Kids are so insensitive. They say mean things to belong to cliques. I hope you didn't let that overwhelm you."

"Yeah, it affected me, sure. But I never let on to them how much their taunts hurt. I returned their barbs with jokes when I could. What blew my cool and set me off happened when I was sixteen. We moved into a new neighborhood." His foot pressed harder on the accelerator, and the speedometer edged past one hundred thirty kilometers.

"As an army brat, my family resettled every two or three years." His voice rasped like sandpaper. "A bunch of guys called me out to play basketball. I thought they made a special effort to include me, so I jammed on my new sneakers and went out." The line between his brows deepened. "I never got to play. They beat me up. Six of them."

"No!"

"Never wore those sneakers again. Couldn't wash the blood out." His jaw jutted. "I got even. I called them out, one by one, and walloped them. That earned their respect." He was quiet, probably reliving the event.

"But the hate didn't end there. Other kids stole my books and kicked spokes out of my bike. Did different things at different times. I never saw who did it. Made me suspect all of them."

"I can understand that."

"Gave me a sense of isolation, of being different. Not as good."

Her heart twisted. Josh had to be almost thirty, a grown man. Yet his past haunted him. "But you lived through that experience. And were stronger because of it?"

"Maybe." He frowned, his eyes intent on the road. His voice sounded detached, as if he were discussing the weather. "In college, Jews don't get rushed into any but Jewish fraternities."

"Oh."

"Bet you belonged to the best sorority!"

She nodded. She'd been popular. Often the center of the 'in group.' Wanting to reach across the grey plush seat in the shadows and touch him, reassure him, console his pain, she stopped herself. She already cared far too much and was way too attracted. She couldn't become further involved with Josh while Ian's life was at stake. She must focus her attention on finding him.

Plus, their religions kept them apart. He wasn't a Christian, nor did he seem interested. Her faith was too strong, her commitment too deep, to let a man with a different belief tempt her. No matter how attractive. Or how every nerve in her body responded to him. Or how much she wanted to nestle close to his protective presence.

"I was right. Sweetheart of Sigma Chi wasn't it?" His grin looked crooked.

"Possibly. But now ... in the Air Force, are things different?"

"Sure. Reformed Jews are Americans first. The Air Force binds patriots of all persuasions."

"Reformed Jews?"

"Yeah. I'm not Orthodox. Orthodox hold to a literal interpretation of the Writings. My folks are Conservative Jews. I'm Reformed."

"I'm sorry. I don't know the difference."

"My folks have services in Hebrew and keep Kosher. But Conservative is more modern than Orthodox."

"And Reformed?"

"Most liberal. We even have women Rabbis. Some Hebrew in our service. Not much."

"Oh."

Josh fumbled with the radio. "Any special music you like?"

"I'd rather talk." Static and the minor keys of muted Turkish music hurt her ears.

"Looks like we're out of radio range anyway." He twisted the dial to off.

Headlights behind them surged closer.

CHAPTER TWENTY-EIGHT

Nicole watched the wide highway wind through the countryside. Few cars traveled either direction. She remained silent now except for occasional comments on the scenery but kept an eye on the car tailgating them.

Josh dialed their speed down to ninety kilometers.

She fought her avid interest in him. With his every revelation, regard for Josh burrowed deeper into her heart. She couldn't help herself.

His hands relaxed on the steering wheel.

Was he willing to continue their conversation? Josh's former sister-in-law was involved with the kidnappers. How much hold did that exotic woman exert over Josh? "And Scott's widow, what about her?"

"Regular little interviewer, aren't you?"

She smiled to encourage him.

"Susan's maiden name was Shamansky." He slanted her a challenging look. "I'll tell you what I can, but you're next, Angel."

His look sent delightful spasms to her stomach.

"Scott killed any *shiddach* my parents wanted."

"*Shiddach?*"

"Arranged marriage. Scott was the oldest. Dad expected to choose Scott's life partner from an orthodox family." Josh tapped his fingers on the wheel. "For thousands of years rabbis told us Jews what to eat, who to marry, what books to read. America challenged that tradition. Scott refused to enter into an arranged marriage."

Josh's voice softened. "Scott and Suzanne met at Cal Tech, Fullerton. My alma mater also. Suzanne seemed a typical California girl. Scott thought her manna from Jewish heaven. He strove to please Dad. But if Suzanne hadn't been Jewish, Scott would have married her regardless." Josh leaned an arm across the back of the seat, settled against the cushion, and grew quiet.

"Please tell me more."

"They were happy for three years. Or so I thought." The speedometer passed ninety-five again. "Suzanne filed for divorce eighteen months ago. Devastated Scott. Then someone murdered him. End of interview. Your turn."

Nicole sighed. She yearned to discover so much more. But it was useless to push Josh. How did he feel about Suzanne? Why did the German police suspect him of murder? Her insides burned to know.

Biting back her questions, her mind still focused on him, she filled in her own history. "I met Paul at the University of Texas. I'd completed my Master's in Archeology and minor in History while Paul taught ground school."

"He was a pilot?"

"Yes. He owned a quarter interest in a Cessna Two Ten and spent most weekends flying. He and three friends owned a business together—some sort of transport business. I never knew what they did. I was busy finishing my Archeology Doctorate and learning how to be a wife. My husband died six months after our wedding. I had only known him three months prior to that."

She didn't want to talk about Paul. Not to Josh.

"*You* rushed into marriage?" He raised his brows. "Hard to believe."

"I was foolish. We were very much in love. Paul had his teaching responsibilities and his business but had scant time for dating. We wanted to be together." She gazed at her clenched hands. "We spent precious little time together after we married."

Josh mumbled something that sounded like "Dumb guy."

"Pardon?"

"Nothing. How well did you really know Paul?"

"Paul was friendly, easy to know. Charming and vocal. He said his life was an open book, and he liked for me to read each page."

"Hmm. No problems in your marriage?"

She smothered the unexpected anger popping up. Not often getting to see Paul hadn't been a big problem. If marriage failed to work out the way she'd pictured, the fault hadn't been Paul's. "None. We were deeply in love. I did agonize over the chances Paul took. He thrived on risk. Loved flying. Enjoyed spending money. He wasn't much for saving. Said life was to be lived." She smiled. "One of his attractions."

Hard to reveal her own inadequacies, but Josh had been open with her. "I'm a bookish person. I take my thrills vicariously. Paul never cracked a book. He experienced life, loved adventure, living on the edge. Paul added zest to every moment. To parties, to conversation ... to love." She couldn't keep the smile from her lips.

"Hard act to follow."

"He was an amazing man."

"You still miss him?"

Nicole hesitated. When she was with Josh, she didn't. "It's been more than a year." Sighing, she gazed out the window. Darkness was falling over the rolling farm land. Ominous black clouds shadowed the tilled fields. Thunder rolled in the distance. The damp scent of growing things combined with the fragrance of coming rain. They hadn't passed a house for miles.

In a field flashing by her window, women squatted in colorful groups on the plowed earth burying seedlings by hand, their covered heads bent together.

She changed the subject, unwilling to share her loneliness with Josh. "The timelessness in this Turkish countryside gives me a sense of serenity."

"Do you still miss Paul?"

She mused at the total, absorbed interest in Josh's voice. A smiling spot of sun touched a herd of cows walking in a row toward what must be their home. A small boy bounced behind them, touching a stick to a swaying rump as he looked over his shoulder at the roiling clouds.

How could she answer? After Josh's vulnerability during the last thirty minutes, she wanted to be honest. Part of her no longer desired to discourage Josh from pursuing an interest in her. It had been too long since she'd been attracted to any man.

"I find it difficult to visualize Paul's face. And I don't think I understood him as well as I thought. There are so many things I didn't know about him. I thought I had years to decipher him. Now, he's a fading dream."

Josh grunted, "I can understand that."

"You miss your brother, of course." If only she were one of those women who opened herself up to a man and the devil take the consequences. But she wasn't. She'd tried that route once.

"Yeah."

Josh slowed to follow a small family in an open wagon clip clopping behind their draft horse. The woman inside jostled with each bump. Her easily read expression spoke of pride in a day's work well done and in being protected by the weathered man holding the reins.

If only her life were that simple. Her thoughts drifted as the horse toiled up a hill on a long rein with head bobbing, pulling the couple toward home.

Josh tapped the horn and passed them.

The four-lane highway curled on before them. They sped between fertile, cultivated fields with the two lanes facing them empty. Shepherds grazed their flocks close to the pavement.

When a flock of silky fat-tailed sheep trotted across the highway, Josh screeched to a shuddering halt.

She grabbed the dash.

"Sorry. Animals have the right of way. Even a sheep dog stops traffic."

"Keeps drivers alert." Nicole pulled out her camera and snapped half a dozen shots.

The sheep meandered across the road, bleating and whisking their short tails.

"The shepherd boy looks to be straight from a Bible story with his staff, head cloth, and robes."

"Yeah. Another David." Josh glanced in his rear-view mirror.

"Our two cars don't hurry that shepherd's pace."

"I don't think the shepherd could rush those sheep if he wanted to." As soon as the last animal flicking his tail set his hind hoofs on the grass, Josh hit the gas.

She was acutely aware of him. He exuded protectiveness and masculinity. Was he as aware of her as she was of him? Whiskers stubbled his cheeks and chin. His shirt collar gaped at the neck revealing the strong column of his throat. Broad shoulders stretched the white fabric of his cotton shirt. Dark hair dusted his muscular forearms. He was an invitation to security on the one hand ... and pure trouble on the other.

The sky darkened.

Josh veered to miss a tractor hogging both lanes. The tractor, driven by a cheerful Turkish man who waved, carried his family. His wife perched on the tractor wheel, her long skirt billowing like loving fingers against the driver's seat. Several tall sons and daughters rode behind on the hitch. The gathering storm didn't appear to trouble them.

The car tailgating them missed the tractor family by inches. The men inside yelled at the tractor family and raised fists.

With dusk, a mist of diffused light showed fog rising from the plowed earth. The road curved and Josh slowed the car. Ahead a village, so primitive it could have been three thousand years old, curled like a sleeping cat. The evening call to prayer echoed from the minaret of a small mosque.

The road narrowed to one lane forcing Josh to slow even more. He drove across a bumpy wooden bridge into the tiny village. Sleepy donkeys were tied to low stone walls, and women walked together from a well balancing water pots on their heads.

Men strolled by, their heavy work shoes crunching the rocks littering the main street. In twos and threes, they headed toward the lokanta, arms around each other's shoulders.

"The people look so happy and free of care."

Josh nodded. "Men get together to discuss the day's events and play board games while the women prepare supper and ready the children for bed." His teasing grin crinkled his eyes.

"Is that your plan for the future?"

"No plans for a wife. Not now. Not ever."

She pressed her hot face to the glass. Well, that cleared the air. No wife in his future. She studied the scenery outside the car window while the refrain played inside her head.

Short, long-skirted, hair-covered women struggled up the unpaved street on thick ankles. They lugged babies, produce, and water pots and looked as alike as gingerbread cookies.

Why should she want to marry anyway? At this point in her life she'd chosen archaeology and remaining independent. But the need for family pierced her heart. She desperately desired a family of her own. She had only Ian, and she might lose him.

She wanted children. A boy with big brown eyes, a handsome nose, and a square chin. A father to teach their son integrity and courage. Josh would make a wonderful father. Why did he not want a wife?

Josh slowed the car to avoid clusters of people rambling past red tile-roofed dwellings needing whitewash. Stone walls and dirt yards enclosed each dwelling. Dusty olive trees sprouted from the rocky soil.

"Did Scott have children?"

Josh shook his head. "No. Suzanne wasn't ready." He pointed. "See that bottle on the roof. That signifies a girl of marriageable age lives inside."

Josh kept diverting the subject from Suzanne. Nicole bit her lip. She must find out more.

His hand, arm lying across the back of the seat, touched her shoulder. "This mirrors a freeze-dried village straight from the Pentateuch. Typical for Turkey. Like it?"

"Absolutely."

Josh slowed on the rutted road. "Years ago, village women were luckier than their city sisters."

"Why was that?"

"In Istanbul and the few other large cities, when a woman left her father's home as a young bride entering into an arranged marriage, she entered her new husband's house never to step foot again in the world outside."

"Sounds as if she escaped one prison for a new one."

"Right. Except her father had allowed her more freedom."

Nicole shivered. Kolya had said she could be kidnaped and end up in a brothel. Never to be heard of again. Much worse than an arranged marriage.

And highly possible in this country with its ancient traditions.

CHAPTER TWENTY-NINE

"Not many secrets here," Nicole said.

Josh braked as a herd of sheep meandered into the street. The spread-out animals clattered into a stable beneath the second floor of a small adobe home. People moved about on the flat roof as if it were an additional room. The mother squatted near an open fire preparing food. Her daughter pulled a long wooden paddle holding ekmek from an outdoor oven.

"Nope. Another reason men keep their women covered." He shifted in the seat to stare over his shoulder.

"Look." Josh pointed. At a large loom, a girl sat beside an older woman weaving dark blue and burgundy yarn. "The design's hundreds of years old. Each village weaves its own pattern, and the rugs are named after the village."

"You love Turkey, don't you?"

"Guilty." Josh grinned.

The Turkish women chatted as their fingers flashed the weaving tool through the wool. Their other hand jammed the wool tight with a comb-like tool.

"I sprang for one of those rugs my last leave in Istanbul. The people squeeze the dye from vegetables and berries. See, behind them hanging on the clothesline." Josh pointed. Large clusters of blue, burgundy and green wool hung drying on the line. "I use my Village Rug in my quarters at Incirlik."

Nicole smiled. "Amazing how a rug warms an impersonal room." How would Josh look in his uniform? Stunning, no doubt.

A granny carried a wide-eyed child in a sling across her sunken breasts. A toothless smile creased her wrinkled face.

How she loved the color and texture of the village. The buildings and the people blended into the rocky hillside reminding her of a picture covered with a film of dust. The babble of voices and soft bleating, clucking, and occasional yip hummed a musical drone. The effect created a quaint time capsule. This was Turkish life—essential, basic, and unchanging.

The last sheep crossed the road.

Josh put the car into gear. "How did you like the traffic jam?"

"Loads better than the ones in Istanbul!" She stared behind them. "But it didn't separate us from our tail."

"No such luck."

"I don't believe in luck."

"We make our own?" Josh raised a rakish brow.

"No. God is sovereign. Nothing happens outside his will."

"Convenient."

The musky odor of wool and lanolin followed the sheep as surely as their fat, stubby tails.

The road headed out to a plateau of verdant, green hills with steep mountains rising around it like lotus petals. She glanced at Josh just as his brown eyes met hers.

"Hungry?"

"Starved." She nodded, though the men in the black sedan doused any appetite she might have had.

"How far's the next town?"

She checked the map. "Over a hundred kilometers."

With a whine of tires on the stone road, Josh executed a U-turn and headed back to the village. "There's no fast food. But the lokantas are speedy. Food's already cooked."

"Let's skip dinner and eat in Antalya."

"This won't take long. We'll drive faster to make up the time. You look beat, Nicole. Food will do you good."

They drove up the hill. Josh parked near a small outdoor restaurant where men occupied the few tables.

The car tailing them screeched up, stirring a cloud of dust. The three burly men jumped out. Their sheer bulk and numbers turned her hands icy.

"Larry, Curly, and Moe." Josh grimaced.

"Hardly. This feels too dangerous to be funny. They give me the creeps."

The Turkish men sitting at the tables looked up as they approached.

"*Iyi aksamlar.*"

Several men echoed Josh's greeting.

"*Iyi bir lokanta tavsi ederbilir misiniz?*" Josh asked.

The men broke into smiles and pointed upstairs with a barrage of Turkish words. One man scooted his straight-backed wooden chair from the table and stood.

Josh nodded, spoke a string of Turkish, took her elbow, and guided her after the man. "There's a restaurant upstairs on the roof. I have no idea how good it is, but we don't have much choice."

Overhead, thunder rumbled.

Josh tightened his grasp on her elbow, stooped, and escorted her into a dim room. The man leading them bowed and motioned them forward. Men sat at a few of the tables, but most were empty. The Turks were polite but ogled her as she walked past. Josh hurried her by an open fire pit where meat simmered. Juice ran down from the slabs of lamb and sizzled into the hot coals. He stopped in front of a display case showing dishes.

"What looks good?"

"Everything." She had no appetite. Ian was somewhere, and she had to find him. Most of the dishes looked appetizing, so she pointed to three.

With a burst of Turkish, Josh ordered their dinners.

The waiter led them up a steep flight of wooden steps, through a dark room filled with unused tables, and up yet another set of stairs. They emerged onto a roof. The man led them past several empty tables to one tucked in a corner.

"It's charming," she said. "But please tell the waiter we're in a hurry."

"Right. Most of the food's prepared, so dinner shouldn't take long."

Josh pulled out her chair.

She sat at a wooden table beneath a tumble of grapevine trellises. The courtyard, hidden from the noise and dust of the street, offered a serene oasis. Behind her ancient walls of crumbling yellow stones cooled in the late afternoon breeze.

Josh lowered himself into a seat across from her.

The waiter brought a lit candle under a hurricane glass, bottled water, and clean glasses.

"No electricity?" Nicole placed the candle in the middle of the table.

"None in the entire village. Most Turks live without electric lights."

"Romantic."

"Yeah?"

In the distance, the boom of thunder rolled through the sky. The orange rays of the setting sun slanted through vine branches leaving sparkling splotches on the table, the walls, and the grape arbor.

"This is like a dream."

"Ordered just for you."

Heavy footsteps thudded on the stairs. Josh stiffened. "Pray your dream doesn't turn into a nightmare."

She watched the rooftop door, but the thudding steps stopped in the room below. Scraping chairs and muted German-accented voices raised the hair on the nape of her neck. The three goons had been seated on the second level. "I prayed, and for the moment we're free."

"Thanks." Josh gave her a crooked grin. "If I were James Bond, we'd eat a gourmet dinner, then flee across the rooftops to safety, eluding the bad guys."

"Can we?"

"Buildings aren't close enough."

The soft dusk and last rays of the sun mellowed day into evening. A gentle finger of light touched Josh's lips and painted them with gold. A shiver of delight passed through her. She knew how those full lips felt in a passing kiss—the lightest, most tentative kiss she'd ever received. She'd like to kiss the sides of his mouth where they turned up, tasting the stubble on his tan cheeks.

Wind-blown and needing a diversion, she opened her fanny pack for a comb.

Josh caught her hand, stopping her. "Don't. You look breathtaking."

She chanced a glance into his eyes. He shouldn't look at her that way. Her heart raced. She stared at her hands, twisted her napkin in her lap, poured their water, and avoided Josh's gaze.

She'd met him only two days ago. But he risked his career, maybe his life, to help her. She'd never experienced this emotion with any man. Not even Paul.

Her emotion had to be tied to her tension, her concern and inability to help Ian. Her exposed feelings left her as sensitive as radar bouncing from object to object picking up every vibration. She sensed his excitement, his vitality, his tenderness ... and his loneliness.

With a flounce and a bow, the waiter brought their food.

She tried not to watch the neat way Josh ate. Not to watch his strong fingers manipulate the silver. Not to stare at the dark hair that dusted the back of his hands. She felt drawn to him, and the table was so intimate. The single candle cast a soft light in the deepening dusk. A bird sang a love song for them.

While his eyes were lowered cutting his food, she ventured another glance at his face. His black lashes swooped over his ruddy cheeks. His hair, dampened by the humidity, curled back from his high forehead. His military cut couldn't control the rebellious waves. His nose, symmetrical and straight, fit his face perfectly. And his full, sensual lips—

She jerked her gaze away.

In a melted caramel voice, Josh said, "This is better. A place for lovers. Would you—"

A brawny man burst through the doorway.

She lifted her water glass and froze.

He swaggered around the terrace as if getting a breath of air.

Their tall, muscular tail, Dead Eyes. Chills shivered her when the man's flat eyes swept over her. She tried to match his coldness.

He strode the roof-top perimeter as if he cased it for a burglary, then catfooted to their table, slid a chair up, and sat.

Josh clanked his silverware on his plate and jumped up, his eyes dark with violence.

"Sitz," Dead Eyes ordered, his voice as emotionless as his eyes.

Josh lunged toward the man.

Dead Eyes fast-drew a gun from inside his shirt. He pointed the weapon at her.

"I said sitz."

CHAPTER THIRTY

"*Sitz! Hande hoch!*"

Josh stared at the cold grey barrel of the 9-millimeter Luger pointed at Nicole's stomach. His insides wrenched, and he almost lost his grip on his emotions. With Nicole in danger, he'd have to obey the thug's order to sit and raise his hands. He walked this dangerous tightrope to keep her alive.

The gunman wouldn't kill her. Meier needed her. But Dead Eyes could wound her. Josh lowered himself into his chair, keeping both hands flat and visible on the table.

Nicole sat motionless, her eyes wide, her mouth ajar. She didn't appear to be breathing. No matter what happened, he wouldn't let her get hurt.

A serrated blade of anger knifed through him. He mastered the emotion and grew icy calm, locking his jaw. Familiar tension knotted the base of his skull. How had he let himself get blindsided? He should have been thinking straight instead of getting distracted by Nicole.

He sized up the gunman. What would the professional tough do? Time distorted into slow motion. Dragging his gaze from the 9mm Luger, he met the assassin's unblinking warning. Death waiting to happen. The jerk liked to kill.

Sweat beaded the back of Josh's neck. His mind raced with possibilities. Boiling inside, he forced himself to appear undisturbed.

The gunman spoke. "W*as ist los, Dummkopf?* The Viper didn't want you two to get lonely. He ordered *Kaymakli Kuru Kayis,* apricots stuffed with cream, for you, *Liebchen.*" Dead Eyes flicked his sharp face toward Nicole. His finger tightened on the trigger, then relaxed.

Josh's dinner clumped into a heavy knot. The muscleman wanted to kill Nicole. The desire radiated from every pore in Dead Eyes' face and in the practiced way he trained his Luger on her. The creep itched to spatter her blood on the white tablecloth.

"Forty-five proof raki for you, Dummkopf Major." The thug grabbed Josh's wrist and held the raw, tattooed half-swastika into the candlelight.

Josh nodded, his face feeling like stone. "Then what?" He jerked his arm free.

"Won't help you to know, Dummkopf Flyboy."

The waiter arrived carrying a tray. As he crossed the rooftop, the gunman snatched a napkin from the table, concealing his weapon. His gaze never left Josh. "One wrong move, Major, and death to the Fraulein."

The server delivered the dessert and drink and left them alone with the assassin. He appeared oblivious to the threat.

Nicole's gaze darted from the gun to him and then to the gunman, her face stamped with worry.

"Don't do anything foolish," he whispered in her ear.

"Trink!" An implicit threat underlined Dead Eyes' barked command.

Josh picked up the potent alcohol and downed the stinging contents in a single long gulp then slammed the empty glass on the table. The liquor burned a trail down his throat and heated his body.

Dead Eyes' attention slid to Nicole. "Eat."

Nicole raised her fork and played with the fruit, taking small bites. But she soon pushed the confection away.

What joke might James Bond crack to calm her fears? Nothing came to Josh's mind. Instead, he diverted Dead Eyes. "What's Viper call you?" The alcohol gave his voice a deep rasp. His senses reeled.

A hard glint appeared in the gunman's eyes. "Gunter."

A finger of sunlight spun Nicole's hair into pure gold. Gunter raised his gun and touched the weapon to her forehead. With the barrel, he traced a line down her cheek.

Josh's gut clenched. He smothered the compulsion to smash his fist into Gunter's grim mouth and toss him off the rooftop. He couldn't risk the moves with the gangster's weapon pressed against Nicole. Fisting his hands on the tabletop, he held himself still.

He needed that 9 mil.

"*Was machst du*? Don't even think about it."

Gunter's voice blew like cold rain down his shirt collar. Josh forced his gaze from the man's hypnotic stare.

"Please." Nicole shrank back from the gun.

Her blue eyes flashed terror. No figuring what she would do.

The thug pulled his gun away.

Josh breathed easier.

"I ride with you to Antalya." Gunter's voice sounded as evil as his eyes telegraphed.

Ice spidered down Josh's spine. Gunter couldn't ride with them. He planned to drop Nicole off and hide her with his friend. Sweat beaded Josh's forehead. When he had Nicole safe, he'd be free to let Meier lead him to Ian. Or he'd offer himself in Nicole's stead.

The waiter arrived with another raki.

"Trink!" Gunter edged the 9-millimeter toward Nicole's face.

"I'm driving." Heat swept through Josh. Stubbornness tightened his mouth. His stomach squeezed into a tighter knot.

"*Gott im himmel!* Viper says trink. You trink."

"I have to go to the lady's room."

Gunter's head snapped toward Nicole. Wrapped in both hard-knuckled hands, he touched the Luger to her chest. "Make it quick. Near the staircase, to da right. Take more dan three minutes and your *liebchen* here gets pistol whipped." He fired his words like gunshots.

Josh partially heard. His hyper-alert body tensed.

Nicole rose and rushed across the rooftop.

Josh curled his fingers. His first moves must be well executed, or he might not survive. Gunter, trained to fight dirty, would be dangerous and vicious. Josh's heart pulsed in his throat in that eternity before a fight when breathing stops.

He reached for the raki and raised the glass. In a lightning movement, he tossed the liquor into the killer's eyes. Gunter blinked and shook his head like a dog shrugging off water.

Josh heaved the sturdy wood bracing the bottom of the table and upended it, smashing dishes, glasses, food, and the lighted candle onto Gunter's lap.

Gunter cursed, pulled away, then got tangled inside the tablecloth. He struggled to rise and targeted the gun.

Too slow.

With the lightning reflexes that'd landed him his jet slot, Josh smashed a hard-right uppercut to the big man's chin and kicked the gun from his hand. He plowed a shattering left to Gunter's lantern jaw. Adrenaline bolted with such callous speed Josh didn't feel the shock to his fist.

Gunter doubled, moaned, and backed away.

Josh followed, pulverizing with everything he had.

Gunter groaned and fell to the rooftop.

Josh leaped atop the bigger man's muscular midsection and beat Gunter's face. Josh fought grimly, grunting and gasping, until he slammed a karate chop to Gunter's Adam's apple.

The killer went limp.

Josh sat back on his heels, his breath whistling in his lungs.

Gunter lay motionless, splayed on the splintered planks of the table.

Josh brushed sweat from his eyes and glanced around the shadowed rooftop. He sighted the Luger near Gunter's hand, scrambled for the gun, slipped the safety closed, and jammed the weapon into his belt. Leaning over the unconscious Gunter, he searched for extra bullets. No luck. Still gasping for breath, he unbuckled Gunter's belt and jerked the leather loose. He shoved Gunter over on his stomach and yanked the dangerous man's arms behind his back and tied the big thug's wrists with the belt.

Light footsteps made him jump and roll. Nicole. He relaxed. "How much of the fight did you see?"

She crept to his side, her face pale but her eyes shining. "Only your karate chop."

His heart skittered. Her expression wouldn't have looked so triumphant if his gamble hadn't paid off. She wasn't expendable to Meier, but he was. "Give me your scarf."

Nicole's hand felt chilled when she passed the silk to him. He stuffed a linen table napkin into Gunter's mouth. He would have preferred to stuff it down his throat. Then bound Nicole's scarf between the thin lips. He rolled the gunman onto his back. "I need something to tie his ankles." Josh swiped at the sweat coating his forehead and dripping into his eyes.

"I hear the waiter coming up stairs."

"Stall him."

Nicole sped across the terrace floor.

He dragged the tablecloth from the mess on the rooftop floor, shook off the shattered glass, wound the linen into a rope and tied Gunter's ankles. Bulky, but the makeshift binding had to suffice.

Nicole's face glowed when she returned. She did appear to enjoy danger. At least, when they made a bold move. "Take Gunter's feet. We'll hide him." Josh nodded to the huge outdoor oven at the far end of the roof.

Carrying Gunter's dead weight would take all the strength he had left, but he hefted the killer's muscular shoulders and Nicole struggled with his feet. The gunman sagged between them, head lolling. Sweat stained Josh's shirt as he wrestled to shove Gunter into the unfired oven. The killer's massive shoulders and bound arms wedged in the door frame. Grunting and shoving, Josh jammed him inside.

Nicole slammed the door shut. Both heaved a sigh of relief.

Breathing hard, he surveyed Nicole. Lovely before, but with her long hair in disarray and her eyes shining, she looked breathtaking. Ripped the breath from his chest.

Take a break, Josh, he warned himself. Keep your eyes off. You have a job to do.

He strode to the edge of the roof. Darkness had come on fast, lit by a pale new moon and the first stars. He squatted above a grapevine growing up the wall to the rooftop. Reaching down to test it for sturdiness, he winced as his smarting knuckles brushed into a tangle of wiry branches.

He turned to Nicole. She shimmered in the moonlight as beautiful as any man's dream of the perfect woman. She made him feel like a hooked fish out of water, gasping for air. Looking at her brought a gut level rush of pleasure that stopped him in his tracks. He heaved himself to his feet and laid his sweaty hand over hers.

And found that wasn't enough.

He grasped her shoulders, feeling her softness, her femininity, and inhaled her clean, tantalizing scent. Gazing at her shadowy eyes, he yearned to fold her into his arms.

Not now. Not here. Not when she's in danger. He snorted at his feelings. Just because Suzanne betrayed Scott doesn't mean all women can't be trusted.

He forced words from his dry throat. "Can you climb down the vine?"

He felt her sharp intake of breath. "I'll try."

She stood so close, her lips inches below his. His hands tightened of their own accord on her shoulders, surrendering to the uncontrollable urge to breathe her scent, to fold her into his arms. He leaned toward the delicate oval of her face and the stars in her eyes and magnetism of her full lips. Something indefinable, sweet and giving, stirred between them. For a crazy instant, he cupped her soft face in his hands, bent his head, and tasted her perfect parted lips. He wanted this second kiss to be just right. Didn't want to overwhelm her. Just a lingering taste. A headier drink than Raki. His world spun. Yep, he'd fallen over a steep cliff. "Go. I'm right behind you."

He braced his foot against the wall and guided her hand as she explored the vine with a foot, slid over the edge of the roof, then swung down, climbing as if she shimmied down roofs for a living. When she was halfway, footsteps thundered on the staircase.

The vine wouldn't hold them both. "Hurry," he whispered. Determination hardened him. She would escape. He would protect her with his life.

"Your turn," she called in a loud whisper.

Seeing her standing safely on the ground gave him the same rush as flying jets through the sound barrier. The rooftop door slammed open. He found a foothold and swung out. The vine bent, groaned, and partially pulled loose from the wall, but held. When he landed next to Nicole, his heart hammering, pain shot up his right leg.

He took her hand and led her along the rear of the building to the corner. He stopped. They crouched with their backs against the stone wall. No sound came from the rooftop, so he guessed the other men had not discovered Gunter. Josh slid his hand along the smooth stone still warm from the sun, ducked his head out. and peeked around the corner. No one in sight. Holding Nicole's hand, he sneaked along the side of the building, stumbling over the rocky ground in the darkness until they came to the street. He checked it out. Only a few locals strolled the area.

"None of the gunmen stayed outside to guard our car. Overconfidence on their part," he panted in her ear, still trying to catch his breath ... and composure. Her response to his kiss lingered on his lips, warm and sweet and filled with life.

"A break for us."

"Yeah. Let's go. Walk as if we're taking a stroll." He sauntered onto the street to their rental car, opened her door, helped her in, then limped to the driver's side. The men playing their games outside the lokanta looked up, waved, and returned to their talk.

His hand shook so it took several tries before he jammed the key into the ignition. He slid into gear, pulled slowly away from the curb to create less noise, and headed toward the highway. No traffic, so he gunned the engine and punched the car up to ninety through the black night. At the *Y* in the road, he turned onto the longer route to Antalya.

"We've a fifty-fifty chance the thugs will head the other way." His pulse slowed when no headlights slashed the darkness behind them. "We bought some freedom—our second break."

"Yes."

Her audible breathing flared a response inside his heart. She'd been superb but was shaken. Was her trembling caused by their escape—or his kiss? In the light from the dash, her eyes looked huge.

"Before I meet the Viper in Antalya, I'll hide you from further danger. Once Viper gets his hands on you, he can force Ian to talk. Once your brother talks ... they won't need either of you any longer."

Her anguish swirled between them.

"What about you, Josh? You're in danger too. Gunter wanted to kill you."

CHAPTER THIRTY-ONE

"They need me." Josh kept his voice calm to steady her, but under cover of the darkness inside the car he wiped his wet palms along the sides of his trousers. The thought of meeting Gunter again dried the sweat on the back of his neck, leaving him clammy. He'd been lucky this time.

"Gunter will hold a grudge." Nicole sounded breathless.

"Yeah, he'll be ticked. So long as Viper needs me, Gunter will have to handle his spleen." Thinking of the killer set his teeth on edge. The man was faster than he'd looked—and stronger. Gunter had taken the stinging pain of the alcohol in his eyes without stopping. The blows he'd laid on the muscleman had been his hardest. He'd had surprise on his side this time. Gunter's gun bulging at his belt barely evened the odds. That animal would be packing again.

"You were limping." Nicole touched his leg. "After you climbed down that vine, you hobbled. Did Gunter hurt you?"

"No. An old injury flared up when I took him down." Josh rubbed his right knee, which ached more then he liked to admit now his adrenaline eased off. He must have twisted his leg when he hit the floor atop Gunter.

"What kind of injury?"

"Parachute jump. Got a steel rod just below my knee. Not quite healed. I'll be fine."

She didn't mention the kiss, but the intimacy sidetracked his thoughts. The lost response the memory brought him detoured his thoughts from pondering his next move.

The night sky darkened, shutting out the pale moonlight and early stars. Thunder rolled nearby. The smell of rain wafted through the open window. He inhaled deeply, willing his tension to drift away. Lightning slashed through the darkness simultaneously with a rumble of thunder. Sheets of water pelted the windshield. He slowed to seventy and raised the window. "Hope the tires are good."

Nicole nodded and edged closer.

He kept the car hurtling through the storm-swept night, away from the tough trio of men who sought Nicole. Up to this point, his value to Meier had kept their hands off her. His own mission had outweighed the Viper's intention to kidnap her. Now, he wasn't sure he was that valuable. He wouldn't risk finding out.

The headlights scarcely penetrated the downpour. Light from the dash illuminated Nicole's face with a faint glow. The click, swish, swish, from the wipers and the drumming rain enclosed him into a cocoon of intimacy with her.

Whoa, slow down. Stop. He dare not think of her. Make your plans. Stash Nicole and get on with wrapping the noose around Meier's neck.

Somehow his strategy for revenge didn't seem important with Nicole in danger. Not since her response to his kiss shook him to his core. He shouldn't have weakened, allowed himself to taste those tempting lips. He'd have to get himself focused back on Meier.

Plus, there'd been Suzanne's plea. She'd said she wanted him alive. She'd insisted he smuggle for Meier. He was sure Suzanne knew nothing about Nicole or Ian. Nor his own plan to gather enough hard evidence against Meier to put the Viper behind bars for a lifetime. Hitching up with Nicole had put him in the right place at the right time.

Now he wanted Nicole free from the whole bait and catch scheme.

He ached to have her out of this mess. And safe. The thought of a single golden hair being harmed sent him over the edge. And he wanted her to keep her innocent faith in God intact.

He knew how to make that happen.

Gunter's turning the gun on Nicole had strung him tight. He massaged the knots in his neck. The forced Raki spread warmth through his body, and no headlights slanted through the rain behind them. The whine of the tires on the pavement, the sway of the car, and the food in his belly worked on him. He rubbed his eyes.

Before he entrusted Nicole to his friend's care, he needed to see she got her documents. "We didn't make it to the American Consulate to get you a new passport or wire for money."

She smiled across at him, her face serene.

His heart warmed and expanded. The magic little world inside the car appeared to work for her. She was so beautiful. He'd dated his share of attractive women. But her spunk, her goodness, her serenity, and now that kiss, drew him like no other woman he'd known. Nicole possessed that indefinable something that set her apart from other women.

He could put his finger on the essence now. Her faith in God. She was intimate with God. He believed in God when he was with her. He'd been searching for God for a very long time.

"I never carry my passport in my purse."

Pleased surprise hit him like an unexpected bonus at Hanukkah. She was smart. And she showed cool sense. He chuckled. "You've got secret hiding places."

"It seemed a good idea." She grinned.

"What else haven't you come clean with?"

Her tinkling laugh reminded him of wind chimes, sweet and musical. In the greenish glimmer of the dash, her face looked mischievous.

He hadn't explained to her that his religion left him unsatisfied. Seeking. Expecting more than he had found. He wanted to meet her God. Yet to go there felt like treading on thin ice. Her God expected surrender. Was he ready to give his heart? He wasn't sure he possessed a heart.

Oh, easy to get high on her, to become addicted. She looked too beautiful, too enticing. The adrenaline rush of his fight, their escape, and the intimacy of the car with them shut in together by the rain stirred him. He couldn't let himself touch her again. He had to get on with his plan and stash Nicole. Now, here tonight, he had to break her spell. Before it was too late. Scott had felt this way about Suzanne.

Long months of betrayal, of grudge, of loss layered his voice with a cutting edge. "Did Detective Pavlik question the staff at the Topkapi? Did he find any leads in Ian's room? Is there a surveillance device planted on this car?"

A hurt expression crumpled Nicole's serenity.

Guilt slashed his heart.

Her face grew stern. "Let me just flip through my notes."

"Sorry." His voice caught. When did his throat get so dry? "But this seems as good a time as any to map our strategy. You're still not going to level with me what happened with Pavlik?"

She was quiet too long. Not telling him everything. He'd been a fool to let his out-of-bounds feelings destroy her mood. He'd blown any chance to unmask Pavlik.

"There's nothing to tell."

Anger jabbed him. "So Pavlik let you waltz off to Antalya without police protection?"

"The note said not to involve the police." She sounded tired.

His anger hadn't worked. He still craved to draw her close and let her rest her head on his shoulder. Instead, he concentrated on driving. His leg hurt as if demons jabbed his knee with hot irons. He pulled his right hand from the steering wheel and sucked his knuckles. The sweet metallic taste of blood rolled on his tongue.

He wanted to be done with secrets and be honest with her. Confess his mission had been revenge. Justice. But he couldn't tell her he was CIA. He'd been too indoctrinated. No one outside immediate family and General Galloway were cognizant of his real job.

He sorted through the tangled strands of what he knew and what he needed to discover. Not keeping his mind on business could be fatal for them both.

This mission gave him a purpose larger than himself to live for, offered him a place to channel his destructive passion. He'd yearned to kill Meier when he'd seen Scott's body stretched out in the morgue. He'd wanted to punish Suzanne for tearing out Scott's heart. Now, his entire focus had shifted. He wanted Nicole safe and Ian found. And Meier behind bars. In that order.

He tried to convince himself otherwise but knew he lied.

"It's late. Can you sleep?" He gripped the steering wheel to keep from touching Nicole.

Her head, lounging back against the headrest, lolled with the car's movement. Long lashes shadowed her cheeks. The dim light glinted on the gold in her hair, spreading around her face like a waterfall. Her classical features looked peaceful with a sweet expression molding her mouth. He fought the longing to trace a finger over the soft contours of her lips.

"Mmm." Her answer trailed away.

He realized she lay in that twilight before sleep, when voices and thoughts waver into dreams.

She's survived a long and difficult three days and had to be exhausted. He snagged his gaze back to the highway, then flicked a glance at his rearview mirror. Blackness followed them.

His thoughts delved where he seldom permitted them to go. After Suzanne left Scott, he'd constructed a well-guarded defense against falling for a woman. Females asked questions to trap him into revealing himself. Even Nicole had. Females looked desirable to entangle him into a relationship. Nicole fit that bill.

He'd vowed never to become vulnerable to a woman. Pain from Suzanne's rejection of Scott had created a terrible treadmill. Like a gerbil, he'd raced that treadmill until he didn't know how to stop. Suzanne's deception burned a hole in his heart so painful he'd had to breathe around it. He wanted no more of that. Love meant pain.

With each succeeding month since Suzanne divorced Scott and Scott had been murdered, Josh reinforced his defenses. Cynicism ruled his heart. He'd been as celibate as a monk.

Then Nicole burst into his life. He hadn't expected capturing Meier would turn out this way. Now serious second thoughts plagued him. He'd believed his job as CIA analyst specializing in nuclear arms sufficient for what he'd set out to do. Had thought his knowledge gave him an edge. Blast the CIA for not sending their analysts to the academy. He didn't know their techniques. Didn't have contacts or backup. The CIA kept him so segregated he knew no one in the covert branch. He was alone in this.

Nicole presented a serious snag in his plans. He hadn't expected her to be so drop-dead gorgeous. Hadn't expected to experience such a strong attachment. Hadn't expected protective feelings for her to interfere with his big plan. Hadn't thought the two of them would be forced to remain together. Visualized the whole mission would be accomplished by now. Before he met her, he hadn't considered Ian's sister as anyone but a lead to evidence. Now he OD'd on feeling responsible for her.

He knew better than to mix emotion with business. His plan had been to do the job and get out. Simple, clean, uninvolved.

When did everything change?

His mind traveled back to their first meeting. At the airport, his first sight of her took his breath away. He'd been butted in his midriff.

The jolt of pleasure she stirred deep inside unbalanced him. She'd worn that short skirt that showed off her mile-long legs. But she seemed unaware of her beauty. Nicole was enough to make any man sit up and take notice, even a hardened woman-hater like him.

True to his Jewish heritage, he'd never considered a relationship with a Christian. She was forbidden fruit.

Yet, her inner beauty intrigued him. No denying the intelligence gleaming in her eyes. She was so smart, she sizzled. Something else attracted him more. Against his will, she captivated him, and held him enthralled. Her faith drew him to her like a heat-seeking missile to heat.

She brimmed with vitality and goodness. There was something more inside her. Calmness? Confidence? An inner glow lit her like a navigation light on a landing approach. And made her different. Something pushed him over the brink and drove him to her.

She'd kept up her spirits when no one met her plane. Even then he'd hungered to fold her into his arms and protect her from Meier and his evil plans.

He rubbed his aching knee.

She hadn't blown her composure as a stranger in a strange land. She was independent and so naïvely trusting. Dangerous for her. He'd been a stooge to give in to his desire to kiss those awesome lips. Stupid. Unprofessional. He'd almost lost her then. His mission with her.

Then their kiss on the rooftop.

A weight settled in his heart. He let his gaze slide sideways to linger on her face. She breathed rhythmically. He glanced down to her graceful neck, to the hollow where her pulse beat, then to her rounded chest rising and falling with each breath.

He touched a tender curl just above the nape of her neck. She stirred, but not before the feathery softness shot an arrow of fire up his arm. He jerked his hand back.

A crazy thought hit him. Meier wanted him to fall in love. That's why he'd ordered them to drive to Antalya rather than fly.

Nah. Too farfetched. Why *had* Meier ordered them to drive? The Viper had known he was with Nicole. A man in love would do anything to protect the woman he cared about.

Even surrender his soul to the devil.

He shook his head. He wasn't in love. And Meier wasn't that smart.

Rain pelted the windshield so hard he barely made out the center white line. The car plowed through axle-deep water. He didn't ease up on the gas pedal.

Nicole stirred and murmured. She slid sideways as her sleep deepened and her body relaxed.

He guided her head to his shoulder, resisting the urge to stroke her cheek. Her hand coasted across her lap to rest on his leg, sending heat jolting through him. The car swerved. He steered it back to a steady course.

Get focused, man!

Miles burned by under the wheels. His eyesight blurred. Despite the rain he rolled down his window so the cooler air would keep him awake. Water splashed his face. His shoulder ached from the pressure of Nicole's body relaxing against him. He slid her on down until her head pillowed on his injured leg. He rotated his shoulders and neck, then rubbed his burning eyes. A glance at his watch showed two-twenty a.m.

Suddenly lights beamed straight at him. He pumped the brakes. Across the rain-swept highway, trucks barricaded the way. A roadblock!

He swerved and fishtailed to a stop. He braced Nicole from hitting the dash.

She woke.

Beyond the trucks' blinding lights, human shadows flickered and swarmed around their car.

An M-16 poked through his open window, aimed at his chest.

CHAPTER THIRTY-TWO

Josh fought a sense of foreboding as dark figures materialized on Nicole's side of the car. Uniforms. Turkish soldiers. Not the Viper then. Not yet anyway.

He gripped the steering wheel. Maybe Meier radioed ahead and paid the soldiers to stop them. A familiar contraction of the muscles at the back of his neck signaled a coming headache.

She looked sleep-dazed and gorgeous, with her luminous blue eyes full of trust, Nicole scooted back to her side of the car. He captured her hand and guided her fingers to the gun protruding from his belt. Closing her palm over the butt, he pretended to snug his arm around her as if she were his girl. He whispered, "Hide the weapon."

His belt loosened as she tugged out the gun. He turned toward the soldier jamming the M-16 through his window and raised his shoulder to block the man's view of Nicole.

In a gruff voice, a sergeant spit a stream of Turkish.

Josh shrugged and held up his hands as if he didn't understand the language. "We're tourists. On our way to Antalya. Are we on the right road?"

Still spouting Turkish, the frowning sergeant asked Josh his name. The sergeant's wet uniform cap sagged in the rain, and he looked miserable.

Josh shrugged again and spoke loud and slow, "Do you speak English?"

The Turkish sergeant jerked Josh's door open, grabbed his arm and yanked him out. With rain slashing his eyes, Josh glimpsed Nicole slide the gun under her leg a split second before the soldier on her side shined his light onto her. The man steadied the beam on her hair as if fascinated. Nicole stared through the windshield at him, ignoring the soldier. She mouthed, "Are you okay?"

He nodded.

The sergeant drew him over to face the blinding headlights.

Josh turned his attention to the tight group of rain-bedraggled soldiers surrounding him.

They talked and gestured with their weapons. One soldier poked his M-16 at Josh's chest.

He raised his hands.

Other men shined more lights in Josh's eyes.

Weariness and strain were fast catching up. His head pounded. Josh questioned the sergeant in English. "What's the trouble?" The driving rain blinded him, slid down his collar, and drenched him. So much for his best shirt, which he'd worn to impress Nicole.

The sergeant answered in Turkish they'd been stopped for a routine car check.

Yeah, right. Explained everything. If Meier weren't behind this, they'd just run into some bizarre bad luck. "I don't speak Turkish." Josh reached into his pocket, pulled out his wallet, and handed his IDs to the sergeant.

The man shined his light on his American driver's license and his military identification. He held them close to his eyes. Like any American sergeant, he yelled for his captain.

Two soldiers patted Josh down while the monsoon pasted his clothes to his body.

A man, probably the captain, stepped out of one of the trucks parked across the highway and sprinted over, water splashing in spurts from his feet. In accented and broken English, he commanded, "You follow truck. You understand?"

Josh nodded. "I'm to follow you. First I want my ID back."

The captain barked an order, and the sergeant passed Josh his wallet.

"What's the problem?" Josh asked, pretending he didn't know.

"Curfew. Follow truck."

He played ignorant. "Are we under arrest?"

The captain's face grew stony. He spouted Turkish as he gestured for Josh to get back in the car.

The captain must have used his entire stock of English words, but he hadn't answered Josh's question. Was he under arrest? His stomach tightened. His head pounded. Was Meier behind this? Josh had to hide Nicole, but this squad of soldiers blocked his way.

The soldier lowered the M16.

Josh slid back inside the car, bringing rain with him. His clothes clung in a sodden, uncomfortable mass. A puddle formed around his shoes as he jammed the car into gear.

As Josh got his car moving, the sergeant and a dripping soldier jerked open his rear car doors and dove inside. Both soldiers carried M-16s.

Was this common procedure for a curfew breaker? He didn't think so. At Incirlik, he'd heard of these roadblocks, but never run into one. From his military experience in Turkey, he knew the soldiers were looking for PKK terrorists.

Blast the luck.

If this were an arrest for curfew, Nicole and he would lose all the time his fight with Gunter had bought them. If Gunter caught up with them here, he'd never get Nicole hidden.

If this were engineered by the Viper, Josh would have no chance to place those phone calls. His head hammered.

From the back seat, the sergeant grunted, "Follow truck."

"Where to?"

No answer. Possibly neither man understood his question.

"What's happening?"

Nicole looked as if she'd been awakened from a good dream to a nightmare. Her eyes were huge. Her lips resembled ripe strawberries. Did she have any idea how appealing she appeared? He flashed a grin to reassure her.

Concerned one of the soldiers in the back seat understood English, he murmured just loud enough for her to hear, "Road blockade. The soldiers are looking for PKK terrorists. Nothing to worry about."

"PKK?" she whispered, barely audible above the pelting rain.

"Kurds fighting for a homeland."

"What do the soldiers want with us?"

"I don't know."

He slowed as one of the army trucks cut in front of them onto the narrow, muddy road. The truck behind them nudged Josh to follow the deep ruts of the truck preceding them. In a line, they lumbered down an unmarked off-ramp toward the dark forested countryside.

Where were they being taken? Josh concentrated on driving the bumpy road, trailing the lead truck's rear lights up a winding unpaved road. Beams followed them cutting windows of light on both sides of the road, illuminating rocky wilderness.

Great place to disappear and never be heard from again. He kept his thoughts to himself. It wouldn't help to frighten Nicole.

Water dribbled between his shoulder blades beneath his soaked shirt.

"Here." Nicole offered her handkerchief and a sweet smile.

"Thanks." He accepted the cloth and wiped his face.

His thoughts whirled. Violating curfew could mean anything from time spent inside a Turkish prison to .... Surely the Turks wouldn't shoot an American Air Force Major. He sighed. Most likely this treatment meant *bakhshish*. His pay-off money was getting thin.

"Do you think the Viper radioed ahead for the soldiers to stop us," Nicole whispered.

His thoughts exactly. His wet hands gripped the steering wheel so tight his battered knuckles seeped blood. "There's that chance."

This road was lonely enough anything could happen. If the Viper sent the soldiers to capture them, his Luger wouldn't be much use against M16s. He knuckled the rainwater clinging to his lashes and took an instant to enjoy Nicole's fragrance scenting the handkerchief crumbled in his fist.

He chanced a look at her. Her back rigid, she stared through the windshield, her hands clasped, her face tight. Poor kid. He should have been on the lookout. Gotten too sleepy, gotten careless. Been speeding too fast.

With some effort he relaxed his posture. Keeping his voice calm and light, he joked, "Our own private escort. Makes me feel like a VIP. Relax. Turks are known for hospitality."

Her expression softened with her smile. Was that a wink?

The sergeant leaned forward, resting his M-16 on the top of the front seat touching Josh's shoulder. Rain from his hat sprinkled Josh's neck. The other soldier's M-16 tapped the back of Josh's neck. The cold barrel shivered the hair on his nape. Just what he needed, a trigger-happy rookie shooting him.

The truck ahead lumbered to a stop. Josh could see nothing in the darkness. He pulled up behind the army vehicle. The truck following blocked them in. In the glare of three sets of headlights, a building loomed between the rocks.

"Uh-oh," he grumbled.

The sergeant reached across the front seat, switched off the sedan's ignition and pocketed the keys.

Anger and helplessness washed over Josh. His apprehension deepened.

Soldiers jumped out of both trucks and surrounded their rental car. The captain trudged over and pulled open Josh's door. A Turk on Nicole's side held his raincoat out to shield her from the downpour and waited for her to get out.

"I guess we go inside," Josh said to her.

"Must we?"

"Looks like it. If we're lucky, we'll be out of here in a few minutes."

"I don't believe in luck."

Weapons clanking and feet sluicing through ankle high water accompanied them through the glare from the headlights to the building. He and Nicole followed the captain inside. Rain thrashed against the tin roof, drowning out other sounds. A match flared, and a private lit a lantern, illuminating the faces of six soldiers circling them.

Nicole grinned at him. Was she enjoying this? At least she wasn't wet and uncomfortable. She hugged the soldier's overcoat around her. She must be hiding the gun beneath the coat, because the room was stifling.

Matches flared as soldiers lit two more lamps, leaving an oily smell in the dank air. The lanterns cast shadows on the walls as the soldiers walked about, their combat boots leaving trails of water on the cement. The main room opened into a primitive kitchen. A closed door stood on Josh's left. Not much of a place.

Thunder rattled the building and lightning slashed the sky. Between flashes and the lantern glow, the soldiers' faces resembled lumbering disco dancers under a revolving light.

Nicole slipped her dry, warm hand into his damp one. The captain's face twisted as he spouted Turkish.

Josh squeezed her hand. "Because of curfew, they want us to spend the rest of the night in this *hotel*."

"Otel!" The captain nodded. "Otel!"

Nicole's eyes widened.

He wasn't feeling too chipper about the captain's idea either. They had to get out of here. Meier could show up any minute.

The fragrant scent of Turkish coffee wafted from the kitchen. Josh heard the rattle of cups above the rain thundering on the tin roof.

The soldiers shucked their dripping coats and stacked their guns. Then the men slumped on the few pieces of wooden furniture and gazed toward the coffee scent.

Their careless attitude showed they didn't think he presented any danger.

Their captain picked up a lantern. His shoes sloshed as he crossed the small room to the closed door. Glaring at Josh, he gestured for them to go inside.

Blast. If he didn't pretend to be Nicole's husband, the Turks would be all over her. He'd have to fight the entire squad. Because of TV, Turks thought unmarried American women promiscuous.

His gut tightened. He wouldn't let himself get blindsided by Nicole's allure while they were alone. He'd stay alert. Too much depended on his instincts and wit. He groaned. Going to be a long night. A wasted night when he could have driven Nicole to safety.

He glanced at her for her reaction.

She stared at the kitchen where the soldier poured coffee into small cups. She must have missed the captain's pantomime. She wouldn't enjoy spending the rest of the night inside a bedroom with him. Blazes, she better hide her discomfort and play along!

To alert her, he squeezed her hand.

Her expressive eyes looked full of questions.

He led her toward the closed door. "Do you want to see our room, darling? Perhaps you'd like to leave your fanny pack there."

CHAPTER THIRTY-THREE

Josh watched the play of emotions on Nicole's face as he clasped her hand tighter, willing her to understand.

She blinked and looked uncertain. Concern puckered her brow, then smoothed. She gave him a semi-mischievous look and purred, "You read my mind, sweetheart. Are you going to bring in our bags?"

The caressing invitation behind her words threw him off balance. Her hand, tucked inside his, exerted enough pressure to suggest interest.

She played the eager wife.

Too much so. Every nerve in his body responded. Her thigh brushed his, sending electric jolts through him, making him uneasy. He began to sweat.

The soldiers watched them, each face expressing a different version of the same idiotic grin.

If they only knew. Irritation grated through him. A single look from her could send him over the edge. He steeled himself and opened the bedroom door for her.

A soldier handed him a lantern.

Josh stepped in behind her and kicked the door shut.

The lantern lit the far corners of the closet-sized room. A narrow bed hogged three-quarters of the space and a wooden chair and end table completed the furnishings. He set the light on the table. He grunted. "No windows to catch a breeze."

Nicole dropped the soldier's dripping coat into his outstretched hand and pulled the Luger from where she'd hidden it inside her fanny pack. Stooping, she slid the weapon beneath the mattress.

He shifted his weight. Feigning easy confidence, he leaned against the door frame, locked a thumb in his belt, and gazed into Nicole's clear bright blue eyes. His heart lunged. She was so dangerous. His heart had little protection against her, rendering him cautious. He'd keep her at a distance. Scare her away if he had to. Whatever it took. Being alone with her undid him.

With her arms locked across her chest, she stood with her back braced against the wall. Being so close, he felt like a jet that ignited its after-burner. He couldn't let her know how she affected him. He narrowed his eyes, lifted what he hoped was a cool brow and smiled with the merest lifting of his lips. His heart thumped. He had to get out. "I need to change these wet clothes. I'll get the luggage."

Nicole followed him out of the tiny bedroom. Someone handed her a cup of coffee. Another soldier stumbled as he offered her his chair. She had that effect on men. She smiled politely and sat.

All the soldiers in the room fixed their eyes on her.

She bowed her head and stirred the coffee in its tiny cup.

The soldiers pulled out cigarettes and matches. After they lit, the room filled with smoke.

"I'll bring in the bags," he said again.

"Fine." She didn't look up.

He hauled their luggage from the trunk through rain pounding as if it intended to float Noah's ark a second time. Sloshing into the cabin he found the soldiers smoking, drinking coffee, and kibitzing.

Didn't they have to go back on patrol? Or were they guarding Nicole and him according to Meier's orders? He had to get her out of here. But how?

He carried the bags into the bedroom, shut the door, stripped off his wet clothes, and fumbled for dry ones inside his duffel. Dry clothes boosted his morale. He checked the Luger and found the weapon loaded with a full magazine. Movements issuing from the main room prompted him to slide the gun back under the mattress.

The outside door opened and closed.

Had the soldiers gone on patrol? If so, he and Nicole could leave. Josh opened the bedroom door and sauntered into the main room.

Two soldiers lounged on wooden chairs—side arms jammed in their belts.

Josh's stomach clenched. He and Nicole weren't going anywhere anytime soon. "I'd like my car keys back." He motioned as if he inserted keys in an ignition and turning them on.

One private shook his head back and clucked. "*Yok. Yarin.*"

Not until morning! Blast. He held up his watch, making circular motions on it as if time were passing.

The two men shook their heads.

Exasperated, tired, and edgy, he forced his voice to sound coaxing. "Nicole, dearest, it's after 3:00 a.m. The soldiers mean to stay until morning when they promise to return my car keys. Won't you come to our room and get some sleep?"

She raised her brows and made a questioning circle with her mouth.

He nodded.

She rose, set her cup on a table, and walked into the bedroom.

He followed and kicked the door closed.

Nicole sat on the edge of the bed, her back straight, her hands clasped in her lap.

"Get some rest. You'll need all the strength you can muster until I get you hidden." He stood as far from her side of the bed as the room allowed. "Chalk this delay up to bad luck." He dropped down on the wooden chair. "If the soldiers stop the Viper's thugs, they might be brought here. It's too risky to stay."

"We're a team, right?" The tone of her voice asked for understanding and support. "Spending the night with you is a real problem for me."

Was the reason because she felt as attracted to him as he was to her?

Her voice softened. "What do you suggest?"

"You rest. I'll listen. If we're lucky, the soldiers will fall asleep, then we'll grab the keys and sneak out."

"It's a plan. But you need sleep too." She stretched, yawned, and reached down to pull off her wet shoes as unconscious as a cat stretching and washing herself with dainty paws. On her hands and knees, she crawled across the narrow bed to the far side.

Pressing his thumb and forefinger against the bridge of his nose, he closed his eyes. "I'm not sleepy. The first place we find that has a phone, I've got to make some calls." He pulled off his shoes. "Alert my commander and a few friends. We need help."

"No police please. Will your friends be discreet?" An apologetic smile curled her lips as she rolled up her sleeves and unclasped her leopard belt. "It's stifling in here."

"Yeah, my guys know how to be stealthy. You won't even know they're around." He studied the closed door. "I have a Muslim friend in Antalya. His father owns a rug bazaar inside the old *Keleici*—"

"Keleici?" She curled on the bed, her head on the pillow and gazed at him with sleepy eyes half-closed.

Forget how adorable she looks. Concentrate. "Citadel. Ancient walls surround the city's narrow streets." He'd spoken too harshly. Situation was getting to him. "You'll like it," he added to cover his snippy words.

She pushed her tousled hair back from her face. "And your friend?"

"Jamel served in the Turkish Army. He'll hide and protect you while I meet with the Viper to negotiate for your brother."

"But you met with Meier in the cisterns—"

"Forget that name. Call him the Viper." Josh leaned so close he could have touched her. A spot of perspiration lay like a jewel in the hollow of her throat. "Knowing that man's name shortens your life."

"Right. But how will your meeting him again accomplish anything? He wants *me* in Antalya."

"You'll be there. He won't know your location. I've got to convince him my service is more important to him than whatever Ian has. Are you certain you don't know what he's hiding?" He leaned his chair back against the wall and rested his stocking feet on the side of the bed.

"I've asked myself a thousand times. I've no clue." Her skirt inched higher as she moved on the narrow bed.

He looked away. "Did your late husband behave differently before he died? Tell you anything?" When she didn't answer, he glanced at her.

She frowned as if thinking about the dead man hurt. "Nothing. I don't think his death was connected with Ian's kidnapping. Paul and Ian weren't close. They hadn't had time to see much of one another." She shook her head, her eyes troubled. "I don't think there's any connection."

"Okay. We'll assume the Viper wants you to make Ian talk. We've got to keep you safe. I'll arrange for Jamel to meet us inside the *Keleici*. You'll slip into his car, and his sister will take your place inside our rental. I'll make certain the Viper sees her from a distance, so he'll think she's you."

"Is she blonde?" Nicole fanned herself.

Sweat encased him. And it wasn't all from the stifling room. "No. But she'll wear a scarf." He yearned to trace his finger along the oval of her cheek, touch the silky skin of her graceful neck, and kiss her irresistible lips.

"How much allegiance do you have to your former-sister-in-law?"

"What?" His chair dropped upright.

She smiled innocently. "I have a right to know. Lives are at stake."

He stood and jammed his hands into his pockets. He would have paced, but there was no room. How much loyalty *did* he have? Suzanne was Meier's wife. The thought usually filled him with rage. Tonight, it didn't.

"Commitment to Suzanne?" His thoughts raced. "A few days ago, I knew where I stood with Suzanne." What had changed? His hunger to put Meier behind bars? His hankering to see Suzanne free from the monster? "I owe her nothing. I'm focused on completing this mission. No matter what it costs."

"I hoped you'd say that." Nicole smiled, her eyes heavy-lidded. "You need rest too. I don't mind if you lie down beside me." The lantern cast deep shadows across her face.

The room closed in. Gripping the iron bed rail to hold himself together, he fought his desire. He would control this situation. Somehow, he'd started to care about Nicole. Long before he'd kissed her in the moonlight. He planted his feet on the floor until his knee ached and sweat soaked his shirt. He didn't dare touch her—he'd never be able to stop.

A glance at his watch told him three forty-five. The stale smell of age permeated the wooden beams, the furniture, and the old mattress. He yearned to cleanse his nostrils with her scent.

"Aren't you planning to rest?" She patted the far side of the bed.

She must think he was an iron man. He gripped the bottom of the wooden seat so hard, slivers pierced his hand. "I'm stepping out to get a drink of water. Need to move. Leg hurts."

"Oh, Josh, I'm so sorry." She pushed herself up on one elbow, lifted her long honey-soft hair out of her eyes, and smiled warmly. "But if Ian's life weren't in danger this would be such an adventure."

"Yeah." He jiggled the door knob. "After we find Ian, we could ...."

He let his voice trail away stopping what he'd been about to blurt. No more adventures for him with this *shiksa*. He jerked open the door and stalked out.

In the kitchen, he gazed over the wooden counter separating the small nook from the main room. Both soldiers lounged in wooden chairs tilted against the wall. The lanterns had been dimmed, and the men appeared to be fighting sleep. He spotted his car keys hanging on a nail beside the entry door.

After pumping water from the old-fashioned hand pump, he gulped a glass. Then he pumped more into an enamel basin sitting on the wooden sideboard. As he plunged his hands in, his bruised knuckles stung. He peeled off his shirt and splashed cold water over his chest, arms, face and hair.

A breeze trickled in. He needed a shower and a shave. One soldier gave him a knowing wink. Grimacing inside, he nodded back.

The soldier's thoughts were on the wrong trail. Man, he was so wrong. Josh reentered the bedroom and closed the door. With any luck, Nicole would be asleep. But she wasn't.

"Do danger and excitement heighten your senses and make you feel more alive?" Nicole sounded drowsy and had turned down the lantern. She appeared to be on the verge of sleep.

"Right." He found he had a half-smile curving his lips. Nicole was as addicted to adventure as he, and she didn't even know it. He slumped on the straight-backed wooden chair, stretched his legs out and lazed back with his head resting against the splintery wall. Uncomfortable. Good, the awkwardness would help him stay awake. His nerves were too tight for sleep anyway. He'd give the guards thirty minutes, then check to see if they'd nodded off.

His lids grew heavy. He drifted as if into shallow water. Needed to jumpstart himself when his battery seeped this low. Couldn't let himself drowse. As he struggled against the drench of sleep, he thought of how Nicole's eyes had danced with curiosity when she'd questioned him about Suzanne. Was more than curiosity behind her question?

The ease of relaxation released his mind to slip to the core of her, the bedrock of goodness he sensed there. A deep yearning unlocked the empty void in his own life. He wanted what she had. He hungered to know the God of Israel in a personal way. Like a Father. Like she did.

CHAPTER THIRTY-FOUR

Nicole stretched in the hard bed. Near her face, a lantern sputtered. The acrid fumes annoyed her nose. The realization of being in a strange place jerked her awake.

Josh. Where was he?

Enough light shimmered in under the door to show him sprawled precariously on the wooden chair. She giggled, then slapped her hand over her mouth.

His dark-lashed eyes flew open, and he wrenched forward. The tilted chair toppled. He landed on the floor in a tangle of long legs.

She tussled with the mirth welling up inside her chest—and lost. Laughter bubbled through her hand until tears filled her eyes. "I'm sorry. It's just so funny to see you on the floor like that." She teased, "You're always so controlled." She bolted upright against the pillow. "Are you hurt?"

He looked groggy—dark eyes sleepy, and shirt half unbuttoned.

"No," he said gruffly. He shoved the chair away with his foot. Groaning, he lurched up to perch on the edge of the bed beside her. She heard the rasp of stubble as he rubbed his hand over his face. He straightened. "Daylight! Why didn't you wake me?"

He leaped across the room and jerked open the door. "Soldiers are gone. We should have been too." He rushed into the main room.

Keys jingled. Josh must have snatched the car keys from the nail beside the door.

She slid out of bed and followed him into the other room.

He paced the empty main room stirring the dingy area's lingering stale cigarette odor.

"Why did they leave?" Relief filtered through her. No room crowded with soldiers. No stacked M-16s.

"Likely reported to their commander they performed their duty." He smiled dryly. "And kept a couple tourists off the road and out of danger after midnight." He strode to the window and gazed out. "Past seven. We've lost any edge we had with Meier's goons." He rubbed the back of his neck as if it hurt from the way he'd slept.

So gallant. So unnecessary. He could have shared the bed. She wouldn't have let anything happen. She didn't sleep with men. Not outside of marriage.

No matter how attractive or how she might be tempted. She stopped herself from walking over to massage his neck. Far too personal in this setting.

He faced her, dark eyes bloodshot, face edged with weariness. "Sorry, my fault. Didn't think I would sleep."

Her heart skipped. Two-day growth of black stubble and rumpled shirt half pulled out of trousers enhanced his already rugged appeal. "You were exhausted."

"Yeah." He buttoned his shirt and tucked in the blue chambray. "We've got a few things to settle before we leave."

She turned toward the kitchen. "Shall I make coffee?"

"Coffee. Yeah. Can't think without coffee." Josh paced, long legs eating up the hut's meager square footage.

She rummaged in the dingy cupboard, found fresh coffee grounds, and figured the intricacies of the water pump.

He talked while she worked. "Okay, let's recap. Yesterday, the gunmen would have checked on Gunter when he didn't reappear or the waiter would have discovered the mess I made of the table. Then the Viper would have searched, no more than five minutes max, and found Gunter."

She inspected the wooden cupboard for food. "Right." No food.

"They didn't guard our rental car while we were inside the restaurant or they would have caught us. But they couldn't have been more than thirty minutes behind us last night." Still looking dead tired and groggy, he jammed his hand through spiked hair. "They were overconfident. Certain we couldn't escape."

The aroma of Turkish coffee filled the cabin. She carried a cup to him and settled with hers on an adjoining wooden chair.

Josh gulped the strong brew. "We reached here about 2:45 or 3:00 a.m." He glanced at his watch. "Some four hours ago."

"If the soldiers had pulled the Viper's men over, they would have been here long ago." Excitement energized her. "Since they aren't, they must have driven past the blockade while the soldiers were inside here taking a rain break. So, the Viper might be in front of us on his way to Antalya." A pressing weight lifted from her chest.

"Precisely!" Josh's grin wiped traces of tiredness from his face.

"But why didn't the soldiers return to the roadblock after they brought us here?"

"Most did. After their break. Pulling us off the road for curfew offered them a chance to get out of the rain." Josh drained his cup. "The roadblock's objective was rooting out Kurdish PKK terrorists. Soldiers usually don't bother tourists. I think we gave them an excuse to take a breather."

"Right. Obviously, the Viper didn't know about the roadblock. So, for now we're in the clear?" Nicole sipped the coffee. "Marvelous. This coffee hits the spot."

"Yeah. We're safe for now. But we can't get cocky. The Viper's musclemen may figure, when they don't catch up, we pulled off for the night." He kneaded his neck. "They might split forces. Buy or steal another car and half might retrace the freeway looking for us while the others head to Antalya." He arched his back and massaged knotted muscles. "Either way ..."

Determination settled on his face. He reached across the table to cup her face in his palm.

A tremor warmed her.

His big hand tipped her chin to look into the smoky brown intensity of his eyes. "I can't figure why Pavlik didn't find us. Is there a surveillance bug on the rental car?"

She jerked back, pulling free. "You're a stone wall. Get over your antagonism against Kolya. You're asking me to choose between police help and ... and your protection."

Josh's expression hardened. He stalked to the kitchen, carried the coffee pot out, and refilled both their cups. "I should have searched the rental car at the restaurant." He shook his head. "Didn't have time. Last night, one of the soldiers locked the car after I brought our bags inside." He slammed his unfinished drink onto the small table and stomped outside.

She ran to the door, watched him slide carefully to his knees on the pavement, then slide on his back beneath the car. He stayed several minutes before he scooted out. After jerking open the car door, he searched the interior, running his hands over every surface. Then, wiping some clinging mud from his pants, he marched to where she waited on the tiny porch.

"I can't find any bug on the car." He stepped closer, face tense with purpose.

She backed away. "What are you doing?" She hoped she was wrong about his intentions.

Josh thundered into the bedroom, grabbed her fanny pack from the table, and dumped the contents on the mussed bed. Finding nothing unusual, he glowered at her, picked up her suitcase, slammed it on the bed, and scattered her clothes, searching all three cases. "No bug." Frowning, he jammed clothes back into her suitcases.

She should be angry, but she couldn't blame Josh. The killers threatened his life as well as hers. Nevertheless, Ian was her first concern. She didn't dare disobey Kolya. The police knew what they were doing. They worked kidnappings all the time. Her heart cried out to tell Josh. But she couldn't take the chance.

When he found nothing, he moved toward her. She backed away from the implacable certainty on his face. And from the glint in his eye.

"No! Don't touch me. I swear I'm not wearing a bug." She turned to run. "I'm not bugged."

"Too late. You lost your chance to be straight with me."

"Wait! Wait! Wait!" She held him off with stiff arms. "Kolya never came near me. Please, Josh. It's your turn to trust me."

She watched his determination waver. But he didn't move away. "Prove it! What else did your friend ... your *trusted* friend, Detective Nikolai Pavlik aka Kolya say?" The word "Kolya" twisted his lips.

Did she detect a tremor of jealousy? Josh jealous? Impossible. "He said ..."

How much could she tell? "Before the kidnappers contact me in Antalya, I am to meet him."

"Where?"

"On the old Roman wall that circles the harbor." She'd revealed enough. Josh need not know Kolya would be disguised and approach her as she strolled the wall.

Josh's intense brown gaze deepened to flashing black. "Did he intimate you might be walking into danger at Antalya?" Josh's lean face showed no tiredness now.

"Yes. That's why it's important I meet with him."

"Anything else?"

She was lousy at lying, so she shook her head.

Josh searched her face, then paced the room. "I couldn't find the device, so we'll have to ditch the car."

"But Josh—"

He jerked around. "I don't trust anyone but myself." His voice gentled, "Not even you. Keeping secrets from me could be fatal. For both of us." He gripped her hand. "Do nothing without first getting my okay."

Beneath the sheer force of his will, she nodded.

He touched her lips with a gentle finger. "Promise me you won't meet Pavlik on that wall."

"But I must."

"I'll meet Pavlik. After I find a phone. I'll contact my friend, Jamel, and arrange for him to pick you up like we discussed. After he hides you, I'll connect with Pavlik." His words turned slow and grating, "You're not safe. Not until I put Viper behind bars."

"But I have to find Ian!"

"I'll find him. I want you out of this."

"The Viper will be furious if I don't show. I can't chance that. He might kill Ian."

"He needs Ian. Ransom money's not his goal. Ian knows something and won't talk. They need you there to threaten your safety which will make him talk."

"But won't the Viper hurt you ... to find out where I am?"

"He needs me too." Josh pinched the bridge of his nose and closed his eyes. "I'm betting that the job he wants me to do makes me important enough ... and not expendable. Not yet."

"And if you're not?"

"I'll never tell him where you are."

Her heart thrilled. "What about Ian. Will they kill him?"

"The way I figure it, Ian's dead if he talks. His only chance is for us to find him."

Something flared in his eyes, something she trusted but didn't understand.

"Ian's best hope is them not getting their hands on you. If Viper didn't need me in his smuggling scheme, he would have snatched you long ago."

Anger and determination raged inside her. At some subconscious level, she knew Josh was right. She mustn't risk letting the Viper catch her. She would have to trust Josh with Ian's life. But his paranoid suspicion of Kolya was ridiculous. "Why don't you trust Kolya?"

"A gut feeling. I learned a long time ago to trust my gut."

Not good enough for her. "Can't we contact the police in Antalya?"

"The Viper has a long reach. If we call in the police, we risk them having been bought off. No. We do this ourselves."

Alone? No way. She would contact Kolya as planned. Police were police. And she and Josh needed help. Besides, though Josh hadn't found it, Kolya had arranged for a surveillance device on the car and had to be close by. She must stop Josh from finding another car. She couldn't risk losing police help.

"Jamel Hasad manages a rug bazaar inside the old Keleici at Antalya."

"And?" She half-listened, forming her plan.

He cupped her face in his torn hands. "Are you listening? This is important."

His touch snapped her to attention. "Yes, of course."

"I met Jamel in his draft days while he served his mandatory two years as a Turkish soldier. He was educated in the States, so he walks in both eastern and western worlds. With his combat training and knowledge of the country, he'll hide you well. Move you if necessary."

"At his Turkish rug bazaar?"

"Sure. Antalya crawls with them." Josh frowned. "One problem. Jamel considers himself a Don Juan. You need to remember that."

She laughed. "Minor problem. Am I to stay with him? Alone?"

"No. He lives above the shop with his family—four sisters, parents, grandparents, and a few aunts."

"Your friend will do this for you?"

"He'd jump at the chance. As an only son, his main job is to keep his sisters from becoming too modern for a conservative Turk to marry. He'll welcome the excitement."

"Chauvinist. I'm not sure I'll like him."

"I don't want you to like him. I just want him to hide you."

CHAPTER THIRTY-FIVE

Pleased Josh hadn't yet found a way to ditch the rental car, Nicole sped down the empty turnpike. For miles, she'd been working up courage to broach what had been on her mind almost from the moment she'd met Josh. Soon he'd leave her with Jamel. She must seize what might be her last chance. She glanced across to where he slumped, eyes closed, in the passenger seat.

"Uh, Josh. I've been thinking." Harder than she'd expected. She felt tongue tied. *Father, please give me the right words.*

Josh opened one eye.

She hated to keep him from catching a few winks, but this was important. "You're headed into danger. I'd feel better if you trusted God to help you."

"Yeah?"

"Do you believe in the Jewish Messiah?"

He mumbled, "You going to ruin a good friendship?"

"Never. I'll always be your friend." If she didn't care so much about him, she would have stopped. "I understand what you told me about what Jews believe that *the Lord our God is one.*"

"*Adonai Elohaynu, Adonai ehud,*" he shut his eye. "The Lord our God is one. We live by that."

"So do Christians."

"What about your Trinity?" Both brown eyes snapped open.

"One Lord, one God, one faith. God is Father, Son, and Holy Spirit just as I am a woman, daughter, sister, and wife—" Her voice quivered. "Correction, widow."

She glanced from the highway to gauge his response.

He still slumped but seemed interested.

Swallowing, she gripped the wheel tighter. "We believe Christ, the Anointed One, the Messiah, is God in every way. He was preexistent as the Word of God during creation when God said, 'Let us create man in our own image.' Christians believe in one God. I believe in one God."

Josh straightened. His lips remained shut.

Interested or hostile? She couldn't tell. "Christ fulfilled every prophesy in your Torah and prophetic writings concerning Messiah's first coming." She let instinct take over her driving, mind occupied with her thoughts. "His virgin birth in the City of David, his triumphal entry into Jerusalem, his betrayal for thirty pieces of silver, his suffering on the cross, even the words he spoke, and the fact his side was pierced. Plus, your Psalm 16 speaks of his resurrection."

Josh hadn't exploded. He seemed to be paying attention.

"In the New Testament, Luke tells us in his gospel the angel Gabriel announced to Mary, the Jewish mother of the Messiah, 'You will conceive and give birth to a son, and you will name him Jesus.'" As Nicole quoted the wonderful words she'd memorized, her heart glowed. "He will be very great and will be called the Son of the Most High. The Lord God will give him the throne of his father David, And he will reign over the Israel forever; his kingdom will never end. ... the baby to be born will be holy, and he will be called the Son of God."

Thinking of Jesus always made her smile. God was in control. The radiance of his holy love warmed her heart and gave her courage.

"When the angel made that announcement to Mary, he repeated the promise made to David in II Samuel 7:16."

Josh sat up. "Yeah?"

She pulled her concentration back to the highway. *What now, Lord, what now?* If only she'd had time to open her Bible. She could think of nothing more.

Josh appeared wide awake and stared at her.

"We believe the 53rd chapter of Isaiah speaks of your Messiah and my Jesus, our savior." God must have given her those words. "Are you familiar with that chapter?"

Josh narrowed his eyes and pinched the bridge of his nose.

She smiled. A sure sign he was thinking. A flash of joy pierced her heart.

His jaw worked. "Not off the top of my head."

"I can quote parts for you."

"Feel free."

"He had no form or majesty that we should look at him, and no beauty we should desire him. He was despised and rejected by men, a man of sorrows and acquainted with grief."

Josh muttered, "I can relate."

"... But he was pierced for our transgressions, he was crushed for our iniquities; upon him was the chastisement that brought us peace, and with his wounds we are healed." How she loved these beautiful, life-giving words. "All we like sheep have gone astray; we have turned—every one—to his own way; and the Lord has laid on him the iniquity of us all."

Josh scrubbed his hand over his two-day stubble. "Jesus was a scapegoat? Like the biblical ceremony of Yom Kippur."

"Our sin offering. Yes."

"Why have I never heard this?" Josh folded in on himself and shut her out.

She wanted to tell him so much more. She bubbled with the joy of sharing her faith. She gave him time to digest what she'd already said.

One thing more to explain before he left to face the Viper and possible death. She couldn't let him go without hearing. She tightened her lips ... whether he wanted to hear or not.

Though she wasn't sure he listened, she began, "A Pharisee named Nicodemus, a member of the Jewish ruling council, came to Jesus one night. Jesus told him, 'No one can see the kingdom of God unless he is born again.' Nicodemus didn't understand."

Josh nodded. "I can see why."

Nicole smiled. "I'm coming to that." She touched Josh's hand.

He sat straight, half-turned toward her, leg bent on the seat.

"Jesus explained to Nicodemus, that just as Moses lifted up the snake in the desert, so he—the Son of Man—must be lifted up, that everyone who believes in him may have eternal life." Nicole squeezed the hand that lay across Josh's knee. "Jesus said, 'For God so loved the world that He gave His only Son, that whoever believes in Him shall not perish but have eternal life.'"

"That's it? Just believing."

She'd never seen Josh so still. "That's it."

His expression closed her out. He slid around and resumed his slump.

Her heart dropped, lead inside her chest. Since the first clasp of his hand, through a growing attraction, she'd fought her unruly emotions. Their kiss in the moonlight had made her believe he cared. Every hope, every fantasy, every dream she'd spun around him burned to ashes.

Today, they would part. She might never see him again. The thought sliced her heart. She sighed. If they did meet again, she'd keep her promise and remain his friend. Nothing more. Not so long as he rejected her Savior.

She couldn't keep disappointment from edging her voice, "A person need only believe in Christ and accept his death on the cross for his sins to receive the eternal life God offers."

Josh sunk lower in the passenger seat, crossed arms over his chest, and closed his eyes.

She surrendered Josh to God. Peace filled the painful, jagged places in her heart.

Father, please keep Josh safe as he faces the Viper.

CHAPTER THIRTY-SIX

At first sight, Nicole fell in love with Antalya. She adored the ancient, well-preserved Roman wall that enclosed the picturesque village circling the beautiful harbor. Boats, bright with flags and colored sails, bobbed in the turquoise water. Beyond the ancient wall, white buildings with red roofs peeked through lush green trees. She could live in a peaceful place like this.

With her brother.

She parked near the water's edge, and she and Josh climbed an ancient stone stairway to street level.

"A hundred steps straight up," she counted, breathing hard.

"See a telephone anywhere?" Josh's voice sounded tense.

"Are there public phones in Turkey?"

"Resort areas like Izmir have them. I thought Antalya might. But I don't see one. This is a main street."

He needed a phone, and she needed to get away from him long enough to meet Kolya. She gazed around, trying to memorize the scenic area. Getting lost could be fatal.

"We'll ditch the rental car and take a cab." Facing the traffic heading their way, Josh waved a hand at the oncoming cars.

She couldn't leave the harbor now. She had to meet Kolya on top of the Roman wall. She pulled back. "I'm hungry." She was starved but not interested in eating with Ian possibly so near and with the emotional distance Josh put between them.

He all but danced on the sidewalk. Impatience seeped from his expression. He glanced at his watch but nodded and pointed to a nearby restaurant perched on the edge of the Roman wall. "This place okay?"

"Fine."

Another restaurant that appeared designed for lovers. Secluded outdoor tables, each beneath its own grape arbor, overlooked the sparkling harbor. Loneliness grabbed her by the throat. Would everything remind her of what could have been with Josh? She followed the waiter to a choice table.

"I have to use the restroom," she told Josh as he pulled out her chair.

He shot her a skeptical look.

"I'll hurry. Order whatever is fast."

"Viper's strongarm goons could spot us and move in." A frown worried Josh's forehead. He glanced again at his watch.

As if she needed warning. "I'll be back before lunch is served."

As soon as she turned a corner out of his sight, she scampered beneath the trees, between the arbors, and up a few stone steps to the top of the ancient wall, beyond where Josh could see her.

Walking the high, narrow Roman sea wall was like striding a paved road built of boulders. She jogged past people strolling arm in arm along its scenic way coiled around the harbor. Where might he be? A stiff wind blew her hair across her face and into her eyes.

Tourists passed in groups and pairs. She came to a bend in the wall. Several old men sat cross-legged on Turkish carpets, throwing long lines over the embankment. Hooks sparkled in the sunlight before splashing into azure water. She dashed past. A woman encased in heavy, black veils walked by.

"Nicole!" The aged, trembling voice drifted from behind her.

She turned. One of the old men reeled in his fishing line, rose from his carpet, and approached. He wore Turkish pantaloons, vest, and a wide toothless grin. Couldn't be Kolya.

"Baruch still in the dark?" The old man took her hand. "Kolya?"

"Good, aren't I?" The detective smirked. "What's his plan?"

"Is it really you?" Even the grey in his eyes seemed faded with age.

"I promised I'd meet you. Stop looking surprised. Walk with me as though I were your guide, you understand." He hobbled along the wall. "Does Baruch have a plan?"

"He ditched the car. He thinks it's bugged."

"Yes. Yes. Baruch's smart. He would suspect." Kolya reached inside the bloused shirt under his embroidered vest. "Hide this in the pocketbook you wear around your waist. If I'm to protect you, I need to know where you are."

She took the small, slender-as-a-dime surveillance device, and slipped it into her fanny pack.

"Have you enough money?" Kolya's voice sounded kind.

"Very little. Josh said his money's getting thin."

He folded her hand around a roll of bills. "You'll want this. Now what does Baruch plan?"

"A friend of his will hide me while he meets with the kidnappers. He figures they need me to make my brother tell them whatever it is they want to know. What do you think?"

"The friend's name?"

"Jamel Hassid. He owns a Turkish Rug Bazaar inside the Keleici."

"But, of course."

Nicole watched the old man, who claimed to be Kolya, scratch the side of his nose with a withered hand. He said nothing for a long moment. "The Viper has not made contact?"

She wished he would use his real voice rather than the cracked voice he had adopted. "No."

"Baruch's plan is good. Let him meet the kidnappers. My men will protect him. Hide this inside his shirt pocket." He handed her another tiny homing device.

She took the bug. She couldn't keep the quiver from her voice. "Do you think my brother's alive?"

"As long as they want information from him, they'll keep him alive, you understand."

"What information? What do they want from him?"

"You don't know?

"No. I wish I did."

Kolya dropped into his own voice, "That would make your brother expendable and be dangerous for you. Better you don't know." He turned to retrace their steps. "Hide with Jamel Hassid. Let Baruch meet the Viper. I'll be close to you. My men will stay with Baruch. Make sure he wears that homing device, you understand. For his protection."

He returned to his carpet, groaning, lowered himself as if he were an old man, and turned his face to the sea.

She ran back the length of the wall, through the trees, and slowed as she approached the restaurant where Josh waited. Their table was empty. Loss jolted her. Their lunch was growing cold. She glanced around. Josh stood at the serving counter bent over a phone. Relief. Just as she slipped into her seat, he slammed the receiver down on its old-fashioned cradle. She picked up her fork.

"Who are you trying to call?" she asked as he walked up.

He sat across from her rubbing a hand through the frown marring his forehead and looking frustrated. "Stateside. A friend at work. Can't get through to him. Where've you been?"

"Attending to nature."

"Jamel's waiting at his shop."

"Then what's wrong?"

"Blasted telephone service. Unreliable as .... Let's finish. I want to deliver you safely to Jamel." He attacked his food.

She ate quickly. How would she place the homing bug into Josh's shirt pocket? If he weren't so paranoid, she could give it to him.

In the end, he solved the problem.

"Here's my wallet. Pay the waiter while I scout the sidewalk to make sure the gunmen haven't arrived."

"Sure you trust me with your wallet?" she teased.

"And my life." He hurried off.

As soon as he was out of sight, she slipped the bug into a zipped pocket inside his billfold. Then she paid the waiter. Josh didn't have much money left. Guilt chewed at her. He'd been honest with her. Should she tell him about her talk with Kolya? He was already frustrated, and he'd not like to hear what she'd done.

Josh jogged through the tables toward her, looking more relaxed. He smiled grimly. "Coast's clear. Let's fire our jets."

She followed him to the street where a cab waited by the curb. They drove through narrow cobbled streets inside the ancient Keleici. Bible-ancient-looking shops lined both sides. Their taxi often slowed to let pedestrians flatten themselves against hand-hewn stone buildings so they could drive by. The driver crisscrossed so many lanes she was lost.

They drove around a corner and through a blind intersection.

Tires squealed. Metal screeched on metal. A car slammed into them.

She fell hard against Josh and heard his head crack against the side window. His reflexes were so fast, his arm streaked around her, catching her and protecting her from being thrown forward against the back of the front seat. Both their knees smashed into the seat.

"You okay?" He had his hands on her shoulders, then probed her back and arms.

"Just shook up, with a bump here and there." Fear gripped her when she saw blood on his temple. "You're bleeding."

He touched the side of his forehead. "Can't do much damage to this hard head. Just a lump."

The car that smashed into theirs steamed and hissed against their front passenger seat. Her insides quaked. Had it hit a foot further back, she would have been badly injured.

Their driver loosed a torrent of Turkish.

"My guardian angel was on duty today." She dabbed at the blood on Josh, her handkerchief trembling. "Thank you, Father."

"Yeah."

The shock of the accident was almost worth seeing the concern in Josh's dark eyes.

"We're going to crawl out your door," he motioned." My side's jammed against the building. Can you make it?"

Shaken, she let Josh reach across her and shove her door open. From beside her, he helped her climb out, then followed. He surveyed the damage while their driver scrambled over the front seat into the back and trailed them out the single door that opened.

"Blast. No way this cab's going anywhere." A bump grew and darkened Josh's temple. "Car's totaled. When the police come, we'll hitch a ride with them, and call Jamel from the police station." He held his head.

The purple bump had to hurt.

A crowd gathered around them and the two disabled cars. Each person had something to say and yelled at the top of their lungs, in Turkish, with excited gesturing.

"Stay here." Josh stalked over to talk with the driver of the other car who sat behind the wheel of his car looking dazed.

Several Turkish men walked close to her and spoke.

Nicole shook her head to indicate she didn't understand. Then she spotted *him*. Standing apart, behind the crowd. Not one of the three men who tailed them, but one so like them, she knew he was one of them. Larger than the others and more muscular, he moved like a truck. Not with agility like the dead-eyed Gunter but with invincible certainty.

And anger. The thug's fury spilled out of him like radiator fluid from the smashed car. And left him steaming. The small crowd around her parted, letting the man truck through. She backed against the building.

He stopped, just short of touching her. "Follow me. I lead you to your brother."

She barely understood his accented words. Shock hit her. She hesitated and turned toward Josh. But a shouting mob surrounded him.

"Alone. Now." The man turned on his heel and strode away.

CHAPTER THIRTY-SEVEN

The truck-man stopped and turned toward her.

Nicole stared at the man up close. He resembled a tank more than a truck. "Is Ian in Antalya?" She squeaked. The tank was frightening. His blue eyes wild with hate, he appeared to verge on insanity.

"No. Come. Now."

"Is Ian with the Viper?"

"No," the man growled. He frowned and looked ready to pounce on her and carry her away. He glanced from her to where Josh stood surrounded by a mob of chattering, gesturing Turkish men.

"I take you to the kid's prison." Tank-man kept his gaze on Josh.

Nicole could barely see the back of Josh's head above the threatening crowd. Had their crash not been an accident? Had this fierce man designed the wreck to separate her from Josh?

"Hurry. Or you be too late." Tank motioned to a car parked halfway up the block.

Chills tiptoed Nicole's spine. "Where are the three men who tailed Josh and me?"

"They follow a decoy. Wild goose chase. They will be on you tail again soon."

"Why are you helping me?" Her heart thumped crazily against her rib cage.

Tank looked at her, eyes flat. "Come." He turned and strode away.

He was almost at the parked car before her feet made her decision. She chased him and screamed at his back, "Where's Ian?"

"Come, you see."

"Let me get Josh."

"Gunter and Jaakov have order to drive Major to Air Base to fly for boss. They catch us if we not leave now." Tank stopped in front of a black BMW, shoved open the passenger door, and motioned her inside.

"Wait. I ... I ...."

"No time." He ran to the driver's side and slid inside. "Franz on way to take you to Viper. You want brother alive?" He slid inside.

She glanced over her shoulder where the mob hassled Josh. She couldn't see him but heard shouts and arguing.

The tank-man snapped on the ignition and jammed the car into gear.

This might be her only chance to find Ian. She jumped in. As she shut the door, Tank gunned the engine and the car roared down the narrow street and squealed around a corner.

A flush heated her entire body. She was committed. What if this man was the one ordered to take her to the Viper? Had she just walked into his trap? *Father, please protect me.*

"What's your name?" she braced herself against the hard, fast turns he made.

"Brun."

Not much help. German like the others. She dried damp palms on her pants. "Where is Ian?"

"At the *Toprakkale* near Adana."

"Toprakkale?"

"Crusader castle. Fallen down. Kid's tied up inside old dungeon."

"He's alive?"

"He alive."

Too good to be true. *Thank you, God. Ian's alive.* Her heart lifted. She rubbed her temples, dizzy with relief. "Why are you helping me?"

Tank Brun frowned, but didn't answer.

"Where's the Viper?" She put her hand on the door handle. "Tell me or I'll jump out."

"With Franz. He follow decoy." Brun took his eyes off the road and glanced at his watch. "By now they know trick and turn back. They find crash soon, pick up Major, then search for you." Brun stepped harder on the gas. Antalya fell away behind them. An empty freeway stretched ahead.

Nicole clutched her aching heart. Abandoning Josh felt as if she left part of herself. The sharp metallic taste of fear for him filled her mouth. "What will they do with Josh?"

"Why you worry about Major? He work for Viper. Tonight he fly mission for Air Force and smuggle old statues into Iraq."

"Stolen from Turkey?"

Brun shrugged his massive shoulders.

Nicole's body went cold. Josh in league with the Viper? No. Never. He'd told her what the Viper wanted from him. Her heart warmed. Josh was an American Air Force officer who risked his life to save others. Tears pricked her eyes. She cared a great deal for him. More than she wished. No, he wasn't in league with the kidnappers.

Whatever happened, when she had Ian safe, she would notify Josh's commander and tell him of Josh's plight. The Air Force could send out their Search and Rescue responders for their major.

If the Turks didn't catch him first. Or the Viper hurt him. Worry squeezed her heart. She had to find a phone. If only she had a cell phone. Oh, she wasn't able to help Josh now. She could only help Ian. She must plan.

Nicole made her voice businesslike, fighting her fear. "Who are you working for? What's your motive in taking me to see Ian?"

Brun continued his stony-faced driving. A vein bulged in his reddened temple.

She tried another tack. "What are our chances? Will the Viper find us?"

"Stepp and me call Viper two times a day by radio. I left after this morning's check-in. When Viper discover he can't reach me, the boss will add two plus two." Brun frowned at the empty highway.

"Stepp? Is he another guard? Won't he contact the Viper?"

"Stepp was guard over Ian. I killed him."

Shock hit her. Her insides trembled. *Oh God, let me have heard right.* "You killed Stepp ... not Ian?" The man beside her was a murderer. And he was steaming mad. Tank's anger showed in the reckless way he wrapped his beefy hands around the steering wheel and jerked it through each turn and curve of the road. The way he stomped on the brakes and squealed the tires.

"Worthless whelp! Stepp in my way. He would radio Viper. Tip him off."

"Oh." More words stuck in her throat.

The BMW raced around a curve, leaning out toward the edge, tires screeching. Nicole saw a precipice looming below with the sea rushing in over rocks.

"He not torment you brother. Not now."

Her stomach squeezed. She shut away the thought of Ian being tortured. Wouldn't think of this angry man killing her.

Her heart hammered in her throat. God was still in control. Plan, Nicole, plan.

Stepp gone, leaving one less man. How many more? Brun must have guarded Ian while three other kidnappers, Franz, Dead-Eyes Gunter, and Jaakov tailed her and Josh. How many more kidnappers were there? "Is anyone guarding Ian?"

"Not now."

She heaved a sigh. But what if Brun lied?

If not, somewhere along the way, the Viper must hook up with his three men. Probably by now, thanks to the crash, two of the kidnappers held Josh. Her stomach knotted. That left the Viper and a man named Franz looking for her. Shivers fluttered down her spine. She clasped her cold hands.

Had anyone seen her and Brun leave the crash? She shut her eyes tight and ran her memory video. Too blurred. Everything happened too fast. She had no idea. She hugged herself to stop her trembling. She breathed easier. She had her surveillance device. And so did Josh. Kolya and his police must be following both of them.

Scrunching her eyes, she hung on while the car lurched down the mountainside toward the sea. She would find Ian ... no, she would *rescue* Ian and then send help for Josh. Brun had said a castle near Adana. That's where Josh said the American air base was located.

A question burned in her mind. "Why are you helping Ian and me? Why are you betraying your boss?"

Brun didn't even glance at her. It was as if she didn't exist. As if she were a means to an end. His eyes remained concentrated on the road. But his chest heaved, and muscles bulged in his clenched jaw.

"You're angry, Brun. Were you upset with Stepp?"

"Himmel, no. Whelp in my way."

Getting information from Brun was like digging for gold in a played-out mine. "Who made you angry?"

"Viper," Brun gritted, ears growing red. He pounded the steering wheel. A vein throbbed in his forehead. Would he have a stroke?

"Is that why you're helping me? You're angry at the Viper? So, you are—"

"Ja, dummkopf. Help you free kid."

A stab of joy hit her. But she didn't like this man. Or trust him. "You're taking me to Ian so I can release him, and we can both escape from the Viper who is hot on my tail?"

"I take care of Viper."

Reassuring. But there was still the other man. "You said Franz is with the Viper?"

Brun grunted.

No more information there. Nicole used both hands to hang on as the car sped around curves. "This castle is near Adana?"

"You talk too much!" He shot her a mean look.

Her insides shuddered at the loud tone of his voice. But she had to make her plans. "How far is Adana?"

"Five hours."

What? She had to drive with this lunatic for five hours! She felt around the seat for a seatbelt, but if the car had one it was well hidden. *Oh God, please don't let us crash. Let me reach Ian in time. Please let me save him.*

Josh had said Incirlik Air Base was at Adana. After she freed Ian, they would need a pass to get on base to safety. Josh said armed Turkish soldiers guarded the entrance, and everyone had to show Military ID or a pass before the Turks let them enter. Even though she couldn't get on base, the check point had to have a telephone. She could call for help.

320

Nicole leaned back on the cushions and tried not to look at the landscape flashing past. Brun held the speed to one-hundred-five kilometers. He must be frightened of his boss to take such chances on this winding road.

"How far is Adana from *Toprakkale*?"

"About fifteen miles." He sneered. "Long walk." His eyes raked her as if he saw her for the first time.

Her hope deteriorated into a forlorn mist. Maybe Brun didn't intend to let her save Ian. Why would he? Maybe he had other plans for her. She swallowed and forced words through her dry throat. "The Viper made you angry?"

"*Kaput!* My heart *kaput!*"

She understood *kaput*. His heart was broken? She stared at the man's sweating face. The knot of fear in her stomach loosened.

"My *liebchen*. Viper took her in helicopter. Not bring her back." He groaned, then whimpered. "Gott in himmel. The Viper took my liebchen. My Vashti."

Seemed Viper collected women. First Scott's, now this man's. "You're getting even by helping me release Ian?" Or this was a scheme to collect her for the Viper and add her to his stable of women.

"Ja."

The man was so upset his mouth worked, but no other words came out.

Could it be true? It made sense. Ian was alive and she was on her way to release him. *Thank you, Father.*

She peeked in the rearview mirror, but the road zigzagged behind them. She couldn't have seen a car even if one had been only a quarter mile back. Somewhere trailing them, Kolya monitored her. Comforting. After she found Ian, Kolya would help them escape. But she mustn't count on him, because the Viper lurked there too. Perhaps Brun wouldn't be able to handle both the Viper and Franz. Perhaps Brun was intent on a suicide mission.

For them both.

CHAPTER THIRTY-EIGHT

The BMW slid to a neck-snapping halt. Nicole pulled in a long breath and unclenched her hands.

"Castle up there." Brun pointed a thick finger.

"On top of that mountain?" Nicole tried to keep the skepticism from her voice. Was this a trap after all?

"Ja. I park close as I can."

Her heart beat frantically as they drove from the placid farming plain up the steep road. True, Crusaders built their fortresses to take advantage of high terrain.

With a swirl of flying stones, Brun swept into a tiny graveled parking area. He braked and swung the wheel, spinning the car ninety degrees. He screeched to a halt in a cloud of dust.

"Out!"

"Where's the castle?"

Brun rolled down the window and pointed up a steep path. "Up. You walk."

Wow. This was unexpected. The two of them were alone, three-quarters up a mountain. Where was the castle? Oh, there. Far above her, boulders and a rock-strewn path led to the suggestion of ruined walls almost hidden by undergrowth.

A desolate spot. Frightful and lonely. But Ian was locked in prison up there. She bolted out of the car. "Let's go!"

With the brake on, Brun gunned the BMW's engine. The back wheels spun, spitting gravel and dust. "You go." He hit the gas.

And she stood alone, choking in his dust.

For a second, she watched his car disappear around one of the hairpin turns, the growl of tires on gravel loud in the silence. Her heart skidded to her knees. Was Brun heading off the Viper and Franz? Or was he leaving her to face them?

Alone.

She was not alone. With Christ's strength, she could do this. One step at a time. She crossed the gravel road and started up the faint path. Her brown flats gave little protection from the sharp rocks and undergrowth, but at least she wasn't wearing heels or sandals.

She had to hurry. Already out of breath, she slipped and skidded over the rocks, using them as steps when she could. Her shoes dislodging smaller stones, she climbed the treeless mountainside. The crunch of shoes on the rocks and the gossip of birds broke the silence.

Breathing hard, she halted to rest. When she looked down, she gasped. On every side, for miles around, a serene plateau latticed with tilled fields as elegantly patterned as a Turkish carpet. Far away, a river snaked across the plain. But there were no towns or trees. Once she and Ian escaped the castle, there was no place to hide.

She took a deep breath. So, this was the Plain of Ossos where Alexander the Great defeated Darius the III, ending the Medo-Persian Empire and ushering in the Greek. She stiffened her shoulders. And here she would defeat the Viper and free Ian. *Lord, cast down these evil strongholds.*

In the distance on the freeway, a car sped away. Brun, returning the way they had come. She hoped. With her directional dyslexia, she was unsure. She memorized the opposite direction, the road to her left, the road to Adana, the direction she and Ian would take.

Grabbing a deep breath of clear air, she forced tired legs up the ever-steepening path. No trees sheltered her from the sun. Sweat filmed her body as she reached some crumbled ancient stairs.

Ahead and on both sides stretched a half-fallen stone wall. It must have once been the stone curtain which separated the grounds from the main castle buildings. Almost there. Her pulse beat so fast she stopped to let her heart slow.

Raw determination spurred her. She had to hurry. The stone steps took her to an arch in the broken wall. Through the narrow arch, more broken steps led up to a doorway. She leaned against the archway to catch her breath.

The closer she came to the entrance, the stronger became the presence of ancient conquerors and defenders. The spirits of long dead warriors lingered inside this half-ruined castle. If the stones could cry out, what stories they could tell.

She worked on up the giant stone steps. Her imagination brought to life enormous steeds, hooves striking against stone, clattering up these stairs. Their knights rode valiantly, hot sun flashing their armor. Hard-muscled armor bearers strode beneath blood red banners. If only she had a knight with her now. She had foolishly left her knight behind.

Heart beating fast, she pushed open one of the double doors and tiptoed into the castle's huge reception hall. Her flats made no sound in the cavernous room. A staircase curved half-way up to what would have been the second level, now ragged walls to an open sky.

She paused at a window. Outside, weeds and bushes filled the grounds all the way to the castle curtain. In the distance stood a single watchtower. Ian wouldn't be there. Too obvious.

She circled the room searching for a staircase. Brun had said Ian was imprisoned inside the dungeon. According to what she knew from medieval studies, dungeons lurked below the stables.

Behind the curved, half-missing stairway, she almost overlooked a heavy wooden door. Her hand trembled as she pulled the leather latch and discovered a wide descending staircase. Her heart leaped. She sped down. At the bottom, she entered a two-story room whose stone walls arched overhead to meet in a remarkably preserved stone ceiling. Enough light seeped into the narrow room to create shadows. She could visualize stalls punctuating the length of the room. Above them must have been a second floor for hay and tack for the horses.

She ran the length of the deserted stable. Nothing. Then she stumbled over a vine-covered passageway. The crumbled steps down ended in darkness.

Excitement charged her tired legs. She descended the steep steps that circled past nooks cut into the wall for lighted torches. If only she had one! The further down she stepped, the darker the passage grew. She felt along a cold stone wall, hesitating when a lizard skittered under her fingers. She groped to where the stairs ended before a low, narrow tunnel.

She stooped to enter and crouched through the tunnel to a chest high door at the tunnel's end. Heart in her throat, she opened the door. Rusty hinges screeched. She jumped back, chills chased her spine. Nerves.

Mildew. Wrinkling her nose at the smell, she peered into pitch blackness. "Ian," she whispered. If Ian were inside, he wouldn't answer. He couldn't hear her. Still she couldn't help herself. "Ian!" she called. Her voice echoed back and landed at her feet, telling her the dungeon must be cramped. If only she had a ray of sunlight, a flashlight, a cigarette lighter, a match. So dark.

"Courage, Nicole!" Shuffling with hands outstretched, she entered the prison. Almost immediately her foot brushed something inert. "Ian!"

She knelt and felt the mass, passing her hands over hair, a face, muscular shoulders. The body of a man. He didn't move. Shudders shook her. "Oh, dear God."

He lay on his side.

He was dead. Gritting her teeth, she felt his shoulder, down his arm to his wrist. His hand was cold, but there were no ropes around his wrists. She forced herself to explore the length of his body, along his leg to his ankle. No ropes. His chest felt wet and sticky. She jerked her hands away and sniffed her fingers. Congealed blood. The smell of death.

But this man had a different build, shorter and more muscular than Ian, hair longer. Relief filtered through her, strengthening her wobbling knees.

Wrenching away from the body, her stomach rebelled. She retched. Then inched past the inert form. The stone roof was so low she hunched her head and shoulders. Stones arched against her back and pressed her bowed neck. She crept forward, sliding her hand against the wall. She touched something large and slimy. Her skin crawled.

She forced her feet forward. The air was almost unfit to breathe. Claustrophobia gripped her. Her outstretched hands brushed thick cobwebs and brought loosened dirt showering on her hair and shoulders. Tiny feet touched her ankle and scrambled over her flats. She jumped back, stifling a scream. She would do this only for Ian.

Father, help me find Ian.

He had to be here. Her groping hands hit a stone wall. She had reached the dungeon's far end.

Disappointment jolted her. Where was Ian?

Okay, she'd have to explore the dungeon's center. She looked over her shoulder at the open dungeon door. There it stood where the faint lessening of the deep darkness. If her poor sense of direction kicked in, she would lose precious time hugging the wall again to find the way out. She hated leaving the security of the wall. To the point of obsession, she despised rats. And spiders. And bugs. Her skin crawled.

She took several tentative steps. Her shoe hit something larger than the clumps of dirt on the uneven floor. She flinched. Were there snakes here too? She slid her foot forward and touched the object again. It moved.

"Who's there?"

Ian's voice! "Thank God, you're alive!" Her heart soared.

She dropped to her knees, found a body part which turned out to be a bare foot and hugged it. She sensed he struggled to sit and helped him. Then hugged him, unable to let him go. Tears, long held back, spilled out and slid between her cheek and Ian's bristly one. He smelled. But to her, his unwashed odor smelled sweet. He was alive! So very alive!

"Vashti? It that you?" Ian's throat sounded dry and his words slurred.

Vashti? Wasn't that the name Brun had mentioned? Answers could wait. She had to get Ian out of this foul place. Smoothing her hands along his arms, she found ropes and struggled to untie them. With her fingers trembling so, the job took a long time.

Hands free at last, Ian felt for her. He touched her face. "Not Vashti. You smell like Nicole. Is it you, Nicole?"

She opened his hand and made her *yes* sign inside his palm. And repeated it. And repeated it. Then got to the business of untying his ankles.

"Nicole! You don't know how I prayed."

His slurred words sent pangs through her heart. They weren't out of trouble yet. Her hands were too busy to answer him.

"The kidnappers never got you. I feared they would."

His words were mumbled. He must be starved or drugged. How would she get him out of here? She finished the last knot. "Come," she signed into his open palm. She bounced up and tried to pull him to his feet. He was too heavy.

He struggled to rise but couldn't get to more than his knees.

"My feet are numb. I'll be okay in a minute. Dizzy too. And thirsty. You have anything to drink?"

"No time. Come," she signed in his hand. Then pulled on his upper arms.

"Can't. Sorry."

She pulled him forward, so he crawled on his hands and knees toward the less dense darkness.

"We're still in danger?"

She tugged harder on his shoulders.

When they reached the door, Ian used the stone archway to drag himself to his feet. He lurched like a Frankenstein.

She positioned his arm across her shoulder and helped him through the tunnel and up the stairs.

Blinking and unsteady, he shielded his eyes in the shadowy stable. Clothes dirty and torn, barefoot, bright blue eyes bloodshot—his hair, matted with dirt, stuck out in all directions. Rope burns branded his wrists and ankles. Bruises marked his face. He'd never looked so good. He was alive.

She couldn't keep from hugging him. And hugging him. He felt thinner. And weak in her arms. But gratitude and happiness gave her renewed energy. Tears slid down her cheeks. With his hand in hers, she signed, "We must hurry."

How would she get him down that rocky mountain without tearing up his bare feet? And how would she get him to safety? Judging from her trip here, there were few towns along the freeway. And from her earlier vantage point at the castle window, she hadn't seen any town nearby. Adana must be the nearest. Somehow, she had to get Ian to safety. Then she'd find a telephone. She'd call in Search and Rescue for Ian and her, and send help for Josh.

First, they had to escape the castle and the mountainside. Neither offered a place of safety, nor a spot to hide.

CHAPTER THIRTY-NINE

As Nicole helped Ian step out from the shaded stable into the roofless main castle room, urgency swept Nicole. Time was running out.

Ian blinked in the bright sunlight and ran his tongue over his crusted lips. "Nikki, you're not alone?"

He looked in no shape to walk, much less run. She faced him so he could read her lips as she signed. "For now. But help's on the way." Pulling the homing device from her fanny pack, she held the bug out for him to see. "The police are following."

"Following? Why aren't they with you?"

"It's a long story, and we've got to hide. The kidnappers can't be far behind me."

"I don't see any place to hide here inside the castle. I ... I can walk. Let's get out of here."

They were goldfish in a bowl. Nicole rubbed her aching forehead. Not many options. This gutted reception room offered nothing. Sunshine illuminated every cranny. The crumbling stairway rose to nothingness, and the double wooden doors led outside. Behind them the stable, although full of shadows, was visible from one end to the other. The steep path down the mountain lay exposed. "We'll make a run for it. Pray the Viper and his men are still far away."

"Right."

"Let's go," she signed and grabbed Ian's hand. He lurched beside her as they crossed the room. She pushed open one of the wooden doors and peeked outside. The way as far as the archway that led to the steep steps was empty. She listened. Nothing. Not even the song of birds. Quiet. Still. The air smelled sweet and the sunshine felt warm after the dank dungeon. "We'll make it." She stumbled across the rocks, her shoulder under Ian as they struggled to the archway.

"Better check, Nikki," Ian whispered, already breathing hard.

She nodded and poked her head around the crumbling bricks. The steep path ran down the rocky mountainside, empty all the way to the graveled area where Brun dropped her. No people, no vehicle. The Viper had not yet arrived. Only Ian's soft pants broke the silence.

Ian crouched behind her on a patch of grass between the sharp rocks. Already his feet bled.

"Your poor feet," she whispered, and motioned him forward.

He read her lips. "Forget my feet. Let's get out of here."

She stepped through the arch.

Strong, muscular arms grabbed her and yanked her against a rock-hard body. She screamed. The man was monster huge. She tore at the hands grasping her. "Run Ian," she yelled, knowing he couldn't hear. Knowing it was too late.

"Scream away, lady. No one around to rescue you," the monster boomed.

On the other side of the archway, Dead-Eyes Gunter, his face battered and swollen, grabbed Ian and slapped him into a full nelson.

Every protective instinct in her howled. She kicked like a bucking mule.

A third man, the man she'd seen in the shadows of the Istanbul cistern, stepped into view. He looked massive, silver hair glinting in the sunlight. Hard lines etched his full face.

"So, Nicole Phillips. The name is Helmut Meier. We meet at last." His voice reverberated above her winded breathing.

The monster's arms grappled her tighter to his rock-hard chest.

She couldn't move. "I can't say it's a pleasure."

"Oh, but it is, my dear. An exquisite pleasure."

"Release my brother before he blacks out." Her traitor voice trembled, but bite hardened her words.

The Viper nodded to Dead-Eyes Gunter.

The bruised man released his pressure around Ian's neck. One evil eye was blackened.

Blood flowed back into Ian's chalky face.

"Take them to the watchtower," Silver-haired Helmut Meier ordered.

The way the giant man issued orders and the immediate obedience the other two men showed, convinced Nicole. "You're the Viper." Josh had mentioned his name by accident and asked her to forget it. She slammed her lips closed.

"Yes, my dear. In some circles I'm known as the Viper. Astute of you to recognize me." He nodded to the monster dangling her in his arms. "Franz."

Monster Franz carried her through the weed-filled Keep toward the still-standing watchtower. Dead-Eyes Gunter, lugging Ian, followed. Her heart pierced her. She'd failed to get Ian to safety. With Dead-eyes Gunter hauling Ian like a rag doll, her brother looked so battered, so helpless. What could she have done differently? Brun obviously hadn't taken care of the Viper. Nor Franz, the monster who manhandled her.

Monster Franz forced her, step-by-step, across a narrow wall. Her heart skittered. A false footstep would send her hurtling twenty feet to the bottom. Safe on the other side, he hauled her up the broken stairs that circled the tower's exterior. She fought Monster Franz, but her efforts felt feeble against the man's enormous strength.

"Gott! Quit kicking." He flung her over his shoulder and toted her like a sack of potatoes up two flights of stairs.

Blood pooled inside her head, and she beat his back and legs until her fists ached.

He didn't so much as grunt or take an extra breath.

Dead-Eyes Gunter shoved Ian's hands up behind his shoulder blades and forced him forward.

Ian grunted with pain.

Nicole winced, feeling his pain more than her own stomachache smashed against Monster Franz's hard shoulder.

Breathing normally after the hard climb, Monster Franz lowered her until her toes brushed stone, then dragged her inside the third floor of the tower. He wrapped one iron arm around her neck and the other around her waist.

She fought for breath. Far below, through ancient archer slits cut into the stone wall, large, wide emptiness glared up. Steps led up to a narrow ledge that circled the room. Floor-to-ceiling windows were spaced at intervals along the ledge where soldiers must have catapulted firebrands down on invading armies. Her heart hammered. Would she and Ian die here?

Daggers of horror fired her nerves.

The Viper nodded toward the center arched window. "Franz, escort Mrs. Phillips to the opening."

She couldn't see Monster Franz's face, but his response galvanized his body. He tightened his hold and lifted her effortlessly.

She grabbed spurts of breath as he carried her up the steps and onto the ledge. He loosened his grip, and she slid down until her seeking toes touched stone.

"Show Mrs. Phillips the view," the silver-haired Viper ordered.

Monster Franz pushed her forward until her head and shoulders jutted outside the floor-to-ceiling window. Her throat constricted. Hundreds of feet straight down jagged rocks protruded from rough ground. She hadn't realized the tower overlooked a sheer mountainside. If Monster Franz dropped her, she would be dashed to death on the rocks.

Monster Franz held her teetering on the edge.

Ian fought Gunter with all his ability. He had to free Nikki. Fear for her pumped his adrenaline, giving him super-human strength. It wasn't enough. Gunter forced him to his knees. Pain from a double hammerlock shot through him. A muscular knee hit him just below the chin and forced his head up. He battled pain and dizziness. He couldn't black out now.

The massive silver-haired man turned toward him. "Talk."

Ian had no need for signing. He read the word on Silver-Hair's thin lips. On the ledge above Silver-Hair, Nikki—spunky, beautiful Nikki—struggled against Monster Man's arms, her toes braced against the window ledge, gazing over her shoulder at him. The sun bronzed the gold in her hair and glinted on the fear in her wide eyes.

His insides quivered as they had not done all during his captivity. "What do you want to know?" he yelled.

Silver-Hair let Ian read his lips. He stood so close Ian smelled his foul breath. "What's the secret of the map?"

Ian had no choice. Nothing was as precious as Nikki's life. "The map shows a secret underground tunnel which leads from the outside of the Topkapi Museum into Sultan Ahmet's throne room." How much should he say? He had to think smart or they'd throw Nikki over the rampart!

"Ah! Yes. Just so. How do I get inside?"

Ian almost heard the satisfaction in Silver-Hair's voice from the way the man reacted. Rage choked him. He pushed it aside. No time for emotion. He had to save Nikki. Think. He must think. But the drugs turned his mind into mush.

"Go on. Where is this tunnel?"

"The tunnel door can only be opened from the inside—for the sultan's escape in case invaders broke through the castle. From inside, he could take with him the most valuable of his collection."

Ian stalled, buying time. A plan. A way of escape. Three to two and they were giants. He could think of only one way out.

"And the doorway is?" Silver-Hair pressed.

"The hour hand atop the watch on the Topkapi dagger points to a jade sailing ship."

"Yes, yes. Makes sense. Stop stalling and get on with it."

Monster Man shoved Nicole further out until her toes dangled over empty space. Her mouth opened in a scream.

"The ship's prow, in turn, points toward the hour hand of the watch."

"Astute. And?"

Ian gazed into Silver-Hair's cold grey eyes. Would the man kill them? Absolutely. "I'll reveal the exact spot where the secret lever to open the door is located after you release my sister and see she's given a car and an hour's head start. You'll kill us both when you learn the secret, so I'm not talking until Nikki's safely gone. I've nothing to lose."

Monster Man cursed and pushed Nikki until she squirmed against him and wrapped her ankles around his legs, clinging to him. Ian's heart pounded in his throat. Despite the agonizing pain Dead-Eyes exerted on his arms and shoulders, he refused to blurt the secret. Nikki's life—

All eyes shot to the door. He turned.

CHAPTER FORTY

Nicole pulled in her first deep breath.

"Well, what have we here?"

"Kolya," Relief washed through her. Her feet hit the solid rock floor. Shock must have loosened Monster Franz's hold on her. She wiggled free, raced across the ledge and down the stairs to the detective.

He opened his arms, and she fell into them. Then he tightened his grip until she could barely breathe against his chest.

"I told you I want the girl, Helmut," Kolya pressed a hot kiss against her forehead. "Did you plan to inform me she'd had an accident?" His voice sounded harsh. "And, the information the lad just relayed, did you plan to withhold from me as well?"

Like a lightening ice storm, Nicole's skin turned frigid. She tried to push away, but the detective tightened his grip on her wrists. She searched his face. Smug. Sure of himself. Grey eyes alight. "What's wrong with you? Why are you acting so strange?" she choked. A sense of betrayal seeped through her.

"You don't remember me, do you?" Kolya smiled.

Icicles drenched her heart. "No." Against Josh's admonitions, she'd trusted Kolya. She'd let him track her all the way here.

"Your late husband, Paul Phillips, God rest his back-stabbing soul, was my pilot. Until he stole my map." Kolya's smile turned grim.

She struggled against the detective's grip. "No. You're wrong. My husband worked for Nathan Parker. An elderly man, effeminate ..." Her words trailed away. Realization trickled over her. Nikolai Pavlik, Kolya, Nathan Parker or whatever his name, was a master of disguise.

Kolya dropped his voice to a rasping tremor. "Your late husband smuggled antiquities for me until he developed sticky fingers."

Her knees went weak. "You killed Paul?"

Kolya's words stung with sarcasm. "Sorry, my dear, but yes. So sad."

"But there was no body at the crash site."

"Simple, my dear. Bullets in a corpse makes a crash appear suspicious. The wreckage burned the area as I planned. I disposed of the remains elsewhere. You understand."

"But why did you kill Paul?"

"He stole my map. The map Phillips, suspecting his death, passed to your brother."

Paul, a smuggler. Nicole shook her head, not able to take in the truth. Yet, deep down her intuition quivered an affirmative. His lengthy absences. His vagueness about his business. His reluctance to include her.

"I staked out you and your brother at your late parents' home for months. My men searched your house time and again but couldn't find the map. Your brother hid the treasure too well. Unfortunate for him."

Puzzle pieces fell into place. The times she'd entered the house experiencing the eerie sensation of being followed. The strange static on the telephone and the many hang-ups. She'd chalked her suspicions up to nerves from Paul's crash.

"Professor Alexandros, God rest his trusting soul, arranged your brother's archaeological job in Turkey. I knew Ian McKenzie would bring the map with him when he came. I also knew with his brilliant mind he couldn't resist solving the cryptograph before he turned the map over to the authorities. Your brother still has explaining to do, you understand." The triumphant eyes shifted to the dead-eyed man restraining Ian. "Gunter!"

Dead-Eyes Gunter jerked Ian straight.

Ian grunted in pain.

Kolya, gripping her wrists like a strait jacket, yanked her with him until he stood a hand's width from Ian.

As Dead-Eyes Gunter held Ian still, Kolya thrust his face into Ian's. "Now, I promise not to kill pretty Nicole." The detective caressed her cheek with a smooth hand. "I've waited far too long for her, you understand."

Kolya's smooth voice turned deadly. "McKenzie, you've told me enough. I too, am brilliant, you see. The secret lever is at the exact spot where the two points intersect." His chiseled features glowed. "At the time of the sultans, the eighty-four carat Spoonmaker diamond was displayed in the center wall. The diamond is no longer there. So, I need only visualize the place where the gem hung to find the secret lever."

Even though Ian hid the shock Kolya's hypothesis evoked, he was too late.

Both Kolya and the Viper chortled. Kolya pulled her close. His savage lips crushed her mouth.

Ian growled, "Leave my sister alone."

She heard him fight to free himself from Dead-Eyes Gunter. She knew he struggled uselessly. When Kolya finally raised his mouth, she felt violated. Dirty.

Kolya smirked at Ian. "So, we know the secret. Unfortunate for you, you understand." Kolya nodded toward Dead-Eyes Gunter. His voice betrayed no emotion. "Gunter toss the lad from the rampart window."

Dead-Eyes Gunter hauled Ian over to the stairs.

SHADOW OF THE DAGGER

Nicole watched the muscular killer drag her fighting brother up the stairs toward the narrow ledge. Caught in a time warp and Kolya's arms, she couldn't breathe.

"Not so fast, Gunter," a new voice called.

CHAPTER FORTY-ONE

Nicole grabbed a breath of air.

Josh's smooth baritone rang out through the tower. "Can we be certain Pavlik guessed the puzzle? Why not keep the boy alive until we put our hands on the secret lever? What's a few more days?"

Kolya turned, enabling her to see around his shoulder. Josh stood outside the door of the tower room, legs spread, cool and unperturbed, a half-smile on his lips.

"So, we are all here." Kolya dropped one of her wrists, flashed his hand under his jacket and drew a gun, aiming the weapon at Josh.

Josh raised his hands but stood easily, a smile playing on his lips.

The Viper spoke from his spot near Kolya. "He's okay, Pavlik. Come in Flyboy."

Josh lowered his hands, strode into the room, and faced Kolya, so close if the kidnapper hadn't gripped her so tightly, she could have touched Josh. He brought a burst of dazzling hope to her heart. But how had he found her?

"Major Baruch, because he loves my wife, has accepted stolen artifacts and passed them to an Iraqi go-between." The silver-haired Viper clapped Josh on the shoulder. "Thanks to Suzanne, Baruch's one of us."

Nicole's heart stopped. Viper's words had to be true. Only the Viper and Brun had known where Ian was imprisoned. For Josh to find them here ... he had to be part of the gang.

The black day darkened as if a Texas norther had blown in. Hope flickered from a tiny ray of light, then sputtered out. Josh, one of the kidnappers. That *was* why the thugs wanted Josh with her. Her heart solidified to ice. And she'd loved him.

But she wouldn't let Josh see her anguish. She wouldn't let him see how much the Viper's words, about him loving his former-sister-in-law, hurt. She jerked in Kolya's grip and, despite her resolve, screamed at Josh, "You deceitful Judas!"

CHAPTER FORTY-TWO

Nicole screamed again and kicked and squirmed against Kolya's iron grip. The master of disguise, diverted by her actions, lost his concentration on Josh.

Josh wrenched her wrist free from Kolya's grasp, pushed her behind him, and using Kolya as a shield, protected her from the other three men.

Her heart roller-coasted to her throat and back.

Josh wrestled Kolya's gun hand up until Kolya's gun touched his own temple.

Her entire being thrilled. Josh. Saving her. How could she have doubted him? Because she'd feared he did love his beautiful former-sister-in-law, and she'd accepted appearances rather than hard facts. Josh had proven, over and over, he was on her side.

But they weren't free yet. From the corner of her eye, she glimpsed the Viper slithering up the steps to where Dead-Eyes Gunter still held Ian. "Josh ... Ian," she pointed.

While Dead-Eyes Gunter still fastened Ian's arms, the Viper seized Ian's neck in a choke hold, pulled a curved dagger from under his suitcoat and pressed the blade against Ian's throat.

Ian, held tight by both men, widened his expressive eyes. He yelled, "Go! Get away! Leave me!"

"Let Kolya go," the Viper ordered, drawing the knife across Ian's throat, trailing a thin streak of red.

"Free Ian or Kolya dies," Josh thundered and tightened his index finger over the trigger.

"Leaving me the entire fortune," Viper gloated. The greed lines in his face hardened.

Before her eyes, the crook transformed from Kolya's underling to his boss. "Think I care about Kolya's life? I've got the map and the answer to the cryptogram." He sneered. "This kid and I are walking out of here. The rest of you, drop your weapons, and fall on your faces."

"Ah, Helmut, what a Viper you are. Not!" Kolya grimaced. "I knew one day you would stand up to me." Sweat dripped from the master of disguise's forehead. He brushed at the gun barrel at his temple.

Josh held the weapon firm.

"I planned ahead for your betrayal, you understand." Kolya gloated.

The Viper stopped.

Kolya attempted to sidle away from Josh's gun.

Josh pressed the barrel behind Kolya's ear, bent Kolya's arm behind the stocky master of disguise, and anchored him in place.

Respect for Josh's coolness burned inside Nicole. What a hero. That the two leading kidnappers fought each other for the treasure didn't surprise her. Both men lived only for themselves.

"Meier, that export-import business of yours," Kolya continued, "that beautiful estate, and that exquisite wife of yours …" He laughed. "… all, all revert to my son in the event of my death." Kolya twisted in Josh's grasp trying to escape the gun.

Josh held him steady.

"You signed the papers yourself. Pity you never learned Russian, Meier."

The Viper's mouth dropped open.

Relief flooded Nicole.

The carved dagger went slack, and Viper-Meier's hand fell to his side, releasing Ian.

Ian straightened, relief on his face.

She frowned and stepped toward Dead-Eyes Gunter, who still wrestled Ian's hands behind his back.

"Gunter, release Ian!" she commanded, her voice only trembling slightly.

Josh ordered, "All you goons drop your weapons." To show he meant business, he tightened his trigger-finger on the gun he pressed to Kolya's temple.

Both Dead-Eyes Gunter and Monster Franz flicked their gazes to the Viper. The silver-haired giant nodded. But with his massive hands clenching and unclenching and his expression blazing a warning, he looked far from surrender.

Dead-Eyes Gunter released Ian.

Rubbing his arms, Ian inched behind Dead-Eyes Gunter and the silver-haired Viper and lurched from the ledge down the stone stairs.

Dead-Eyes Gunter, Monster Franz, and the silver-haired Viper each laid his gun on the stone floor.

Nicole released a long breath. She still feared the men would jump Josh.

"Back against the wall. Turn, face it, hands on the wall," Josh ordered master of disguise Kolya and Monster Franz. He nodded to the Viper and Dead-Eyes Gunter. "You two walk down and face the wall next to Pavlik."

If looks could kill, the four men would have buried Josh. Each shuffled to a place against the ancient bricks.

Keeping his gun trained on the four men, Josh said, "Nicole tell Ian to search them."

Nicole faced Ian. She signed and said, "Please search the kidnappers."

Ian picked up the guns lying on the floor and frisked the men.

Nicole moved toward the men, intending to help Ian.

"Not you, Angel." Josh knelt and scooped up the Viper's gun. He held a weapon in each hand. "You stay behind me."

Ian patted Kolya's tailored suit. Ian discovered a cache of knives and wicked-looking guns still hidden on the four big men. Unarmed, the massive men still looked dangerous. Ian's slenderer frame appeared boyish beside them. Even Josh looked small in comparison. She couldn't believe Josh had subdued, unarmed, and outsmarted all four men.

"How did you find me, Josh?" She took two of the guns Ian handed her.

"Later, Angel. I'll tell you everything I know. Pick up as many of their weapons as you can carry."

She and Ian collected the rest of the guns lying on the tower floor. She yearned to hug Ian but resisted as he trained his guns on the four men.

Josh gathered the weapons and poked them into his belt, Ian's and hers. "Angel, sign for Ian to take you down the mountain. Go for help. Incirlik's the closest place." The protective love in his dark eyes melted her heart.

"You'll find an SUV parked half a mile from the graveled area on the back side of the mountain. Before you leave, grab my wallet from my pants pocket. ID's inside. Drive to Incirlik Air Base and telephone at the guard check point for General Galloway. I'll hold these thugs until you send reinforcements."

She glanced at Ian. From the determined look squaring his jaw, he'd read Josh's lips. Resolve fired her as well. "We can't leave you here alone, Josh. It's four against one, and I don't trust any of these jerks."

"Just go, Angel. I—"

"I'm staying. Nikki, go and—" Ian started to protest.

Footsteps interrupted, clattering on the stone floor behind them. Men dressed in camouflage fatigues carrying M-16 rifles burst into the tower. Josh's eyebrows rose.

"What the—"

"Appears we're just in time, Major." A young Air Force lieutenant trained his rifle on the quartet of criminals. "Search and Rescue here."

A sliver of disappointment slashed through Nicole's relief. The three of them could have managed to transport Kolya and his men to jail.

Josh slanted an eyebrow at the lieutenant but held his guns on the criminals. "How'd you know we were here?"

"Squinty little guy with glasses flew in an hour ago by helicopter. Claimed he was CIA. Said he's been tailing you since you left the States. Saw everyone headed to this castle and thought you might need help. Seems he was wrong." The young face under the blue military beret grinned. "CIA said they were chasing the intelligence behind the Viper. One of these guys him?"

Satisfaction energized Josh's voice, "Yeah. We got him." Josh shoved the gun against Kolya's back. "That's him." He motioned to the silver-haired Meier, "And the Viper."

"CIA?" Nicole squeaked. She would lose her cool if she didn't get some answers.

CHAPTER FORTY-THREE

Later that night after a shower and a short nap, Nicole gazed with avid curiosity at the two men she loved best. Seated with her inside a Turkish restaurant, Josh and Ian lounged on bright red pillows before a low table. Colorful, thick carpet cushioned her feet. Background Turkish music teased her ears. From their upstairs window, she could see across the street where four armed Turkish soldiers guarded the entrance gate to Incirlik Air Base. For the first time since she'd arrived in Turkey, she felt secure.

Josh must have noticed her gaze.

"Although you and Ian can't go on base without a military ID, someday, I'll take you there." His grin looked confident and relaxed. And handsome.

"Soon. I want to see what those soldiers guard." She sipped her water then leaned forward. "Tonight, I need answers. Start at the beginning. Ian, how did you get the map Paul stole?"

Ian nodded. "Paul came to the house the night before Meier murdered him. Nikki, he handed me a book and told me to take care of it. I thought that odd since Paul wasn't a reader. As soon as he left, I leafed through it." Ian smiled grimly. "I found the map tucked between the pages and recognized its value." He fingered the roughened rope burns around his wrist as he talked. "Paul had attached a note saying his employer, Nathan Parker—or Kolya as you know him—would kill to get the map."

Ian's hands appeared steady as he signed his words while he spoke. Happiness settled in. The drugs the kidnappers gave her brother had worn off.

"Paul had slipped me the map because he suspected he was in danger." Ian looked tired, but relaxed. "After the plane crash the next day, I hid the map. I didn't know Paul had stolen it. Didn't figure him for a thief."

"But Kolya said he searched our house many times."

"Right, Nikki. I'd taped the map to my chest. I planned to hand it over to the police, but after the job offer from Professor Alexandros to work the dig in Antalya, I decided to return the map to the Turkish authorities." He gave her a crooked grin. "Then I couldn't resist solving the cryptogam. I never thought I'd put you in danger."

Ian's blue eyes beamed repentance.

Nicole leaned over and hugged him. And with her arms around his dear shoulders, she had to kiss his cheek. Could she ever bear to have him out of her sight again?

He coughed, tried to free himself and generally appeared uncomfortable.

She let him go.

The waiter arrived with ekmek and honey. They dipped their bread and ate like starving POWs. Nicole didn't know what she hungered for more, food or answers. She licked honey from the tips of her fingers.

To center her thoughts, she gazed at the Turkish wall hangings and the swag lamp lighting their secluded nook, then turned to Josh. Shadows circled his eyes, but unlike Ian, ruddy color flushed his face with health. She wanted to caress Josh's lean cheek and press her lips to his so very inviting ones. Instead, she concentrated on fitting the puzzle pieces together. She took a deep breath. "I don't understand your part in all this, Josh."

Josh looked as if his mind lingered elsewhere. "This whole business started a long time ago. While Suzanne and Scott were married." He sighed. "Meier ... known to you as the Viper, offered me a job. He wanted me to deliver certain mosaics to Iraq. Stolen ones. Just stow them aboard my plane before a routine training flight at Incirlik and hand them over to a fence who'd wait for me at a landing field in Jordan. Easy, safe, lucrative, and very illegal. I declined."

Josh lifted the tiny cup at his right hand and sipped his strong coffee as if he needed the caffeine. He rubbed his forehead and frowned as if he weren't happy with himself. "Soon after, Meier murdered Scott. But I had no proof except Meier had promised to hurt me if I didn't work for him. Then he married my sister-in-law." Josh pinched the bridge of his nose and narrowed his eyes. "I had to get revenge. Justice, I called it. I investigated Meier and discovered he ran many illegal Turkish artifacts through Jordan, which freed them to go from there to European markets." Josh's intense brown eyes gazed into hers.

She loved how his gold-flecked eyes, outlined with dark lashes any woman would envy, were so masculine. The expression in them brooded. Was he unsure she understood his motives? Did he understand them himself?

"I was about to turn Meier over to the Turkish authorities when I discovered he used his profits to buy weapons from Russia and sell them to Third World countries. To some fanatic splinter group intent on terrorism."

He leaned toward her, face tight.

Her stomach quivered at the steadfastness in his scrutiny.

"This international arms trade landed Meier under the heading of CIA business. But I had no proof against him. Anyone who possessed hard facts against Meier ended up dead."

"After seeing the man face to face, I believe he's ruthless." Enormous relief flooded her knowing the military had flown the four men to a secure federal prison. "He'd let nothing stand in his way. I'm glad I didn't know how easily he killed when we were searching for Ian."

"Yeah. I didn't think that knowledge would let you get so high on the cloak and dagger stuff." For a moment Josh grinned and seemed his old self.

"Nikki's always liked intrigue." Ian leaned forward, his face alight with interest as he read Josh's lips, then hers.

"Go on. If you had nothing to tell the CIA, how did they become involved?" Nicole bounced on her seat.

"When the report arrived at my CIA Station at Langley specifying the authorities suspected an art dealer headed Ian's kidnapping, gut level intuition told me Meier plotted the scheme. I wanted to nail him."

His eyes looked warm as melted chocolate, but something indefinable stirred behind them. Something was cooking. What? He'd said— Then it hit her. "*Your* CIA Station at Langley?" Her stomach dropped.

"Yeah." Josh cocked an eyebrow. "You just received Top Secret Clearance with this knowledge. Don't leak it."

Her mouth fell open. "You're with the CIA?"

"Wow, Central Intelligence Agency!" Ian pumped a fist in the air.

"Shush. I'm an analyst. A desk jockey. Nothing dangerous."

"But you said you were Search and Rescue." No wonder Josh was so knowledgeable, so steady under pressure, so ... able.

"I am. Two weeks to a month out of the year. Air Force. Reserve status. I never lied to you, Angel." His even, white teeth flashed.

"Just misled me."

He nodded. "I had to. I joined the CIA after Meier murdered Scott. I wanted to be an agent, but the Agency assigned me to analysis. I had to keep my CIA identity secret. We all do. Only close family are told." His eyes lit with eagerness. "I've made a decision."

Nicole realized Josh was no longer preoccupied. In fact, he quivered with enthusiasm. Was she ready to hear what he wanted to share? She needed more answers first. "You never worked for the Viper?"

"Never." His hand folded over hers.

"But after we separated at the crash, how did you find us at the castle? I was certain the Viper gave you directions. How else could you have found us? Only he and Brun knew where they imprisoned Ian." She thought a second. "And Stepp. But he's dead."

Josh chuckled. "Lieutenant Stanley of Search and Rescue mentioned a squinty little CIA guy who arrived in a helicopter. He was the man you and I christened *Ducky.*"

At her blank look, he explained. "You remember, the man we kept running into at Istanbul. Glasses. Loud shirt. Waddled like a duck."

A light bulb glowed. "You're kidding. He's CIA?"

Josh flashed his lady-killer grin. "Yeah. The day I left Langley for Istanbul, my fellow analyst and friend, Hal, also read Ian's kidnapping bulletin. Hal knew I wasn't due to report to Incirlik for another three months. So, he multiplied two times two."

"Brilliant."

"No, it's just what analysts do. Analyze. Anyway, Hal went to our Director of Intelligence and voiced his suspicions. Our DI hotfooted it over to covert operations, and they informed my director they had Meier under surveillance and were expecting him to lead them to the mind above the Viper. They didn't want me to snag the net." He squeezed her hand. "To keep me from flat-heading their plan, they sicced Ducky, aka CIA Agent Joe Grimes, on my tail."

He frowned and some of his high color faded. "When I lost you after the smash-up in Antalya, I spied this Ducky character loitering near the wreck, grabbed him by the shirt collar and smashed him against a stone wall, certain he must have seen where you'd gone."

"Ducky spilled his guts. Told me he was CIA, and he saw you hop into a black BMW with some huge bruiser, and you'd headed east." Josh shook his head and a haunted expression settled on his face.

He looked as lost as she'd felt when she'd left him.

"I was fuming. And worried sick." He gulped his coffee. "I *borrowed* the SUV from an uncooperative bystander and gunned it after you. Never spotted the BMW until ..." He stopped.

From across the low table, he caressed her hand with gentle fingers. "You sure you want to know?"

"Certain."

"About ten miles west of Toprakkale Castle, just before the land plateaus out, I found the BMW at the bottom of the last cliff. The thug sat behind the wheel, a bullet in his forehead."

She stifled a cry, then whispered, "Brun."

"Whatever his name was, yeah." Josh hurried on. "I didn't know which way to head to find you. So, I trekked back up to the road and studied the car tracks. Skid marks and knocked-down bushes indicated the car had come from the east, from the direction of Adana. Didn't make sense. Why would the brute have turned around? And why had he been shot?"

She could picture him standing alone on the cliff, the wheels spinning inside his head. And from his bleak expression, realized he'd been devastated.

For her.

"I knew the Viper's MO was to kill anyone who stood in his way, so this guy had to have taken you somewhere the Viper didn't want you to be. Where, but to your brother?" He swallowed as if remembering was torturous.

"Okay, so I was on top of that hill and I looked east, in the direction the dead man had come from, and saw the mountain rising out of the plain with the ruins on top. I'd visited the castle last year during my annual training and figured the out-of-the-way spot could be a prison. So, I gunned it up there praying I'd gone to the right place ... and I wasn't too late." His expression told her he'd been frantic.

"Great analyzing!" Ian clapped Josh on the back.

Josh grinned. "Didn't take any major deduction to figure you and Nicole might be inside the castle."

The waiter brought steaming dishes of savory Turkish food.

Josh and Ian ate like lumberjacks.

She picked up her spoon, thinking over what Josh had said. "But the Viper told Kolya you were one of them."

"Sorry." Josh wiped his mouth with his napkin. "When I met Suzanne at the Topkapi she gave me an authentic Hittite Lion Statuette, which Meier wanted me to pass to his fence in Antalya. I took it to prove I accepted Suzanne's proposition of my working for Meier in exchange for your and Ian's lives."

Her stomach clenched. "Did you give the artifact to the crook in Antalya?"

"No. I passed off a copy I picked up when we ran through the bazaar. The real one is priceless and belongs in a Turkish museum." Josh started eating again.

"Why did Kolya believe the Viper when he claimed you were one of his men?" She remembered the depth of blackness she'd felt.

"Crooks think anyone can be bought. A man who can't, staggers their mind." He winked. "Besides, I used that little microphone you slipped into my wallet. In Antalya, I left a message on Meier's answering machine telling him I'd handed over the statue. I made sure the microphone overheard my words."

"Microphone? Not a bug." She no longer felt hungry.

"Yeah."

"But why did the kidnappers want you with me?" She toyed with her grape leaves stuffed with ground lamb.

"Part of my bargain in the Istanbul cisterns. They told me if I delivered you to Antalya, they wouldn't take you." He grinned at Ian. "I stipulated Ian had to be kept alive and not minus any of his parts. Meier only trusted a few men for this job, and two of them were guarding Ian." He winked at her. "Viper kept us together, so we'd be easier to shadow."

Laying down his fork, he ran a hand through his short hair and leaned forward. "When Professor Alexandros's body washed up on the beach at Antalya, the CIA almost stepped in. But our old friend, Ducky, persuaded the chief I was their best chance at getting the mastermind above the Viper to come out of the closet. Kolya's clever. He blew this one, because he wanted you, Angel."

She shuddered. "I never knew it. And I trusted that man." Her cheeks burned. "Even when you advised me not to."

He hunched over, flashed her a villain's evil grin, and said in a mock hollow voice, "You must learn to trust me, Angel."

Ian laughed and asked, "Darth Vader or Count Dracula?"

"Sounds like Josh's rendering of the villain in the *Perils of Pauline*." Nicole looked fondly at the two men, folded her napkin, and laid it beside her plate.

Josh finished eating.

Ian leaned on his cushion and rubbed his belly. "That was good."

"You ate enough for three archaeologists." She grinned at Ian. "You need to gain back that weight you lost. Weren't you hungry, Josh?" She squeezed his hand to keep from smoothing the tired lines from Josh's face. "You took incredible chances for us. How can I thank you?"

"You can thank me later." He picked up the bill. "Right now, I've got to walk you two to your pensione. Ian looks ready to sleep standing up."

While Josh strode to the old-fashioned cash register, Nicole took advantage of Ian's semi-somnolent state, her mother hen instincts clucking. "Who is Vashti?"

CHAPTER FORTY-FOUR

Nicole waited.

Her question woke Ian. His color rose. "A girl who helped me when I was imprisoned by the Viper."

"Was she one of the kidnappers?"

Ian raked his fingers through his thick blond hair. "I don't know. She spelled words in my hand when I was blindfolded. We ... we connected." He blushed to the roots of his hair. "She gave me water and fed me." He fiddled with his spoon. "I don't think the men treated her well. I got the impression she didn't like the kidnappers. Then she must have left with the Viper. She never came back."

A vivid picture flashed through Nicole's memory. A beautiful innocent face with dark, compassionate eyes. Inside the Harem, the young girl who'd mesmerized the men with her seductive dance. Nicole almost blurted the belly dancer had belonged to Brun. Brun had betrayed his boss for Vashti.

She'd go over these things with Ian when he was better able to handle it. After he'd rested.

Josh returned and offered her a hand up from the cushions.

"Are you proficient locating missing people?" Ian asked Josh as he followed her and Josh to the door.

"I can access the CIA computer and locate anyone."

"I'd like to find a girl," Ian blushed.

Nicole recognized that dogged look on her brother's face before. When Ian determined to do something, he left no stone unturned until he uncovered his goal. His persistence would make him a good archaeologist.

She sighed. The girl at the Harem could prove to be a mighty complication. She'd just gotten Ian back and wasn't ready to surrender him to another woman, especially a girl connected to kidnappers, a Muslim who'd been intimate with that nasty Brun. A girl who made any man she wished turn into putty when she danced. With Ian's hearing problem, would the beautiful girl look at him twice? Most girls didn't after they discovered Ian's impairment.

"What do you think, Josh, can we find a girl named Vashti?" Ian persisted.

"When I get back to the Langley office, I'll check her out. Got a last name or is Vashti all you have?"

"That's it."

"Josh, the belly dancer. The guide called her Vashti." Nicole snapped her fingers. "I'm sure she must be the same girl."

"Yeah, okay. We'll start there."

They stopped at the door where Mujdat, the owner, stood holding a vial. He poured rose water over their hands and told them, "Go with God."

Outside, the night was black except for streetlights. They strolled the length of the balcony, down the steps, and into the balmy evening. Josh slipped his arm around her waist to guide her along the sidewalk. In the distance behind the guard post, the deafening thunder of jets flamed, as a fighter plane took off from the military runway.

"British Tornado," Josh identified the plane by sound.

In the silence following the jet's departure, a muezzin called Muslims to prayer. It was late and the street was empty. Their footsteps echoed in the stillness. Too soon, they reached the old pensione where she and Ian were spending the night. Tomorrow,

Josh would drive them to the Havaalani. If only she had more time with him, she could try again to tell him about the Lord.

When Josh returned to the states, he would fly to Washington DC. She and Ian would return to Dallas. Her thoughts wandered to the day they'd met. To the day he kissed her. That kiss had been more electric than any kiss she'd ever experienced—that sweet kiss in the moonlight.

"I'm off to bed." Ian smothered a huge yawn.

That had to be for Josh's benefit. Ian never yawned. Even when he was dead on his feet.

"See you two tomorrow. We'll be ready for you to drive us to the Havaalani by ten a.m." Ian's voice sounded suggestive.

Nicole grunted under her breath. Was Ian up to something?

"We'll land in Dallas in twelve hours."

Was Ian egging her into staying longer with Josh? Ian suffered from a huge case of hero worship. She'd never expected her brother to react that way.

"I'll be back in Langley, but I'll keep in touch." Josh shook Ian's hand, then the two men hugged.

"Night, Ian." She kissed his cheek and hugged him.

Ian took the spiral steps up, two at a time.

Her heart leaped, glad to have him safe. *Thank you, Lord.*

Ian's door closed.

Shop lights from the street cut shadows in Josh's face, making him appear aloof. She hesitated, new at this. Then blurted, "Would you like to come up? I have a quiet balcony overlooking a garden. I'll make coffee."

He took her arm and they started up the steps. "No coffee."

Her hand trembled as she inserted the key.

Josh shut the door behind them.

She switched on a table lamp, kicked off her ruined shoes, and padded through the bedroom to open the balcony door.

He followed her, so close she inhaled his after shave and felt the magnetism that made him so self-confident. She fought her overwhelming desire to nestle close to him.

Balmy air welcomed her. Moonlight spilled over the railing and played games on the empty balcony. The sky shimmered with tiny points of starlight. She was as nervous as a teenager on a first date. How could she say goodbye? To break the silence, she teased, "Do you fly to the stars?"

"Not that high. But they seem close." His voice sounded husky. "I'll take you up for a moonlight ride. You'll see."

Was promise in his voice? With each breeze, the scent of gardenias wafted to her. Next door in Ian's room, a radio played a love song. "Ian, acting the matchmaker," she whispered.

"Jews use matchmakers. High success rate." He stepped closer and slipped his arms around her.

She twined her arms around his neck. "Ian's my only family, so he's protective and responsible."

"I think he's willing to pass on his responsibility." Josh ran his fingers through her hair, leaving her feeling electrified.

"My family's big enough for both of us. Aunts, uncles, cousins. They'll love you."

His tender voice reached to the deepest responses of her heart. Spoke to her innermost being. She mouthed the question, hardly daring to breathe, "Love me?" She tingled all over.

"I do. Angel, I fell in love with you at the Havaalani. The first moment I saw you."

Her world exploded into the brightest future she could envision. She adored the firm curve of his lips. But ...

"The minute you walked into the airport, you walked right into my heart." He unclasped the necklace he wore and placed his Jewish letters spelling *To Life* around her neck. Then he cupped her face in one strong hand and tilted it. She delighted in his moonlit eyes. But ...

"When I fall in love, it lasts forever. I'm a forever kind of guy, Angel. And I love you." He traced her mouth with a gentle finger.

She thrilled at his words ... and to his touch. She cherished his touch. But ...

He nuzzled her neck. She loved the invigorating masculine smell of him. And his warm lips. But ...

When he pulled away, he smiled his oh-so-devastating smile and slid to one knee. "I'm an old-fashioned kind of guy." He took her hand. "I'm looking for one faithful wife, a house somewhere between Dallas and Virginia and as many children as we can afford. I love you. Will you do me the honor of becoming my wife?"

Reality hit her so hard it stole her breath. She couldn't marry Josh. No matter how much she wanted to. "I ... I can't." Slivers of pain bit into her heart.

"Can't or won't?" Tension stiffened his face.

"Can't. As a Christian, my Father God forbids me to become yoked with unbelievers. You do not accept my Savior, so I can't marry you." Would her shattered heart ever mend?

He relaxed and grinned. That special lady-killer grin of his. "I wasn't ready to share with you yet. Something so personal. But we want to start this journey together with honesty."

Hope fluttered in her heart.

He cleared his throat. "I'd been thinking since I met you, I had to forgive my sister-in-law and get on with my life. But what she did ... divorcing Scott hurt too much. I couldn't. I still wanted my revenge against Meier, but that dissolved with the need to find Ian." He stood.

Hope fluttered in her mind.

"From the beginning, I saw in you a woman I trusted, loyal and not motivated by greed, and a woman with the same dreams for family I'd given up. Your faith guided me like a directional VOR guides an airplane to a safe landing." He released her enough to gaze into her eyes. "And you had something else ... undefinable ... elusive. I didn't know what it was until you told me of your God. Then I knew. A personal God, my Messiah. I'd been searching all my life. I mulled over everything you said as we drove to Antalya." He drew her close and traced her features with a gentle finger. "Your words have been an undercurrent in my thoughts since I met you."

"Then when you disappeared, and I found the wrecked BMW with the dead man ... I was afraid you'd been hurt."

She felt the shudder pass through his body.

"There at the top of the cliff, I knelt and cried out to God."

His arms were a fortress surrounding her. Tears pricked her eyelids.

"I prayed for your safety. Then I opened my heart and life to Messiah. I experienced joy and peace. Even before I knew you were safe."

Moonlight glinted on the tears pooled in his eyes.

She could gaze into his eyes forever.

He kissed her.

His warm, tender mouth sent electric shocks through her. She had trouble thinking. Her thoughts scrambled. But she had to tell him. "I guess I'm a bit slower. I didn't realize I loved you until I abandoned you at the car wreck. I never wanted to leave you. I felt I left part of myself."

"Then never leave me again. You brought meaning into my life. And healing. I've seen you thinking of others. I've seen you risk your life for someone you love."

She ran her fingers through his dark hair as she had wanted to for so long. Then stroked the back of his just-right neck and caressed his unbelievable shoulders. She loved to feel the strength of him. "And you, my love, risked your life for Ian and me. How could I not love you?"

He tipped his head with tantalizing slowness and met her lips again.

She'd read of kisses being sweet, of tasting like nectar and honey. But his! His left a trail of sweetness mixed with the licorice scent of anise seeds on her lips. His kiss warmed a path straight to her heart making it swell with love. His full, warm lips tasted like home.

She never wanted to leave home. "Fireworks." Lights exploded inside her head with her eyes wide open gazing into his.

"Yeah. I know what you mean. For me too," he whispered. "One thing though. No more secrets between us." He pulled her into his broad chest.

"No more secrets."

He knelt again in front of her and took her hand. "Will you be my wife?"

"Yes. Oh, yes."

He rose and tugged her into his arms.

She kissed his so-kissable mouth again. "Yes. I want more than anything in the world to be your wife." His heart hammered. How she loved his heart. "But I believe in long engagements."

He frowned. "How long?"

"Long enough to make certain."

He kissed her, short and sweet. "How long is that?"

"A year?"

He fingered the hair around her ear, sending delicious prongs of anticipation through her. "You're worth waiting for."

She reconsidered. "Maybe six months."

"I'll wait as long as you want." He nuzzled her ear. "You're one in a million. I can't believe I found you."

"And so are you." She whispered, "Have you forgiven Suzanne?"

"When I've been forgiven so much, how could I not?" His face looked so relaxed. His mouth caressed hers in a way that sent delicious shivers through her. When he pulled away, she wanted more.

"You know what else?" he asked.

"There's more?"

"I'm no longer an outsider. There's no fence between me and other people. Between me and Christians. Between me and God."

"And not between you and me," she added. Joy sloshed over her heart and warmed her soul. Could anything be more perfect? Or make her happier?

"My DI thinks I should go covert, become an agent."

Shock waves bounced her to her senses from where they'd been scattered to the heavens.

"An agent? Undercover? Get the bad guy?" Her heart beat faster. The idea held enormous appeal. "I could help. Be another Amanda Greene, Detective, except I'd be Nicole Phillips, Archeologist/Detective. CIA Assistant."

"Yeah. But you'd be real and she's fictitious. Nicole Baruch, AD."

"I'll think about it," she teased, already planning their first case. She and Josh would ransack Turkey for the missing Vashti.

Dear Reader,

I hope you enjoyed *Shadow of the Dagger* as much as I loved writing about Josh, Nicole, and Ian. I'm certain you will enjoy my other stories.

I find it such a pleasure to speak with my readers. Please visit with me at www.AnneGreeneAuthor.com, and www.facebook.com/AnneWGreeneAuthor. You can also subscribe to my newsletter so we can keep in touch. I enjoy discovering what you think about my books.

Thank you for reading *Shadow of the Dagger*. Consider telling your friends or posting a short review on Amazon or Good Reads. Word of mouth is an author's best friend and much appreciated.

ANNE GREENE delights in writing about alpha heroes who aren't afraid to fall on their knees in prayer, and about gutsy heroines. Enjoy her *Women of Courage series* which spotlights heroic women of World War II, Book 1, *Angel With Steel Wings*. Read her *Holly Garden Private Investigating series, Handcuffed*

in Texas, Book 1, *Red Is For Rookie.* Enjoy her award-winning Scottish historical romances, *Masquerade Marriage* and *Marriage by Arrangement.* Anne's highest hope is that her stories transport you to an awesome new world and touch your heart to seek a deeper spiritual relationship with the Lord Jesus.

Visit with Anne at www.AnneGreeneAuthor.com, www.facebook.com/AnneWGreeneAuthor

ANNE W. GREENE

ENJOY CHAPTER ONE OF ANNE'S BOOK,
HOLLY GARDEN, PI: RED IS FOR ROOKIE

LET YOUR LIGHT SO SHINE BEFORE MEN THAT THEY MAY SEE YOUR GOOD WORKS AND GLORIFY YOUR FATHER IN HEAVEN.—MATTHEW 5:16 (NKJV)

CHAPTER ONE

"Ever notice that Cupid rhymes with stupid?" Hands jammed on my hips, I surveyed the five-star hotel ballroom decorated with porcelain cupids and scarlet hearts.

Here I was, Hollyhock Garden, clad in strappy, spiked heels, valentine-red dress, diamond earrings, and shaking knees … working undercover security. Hired by my mother—the same dear lady who saddled me with my name.

My friend, Temple Taylor, grinned at me, twin dimples in her milk-chocolate cheeks. "Only you would rhyme Cupid with stupid."

My heart stuttered. "Yeah, with me being stupid." I moved to the ballroom's center to watch the first trickle of invitees enter. To get my mind off my lost love, I quipped, "If only my fourth-grade Sunday school students could see their teacher now. They picture private investigating as dangerous."

Amusement flashed across Temple's exotic face. "That is sooo you! Your mom spins the world to make this Meet-a-thon happen—" Temple swept her arm to encompass the softly lit ballroom filled with white-clothed tables. "—melt-in-your-mouth chocolate hearts, glittery valentine cards, tables assigned according to professions for the eligible bachelors, and you want more excitement."

My left eye twitched like it does when I'm stressed. "Who'd have guessed Dallas had so many lonely executives? Thus, the need for tight security."

"Right. Not even the rich want to be dateless on Valentines."

My stomach flip-flopped. Dateless. "Rub it in."

To help me forget my own lack of a male love-of-my-life, I roved around the room reading a few of the designated professions etched on placards above centerpieces of roses and candles flagging each table. "This sign reads *Attorneys*. This one *Physicians*." I pointed. "That one's for *Architects*. And—"

"Honey, you can bet your white bod that this dinner bash beats a dating service."

"Yeah, for lonesome work-a-holics who don't have time to look for dates." I buried my nose in the sweet fragrance of a velvet-textured rose. "It's sad."

My friend gave a throaty laugh. "Sad nothing. Your mom's created a meet market. We can shop 'til we drop."

I gave Temple a *yeah, right* look. "Shop all you want. Tonight's strictly business for me."

Temple smiled with the same dimpled sincerity that gained her more friends than she could text in a single lunch hour. "You don't have to buy. Window shop. You look smashing in that red dress. It's time you stop languishing. This holiday's created for love. Make a new start."

I rolled my eyes. "New risk more like." Hugging myself to hide feelings of rejection still clinging to me from my last romantic venture, I shifted to the next table. "I'm here to work. Garden Investigations doesn't need any more bad publicity. A splashy robbery pulled off under our noses tonight would close our doors."

Temple tapped one of the table placards with a coral-tipped nail. "Hey, girl, I noticed your mom didn't invite any of your new spy-buddies from work."

"Just Matt. He's my backup tonight."

Matt Murdock, my next-door neighbor and life-long pal, had worked for Uncle Robert at Garden Investigations a year longer than I. After Dad's murder, Matt hovered over me like a too-protective brother. I liked working with the sweet nerd but hated him butting his nose into my non-existent date life.

Holding up my black sequined evening bag with its noticeable bulge, I joked, "What we don't need tonight is someone besides Matt and me packing weapons."

Temple's almond-shaped eyes twinkled. "What you need in that purse is lip gloss and Tommy Girl perfume."

I snorted. Even Temple wanted me to date. I shook my head until the few strands of hair framing my face tickled. I had yet to succeed in love, but I had high hopes for my shiny new career of detecting.

"What I need is a real client. Someone other than my mom. I need a case."

The seven-piece orchestra climbed the stairs to the small stage, settled behind their instruments, and began to warm up. With the first bars of a romantic song, a few smartly dressed men sauntered inside. They passed us and tossed Temple and me appraising glances. I squirmed in my high heels as several women in designer gowns glided in, their evening Jimmy Choo's shimmering against the blue carpet. *And these women are also dateless?* I made a wry face and scanned the growing crowd. Diamonds everywhere. They sparkled on long feminine necks, elegant wrists, and tiny ears. Gold came in second. This gala offered an open treasure chest. The only thing missing—a sign inviting pirates.

More and more men roamed into the room. Along with expensive aftershave, I almost smelled testosterone. Some wore tuxes, some dark suits. Most ambled toward their assigned tables, trying for the cool look, but appeared as uneasy as trapped lions. Some resembled cuddly, tux-suited bunnies with rounded tummies and others penguins with polished heads. A few simulated antelopes about to flee the watering hole. No warthogs to be seen.

I glanced toward the door. "Looks as if everyone's here. I better get with it." I sucked in my lack of theatrical presence and headed toward the stage.

Silently praying I wouldn't break my neck, I tottered up the three steps, crossed the strip of floor in front of the musicians, and clutched the hard sides of the glass lectern. Most days I wore jeans and tees, so I felt exposed in the short dress. Knees pasted together, I produced a smile and spoke into the microphone.

"Good evening."

My soft words boomed over the elegant crowd. I swallowed and prayed my voice wouldn't tremble. "Welcome. The Dallas Ladies Auxiliary is so pleased you accepted their invitation to this evening's Valentine Meet-a-thon." I wiped a clammy hand on my velvet-covered thigh and watched numerous men slink through the rose-scented room like robbers casing a glamorous bank.

"If the rest of you gentlemen will kindly find your seats, the ladies can begin making rounds." I took another breath and hurried through the rest of Mom's ridiculous instructions.

"Each lady will choose a seat next to a gentleman of her choice, dinner will be served, and if an interest sparks on either side, business cards will be exchanged." I pried one hand loose from the glass and waved it in what I hoped was a graceful, welcoming gesture. "Now, relax and enjoy your evening."

I again navigated the steps in my short dress and tricky shoes. Feeling inadequate to begin my first field job, I hit level ground and beelined to the pillar Temple stood beside. "How was that?"

"You did well …." Temple's smile looked encouraging.

I nodded, then blurted out what was uppermost in my mind. "You know what?" I scanned the crowd for problems and tried to erase the uncertainty from my face. "Sometimes, I think I'm crazy to become a Private Detective. How can I be a light while working in the sinful underbelly of society?"

Temple snorted. "Come on, Holly. "Don't look so upset. I believe in you."

"Yeah, but ... well, I've agonized about this job. Sometimes dirt rubs off."

"If a place is dark, even a flickering candle sheds a lot of light."

"You don't think the dark will douse the candle?"

"Not your candle."

"But what if I don't have what it takes?"

"Trust me. You do. Now, I'm off to dig for gold. You're on your own." Temple blew me an air kiss, waved a finger, and slipped past me to undulate, like a sun-blessed wave, among the tables. Her fifties-style, shimmering gold sheath caught every male eye. Men's faces acquired that stunned, slack-jawed look they got when they first gawked at Temple, no matter what outfit she wore. My friend wafted irresistible female pheromones. Males dug into tux pockets for business cards, stood, and flaunted them at her.

I leaned against the column. *Lord, please let something more exciting than singles finding mates happen tonight.* My matchmaking mother finagled this evening to get me out of Uncle Robert's hair. But knowing Mom, she had a dual purpose going here. Mom wanted her adventure-loving daughter married. I wished she'd cut me some slack. My new career demanded all my attention.

Matt waltzed over, a grin on his intelligent, computer-geek face. "See anything suspicious, Garden?"

For the nth time, I eyed the room from end to end. "Not yet." The atmosphere had taken on a texture of intimacy, with the candlelight, scent of roses, and romantic music doing their number on the senses. Men eased into their personalities-on-display roles as ladies slipped into empty seats next to them. Business cards appeared like snow on the Alps. "You spot any trouble?"

"Nope." My old friend locked his gaze on one particular young lady.

I'd often thought he preferred blondes, and this one looked stunning in a black strapless above-the-knee Vera Wang creation.

I gave Matt's arm a friendly poke. "I'm guessing you want to police her side of the room." A sisterly type of happiness made me wink. "Just keep your mind on business."

"Right." He straightened his tie. "You're always looking out for other people. Why not bat those eyelashes at me and catch yourself a gent?"

Amusement gleamed in his eyes, revealing the teasing boy still strong inside the man he'd grown into, so I lapsed into one of the pretend voices we'd shared through the years. "Get on with ye."

"Somebody's got to keep ye out of trouble." He grinned, one eye on security, the other on the blonde and took off.

After he left, I surveyed the guests and tried not to fall under the room's romantic spell. Some nifty red sports car types revved their engines among the black BMW guys parked at the tables. Glittering, perfume-scented women surrounded them, intent on test driving. Drivers had all evening to check out the offerings.

So, I glided into the effervescent scene praying I knew what I was doing.

I kept both eyes wide, searching for sticky-fingered men or women seeking treasure more tangible than a relationship. I prowled my half of the bustling room, eye-frisking each guest for a concealed weapon.

Soon waiters removed empty salad plates and began serving the prime rib. The room crackled with barely controlled hormones. Women glowed. Men preened. Peacocks performing a mating dance.

Looking for trouble, I wove around the full *Engineering* table and passed the glittering-women-double-seated *Physician* table. Everything appeared to be going without a hitch … until—

A delightful breeze of suspicion flitted through me. Hair rose on the nape of my neck. Something wacky at the back of the room. I glanced over to see if Matt, working security on the ballroom's other side, noticed. He looked busy separating two gentlemen from commandeering one apparently special lady.

My tickle of wariness itched as I approached the rear table where four burly men, dressed in matching black tuxes, red bow ties, and red cummerbunds, their long hair flicking their shoulders, sat glowering. Temple must have picked up on the men too, because she sashayed to my side.

I whispered in her ear, "Mom didn't arrange that table. Get a load of their placard, *Champion Wrestlers*. It's not professionally lettered." A creepy sensation crawled over my skin. "Mom has zero interest in athletes. She absolutely wouldn't invite wrestlers." What was happening here?

"Mumnn. Maybe she missed a good thing."

Excited goosebumps stood at attention on my bare arm. "No socialite tire-kickers are shopping among those musclemen." Their table of pretty-faced wrestlers with juiced-up muscles remained an island of loneliness in the crowded room. "Wonder why they came?"

"They each paid their five hundred bucks or they wouldn't be inside." Temple took a step toward them.

I put a hand on her arm. "Don't." Tugging Temple with me, I backed away from their table. "Look at those scowls. Those guys need an attitude adjustment."

"Spoilsport."

I smiled. "I might find a client there. After they chill. They're the kind of semi-shady guys who hire surveillance." My smile grew to a grin. "Or protection."

Temple pushed her generous lips into a mock pout. "I can just see little ol' you protecting those mountains of muscle."

I huffed and tried to toss my hair, forgetting I wore an upsweep. "Gate crashers or not, those wrestlers aren't causing any trouble. I'll keep them high on my radar screen and check with Mom when she arrives. She's doing her usual late, dramatic entrance."

"Since I'm not prospecting for muscles, I'll get back to my mining." Temple winked and sauntered toward more promising tables.

As I turned away to retrace my surveillance route, my gaze swept across a man I hadn't noticed before. He stood near the ballroom door with his back to me. I did a double-take. An off-duty cop. I could spot one a mile away. The way he walked, stood, and observed his surroundings. A cop couldn't disguise his identity. Calm, professional, strong, he looked as though he controlled the world. With legs braced wide, right foot behind, he kept his piece away from the crowd. Even from the rear, the guy looked cocky.

Someone touched my shoulder. I jumped. While I'd been eyeing the cop, Matt had crossed to my side of the room.

"Who invited the police?" Matt jabbed a thumb toward the ballroom door.

"My question exactly. Maybe one of the rich types demanding extra protection. Or maybe the cop's moonlighting as a bodyguard."

Matt rubbed his clean-shaven chin. "Maybe. Don't know."

"Whatever. I'll find out."

"You do that." Matt sauntered back to his side of the ballroom.

I planned to check the cop out but didn't want to meet him this way. I had an image to project. I was an investigator. A professional. Strong. Independent. Cool. Granted, I had a lot to learn, but I sure didn't want to be seen on Valentine's night appearing to shop for a man. In a town as closely-connected as Dallas, if we met in the line of fire and I had no doubt we would—he'd never take me seriously. Some time tonight I'd inform him I was actually working.

I policed my half of the room then headed back toward the *Champion Wrestler* table.

Big, warm fingers grasped my arm with just enough pressure to make me brake and take notice. The dark-haired, fine-looking man extended his other hand. A sense of recognition nagged me. But I didn't know him.

He sat with his back to the wall at the *Attorney* table catty-cornered to the wrestlers' enclave. I shook his waiting hand, feeling warmth and solid strength I hadn't expected to find in a lawyer's grip. He wore his dark suit like other men wore uniforms. Daring. Proud. Indomitable. Candlelight reflected mystery in his brown eyes. With the kind of smile you see on a man given an unexpected dish of ice cream, he stood and offered me the empty chair his polished wingtips had guarded. With the chair now free, a bevy of females flew over from different tables and circled him.

"Sit a while."

His compelling expression excluded everyone in the room but me. I didn't want the invitation, but my feet, aching from the unaccustomed spike heels, did. So, I slid into the seat.

"Thanks, but just for a minute."

Sophisticated women glared—shoppers vying for the attorney's attention. He flashed them a smile and motioned to the nearby *Champion Wrestler* table. "Those men want to meet you."

"I'll be back." One woman, wearing heavy eye liner, trailed her hand along the top of the attorney's chair and threw him a seductive glance before she moved away. The other ladies stepped over to the strong men's den.

"Thanks, man." One wrestler nodded, his long blonde hair falling into his square-jawed face.

I turned to the attorney, a real James Bond type. Unwanted sparks ignited my insides. Too intense to be handsome and too electric to be ignored, he was big, tense, and concentrated. I'd never met a man who looked so ready for adventure.

Here was trouble masquerading as charm.

"They're gonna love this at the office," Bond drawled.

I blinked. The heat in his eyes warmed me like sun-melted chocolate. The challenge in his steady gaze stiffened my backbone.

"The office?" I noticed the bulge under his armpit not quite hidden by his well-fitting dark suit jacket. Tingles trilled my spine.

"Stryker Black. You're Holly Garden."

Recognition hit me. The out-of-uniform cop I'd spotted standing in the foyer with his back to me. How had he settled in so quickly? His proximity caused my eyelid to do its thing. Most people never see my twitch. I hoped Stryker didn't. The quivers make me look unprofessional.

"How do you know my name?"

"Looked up your file at our office."

Suspicion brought sudden anger biting into me like the Genesis serpent. To keep my temper in check I whispered. "You're a police officer?"

"Used to be. Now a PI. Ace Investigations."

I shot to my feet, snagged a four-inch stiletto on the chair rung and lurched forward, catching the table's edge to keep from landing in his lap.

"I knew it!" Mom again.

With my nose inches from his ear, his masculine scent broke through my protective aura. Trying not to breathe in his woodsy, nautical aroma, I scooted away.

Because I wasn't breathing freely, my whisper sounded weird and nasal. "I want you to leave. At once."

"Why should I?"

I stared and forgot to lower my voice. "You're not needed."

The four lawyers seated around Stryker perked up. Fat and thin, they gazed at me like I was a valuable bequest in a contested will. One leaned so far forward on the table his French cuff dipped into his coffee.

Stryker remained cool. "I'm sure you're acquainted with a lady named Violet Garden."

My palms turned sweaty.

My own mother thought I couldn't fill Dad's shoes. She thought I didn't have the guts to be a detective. She thought I'd fail. Knees weak, I slid back into the chair and gazed down. My fingers itched to fiddle with the clasp on my glittery bag, but I held them still. I couldn't let the PI see how his words curdled my self-esteem.

"Security was the word Ms. Garden used."

I spoke low, not wanting anyone else to hear. "She didn't. She couldn't." I clamped my lips. He didn't need to know how his words upset me.

"Hard to believe?" He gave me a hard-boiled, tight-lipped Bogart smile.

Sitting so close, he didn't look like a cop. Or a PI for that matter. More like a very, very sexy bad guy. Mafia or something. My throat closed. How could Mom do this to me?

"Mom asked for you? Personally?"

"She asked for Ace's top man." His dark eyes spoke of secrets, hinted of danger. Pulled me in even as they warned me off.

I whispered, "Luck of the draw?"

We'd been talking in hushed tones, but now the PI, a beguiling smirk on his face, spoke louder. "I won the lottery."

One lawyer said, "I've got to remember that line."

The other lawyers grunted agreement.

Their responses helped me regain my poise. I turned back to the PI.

"Okay, you work for our competition ... and you're here?" I'd staked out Ace Investigations to see what I was up against, so why hadn't I laid eyes on him there? And he *was* an eyeful. Plus, he was feeding me a line. And good at it. Too good.

I scooted my chair away from him. Not that long ago I'd been dumped by another charmer. I wasn't about to nibble this bait.

Even if I had wanted to chance another romance, God had laid out other plans for me. I had a new vocation. I had Dad's murder to solve and his reputation to sanitize. I needed to prove to the city of Dallas and the entire police force that Dad hadn't been a dirty private investigator. If I failed, our investigative firm would dribble on down the drain. I lifted my chin. Even if I had time to spend with a man, I'd never choose this smoothie. But I did need to size up the competition.

Investigator Rule Number One – know your enemy

So, I did an about face and turned on the sugar. "Stryker, is it?" I smiled sweetly. "I thought I had every PI in Dallas pegged. Glad to meet you."

Stryker's focused expression didn't change. "Likewise." He laid a strong hand on my bare arm, raising the hair with a single light touch. "Stay a minute more. Tell me about yourself."

A male voice interrupted Stryker. "Let's be judicious here. Fair's fair. There're four attorneys at this table and one lovely woman. Time to share. My name's Jeff Davidson of Davidson, Hillyer & Greene. I'm sure you've heard of my firm. And this is ..."

While Jeff introduced the other three suits, Stryker leaned back and scanned the room, doing his security thing. With me quickly shaking hands around the table, the trio of women who'd huddled around Stryker earlier made their move. Rising from the nearby *Champion Wrestler* table as if directed by an unseen choreographer, they mobbed Stryker.

I sucked in a breath. His mouth hanging ajar, Stryker looked stunned. Three wrestlers stood too, pushed aside their chairs, and towered over Stryker. I glimpsed Matt striding across the ballroom toward us, security face on.

The big blond wrestler, who seemed to be their leader, rasped, "We wasn't just twiddling our thumbs over here. We was talking with these ladies." His expression looked downright testy. He raised a fist, looking about to deck Stryker.

The three glamour girls stepped away from Stryker and melted into the crowd.

Prepared to intervene, I grabbed my purse and wriggled to the edge of my seat, curious to see what Stryker would do. This scene was plain screwy. Were the wrestlers *trying* to pick a fight?

Stryker's face grew leaner, showing clear bone definition. A paper-thin scar slicing through his cleft chin whitened. He stood and faced the three muscled men, their crimson cummerbunds flashing.

"So?"

"So, we want our ladies back."

"Take them."

"Cool it, you guys." I unclasped my purse, thinking I might need my gun.

The fourth wrestler jumped to his feet, tipping his chair backward. It landed with a thud on the carpeted floor. A solid wall of red cummerbunds circled Stryker. I shot off my chair. One mat-pounder grabbed my arm and hauled me toward his table.

"We want this one too."

I jerked my arm loose. My abrupt movement caused my ankle to turn in one of the tricky stilettos.

"Yow!" I stumbled. Before I could catch my balance, I lost the shoe on my twisted ankle, and fell to my knees.

Events fast-forwarded. Two wrestlers pummeled Stryker. Someone kicked my evening bag. On hands and knees, I chased it under the *Attorney Table* to rescue my gun. I glimpsed Matt confronting the other two wrestlers and attempted to squirm out from under the table to escort the muscle jocks to the nearest exit. Crouched on hands and knees, my dress tightened around me like shrink wrap and stopped me cold.

A lawyer squatted beside me. "Let me help—"

One of the wrestlers slammed him backward with an open palm. With a crash and tinkle of broken glass, the table flipped onto its side. A white and silver rain of crockery and cutlery poured down. A plate of romaine lettuce and blue cheese dressing slapped against my thigh, releasing the odor of salad-splashed velvet. My vision slowed as if I starred in a surreal movie. Mind scanning possible actions, my skirt creeping higher above my knees, I crawled free.

Was this a diversion for a robbery? I had to take control. Still on hands and knees, I smelled something acrid and sulfuric. The lighted candle centerpiece smoldered at the edge of the tablecloth. With a soft whoosh, flames leaped to life. I grabbed the closest thing at hand, a large slab of prime rib probably from the same uneaten place setting as the salad and beat the flames with the semi-rare meat until they died in wisps of smoke beneath charred beef. Smelling cooked steak mixed with scorched hair and fearful of what I would find, I touched my eyebrows and bangs. Crispy but still there.

Gasps and murmurings told me the crowd grew around us. Heavy feet shuffled, and I jerked my hand back to keep it from getting trampled. Fists struck flesh accompanied by grunts and colorful language. I couldn't believe such a brouhaha erupted in our little corner of the big room with so little provocation. Something smelled fishy, and it wasn't the shrimp cocktail sauce dripping onto the carpet. I was about to spring to my feet when a body thudded to within an inch of me and lay still.

Stryker. One look at Stryker's bloody face and I all but keeled over him.

My pulse spiked, pushing me into Unthinking Mode. Okay, so I lost it here. Thoughts of my job flew out the window. But only for a few seconds.

Still on my knees, I fished in my clutch for my cell, and dialed 911. Dead zone. Resisting the urge to throw the instrument at a wrestler, I dropped the useless thing back into my purse.

As quickly as the commotion started, it ended. The dull thud of fists on flesh died. Fingers and knees digging into the thick carpet, I lifted one hand and pressed two fingers against the carotid artery in Stryker's muscular neck. Warm skin. Steady pulsing.

Lord, please don't let him be badly hurt.

With all quiet above me, I assumed Matt held everything under control. I loosened Stryker's red power tie and rubbed his big, limp hand between both of mine. His lashes, fanned across those high cheekbones, looked longer than any man had a right to own. Other than being a little bloody and lying motionless, he looked fine. Too fine. But I didn't have to remind myself that Mom hired him. A twinge of joy that it was him, not Matt or me lying on the floor, layered in an uncomfortable guilt that squashed the relief, so I said another quick prayer for the competition PI.

He groaned and his eyelids fluttered.

Men's polished dress shoes, accompanied by glittering high heels, moved close enough for me to touch. One wrestler squatted next to me. "Here, let me—"

"No. Don't touch him." I swatted the man's beefy hand away from Stryker.

Stryker opened his eyes, relieving my worry about him. But Mom would arrive any minute for her grand entrance, and I desperately wanted her to gawk at *her* security being carried away in an ambulance.

So, I said to the wrestler, "I've got to call EMS."

Furor at the ballroom doors made me look up. "That was fast. Matt must have gotten through to EMS." But doubt nagged my brain. Too fast. Way too fast.

Before I could follow up my hunch, the crowd opened and two blue-uniformed men, carrying oxygen paraphernalia, a stretcher, and a medical kit hustled to the table.

The EMS team ignored Stryker who lay concealed by a drooping tablecloth, with only his long legs and feet protruding. One Medic knelt beside another stretched-out body. I struggled to my feet, red dress hiked almost mid-thigh, to identify the victim.

"Matt!" I rushed over in time to see the medic jab a syringe into my co-investigator's limp arm.

Electrical impulses spiked my nerves. I'd never seen an emergency team do that. The first medic finished a cursory check for broken bones, then both men heaved Matt onto the stretcher and hustled him through the crowded ballroom.

Juggling on one four-inch heel and one bare foot, I elbowed my way through the crowd after them. "Which hospital?"

They mumbled something incoherent and disappeared through the hotel's exterior door.

Lord, please take care of Matt. He's a good friend. Keep him safe.

I started after them.

The blond wrestler clutched my arm, stopping me from following them out to the ambulance. Then he smiled crookedly, straightened his bow tie, and righted his cummerbund.

"Don't look so worried, the PI's in good hands."

I stiffened. "How do you know Matt's a PI?"

The wrestler frowned and clamped his lips.

Shivers snaked up my spine. Something was very wrong.